Robert Owen Minearo

A True
Heart

Journey to the City of Light

A Spiritual Novel

Gallagher Close Publishing and Communications, LLC

© 2020 Gallagher Close Publishing and Communications, LLC

A True Heart, Journey to The City of Light. Copyright © 2020 by Gallagher Close Publishing and Communications, LLC. Copyright © 2020 Robert Owen Minearo. No part of this book may be reproduced, stored in a retrieval system, or transmitted in any form or by any means, digital, electronic, mechanical, photocopying, recording, or otherwise, or conveyed via the internet or a website without prior written permission of the publisher, except in the case of brief quotations embodied in articles and reviews.

Cover Design by Charlie Allnut
Front and Back Cover Image © iStock
Cover Design © Gallagher Close Publishing and Communications, LLC

All inquires should be sent to: Publisher
Gallagher Close Publishing and Communications, LLC
P.O. Box 333, West Wardsboro, Vermont 05360

Printed in the United States of America

www.gallagherclosepubishing.com

Library of Congress Cataloging-in-Publication Data
is on file with the Library of Congress.
ISBN: 978-1-7348283-1-3 (Paperback)

2020 First Edition-Paperback

Thank You

Ian and Pecky

For the many adventures
we took together

A True Heart

Journey to the City of Light

ᘓ

I wrote this spiritual novel for my
seventeen year old self. I wish I had it
to read during those dark days.
My hope is that anyone in a dark place
learns to hear their authentic self.

Cʒ

A True Heart

Journey to the City of Light

Cʒ

A True Heart

CG

Chapter One
Home

I
n a valley of two green mountains towering above the forest floor, and near a wild river that gushed into a blue lake, grew an apple tree that had seen many decades. The apple tree's great trunk was rippled and knotted like the face of a wise old man, and its branches stretched out like fingers touching the sky with its leaves, creating a tapestry of colors.

Ever since the apple tree broke free of the earth to move towards the sky, it was alone and invisible in the deep woods because without loving eyes to look upon such a magnificent tree, it didn't exist.

In time a village grew up at the base of the two green mountains. Near the town, a small home was built near the apple tree. It was a modest dwelling with white clapboards and green shutters and a green metal roof that was angled steeply so that the heavy snow in winter did not burden the home. Attached to the house was a large barn with cedar shingles that had grayed over the years from the sea air moving up from the coast.

One day, a most extraordinary child stood before the apple tree with exceptional love in his heart for all things. The boy, named Ian, was a small fellow with skinny legs and piercing green eyes. He lived with his mother and his father in the little house. His mother had her heart and mind bound to the goodness of the earth, and his father was a man of the sea and beyond. His parents had always been of a different mind from each other, but they found common ground with their love for Ian.

To the south side of the house was a field with a garden with rich dark earth and sun most of the hot summer day, where Ian's mother grew the tomatoes, corn, basil, and other vegetables and herbs that complemented their meals. An overgrown well-picked rhubarb patch lined the edge of the garden.

The north side of the house overlooked the wild river of rushing clear water filled with an abundance of fish. On the other side of the river was a path that led deep into the forest. Ian's father would walk there with him until the stars began to come out, and they would return to their small home and dinner that Ian's mother had made with their garden's bounty. The end of the path had yet to be discovered by the little boy.

All children are given a gift of purpose when they are born. The gift of purpose given to Ian was a true heart. The kind of heart that was beating in Ian's chest is given to few. There is a quality in a child who possesses such a heart, which cannot be seen but only felt, and from the moment of Ian's birth, this mark was apparent.

When Ian was three years old, the family traveled to Boston, Massachusetts, to see a new ship built for Ian's father, Eli, to command. It was November, a frigid wind was blowing in from the north, and the streets were almost empty of people. Eli often joked that Boston was one of the coldest places he had ever visited on the earth.

Eli, Anne, and Ian were walking down an alley leading toward the seaport, a thin layer of snow crunching under their feet. When Ian ran off towards the park for no apparent reason. In the park, there was a pond surrounded by gardens that the family had boated in only a few months earlier, the warm sun shining on them. For some reason, Ian ran directly towards the pond, breaking through the thin ice that edged the water.

Without hesitation, Eli ran into the pond to retrieve Ian. The water was only waist deep, and Eli quickly pulled out his pale, limp son. Anne rushed up to them, and together the father and mother shook and pounded the water from their son's lungs. He coughed then wrapped his shivering wet body around his father, his thin arms and skinny legs tight against his father's warmth.

They rushed back to the hotel and put Ian into a hot bath. The incident seemed not to distress Ian at all, and to this day, his parents cannot make sense of why Ian did what he did.

The next day Ian started to radiate an energy that permeated his whole being. Eli and Anne could feel the warmth emanating from Ian's body as it began to shine brighter and brighter until Ian almost became translucent. It lasted for a moment, and then Ian's radiance began to subside, but a soft warmth and brightness surrounded Ian from that day.

Before they left for home, they visited the Boston Aquarium. Ian was fascinated by the colorful fishes, the sharks, and the starfish. But when they got to the giant ocean tank of penguins, Ian stood dumbstruck. His eyes widened, and then he yelped with joy. He plopped himself down in front of the exhibit and watched the birds for hours with delight, talking to them, laughing, and sometimes even dancing in front of them.

His parents suggested looking at the other fish in the Aquarium, but Ian was content to sit with the penguins. "These penguins are my friends, they talk to me," he said happily.

Shortly after, Eli brought home from his travels, a life-sized emperor penguin made from a soft wooly fabric. Ian's radiance seemed to grow brighter as he hugged the sweet penguin to his chest. "This penguin is called Pecky, short for Peckerage, but he likes Pecky better," Ian declared. Anne and Eli looked at each other with startled eyes when Ian named the penguin Pecky.

Some could see the light emanating from Ian's soul, but many could not, and those who couldn't only disparaged Eli and Anne for believing that their child was so unique. Anne would say that maybe Ian was baptized that day in the frozen pond, and his compassionate soul was then released to do great things in the world. Anne always sensed Ian was an exceptional child who belonged to a bigger world than their small village nestled in the valley of the two green mountains.

Over the years, Ian's great compassion and exceptional gifts were remarked on by the people of the small village. The people kept these stories among themselves, not wanting to awaken an evil in the world that may try to dampen the light that shined so bright in Ian's heart. In truth, stories about Ian became a point of honor for the villagers. They would tell the stories of Ian over and over again. One such story was when his mother, Anne, was deathly ill and was healed by a touch from Ian's hand.

Eli was away at sea when Anne one day came down with a fever. She rose from bed dizzy and swaying and carefully walked down the stairs to the kitchen to put out a spoon and bowl and the cereal and milk for Ian's breakfast. On her way back to bed, she looked in on him. He was still asleep, and his tousled golden hair was all she could see of him under the covers, except one small arm that draped over Pecky, who was almost as big as he was.

She went back to bed and fell asleep, only to wake when Ian came into the room and stood by her bed. "Mommy, it's morning!" Anne smiled at her little boy and told him to eat his breakfast that was on the table. "And put away the milk when you are done."

"I already did!" Ian sang out happily. Ian was barely five, but he often did or said things that made Anne feel that he was much older. Ian left her to sleep again, but he would climb the stairs to her room to check on her and ask, "Mommy, are you okay?"

"Yes, dear, but I can't get up to get your lunch. Are you eating anything?" Anne was a mother who felt that food was a form of love, and she loved her family. Ian assured his mother that he was okay and was finding something to eat.

"That's good, dear. Go down and watch TV, as long as you want, just for today. I need to rest and get better." She watched her son skip out of the room and let out her breath in a prolonged racking cough. Anne didn't get better; she started to get worse with a high fever and sweats.

She slept and woke, each time worried about her son. Hearing his laughter, as he watched television from the living room below, she was relieved and slept again. Ian would often climb the stairs to her room to check on her.

Neighbors were unaware of Anne's dilemma, and Ian was too young to think to go for help. Anne tossed in delirium throughout the night, coughing and feverish.

On the morning of the second day, Ian walked into his mother's room and stood next to the bed, looking at her sadly. She was sweating and had labored breathing. An expression came over Ian's face, like the look an old man might have for his beloved child.

A glow started to emanate from Ian's body. The glow became brighter until Anne opened her eyes, saying, "Honey, what is that light? It is hurting my eyes."

Ian gently touched his mother with his small and delicate fingers. As he tenderly stroked her face, the pain left her body, and she lifted her head from the pillow to stare at her son as the light about him diminished. She felt as though she'd just awakened from a good night's sleep.

Anne sat up and looked at Ian for a long time. She did not fully understand what had just happened. "Honey," she told Ian, "I've been gone somewhere dark for a long time, and you brought me back."

Ian smiled, putting his little arms around her. "Mommy, I'm hungry, can you make me breakfast?"

It occurred to Anne, as she rose and pulled on her bathrobe, that Ian was not aware of what he had just done, that perhaps his concern for her brought out something in Ian that was dormant. She looked at Ian and smiled. "Yes, I'm famished! Let's go down and make some pancakes."

Anne watched Ian intently as he skipped down the hallway. She wanted never to forget how beautiful Ian was at that moment. She desired to hold it dear to her heart forever.

As they reached the living room, she stopped and stared. Ian had placed his tiny green table, and little yellow chair in front of the television, and on the table and about the floor were piles of ice cream wrappers and sticks. Ian had just been eating his favorite food, popsicles, since the previous morning!

The sight of the popsicle debris made Anne laugh so hard that she had to sit down. Ian joined in, and they both had a good belly laugh. The popsicle story always brought a smile to Anne's face and to those who heard it.

Other stories were told of the little boy's gifts. He was outgoing and friendly to all, and when his parents went to town, he would stop and talk to people in the aisles at the grocery store and the checkout. He would skip around the local diner where a family was eating and plop himself down next to people at any table, putting Pecky on another chair to stay close. "Who wants to read to me?" he would ask. Or, "How do you like your dinner tonight?" he'd say to some surprised diners. Often, he would sing a song that he had learned that day and then ask if he should sing another. His sweet high voice was so lovely to listen to that soon the whole diner would be quiet to hear him sing.

He would hug waitresses, or his parents' friends, or town folk, and often they would smile and laugh and hug him back and feel happy. People in town considered that they were his family, that Ian's happiness at seeing them was a high point in their days, and his joy at being in the world crept into their world, too. But not always.

One day when Ian was still young, he was playing in the living room with Pecky while Anne and her roommate from college, Lynne, talked in the kitchen. Ian got up, walked over to Lynne, and placing his hand on her belly announced, "It's a baby girl, a sweet little girl."

Lynne froze in astonishment with Ian's announcement, and sputtered, "How does he know? I'm only a few weeks pregnant. We just found out. I haven't told anyone, even my mother, and how does he know it's a girl?"

Anne was taken aback by Ian's prediction. She looked at Ian and her friend for a moment before she answered, "I don't know. I don't think Ian understands how he does it." Then Anne smiled and laughed and hugged her friend. "Congratulations! You are going to have a baby girl!"

This experience so upset Lynne that she didn't visit again, and the friendship began to fade away. Lost friendships were one consequence of those who witnessed Ian's abilities and couldn't understand.

There were other things about Ian that were different. Often Anne would hear Ian singing or chattering happily in his room. Checking on him, she would see him playing with Pecky, talking, and gesturing as if with someone. If she asked him who he was talking to, he would smile and say, "My friends, Mommy."

Anne was concerned that maybe Ian had an over-active imagination, but Ian would talk about things, things she couldn't fathom how he would know.

One day Ian insisted on visiting an elderly woman who lived nearby. Sarah's husband, Victor, had died from pneumonia a few weeks earlier. They had known Ian all his life and had had many visits from Ian as he explored his town. He would often show up at their home. Sarah or Vic would open the door wide for Ian and Pecky, saying, "Come in, come on in!"

They would listen to him go on about his day or his adventures. Sarah made cookies regularly, counting on one of Ian's visits. He would politely take the offered cookies, always saying "Yes, please," to an offer of seconds, and then would talk and laugh with them and ask more questions than any curious kid could even think of until Vic would throw up his hands. "I give up! I have no more answers, young man!" And they would laugh, and Ian would hug them when he left.

Sarah was more than happy to have Ian and Anne's company that day. She ushered them into her living room, and Anne sat down on the chintz couch. Ian stood by the couch a moment, then walked over to Sarah and put Pecky in her lap. He took her wrinkled hand, looked at Sarah solemnly, and said, "Victor wants me to tell you something important."

Sarah was distressed to hear this from Ian and wondered if this little boy is making up stories, but she indulged him. In a soft voice, she asked, "What did Vic want me to know?"

Ian kept her hand in his and leaned into her shoulder. He looked up at her, and she felt a warmth of joy in her that she hadn't known would ever happen again. "Vic bought a life insurance policy years ago," Ian told her. "You'll find the policy in the bottom of the red chest you keep the blankets in, in your son's room. He put it there for safekeeping but forgot to tell you about it."

Sarah's face froze for a moment, then she gave Pecky back to Ian, got up, and walked upstairs to her son's old room, who was now a man with a family of his own living far away. Sarah kept the room as her son left it, more than thirty years earlier.

She returned downstairs, holding the life insurance policy. Sarah quietly said, her voice shaking, "This is enough to let me keep my house and live here until I die. I have been so worried about it. I didn't want to move from my home, and now I don't have to. I don't know what to say or how to thank you."

Anne looked at Ian, who was holding Pecky and looking at Sarah with bright, happy eyes and a sweet smile on his face. Sarah knelt, reached out, and pulled Ian to her. His arms went around her neck, and they hugged for a long minute, with Pecky squished in between them.

As Ian grew older, unsettling visions and dreams of future events began to trouble his mind. Ian would often awaken in the middle of the night, scared and sweating. His parents took him to the doctor, but nothing was wrong with him physically.

They didn't know what to do for Ian other than support him and try to soothe him when he would get upset. Both of Ian's parents understood their son was unusual and had many gifts, and now many burdens.

Anne worried about Ian. He was young, and she knew that someday he would be old enough to be aware of his gifts but not mature enough emotionally to handle what was going on in his mind and soul.

In his dreams and even at times when he was awake, Ian would have a vision of a City of Light surrounded by jungle and a field of roses. He would have nightmares of a malevolent force that lived in shadows and controlled lost souls. He would hold Pecky tight and feel comforted by the big penguin. He told his parents that Pecky took away his bad dreams.

His parents thought it odd that something so simple could comfort Ian, but all Ian's parents cared about was his happiness. Anne often worried about something happening to Pecky, and she laughingly called Pecky her second son. When Pecky did get left behind at a neighbor's house or in the village, the animal was always quickly returned to Ian, as everyone knew how vital the penguin was to the boy.

On Ian's twelfth birthday, however, things changed. Ian started to act like an ordinary young man. He gradually stopped talking to his invisible friends, and his visions or nightmares diminished into nothing.

Ian's mother came into his room one day to find it stripped of all toys. Even Pecky had been put away in his closet. "I don't need him anymore," Ian said flatly.

The sparkle that emanated from the young Ian vanished. He talked less with neighbors and not at all to strangers and stopped the comforting hugs he had once given out so freely. The laughter that once spilled out of the happy boy was now contained and stiff.

Ian became an average young man making friends in his new upper-level school and even having his first seventh-grade crush.

Warm and loving stories of Ian still were told by the people in the village, but over time the stories became more made-up than true. Even Anne and Eli began to wistfully put away memories of the magical light that surrounded their young son. Ian's golden youth was just a sweet and lovely dream. Eventually, they just stopped talking about Ian's younger life and went through their days without magic. ○ઝ

ෆ

Chapter Two
A Change of Heart

On Ian's sixteenth birthday a dark cloud descended on his heart. Ian was like many sixteen-year-olds, laconic, moping, and questioning the world around him. The angst and emptiness that Ian suffered was far worse than most his age.

His parents could see that Ian was pulling away from them and isolating himself from his friends. The past four years had been uneventful, ordinary even. They wondered if Ian's joyous sparkle would ever come back, and now the boy was even more morose.

Anne knew in her heart that Ian was exceptional. She knew that he was destined for greatness and burdened with a responsibility mysterious to her. Ian pulled away from his mother the most. The deep connection they had diminished, and Ian wounded his mother by rejecting her love and shunning her embraces.

Ian's father was traveling the world during most of Ian's childhood. The connection Ian had with his father during that time was simple. When he was home, his father took him to amusement parks and camping. Eli was a distant figure to Ian, even when they were together, as he rarely spoke of his travels or anything of importance. Ian looked up to his father, felt his stern love, and yearned for his time and attention when he was at home. The distance between them was bridged when they were together, but it was never eliminated. For some reason, Ian never confided in his father, and both felt that lack of connection, despite their love for each other.

From Ian's infancy, Eli seemed baffled by the closeness between Ian and Anne. Ian had always gone to his mother for comfort, but now that he was pushing her away, he needed his father more than ever.

That summer of Ian's sixteenth year, Anne advised Eli to take Ian on a camping trip. "You've got to talk to him, Eli. He needs you now, you know that." Eli could see that his son was greatly troubled, and his concern for Ian grew.

Eli packed their gear and strapped the canoe on top of the car, while Anne packed a large hamper of food that Eli and Ian usually didn't eat much of on their camping trips and ditched before they got home. Ian was disinterested in the proceedings and could barely pack his toothbrush and underwear without his mother's prompting.

The long car trip to New Hampshire with Ian was not unlike what Eli expected. There were extended periods where not a word would come out of Ian's mouth, and maybe too many words came out of Eli's.

"Your mother said you might be going to Block Island with some friends at the end of summer?"

"Yeah."

"Who are the friends you're going with?"

"You don't know them."

Eli drove several miles with an annoyed look on his face. "Yes, I understand that I don't know them. That is why I asked you who they were."

Ian glared at his father and replied, "Just friends, no one important."

Eli thought to himself that if this were the level of the conversation for the next four days, it was going to be a long camping trip.

The conversation lightened when the two reached the campsite near Squam Lake. Eli and Ian got busy setting up the tents, laying out their sleeping bags, and gathering twigs for the fire pit.

They had bought a bundle of campfire logs on the road, at the same farm stand near the lake that they always did. A man sat on a beach chair by the front screen door reading the paper as they came in, and his face lit up when he saw them.

"Long time, no see!" He got up to shake hands with Eli, then opened his arms to hug Ian, but in a flash instead stuck out his hand to meet Ian's grip.

"My, ya've gotten to be quite the young man," he said, peeping into Ian's face as if to catch the youngster that used to be there. "I'd'a hardly recognized ya." His smile faltered a bit, then he turned to Eli.

"Need bait? Wood? What'll do ya?"

Eli and Ian had the routine down so well that the campsite was set up before the sunset, and the supplies they got at the farm stand, including ice for the cooler, a six-pack of Narragansett, and hamburger and buns, were put away. After dinner and s'mores, Eli made sure everything edible was in the trunk of the car, having an aversion to bears and a conviction that bears were waiting in the woods to get their dinner.

The last time Eli and Ian had gone camping together was when Ian was eleven, at this same spot, and he brought his friend Tom. It was easier to entertain Ian at that age with a friend to occupy his time. But this would be the longest camping trip of Eli's life if he couldn't get Ian to relax and talk.

Eli had the next morning planned. They started with a drive to a diner in town for breakfast. Then they bought sandwiches and drinks to go from the deli for their lunch and returned to the lake. Eli rented a speedboat and taught Ian to drive the boat around the lake. Ian seemed to have fun and even laughed when they carved some circles in the middle of the lake.

After lunch, they rented a fishing boat and went to a secret cove they'd had luck with in the past. Once Ian caught a 10-pound trout in the cove, and from then on, it was their place. But they had no luck that day, not even a nibble. The silence in the boat was oppressive.

In the evening, the two ventured into town again to indulge in hot dogs and root beer floats at the drive-in and then went to the cinema to see a movie.

The next day Eli planned little except for swimming by the campsite. Eli knew that this was his chance to reach Ian, that once they went home again, Ian would isolate himself from his parents and maybe his close friends.

As the day went by, it seemed to Eli that Ian was getting more and more agitated about something. It appeared that Ian was in conflict, and the absence of distractions was bringing up something dark in his heart that he was unable to suppress.

After dinner, Eli built a massive fire in the fire pit. He placed his old grey wool army blanket near the fire and a small cooler of Narragansett cans next to that. Eli and Ian sat on the blanket next to the fire for a long time, not saying a word to each other, watching the sparks from the fire rise and fade away into the starry night.

Late in the evening, Eli looked over at Ian and saw tears rolling down his son's cheeks. Ian put his face in his hands and began to weep quietly. Trying to contain his tears, Ian looked up at him.

"What is this place?"

Eli looked sadly at his son. "I don't know," he said, confused. "Do you mean where we are now?"

Ian took a deep breath and sat back against a log. With a cold stare, Ian said, "No, Dad, I mean, what is this reality?" He stopped a moment, looked down, and softly added, "I don't feel at peace with my life."

Eli thought long and hard about what to say next. "I thought the conflicts you had when you were younger were gone?"

Ian let out a hard laugh. "No, I never found peace. I just was able to fake it for the past few years."

"Why did you start to fake who you are?"

Ian let out a sigh. "Remember that girl I fell in love with when I was twelve? Ellen? We started going together the next year. She wasn't at all interested in my thoughts or my ideas of the world. She was mostly interested in herself and me being what she wanted in a boyfriend. She wanted to tell me how to do everything, you know, right, so that we'd fit in with all the other couples at middle school. That's why I only lasted the school year with her."

Eli looked at Ian with concern and asked, "What about your friends? Have you talked to them about this?"

Ian let out another unpleasant snort and replied, "My friends are only interested in playing video games and talking about video games. They have no interest in talking about anything else, especially in understanding the mechanism of the universe."

Eli looked at Ian with empathy and a bit of a surprise. "I am so sorry, son, I have no idea the anguish you've suffered." He wrapped his arms around his knees and stared into the fire, then looked at his son. "You think about this reality and the mechanism of the universe?"

Ian had a grave look on his face. "That's all that I think about, that and sometimes the dreams, you know, and nobody at school wants to hear it. I'm practically an ostracized person there."

He looked up into the starry sky and said carefully, "For some reason, I know that the world outside of us is only an illusion. I have known it since I was a child. I would often go into my room when I was four or five and ponder if there was some secret place behind the walls.

"Spirits would show up in my room late at night and want to talk. They never scared me, but I couldn't understand what they wanted from me. I just wanted to be a normal kid with friends and maybe a girlfriend or two before I went off to college."

Eli moved closer to Ian on the blanket and draped his arm across his son's shoulders. "Your mother hoped that the turmoil of those years went away. We had no idea that you were still dealing with so much."

Ian seemed to be lighter after disclosing his thoughts to his father. He sat with his father's arm around him for a long time. He couldn't remember when they had last done this, probably when he was a little kid. He was overwhelmed with missing his father, the man sitting next to him.

Ian turned to his father. "So, what do you think is this reality, and why are we here?"

Eli deliberated on how he was going to answer his son's question. Eli understood more about the subject than Ian knew but understood that Ian needed to work these things out for himself.

Ian looked over at his father. "Dad?"

Eli looked back at Ian with a weary smile. "I don't know why we are here. Here in this universe. What I do know is that you are an extraordinary young man, and you are destined to have a profound understanding of what this reality is and why we are here."

He stretched over to the cooler to grab another beer, cracked it open, and took a swallow. "Ahhh, that's good." He turned to Ian. "I believe that maybe your purpose in this life is to find the answers to many of the questions asked throughout history. I believe you have the potential to be a great teacher of humankind."

Ian let out a snort and replied, "Lighten up, dad. I would be happy if I just knew my next move in this cosmic drama."

Eli laughed. "Sorry, son, I got a little heavy." He paused and said seriously. "Do you still have the dreams, the visions of the city surrounded by fields of black roses?"

Ian looked down at something interesting on the grey blanket. Finally, he answered, "Yes, the visions have never gone away. They don't come as often as when I was younger, though. I think I block them because when I was a child, the visions came with a dark figure.

"The image of the city with black roses doesn't bother me. What does scare me is that dark figure. I always feel that it is aware of me and wants to stop me from some unknown journey I'm destined to go on."

Ian lapsed into silence, thinking about this vision and others he'd been having. He wondered how much to reveal to his father, whether the crocodile or the penguin he'd been envisioning would be dismissed by his father as just dreams or would be taken seriously.

He hesitantly offered more information to his father. "I've also started to dream about a big tall penguin." He laughed. "I think I spent too much time with penguins in my room and at the Boston Aquarium when I was younger. I can't tell you why I needed those penguins, but I remember feeling comforted."

Eli didn't laugh or even smile. He stretched out his legs toward the fire, took a big sip of his beer, and sighed. "Ian, I know that you are going on a journey. There is much that you do not know about me and my work and what I have been doing over the last twenty years. I can say, I have confidence you will be able to handle what lies before you, and yes, you will be able to deal with those in shadow."

Ian looked solemn and lost in thought. He was not used to hearing compliments from his father, who was taciturn at best.

Eli softened his tone. "Always know that your mother and I love you and we are proud of the young man that you have become. We will always be here as a support for you."

He continued, steadily speaking as if to get what he had to say out before he could change his mind. "Many parents might consider their children to be extensions of themselves, always trying to meet their expectations. That was never how your mother and I felt about raising you. We don't want to live vicariously through you. We don't want you to have to meet our expectations. What we want most is to be a support for you, so that you can find your path.

"I do have my ideas about the questions you asked. Unfortunately, the answers to those questions are so broad that you will only find the answers in your own heart."

Eli put his hand on Ian's. Ian, usually uncomfortable with affection, felt the solace. And the two sat by the fire, looking at the stars.

The next few days seemed to go by fast. Ian and his dad didn't talk about anything more than girls, what kind of car he would like someday, and where he might want to go to college.

Eli and Ian felt a finality on the camping trip. They both knew that this was the last time they would go on a camping trip while the three of them, his mother, father, and Ian, lived together in the peaceful little house in the mountains.

Even though Ian was destined to follow another path, the bond of understanding that formed between Ian and his father on the camping trip would only grow stronger over the years.

•••

Eight months later, on his seventeenth birthday, Ian awoke to a powerful feeling of strength and purpose in his heart. He somehow felt that he had transcended his consciousness to see the world in a whole new light. It was as if he had walked through a door from one life he had lived to another where the whole world opened to him. He felt that all the years of uncertainty might be over.

Ian's parents could see that their son seemed lighter and happier. At first, Ian's parents thought that perhaps he was in love again, but the kindness and compassion he now showed to his parents and friends was more encompassing than what a passing crush might produce. For no reason, Ian would come up to his mother or father to give a big hug, and say, "Thank you for everything." Anne received these embraces casually as if they were normal, but her joy at Ian's happiness and love filled her heart.

For Ian, the world was coming alive to him in a way that he never thought possible. Ian's heart waking up did more than give him strength. He started to hear subtle voices from all creatures, large and small. He began to hear conscious sounds from the birds in the sky, and even the moss on the rocks had a voice that seemed familiar to him. It was if he remembered all that he had forgotten.

Visions of a city in the jungle and friends he didn't know started to flood his mind once more. The field of roses and the daemon also filled his mind, although he didn't back down from them. These visions, Ian knew, were a portend that he would soon have to leave his beloved home.

He felt stuck between his two worlds—a world that he knew and loved and another world where he must go. Nothing is more painful to a soul than to be between worlds without control.

Ian knew he did not have to hide his feelings from his family anymore. He started to talk openly about his ideas, visions, and dreams. He talked with his friends and with those in the village who had known him since he was born. At first, they didn't know what to make of this young man. Some pulled away from Ian, but many in the village embraced Ian's compassion and kindness. Ian did lose some of his friends who didn't want to delve into quantum physics or the nature of reality with him, but the friends he did keep become better and more dedicated to Ian than before.

Strength was building in Ian's heart, but the conflict between his peaceful life in the village and the life that he was destined for was burdening his soul.

The heat of summer broke in late September. By early October, the leaves started to radiate fall colors. Ian knew with the turning of the leaves, something magical was about to happen. It was not the feeling of the vision, but the anticipation that his life was about to change.

Ian's foresight burdened his parents. Eli and Anne knew that once Ian left for the larger world, he would never be the same, and he would not fit in the small village nestled in the valley of the two green mountains. ଓ

CƷ

Chapter Three
A Late-Night Visitor

There was nothing different about the night Ian heard a knock on the door, other than a cold breeze that was moving down from the north to remind the people who lived in the village below the two green mountains that winter was on its way.

Ian was awake in his bed long after his mother finished her work and retired for the evening. A knock sounded like a tree branch from the mighty apple tree tapping against the side of the house in the wind. But when the bang became more deliberate, Ian knew it must be a visitor at their door.

Many who lived at the edge of a vast forest might not open their door late at night, but Ian was brave beyond his seventeen years. He opened the door wide, and before him stood a most unusual sight.

An emperor penguin with a red bow tie neatly tied around his rather muscular neck, stood there straight and tall, taller than Ian. The penguin had a monocle in one eye with a red ribbon leading down to a pocket on his elegant vest of purple satin.

Although thoroughly astonished, Ian could tell from how this creature stood that he possessed great strength. He also could sense that this penguin possessed a high intellect and an enormous capacity for compassion.

The emperor penguin looked fondly down at Ian, and asked, "Have you water on the stove for a spot of late-night tea?"

Ian was dumbstruck at the sight and sound of this penguin. But the previous months of awareness, the sense that animals and birds were voicing their thoughts for him to hear, and especially the memory of his visions of a penguin brought him instant comfort.

The emperor penguin remembered his manners. "Sorry, dear boy, first things first. I want to introduce myself formally. My name is Peckerage Hornblaster III, Esquire. I'm delighted to make your acquaintance."

"Pecky!" Ian took a deep breath of joy.

"Yes, all my friends call me that, and you certainly are a dear friend," Pecky said as he brushed by Ian and went straight into the kitchen.

Ian watched in silence as Pecky deliberated on either Earl Grey or chamomile tea, but finally said, "Earl Grey will have to do because we need to stay awake for the journey ahead."

Ian woke up from his daze. "Journey? What...?"

"Why, to England, of course. Tonight," Pecky replied.

"I can see by the bewildered look on your face," the regal penguin continued, "that you have no idea why I'm here or where we are going. I don't spend as much time around human folk as I used to, and I forget that most, if not all, people lack the vision we penguins take for granted."

Ian stood there, confused and mute. Pecky sighed, made two cups of tea, and placed them on the table. He gave a piercing glance at the tow-headed young man seated in front of him. He took a deep slurp of his hot milky tea and continued, "The best place to start with any story is the beginning.

"I have been friends with your father and mother for many years. When you were born, you had the mark of a true heart. You don't remember, but I was here on that cold February day when you were born.

"Since your seventeenth birthday, you might have started to rediscover your differences from your friends and family. This 'heart awakening' happens to all who carry your gift when they turn seventeen. You begin to understand your gifts, but, of course, there is a price, and that is the longing to fulfill your divine purpose."

The wind had picked up outside, rattling the metal roof of the little house, so Ian leaned closer to listen to the imposing penguin. Ian sipped his Earl Grey tea and took a bite of a butter cookie that his mother had made earlier in the evening. He slathered a good helping of Anne's strawberry-rhubarb jam on each golden wafer before diligently consuming it. He was full of questions but too confused to ask anything. Sitting at the table with cookies and tea was calmingly normal in the circumstances.

Pecky continued, "My job is to help you become aware of your inner self and to fulfill your divine purpose. Our journey together is also my path, which I began to fulfill during my training at University of Oxford, England—from which of course, I graduated Summa Cum Laude." Pecky made a slight adjustment to his bowtie with a large flipper. "Ah-hum." He looked over at Ian's rhubarb covered cookie, and, when Ian smiled and gave it to him, he flipped it into his mouth and swallowed it in one gulp.

"I know," he resumed, smacking his beak, "that your father has kept you shielded from his true avocation. You have always known your father to be a sea captain, but he is much more than a sailor. He is part of an ancient secret order.

"Nine months ago, a classmate from Oxford, Sir Rupert Nightingale, trekked across the Antarctic plain to visit my family and me in the great City of Penguins, Penderby. He told us a story of an Ancient City lost in the jungles of Africa. As the story goes, the Ancient City has within it the power to heal all of humankind. The city is known as the City of Light."

The moment Ian heard of the Ancient City he felt an overwhelming feeling of longing—a longing that was a key to his future. He had been waiting for a sign of what was next for him.

"The City was only a legend told by eager explorers, a myth," Pecky continued, "until an old persnickety crocodile surfaced in England with an actual map, it is told, to the Ancient City. This crocodile may be five hundred years old, which is old even for a tough Nile croc."

"The crocodile!" Ian exclaimed. To hear of the crocodile startled Ian. Things were falling into place from his past visions and experiences.

"Mmmm, yes." Pecky gave Ian a searching look. "Rupert planned an expedition to find the City of Light. He left Penderby six months ago to meet your father's ship in Brazil, where they would both continue to Africa, and, hopefully, to the Ancient City."

"We haven't heard from my father in many weeks!" Ian said. "Do you know where he is now?"

"Regularly we would receive word of their journey—that is," Pecky said sadly, "until over a month ago when all contact ceased, and no one has heard a word since. It was as if the African jungle just swallowed them up."

"So, you see, my dear boy, you and I need to go on a journey to find your father and maybe even an Ancient City. On this trip, I need a true heart. Of course, you must go on this journey willingly and with an open mind. So, what say you, are you up to the challenge?"

Although his path was clear before him, Ian also felt, fear and doubt. He knew he had to leave and was worried that he might not return. Ian knew how troubled his mother was at the lack of communication from his father, and now he, too, was thinking the worst that might have happened.

Something deep down worked its way up into his mind. A renewed sense of self sprang from his heart that stated, "This is your destiny."

Ian merely said, "When do we start?"

"Good show," said Pecky. "We start after we finish our tea and these delicious butter cookies, of course."

The first thing on Ian's mind was his mother. Any mother who wakes to a letter explaining that her seventeen-year-old has gone on a journey to Africa would be distraught, but Ian's mother knew her son possessed a gift that belonged to all. Ian knew that she would understand.

Ian gathered a few belongings that he would need on his journey and wrote a short loving letter to his mother. He thought it best not to mention circumstances behind his father's lack of communication, as she was already so worried about him. Ian did remark that he was with Peckerage Hornblaster, III so that she would know he was in good hands.

Ian opened his front door, turned around, and looked at his beloved home. Then he stepped through the doorway to start his long journey.

•••

It occurred to Ian as he and Pecky walked in the brisk wind down the familiar path toward the forest, that if they had to walk to Africa, it was going to be a long journey. Ian turned to Pecky and asked, "How are we going to get to Africa?"

"By sleigh, of course," replied Pecky.

At the edge of the sloping glade that bordered the forest, a large sleigh, sitting amid autumn's remnants of goldenrod and Queen Ann's lace, glowed in the light of the harvest moon.

The sleigh appeared to be old but in excellent condition. The runners were painted bright red, and the sides of the sleigh were highly varnished tiger maple.

There were two cushioned seats upfront and three rows of bench seats in the back. When sat upon, the slightly weathered cushy red leather seats made a crinkly sound. Draped over each bench seat was a thick wool blanket.

There was a cargo hold with an oak cover in the rear of the sleigh that had many drawers, and one big bin in the center.

A peculiar object rose from the floor next to the driver's seat. It was a lever made of gold, to the right of the two golden foot pedals, and the grip at the top of the lever was a ruby the size of a clementine.

"Seat belts are always required when the sleigh is in flight," Pecky cautioned Ian.

The only response Ian could muster was, "Flight?"

"Yes, flight. How else did you think we will be able to arrive in England by early morning?"

Pecky patted the side of the sleigh as if it were alive. "This sleigh was a gift to my great-grandfather from a good friend, and it's been in the family ever since. It's useful to travel around with, I might add."

"Pecky," Ian laughed, "The sleigh looks like what Santa Clause might fly!"

Pecky smiled. "Yes, Hans Muller was a good man, but I wouldn't call him a jolly old elf. He was a German physicist who lived in the early 1800s. He studied zero-point energy.

"Hans created a device that becomes lighter than the energy that surrounds it and he built this sleigh to travel on flows of energy. Electromagnetic energy flows from the North Pole to the south, creating different frequencies of energy throughout the world. The sleigh travels on these flows of energy. People utilized sleighs for winter transportation in 1820, thus, Muller felt, a sleigh with runners was ideal to transverse the fields of energy.

"I do believe that some of the folklore about your Saint Nick is when young children saw Muller test fly the sleigh around the Netherlands and Germany."

Pecky settled his ample bottom in the driver's seat. He placed his webbed feet squarely on the two golden pedals in front of him and rested his flipper on the ruby sitting on the golden lever.

A moment later, translucent green lights glowed from the bright red runners under the sleigh, and with a lurch forward, the sleigh started to rise.

Pecky skillfully guided the sleigh between a couple of tall trees that stood at the eastern edge of the glade. Then the sleigh slowly rose above the forest.

Ian spotted his house as he and Pecky flew above the village. The moon's light illuminated the town below, and he could see his home. The kitchen light was still on, and the pale stream of smoke floating out of the chimney was caught by the wind and disappeared into the night.

Pecky steered the sleigh southeast towards the mighty Atlantic Ocean, and it wasn't more than fifteen minutes until they reached the shoreline.

"Pecky, do you think I will ever return?"

Pecky looked down at Ian with a warm smile and replied, "Yes, you most likely will, but when you return to the green mountains, you will have changed. You will find that the home you love will look different and feel different, but that, my dear young man, is the nature of growing up and going on such a journey."

As the sleigh quickly traveled over the sparkling black ocean, Ian pointed out a brilliant set of stars in the east. "Oh, Pecky, look at the stars!"

Pecky looked over in the direction of the stars and replied, "Yes, Orion's belt and surrounding Orion are Betelgeuse, Rigel, and Sirius."

"My father used to point these out to me when we were on camping trips. He felt that any son of a sailor should know how to navigate by the sky."

"Quite right, your father. Well, these are merely some of the stars I will use to navigate our way to England tonight. I primarily use Sirius and the bright north star, Polaris."

Ian looked to the north and followed the handle of the Big Dipper to the brilliant Polaris, the first of the stars that his father had shown him as a boy. He missed his father acutely, and now he was worried about him. He wondered where in the world his father was and if he and Pecky would be able to find him.

They flew rapidly over the endless water while Ian thought of this and other news that he had learned from Pecky. Then he asked, "Pecky, how is it that you speak English?"

Pecky looked at Ian thoughtfully, formulating his response, "I was wondering when you were going to ask.

"First of all, I am not talking English; I am speaking my native tongue. Ian, I have not changed. What has changed is your perception of me and your understanding of my language.

"One of the important gifts you possess is the power of hearing. For the last few months, you have heard the world in an all-new way."

"Yes," said Ian. "Once I turned seventeen, it seemed as if the whole world was talking to me. I don't know how it happens, but it is like I am a part of everything now."

"Well, Ian, consider how Latin is the base language for all the romantic languages. What you are hearing is the principal language of the universe, which is a single vibration of energy.

"The concept is not unlike computer languages that initiate with binary code. You hear the binary code of the world, and because you can hear the base language, everything and everyone in the world is talking your language.

"Your heart is translating everything you hear around you into a single conscious understanding that your mind is interpreting as language. Does this make sense to you?"

Ian reflected on this moment. "Yes, it is not unlike what I learned in art class last semester. My teacher explained the way our minds interpret light. That white light is made up of all colors, and our eyes are primarily prisms separating the light into different colors that our mind interprets as reality."

Pecky looked at Ian with delight and replied, "Yes, that is exactly right. I am so pleased that you have understood this concept. It is important during our journey that you start to understand and embrace your gifts."

Ian sat back in his seat, looking up at the stars considering what Pecky just told him. He knew Pecky was right, that he had changed—stretched, perhaps into a bigger world.

Ian turned to Pecky, "Pecky, what is your home like?"

Pecky sighed and took his time to respond, but finally said, "My home is a hard place to describe.

"Penderby is a large white expanse nestled between a row of magnificent silver white mountains that shoot up into the sky. A bay of crystal-clear water that is teeming with life.

"In the morning, when the sun comes up, it sparkles in a rainbow of orange, red, and blue over the many icy islands that speckle the bay. When the sun sets, there are long purple shadows cast on the white landscape from the surrounding mountains.

"To you, Penderby might seem to be desolate and foreboding, but to those who live there, it is a beautiful home like no other. What makes Penderby a home is the community of family and friends who accept and love each other.

"I have realized how special my home is from my many travels. Sometimes you need to go away to appreciate what you have."

Ian considered what Pecky said. "I think I understand what you mean. For many years I took for granted my home in the valley of the two green mountains until I turned seventeen, and I somehow knew I would be leaving soon.

"I cherished each moment I was fishing, walking through the woods, or just hanging out with my friends. I was trying to live each moment there, but I knew something was pulling me away. I think I knew that you were going to arrive one day soon. I did not want to accept the inevitable."

Pecky replied, "Ian, growing up is hard for everyone. Change is the fire that we all must walk through to realize our greatest potential."

Ian looked around. They were many miles out to sea, and the ocean surrounded them as far as the eye could see. He looked down and watched the shadow of the sleigh, created by the large glowing moon, move against the calm ocean below. He thought of his home. He thought of his mother waking to his absence and his father somewhere lost. Ian considered it must be the cold night air making his nose water and his eyes tear. ❧

☙

Chapter Four
Queen Me

Aspectrum of colors spread across the vast ocean in front of the sleigh as the glowing red sun broke at the point where the dark sky met the emerald sea. A light breeze traveled over the sleigh, gently waking Ian to a new day and the next leg of his journey.

Ian sat up, a sleepy look on his face, and pulled his blanket tight about him. Still half asleep, he first imagined himself in his soft bed in his home under the apple tree, but in an instant recalled all that had happened the night before. He quickly looked around.

Pecky was buckled in his seat next to Ian with his head tightly tilted down and tucked under his right wing, snoring and making gurgling sounds. Pecky's presence assured Ian that the night before was not a dream.

Ian could see the ocean in every direction. The sleigh was speeding along in a straight line. Ian was concerned that no one was steering, but it seemed they were flying without any problem.

Deciding not to take any chances, however, Ian softly nudged Pecky in the ribs with his left elbow to wake him up. At first, it increased Pecky's snoring, but after another good nudge, Pecky sputtered awake with a bit of a startle.

"What, huh?" replied Pecky. "Oh, my dear young man, I had a frightful dream. I was back in Penderby, and my wife Penelope was standing on the beach crying. She was trying to tell me something, but I could not quite make out what it was she was saying. I do hope she's okay. You know it is said dreams are doorways into our soul."

Pecky continued, "I hope you slept better than I. I always have a hard time sleeping in flight. By tonight we will be able to sleep in cozy beds with crisp white sheets and bed warmers to keep us nice and toasty."

Troubled, Ian replied, "I slept well, thank you. I was little concerned to find you asleep, and the sleigh driving itself. Do you even know where we are?"

Wide awake, Pecky now composed himself and calmly said, "Not to worry, the sleigh has a reliable autopilot, and yes, I know exactly where we are. I can see the coast of Ireland on the horizon. We should be in London in time for a late breakfast. I could use a cup of Earl Grey right now. Mmmm, Marmite, kippers..." He trailed off with a wistful look on his face.

Ian asked, "Pecky, I've been wondering. How are we going to fly into London without anyone seeing us? I mean, won't it be strange to see a large emperor penguin flying a sleigh above the streets?"

Pecky smiled. "Not to worry, no one will see us—at least no one who would make a fuss about it."

With a confused look, Ian said, "I don't understand—how will no one see us?"

Pecky thought for a moment, formulating the proper words. "Ian, what I am about to tell you is crucial, so please listen carefully. It's all a matter of the heart. You see, when children are born, they have open hearts and open minds. As they grow up, the world creates restrictive barriers that, in time, close off most people to what lies beyond what is taught as the norm.

"Most adults become so focused on being accepted or loved by their peers that all they think about is obtaining those things, such as money and power, which will help them achieve that one goal.

"The good citizens of London are not going to consider for a moment that we even exist. They are going to go about their day with heads down, and hearts closed, focused on what they think will make them happy."

Ian watched the penguin as he spoke and thought of many of the good citizens of his village.

"There is a story that was just recently told to me that might help you understand this vital concept a little better.

"When Christopher Columbus first discovered the new world, the three ships in the harbor were invisible to the native tribe that lived near the beach because they had no concept of such things. At first, the shaman saw only ripples in the water, but he didn't know where they had originated.

"He came down to the beach every morning to examine the movement of the water. After many days he finally traced the ripples back to the ships, and, because he had an open heart and mind, he finally was able to see the ships.

"Many things in this world happen all around us that few see because they lie beyond the barriers in our hearts."

Ian thought for a moment and said, "It's funny, Pecky. In my mind, I don't understand what you mean, but in my heart, it makes perfect sense.

"When I was little, I would play out in the forest near my home for hours. Every so often, I would see something out of the corner of my eye.

"Once I thought I saw a tiny bearded person walking through the forest, but when I approached the creature, it looked more like a piece of wood. As the years passed, most of my friends lost their imagination for such things, but not me. I kept seeing creatures out of the corner of my eye."

"Ah, yes, the creature you speak of does exist, and it did not turn into a piece of wood to escape your view. What happened is that your mind turned the creature into a bit of timber, because the concept of another being walking through your forest was more than your mind wanted to grasp or accept at the time.

"In many ways, the world around you only reflects how you see yourself. If you are cut off from your heart, then the world will support how you feel by cutting you off from all that is wonderful around you.

"Ian, the universe believes in abundance; it is only people who believe in scarcity. So, if you ever have a choice, remember: Listen to your heart. It will show you an abundant world that your mind might not be able to comprehend."

Ian sat back in his seat and contemplated the information that had been given to him. He watched the shore of Ireland quickly meet the rushing sleigh.

The lush green landscape swiftly passed beneath them. Pecky flew only five hundred feet off the ground to avoid passenger jets and small aircraft. Pecky told Ian that the people below didn't see them, but they surely would feel it if the sleigh crashed into an oncoming flight.

Below the sleigh Ian saw patch-quilt designs of different farms, tiny, charming villages, and people moving about their day, oblivious to the giant emperor penguin flying overhead.

Then they were over the choppy water that lay between Ireland and England. Pecky steered slightly to the northeast towards London, eagerly anticipating a hot breakfast.

It wasn't more than a few minutes before Ian and Pecky saw the tall buildings of London loom on the horizon. Ian was surprised at how small the British Isles are.

Pecky steered up the River Thames towards the center of London. Ian was quite enchanted to see Big Ben, the stately buildings of Parliament, and the giant wheel alongside the river. He considered words alone could never describe the beauty of London from five hundred feet off the ground.

When his stomach rumbled, his focus changed from sightseeing to food. Ian turned to Pecky and said, "I'm getting hungry, Pecky. Are we there yet?"

Pecky chuckled. "Look straight ahead over the top of those buildings near the park. That is our destination."

Ian looked at what appeared to be Buckingham Palace. He thought it an odd coincidence that his class at school had been studying English history for the last month. In his wildest dreams, he never thought he would have the opportunity to have breakfast at Buckingham Palace.

Ian asked excitedly, "We are going to meet the Queen of England?"

Pecky looked at Ian with a bit of a smirk, and said, "She's quite sweet when you get to know her, but remember whenever you are around the Queen in the presence of others, she is to be called Your Majesty, or Ma'am, like ham." Ian thought of a large plate of ham and eggs. His stomach was taking over.

"She and I go way back to my days at Oxford," Pecky was saying. "To her close friends, she is known as Lilibeth, and I'm sure you two will hit it off nicely."

Near the horse barns on the south side of Buckingham Palace sat a solitary figure on an iron bench. Daniel was an old Australian Aborigine. No one knew his age or how he came to be the head horse master at Buckingham Palace. He did have a way with horses that was almost miraculous.

Daniel had deep-set blue eyes in his craggy ebony face and a shock of curly white hair covering his head. His voice was soft, almost a whisper. He only talked when there was something important to say, and when he did, people focused their attention on what he said.

Pecky steered the sleigh into the horse barn and came to a stop in the usual stall prepared for his arrival. Daniel was whittling a piece of wood when Ian and Pecky walked out into the hallway.

Daniel looked up. "Pecky, I am glad you had a change of heart."

"So am I, Daniel, so am I. And may I introduce my young friend, Ian?"

Daniel rose from his chair, giving Ian a warm smile and a gentle pat on the back. He directed Pecky and Ian to a wrought iron-banded door at the back of the horse barn, pulled an old skeleton key from around his neck, and placed it in the lock.

Through the opened the door, Ian could see a dark stone-lined passageway steeply leading down a series of steep steps into a tunnel below the barns. Daniel pulled out a flashlight to lead Ian and Pecky through the dark tunnel.

The musty passageway reeked of the ages. As Ian walked through the tunnel, he imagined the kings who used it for adventures, escapes, and for ill deeds.

"This shaft led to torture chambers in the bowels of the palace," Pecky explained, "and it was only in the last hundred years that it was finally closed off from the palace. Unfortunately, it didn't close off the history of those cruel acts that men do to others. And now the instruments of torture have only become more sophisticated."

They strode past dark wooden doors belted with iron, some with small barred windows. Ian turned to Pecky and asked, "Pecky, what did Daniel mean when he said he was happy you had a change of heart?"

Pecky looked a little embarrassed. "It's silly, Ian. It's a well-known fact that we penguins consider ourselves world-class checker champions. We often spend the cold months of the Antarctic winter playing checkers, and in the spring, we have our big Tournament of Checker Champions.

"When I was last here, Lilibeth and I played a brisk game of checkers, and she defeated me three games out of four. Just before she defeated me again, I made an excuse to leave for home."

Pecky paused to check his toes intently for a second. "I have felt distressed since, and I need to resolve the situation. You see, Ian, sometimes we let the darker angels of our nature take hold of our reason, even for silly things."

Daniel was silent while Pecky and Ian talked, but his slight smile indicated that he heard everything said. They walked up stairs that seemed to go on and on. Finally, they walked into another hallway that ended at a large wrought iron-banded door. Daniel opened the door with his skeleton key, gave a warm glance at Pecky and Ian, turned, then walked back down the stairs and out of sight into the tunnel below.

The door led to a modest room that seemed to be an entryway to a small apartment in the palace. Near a large window with yellow curtains, there was a small table with white and purple flowers in a vase. On the window box seat under the window sat an elderly woman wearing a floral nightgown. Ian thought for a moment that this woman might be one of the Queen's ladies because she seemed fragile and small, but when she gave a warm smile of greeting to Pecky, he realized that this delicate woman was the Queen of England.

Pecky gave a remarkably graceful bow to the Queen, and they looked at each other, then laughed heartily.

"This is the young man I was telling you about," Pecky said, indicating with a flipper towards Ian. Startled, Ian bowed down and said, "I'm quite honored to meet you, Your Majesty."

Elizabeth II inclined her head slightly and said, "I'm quite glad to meet you, my dear young man. Please let's retire to the sitting room to hear what you two boys have been up to." Elizabeth then turned to Pecky and gave him a warm pat on his flipper.

Up close, this woman wasn't fragile at all. Ian could see the strength of a mighty monarch in her eyes. Her voice had the power of purpose and a sense of knowing.

They all walked into the adjoining room where there was a small fire in the fireplace. On a linen-covered table, the Queen had a bottle of port and a dish with pickled herring for Pecky.

Ian watched Pecky as he and the Queen caught up on past and current affairs. The relationship between Pecky and Elizabeth was warmly intimate. It was like watching his mother gossip with one of her close friends. It surprised him that even the Queen of England liked a good scoop from time to time.

Elizabeth finally turned to Ian and said, "What have I been thinking! You must be famished, young man. Sometimes I get lost in conversations when Pecky is around. So, let us adjourn to the kitchen and a hearty English breakfast." Elizabeth directed Pecky and Ian to the small kitchen attached to her apartment. To the relief of Ian, everything was waiting for them on the table when they entered the room. "This is wonderful, Ma'am, I'm starving!" Ian exclaimed.

"Spoken like a true teenager! Ian, please call me Lilibeth while we are in these quarters, all my friends do, and I hope you and I will be great friends. When we are in the castle, you will need to call me Your Majesty to keep the decorum of my position in the realm of England.

"Pecky, we have prepared all your favorites: kippers, kedgeree, and toast with Marmite, as well as some good English black pudding, grilled mushrooms, eggs, toasted crumpets with marmalade, and plenty of tea."

Ian's eyebrows rose as the Queen recited the menu. It certainly was a lot of food, but what was it? He didn't fancy eating "black pudding" on an empty stomach, but being a hungry teen, he was game for anything. Pecky, on the other hand, was clapping his flippers together and smacking his beak as he noted all the treats laid on the table. "My, my, Lilibeth, you've outdone yourself!"

Over breakfast, Lilibeth and Pecky continued to talk of glorious days past. It seemed to Ian that adults often forget the difficult times and only remember the good times.

When they had eaten their fill, the Queen, Pecky, and Ian returned to the sitting room where a crackling fire warmed the room, and big toile-covered chairs invited them onto their depths to relax. Between two chairs was a small table with a checkers game still in play, black and red disks dotting the board.

When they had all gotten comfortable in the cushy chairs, Pecky turned to the Queen and said, "So Lilibeth, what is the significant information you must tell me?"

The Queen replied, "I have to be honest, Pecky. I used that excuse to get you here so that we could continue the game. I do have some valuable information you need to know, and there is someone I would like you to meet."

Lilibeth continued, "Rupert's expedition to the Lost City wasn't the first. Twenty years ago, an English explorer, Gabriel Dutchberry, discovered a golden map in the national museum, which was given centuries ago by whom, well, no one knows.

"Gabriel set out on an expedition to darkest Africa and never returned, but ten years later, one of his servants surfaced in London with a tale of an Ancient City. He talked about a City of Light that had great magic for healing but couldn't remember where the City was or how to get there. The poor man was half out of his head with what he had gone through, but he did have the map to the City. However, no one knew how to use it properly. It was a queer map, not our sort of map. The map disappeared soon after, and no one knew what had happened. I suspect that the nasty old crocodile you are going to visit has the map."

Ian was listening attentively. He was having a powerful déjà vu listening to the Queen talk of maps and ancient cities and felt a determination in his heart to follow the path she presented. "There is something else. I don't want you to be worried, but there is information that other forces don't want you to reach the Ancient City. Something dark is surely afoot. You and Ian need to prepare for your journey ahead. The council has whispered the name Legorian."

Pecky replied, "I appreciate your concern, but I have no other alternative than to find out what happened to Ian's father and locate the City of Light.

"More will be uncovered, as my heart tells me, on the path to the Ancient City. Also, Ian will be by my side, which comforts me to no end." He placed a flipper on Ian's shoulder and looked down on Ian fondly. The Queen nodded and smiled to indicate that she agreed.

"Who is this person you would like me to meet?" Pecky asked.

"She will be joining us for dinner, so what say we finish that game." Pecky and Lilibeth turned to the checkerboard laid out. Lilibeth made the first move. She yelled out in delight, "Queen me!" They looked at each other and broke out in laughter. ❧

CR

Chapter Five
Friends in the Dark

I an watched as Elizabeth and Pecky played checkers for almost an hour. He was happy to sit there, taking in the newness of everything. It was strange that only the day before he'd been in his familiar bedroom and now, he was in Buckingham Palace with a giant penguin whooping it up over checkers with the Queen of England. A strange thought popped into his head, "You have friends who are waiting for you in the dark."

Ian thought this curious, and almost said something to Pecky, but before he could, Pecky looked up at Ian and said, "I'm surprised that you haven't asked the Elizabeth for permission to explore the palace."

Ian considered that most wouldn't pass by such an opportunity. He turned to the Queen and asked, "Would it be alright if I walked around the palace?"

The Queen said, "I wondered when you would ask. Ian, remember that Buckingham Palace is old and has many secrets. Please do not go through any hidden passageways you might stumble upon because you never know where they may lead, or what might be waiting for you on the other side."

Ian wondered if she were joking, or worse, serious. He assured her that he would keep to the main halls.

"Many people have seen ghosts walking the halls of this palace," the Queen cautioned, "and since you are sensitive to such things, you might see more than you want. My lineage goes back many hundreds of years, and many of my kin have done unspeakable acts of torture to the people who we now try to serve."

Elizabeth stood up and walked over to a bookshelf at the far corner of the room. She pulled out a small wooden box from the top shelf. The box was old and worn, with carved dragons on all four sides and a gold crown etched on the top.

Elizabeth opened the cover, took out a beautiful gold pocket watch, and handed the watch to Ian. "This watch has been a possession of the British Empire for more than three hundred years. It came back from the farthest borders of our eastern empire. It holds a special power. It never needs to be wound, and it keeps perfect time no matter where you are."

Ian looked down at the watch and saw that the face had one large set of hands and three small sets of hands with Roman numerals, which to Ian had no apparent purpose. The gold that surrounded the watch was a pale yellow with a delicate etching of a fierce dragon on the back.

Elizabeth continued, "I am entrusting this watch to you for your journey with Pecky because I know it will bring you back to me safe." She explained to Ian how to use the watch to calculate time.

"Thank you, Ma'am. This watch is very..." Ian stopped at a loss for words. The Queen smiled. "Now, run along, young man, and make sure you are back in the apartment by no later than six for dinner."

Ian slid the watch into the front pocket of his coat, said goodbye, and then headed for the door into the main hallway.

The contrast between the monarch's apartment and the main hall was so extreme Ian felt as if he had passed into another time and place. Her apartment was bright and sunny, not unlike any home of a kindly grandmother, but the main hallway was formally ornate with high ceilings and stone floors covered with thick carpets.

Old tapestries lined the walls, and there were suits of armor positioned along the corridor. Ian thought it odd that nations display objects from the height of their power. They must do this to remind themselves of their days of glory.

The rooms that lined the hallway were spotless and decorated with traditional furniture. Even though wealth filled the halls, Ian felt an emptiness permeate the palace.

Ian wandered through the palace for most of the afternoon. On the first three floors, he found business offices with many people coming and going looking quite busy; in fact, they didn't seem to notice him at all. There were many museums throughout the palace. When Ian ventured onto meticulously maintained palace grounds in the front, he noticed that the Queen's apartment was not on the top floor. He could see a row of windows right above. He thought this strange because he didn't notice any stairs leading to that floor, even though he thoroughly checked each room.

A voice deep inside him said once more, "You have friends who are waiting for you in the dark." He knew he could feel in his heart that something or someone was waiting for him on the top floor, and now he felt compelled to find a way up to that floor.

As Ian was about to search, he heard a voice from behind that broke his concentration.

"Hello, Ian." He spun around and saw standing in front of him a striking young lady. Her hair was dark red, and her eyes were piercing blue. She was slightly taller than Ian, probably no more than a year older.

Something else struck Ian more profoundly than words could communicate. There was a connection with this young woman that defied time and space. He felt connected to her, felt a shared destiny.

"How do you know my name?" Ian stammered. "Who are you?"

"My name is Beatrice, but most call me Bee. Not B-E-A, but B-E-E, because my grandmother says that when I was a baby, I was always quite the busy bee. As far as knowing who you are, the whole palace was informed about you before you arrived with Pecky. It has been a long time since someone like you has visited Buckingham Palace, and we were all excited to meet you."

"It's nice to meet you as well, Bee." Ian had regained his composure. "Maybe you can help me find the top floor. It has piqued my curiosity."

A stern look came over Bee's face, and she said, "Oh, I don't think that would be wise. That floor has been shut off from the rest of the palace for many hundreds of years. There is a rumor that it's haunted.

"However, I know of a secret passageway that leads there. I discovered it a year ago but have yet to venture into it."

Ian considered Bee's information, "My heart tells me that there is something or someone waiting for me on the top floor, and they need to tell me something important."

Bee replied, "I feel that too." She sighed. "I guess we need to explore the top floor."

The two of them slowly walked up the winding stairways from one floor to another. When they reached the sovereign's floor, Ian turned to Bee. "Will you show me where the secret passage is?"

Concerned, Bee said, "Are you sure you want to venture up there? I still think it might be unwise, although..."

Ian said with determination, "Bee, I have to do this. I feel that I couldn't continue with my journey without the information I will learn on the top floor."

"Yes, I know," Bee said.

Bee walked down the hall to a colorful tapestry of Henry III, who ruled England eight hundred years earlier. She lifted the tapestry, and behind was a small hole between exposed bricks. It looked as though a couple of blocks had merely fallen out.

Bee reached in the hole, felt around, and pulled a wooden lever she lo-

cated there. Instantly an outline of a door broke in the brick wall and moved
forward. Bee pushed at the door, exposing a short tunnel that led to another
smaller wooden door.

The door was made of hardwood and looked like it had not been opened
in a hundred years or more. There were thick spider webs around the edges,
and the wood had warped from the heating and cooling of the seasons.

Ian and Bee looked at each other with a little bit of fear, but both knew
they needed to move forward. Ian reached out to pull the simple iron latch
that held the wooden door tightly secure. To their astonishment, the door
opened with their first try, making a whoosh sound as if the pressure had
built up over time and was released. Behind the door was a narrow staircase
leading up.

When he put his foot on the first rung of the stair, Ian felt a heavy weight
on his heart. He could feel sadness and anger, and then he got cold chills and
started to sweat.

Bee, just behind him, touched his hand. "I felt it, too."

At the top, they could see only a dim light shining through cracks in
boarded-up windows. As their eyes got used to the dark, they could see that
while the top floor was similar in layout and architecture to the other floors,
it didn't have tapestries or suits of armor, and the brick walls were shedding
their plaster and paint.

There were old rugs, and sheets slung over furniture that looked to be
hundreds of years old, and, in one room to the side, plates, and tableware left
out on the round dining table as if people were in a rush to leave.

There was something else. Ian turned to Bee and quietly said, "I feel
something terrible happened here." Bee nodded in agreement.

As they almost tiptoed through the main hallway, they heard, faintly, children giggling and laughing. The sound seemed to be coming from outside.
Continuing cautiously down the corridor, they heard footsteps running, like
children playing, but they didn't see anyone.

They heard giggling and laughter again, with a distinct voice crying,
"Ready or not, here I come!" They followed the sounds to a room that looked
like an old nursery, with tall bright windows that shone brightly onto gray
walls and a dusty floor. There were two small wooden beds on either side of
the chamber with horsehair mattresses, covered with torn and tattered sheets.

There were old wooden toys on the floor, and children's clothing
thrown about the room. There was a stillness in the room that was different
from the rest of the floor, and they both felt a presence, and they both
had an eerie feeling.

From behind them, a voice said, "Would you like to play with us?"

Bee and Ian turned and saw two children sitting on one of the beds, looking right at them. There was a little girl with long ringlets about six, and a little boy no older than ten. They both wore unusual clothing, and their pale, almost translucent skin glowed in the sunlight from the windows. Ian and Bee stood frozen with amazement at the specters in front of them.

The boy said, "My name is Thomas, and this is my sister Sarah. What are your names?"

Bee paused for a moment and said, "My name is Bee, and this is my friend Ian." Ian and Bee realized that these two children were the ghosts that occupied the top floor and it was these small beings who would give Ian the information he needed

The two pale children sat down on the floor and started to play with a carved wooden horse and a porcelain doll. Again, the boy asked Bee and Ian if they wanted to play with them.

Bee sat next to the two ghosts. Gently she asked, "Thomas, what are you doing here? Why are you here?"

Thomas looked at Bee, then Ian and said, "I do have something important to show you, but I'm scared."

"Thomas, what are you afraid of?"

Thomas looked at Ian with a frightened look on his pale face and said, "I'm so afraid that he will find us." Then Thomas calmed down, and now with a mischievous look on his face, he said, "It's a beautiful day, can't we just play?"

In that instant, the room around Ian began to transform, and in a moment, the room became a beautiful little nursery with the windows wide open and sunshine pouring in.

The gray that covered the walls was gone. Instead, there were murals of beautiful ladies in elegant gowns waving to armored knights on horses. There were yellow brocade curtains at the windows and a beautiful red and blue rug covering the floor.

A loud explosion outside the walls of the palace startled Ian. He looked around for Bee, but he was alone in the room. Something significant had happened, Ian knew, and he was aware that this was part of the information he was supposed to know before he could move on with his journey.

Ian quickly got up and went to the window. To his amazement, there was a small army of warriors on horseback just outside the gate to the palace. In front of the force sat one warrior on a black stallion wearing a suit of black armor. The soldier's helmet shadowed his face so Ian could discern no facial features.

The sound of children playing in the room made Ian turn around, where he saw Thomas and Sarah playing in the bright sunlight. Their skin and hair were not pale anymore, and they both had life in their eyes.

Thomas approached, and Ian asked him, "What time is this?"

Thomas looked up at Ian with a puzzled look on his face and said, "It's morning, of course."

Ian pulled out the pocket watch the Queen gave him and looked closely at the hands. The main set of hands read 5:10, but Ian calculated the three sets of hands in Roman numerals and came up with 10:00 in the morning. He thought for a moment and considered that perhaps he was reliving some past vision of time and space. This concept made perfect sense in his heart, but his mind was having a hard time grasping the idea.

Ian asked Thomas, "What year is this?"

Thomas looked at Ian blankly. "Year?" Ian quickly revised his question. "Yes, who is the monarch?"

"Why King Henry, silly, King Henry II." Thomas gave Ian a look that a child who has one-upped an adult would give, a kind of smirk, and returned to Sarah.

Ian looked out the window and stared at the dark figure on horseback. In his heart, he knew this was the reason for his visit to the top floor. When he turned back, it was to a gloomy room in disarray once again, and the two pale children were on the floor with their carved horse and doll. He looked down at his pocket watch and noticed that the small sets of hands had moved back to their original positions.

Ian sat on the floor by Thomas and asked him, "Who was that dark warrior?"

With a grim look on his pale face, Thomas said, "His name is Legorian. He guards the Ancient City. The city you and Pecky want to find. His purpose is to keep humanity away from the City of Light. He has been in this world for a long time and has become good at deceiving and intimidating all who take the journey."

It's surprised Ian that Thomas knew of his travels and that he talked in such an adult fashion.

"Why did I see an army just outside the palace walls?"

As Thomas played with his horse, he told Ian that Legorian had come for his family, because his father had found the Ancient City and brought back a golden map and a black rose. Thomas looked up at Ian and said, "I fear he has also come for my sister and me."

Ian felt sadness and anger well up in his heart again. He now understood that Thomas and Sarah had suffered by Legorian's hand.

Bee was sitting quietly on the floor next to Sarah. Getting to his feet, Ian glanced at his watch, motioned to Bee, and said, "Thomas, it's time we go. I'm sorry that we didn't get to play, maybe Bee and I will visit you another time."

Thomas stopped playing and looked up at the two. "I would like you to visit. My sister and I sometimes feel lonely and would like some friends to play with."

As Ian and Bee walked out of the room, Thomas stood up and said, "Wait! There is one more thing I need to tell you about Legorian. His appearance can change, and he may trick you into believing he is someone else. His real self, which lies just below the façade, can never change, so you should always trust your heart."

A vision of Legorian on his black steed crossed Ian's mind and heart. All he could see was a shadow behind the armor, or maybe, he thought to himself, Legorian was a shadow.

Ian and Bee waved goodbye to Thomas and Sarah. As they walked down the stairway, they said nothing of their experience together. When they got to the main hallway, Ian and Bee looked at each in complete understanding, then went their separate ways.

Ian reached the dining room of the Queen's private quarters just before dinner. He greeted Pecky and the Queen, who was in a smart blue dress with a triple strand of pearls around her neck. Pecky held a chair out for the Queen, and they sat down. The fourth chair at the table was set, but conspicuously empty.

Pecky looked at Ian with concern and said, "Ian, you have hardly said two words since you came back from exploring the palace. Are you feeling okay?"

With a troubled look on his face, Ian said, "Sorry, Pecky, I just have a lot on my mind and need to work out a couple of things."

"As long as you're okay." Pecky then turned to the Queen and said, "So Lilibeth, where is this person you want us to meet?"

The Queen looked a little frustrated and said, "I can't understand why she is so late. It's not at all like her. Well, let's start while the food is hot."

As they began to eat their first course, the door to the Queen's apartment opened behind Ian. Elizabeth, relieved but still, a tad displeased at the wait, said, "Here she is now!"

Ian turned around, and before him stood Bee with a smile on her face.◈

❧

Chapter Six
Crocodile Tears

The sun streamed through a tiny slit between the closed brocade curtains. Pecky lay in bed quite content to be nestled in such soft sheets. He was never one to let pass an opportunity to luxuriate in the simple pleasures of life. Even though he missed his frozen home, Pecky felt that he could take comfort in his present surroundings, if he must.

Pecky lay in bed for a while, reflecting on the festivities from the previous evening. He could still taste the dry port and pickled herring on his tongue barbs. The conversation had gone long into the night, and during the wee hours, the Queen disclosed information to Ian and Pecky that surprised them.

Elizabeth revealed that Bee was a pure heart and had been preparing for a moment in her life when a twist of fate would take her to the City of Light. The Queen was sitting next to Bee on the couch in front of the fire and took Bee's hand in hers while she talked. "A pure heart is one lifetime away from becoming a true heart. We all live many lives to reach our final self-realization."

"I don't fully understand yet, but I have a deep connection with the City of Light," said Bee. "I need to accompany you, Ian and Pecky, on your journey to exorcise a ghost that haunts my mind."

She said no more about it, and Pecky could see that Ian did not want to ask the questions that filled his heart. Pecky had been on many adventures during his life and knew that part of the voyage is the twists and turns that unexpectedly arise on the path to a destination. The Queen's disclosure about Bee was startling at first, but now that he had time to think about it, he realized it made perfect sense.

A loud noise in the next room startled Pecky out of his thoughts. It sounded like a door slamming and feet stomping. Pecky knew that Ian was in the next room and quickly jumped from his warm bed in case Ian was in some trouble.

Pecky rushed to the next room, putting on his purple vest as he ran through the door. Entering Ian's room, he was surprised to see Ian standing by his bed, packing his bag.

Ian quickly turned around. "Good morning Pecky, I hope I didn't wake you."

"You didn't wake me," Pecky said with concern. "You just brought me out of a daydream."

Ian stood by the bed with a worried look on his face, but when he didn't say anything, Pecky prompted, "What's on your mind, Ian?"

Ian cleared a space on his bed and sat down. "You told me that I had a special gift of sight, but I feel unclear about a lot of things."

Pecky sighed and then sat down on the bed next to Ian. He patted Ian's back with his flipper. "Ian, each one of us has the potential to know our own heart, but it takes a brave heart to face the uncertainty of the journey."

Ian looked frustrated and muttered, "I don't understand."

With a loving smile, Pecky said, "You don't need to know right now because learning is part of the journey."

Pecky continued, "One thing that you should understand is that when someone becomes confused about their path, it's fear and doubt that stands in their way. What are you fearful of, Ian?"

He looked down, then turned to the penguin. "Pecky, why didn't you tell me about Legorian?"

Pecky let out a loud, "Oh!" He considered for a moment what needed to be said, then stood up in front of Ian, laying both flippers on Ian's shoulders. Looking directly in Ian's eyes, he said. "Throughout our journey, many things will be revealed. If I had told you about Legorian before you were ready, it would have been hard for you to understand. I can only act as a guide for you, but the nature of our journey will take shape as you decide to open your heart. Legorian is only a small bump in the road and will only take on power over you if you give that power to him."

"I know I can trust you, Pecky," Ian replied. "I know that deep in my heart."

Pecky sat down on the bed and with a cheerful smile, said, "Trust is a good place to start."

A knock at the bedroom door startled both Ian and Pecky. They turned around to see Bee standing in the doorway, smiling. "Are we going soon," Bee said, "or are you two going to laze on the bed all day?"

Pecky turned to Ian and said, "What do you think, Ian, are we moving forward on our journey?"

Ian replied with resolve, "I'm ready, Pecky."

Pecky jumped off the bed, "Good show! Now let's get some breakfast, I'm famished."

At the breakfast table, the dark cloud that had been over Ian earlier seemed to have vanished, and good conversation was exchanged over a massive breakfast of eggs and bacon, grilled tomatoes and mushrooms, and lots of hot milky tea. A special tray of kippers, herring, mackerel, and serwin, with a side of cockles and mussels, was placed in front of Pecky, who swallowed several whole before the butler had walked away, as the Queen looked on him fondly.

The trio discussed the next leg of their journey with the Queen, and what provisions they would need. Pecky knew that there was a bothersome detour to make before traveling on to Africa, and that was to the home of one persnickety crocodile.

After many hugs and goodbyes with the misty-eyed Queen, the travelers made their way to the sleigh, newly spiffed and shined, in the horse stall. Daniel stood by as they settled in, and Pecky expertly guided the sleigh through the massive barn doors. As they rose into the brilliant blue sky, Bee and Ian could see Daniel waving goodbye from the barns near the palace.

Buckingham Palace rapidly disappeared in the distance as the sleigh traveled almost directly north towards the North York Moors.

Ian could tell how delighted Bee was to take part in this adventure to the Ancient City. He noticed something else about Bee that had eluded him earlier. Bee always seemed to be at ease with her surroundings.

She tended to see things that Ian hardly noticed, and she found beauty in what appeared to be mundane. Sometimes Ian found himself tongue-tied around Bee, but he also felt great comfort in her presence, because Bee was such a kind person.

The meadows of green and villages dotting the English landscape seemed to hypnotize the travelers. But when they finally neared their destination, both Bee and Ian noticed a significant change in the landscape. It was a vast green expanse with no trees or houses in sight. There was a thick fog moving in.

Pecky landed the sleigh on top of a ridge with nothing in sight as far as the eye could see, except wet mounds of heather stalks that have long since flowered. Fog was moving in thick around them.

Ian chuckled nervously. "Are we there yet?"

Bee, too, seemed uncomfortable. "We'll be hearing the baying of the hounds of Baskerville in a moment," she muttered.

Pecky stayed in his seat and turned to Bee and Ian. "I have something important to talk to you about, so you need to listen carefully." Bee and Ian glanced at each other with concern.

Pecky continued, "The crocodile we are about to visit is old and tricky. He is a Machiavellian sort that takes winning seriously. He hasn't lived this long without fine-tuning his talent for persuasion. His name is Sobeck. The Queen believes that he has the map to the City of Light. Sobeck contacted her to broker a trade. We don't know what he wants, but I'm sure it will be costly.

"The one thing to remember when you are in his presence is that he is not your friend, no matter how charming or gracious he may seem. He is a survivor, and a grasper of power and victory, even at the cost of your life."

Pecky could see that this information upset Bee and Ian. Penguins live a dangerous life, leaving little room for subtlety, especially when lives are at risk.

Bee and Ian sat back in their seats with a lot on their minds. Pecky would not caution them thus without the real chance of danger.

The sleigh took off, with Pecky flying it close to the ground not to give Sobeck any warning of their arrival.

On the near horizon, a house appeared out of the fog. It seemed out of place in the middle of marshland that stretched for miles in all directions.

As the sleigh got closer to the house, they could see a beautiful stone cottage with bright green shutters. A white picket fence surrounded a lush garden of flowers in the front of the house, and an abundant vegetable garden in the rear of the house.

As they got close, they could see that it was much larger than a regular abode. Bee wondered if it was the right place, "I mean, really! A white picket fence?" but Pecky pointed out the large black mailbox with the name Sobeck printed in elegant letters.

"Why would a crocodile need a mailbox, especially in the middle of nowhere?" Ian wondered, but considered that the box was no more unusual than the house or the garden.

After the sleigh touched down, Pecky took the ruby knob off the top of the golden lever and tucked it neatly in his coat pocket. "You can never be too cautious," Pecky advised, "especially around a crocodile," and they walked through the gate that led to the front door.

They noticed Sobeck's beautiful rose garden lining the path, and the enticing aroma of the flowers tickled their noses. There were red roses but dappled throughout the front yard were bushes of white and yellow roses, and in the corner of the garden, Ian spied one black rose.

The flower shone with a deep luster that Ian had never seen before. His heart told him that the rose held some power, but Ian questioned his own heart, because how could a rose have any power?

The climate around the house was different than that of the chilly air of the moors with its gusts of wind that cut to the bone. Here, the air was warm and humid, with a feeling of stillness.

The front door was bright red and towered fifteen feet high. The ornate doorknob was at Pecky's eye level, and to the left of it was an elaborate brass buzzer with a bird etched in the center.

Pecky turned to Bee, "Would you be so kind as to ring the bell, my dear?" Bee stood on her toes and pushed the button. In the depths of the house, the buzzer created a loud chirping sound like a bird in distress. The bird's call wasn't familiar to Pecky, but it did rile his feathers a tad.

A moment later, a loud rhythmic clicking could be heard coming from a distant part of the house. It got louder and louder, click-click, Click, Click, CLICK, CLICK, until it was directly on the other side of the door. The door-knob slowly turned, then swung open.

In front of the travelers stood a large grayish-black African ostrich. Pecky, Bee, and Ian stood on the front porch staring in wonder at the tall, elegant bird.

The bird looked down at the surprised trio with disdain, and said, "Master has been expecting you. Please follow me into the drawing-room."

They followed the odd bird into the house. The winding hallway was decorated not unlike a kindly grandmother's house with flowery wallpaper, delicate lace doilies on finely finished tables, and paintings of flowers on the walls. The faintly boggy smell that permeated the house was disconcerting.

Most intriguing were the portraits of people grouped in formal posed photographs, not unlike wedding photographs. Bee thought it strange that there didn't seem to be one picture of a crocodile.

They entered an expansive drawing room with large open windows that did nothing to dispel the dampness of the air or the slightly fetid aroma of the room. At the far end of the room, in a cushy leather club chair in front of a softly glowing fireplace, was an eighteen-foot crocodile sitting with muscular legs crossed and tail snaked around the chair.

Sobeck was smoking a pipe and wearing a crimson flower-patterned smoking jacket with a bright yellow ascot around his rather large and scaly neck. A matching yellow hankie was peeking out of his breast pocket. Perched on his long and horny nose was a small pair of tortoiseshell reading glasses.

As they entered the room, Sobeck cleared his throat and in a thick gravelly voice said, "Welcome, my dear friends, to my humble abode. I can tell you are tired and hungry from your trip. To your left you will find refreshments that I hope will tantalize your palates." He smiled a wide predatory smile and gracefully waved his hands in broad strokes to highlight what he was saying.

Ian glanced over to the food. A plate of cookies, a pitcher of iced tea and a bowl of lemons lay on the left side of the table. Next to a vase of Sobeck's roses, was a large platter with an even bigger slab of extremely rare roast beef hanging off the ends of the tray, the juice dripping red onto the crisp white tablecloth.

"Please rest yourselves on my comfy couch, and my most reliable companion will tend to all of your needs." Sobeck inclined his head towards the ostrich, standing on long knobby legs next to him. The ostrich, standing still and wary as if he were trying to be invisible, gave each guest an appraising look, his long eyelashes fluttering over deep beady black eyes.

Ian leaned towards Pecky and whispered, "This isn't at all what I envisioned. I thought we would find Sobeck in a swamp."

Pecky didn't say a word. He stood like a statue, keeping his eyes firmly on Sobeck. He could see that the couch that Sobeck offered them was too close to Sobeck for comfort, and he graciously replied, "Thank you, Sobeck, you are too kind, but my friends and I prefer to stand."

Sobeck curled his long lips into a pert, carnivorous grin, enough to show some of his razor-sharp teeth, and the shine of one gold tooth in front. Pecky thought this tooth strange, as crocodile teeth are sturdy as steel.

"As you like, my dear friends, " Sobeck replied. "Please don't hesitate to ask for anything, because my only wish is for your happiness."

Pecky took this opportunity. "We would be delighted if you handed over the map to the City of Light," he said, looking straight at the old crocodile.

This direct request put Sobeck off guard, and he burst into laughter. He slapped a pointy little hand on his massive thigh repeatedly, and finally caught his breath long enough to give Pecky an enticing look.

Sobeck straightened his jacket lapels. "You are direct, Pecky." Sobeck lifted his hand in the air, pointing at Pecky with his stubby finger moving up and down, punctuating his words in an accusatory manner.

Sobeck smacked his jaws. "Yes, yes, directly to business. Well, Pecky, then business it will be. Yes, I do have the map, and I intend to keep it. That is unless you bring me something that I desire.

"You must understand, Pecky, I am a crocodile with many delicate tastes, and these desires make my life in this lonely dwelling worth living. It might seem advantageous to live such a long life, but life can become bleak when one has seen and done too much."

Sobeck put his head in his hands and started to whimper. Ian could see great tears like chandelier glass coming down Sobeck's face, and he felt a great sadness in his heart. He also felt something else from the crocodile, something he felt before, but couldn't quite place.

With a need to comfort him, Ian started to move towards Sobeck, but just as he got close enough to smell Sobeck's foul breath, Pecky grabbed him from behind.

In that instant, Sobeck, still sitting in his cushy chair, lashed out at Ian, with his mouth wide open, pointed teeth shining in the bright sun streaming through flowered curtained windows of the drawing-room. He snapped his powerful jaws so close to Ian that he felt his fetid breath on the back of his neck.

Missing his prey, Sobeck let out a terrible groan that sent shivers up Ian's spine. Then, in an instant, Sobeck grabbed the patient ostrich standing next to him and jammed the bird in his mouth. With a horrible grinding sound, Sobeck consumed whole his "most reliable companion." Bee gasped, a look of shock on her face.

A long drop of crimson blood trickled down Sobeck's greedy chin. He pulled out his bright yellow handkerchief and wiped his face, and then daintily tucked his handkerchief back into his breast pocket. Without missing a beat, Sobeck continued, "I see we have an understanding now so that I will get directly to the point. Then I would ask the lot of you to clear out of my home.

"I seek a flower, a precious rose. This rose belongs to an adversary of mine. Why I want this flower is my own business, but I won't give up the map to the Ancient City without first receiving the flower."

He paused, then cleared his throat with a clammy snort. A bit of black feather floated out. "The flower I seek is a match to the black rose in my front garden. The gentleman in possession of this lovely flower is Lord Claridon. He resides in his castle on the Scottish Highlands north of Edinburgh.

"The rose, I am told, is in a secluded garden in the center of his castle. If you bring back the rose, I will give you the map, and everybody will be happy, except Lord Claridon, I assume, but that is not my concern."

With no expression, Pecky replied, "Do we have your word?"

Sobeck was looking directly at Pecky with a sly look on his face, "You have my word, so now I would think you can find your way out, as my most reliable companion is unavailable." Sobeck flicked his gnarled wrist in the direction of the front door and then stared off into the dying embers of his fire with a forlorn expression.

Pecky, Ian, and Bee quickly left the room and headed out the front door, but not before they noticed another ostrich in the hallway. The ostrich didn't say a word, just turned around and clicked away on the shiny wooden floor.

They silently walked towards the sleigh, breathing in the fresh air of the moors. Pecky positioned the red ruby knob on top of the lever and lifted the sleigh off the ground. He turned to Bee and Ian and said, "There is no time to waste. We must make our way to Lord Claridon as soon as possible."

As the sleigh rose, speeding north towards Scotland, Ian mused about their visit to Sobeck, then suddenly remembered where he had felt the sensation he earlier felt with the crocodile. He turned to Pecky and said, "Pecky, Sobeck felt like Legorian, not totally, but enough that I recalled the sensation. Thomas told me that Legorian could take on different forms and that I should always listen to my heart no matter what someone appeared to be."

Pecky quickly looked over at Ian and replied, "Good, Ian, you're starting to know your own heart. That's a bigger step than you might know."

Dark storm clouds accumulated on the horizon as the sleigh continued its journey north towards the Scottish Highlands. Pecky knew that they were in for more than just heavy rain.∛

CS

Chapter Seven
Moon Over Edinburgh

A distant sound startled Ian from his daze. At first, he thought the sound came from his dream, but awakening, he remembered once again where he was, and where they were going.

He quickly sat up and looked around. Pecky had the canvas top up that protected them from rain, but the rain had stopped, and it was a clear, crisp night. Bee was awake and gazing at the rugged landscape below of vast fields and jagged mountains. Low in the sky, a full moon was rising, and then in the distance, he heard the strange sound of clashing metal, once again.

Pecky was examining papers in an old leather briefcase he kept under his seat. When he noticed Ian looking at him, he quickly put the papers away and greeted Ian with a warm smile. Ian thought it strange that Pecky might be keeping secrets, but let it go. He asked Pecky, "Did you hear that strange sound?"

In classic Pecky form, he replied, "Nothing's peculiar, my dear boy, when you know its source. What you heard was the changing of the guard at Edinburgh Castle. I believe it is midnight, and the Black Watch is coming on duty. The Black Watch is made up of those poor souls who stand guard on the castle walls from midnight to four in the morning. In history, it is when the castle has been most vulnerable, and so many good men have died."

The travelers looked out on a spectacular sight as the sleigh flew closer to Edinburgh Castle. A single figure stood guard on the highest wall silhouetted by the yellow moon. It was a piper playing a soulful pibroch, a piping tune, on his bagpipes, seeming almost in time with the swaying of the heather in the wind, a colorful carpet of flowers on the Highlands as far as the eye could see.

Ian knew that he would never forget flying above Edinburgh Castle, hearing the mournful piping of the bagpiper outlined on the ramparts in the light of the moon. He considered that there are moments in life that are indelibly transfixed in our minds forever. These precious moments make up our lives like a spring of water in the desert, sustaining one enough to weather the long journeys in between.

Bee looked away from the piper to ask, "Pecky, where are we going to spend the night?"

Pecky replied, "The best place to spend a night with such a full moon is in the home of the beast that roams the Highlands tonight."

Bee looked at Pecky with a puzzled look. "Pecky, I don't understand."

"We are going to stay at the castle of Lord Claridon. His castle is near the town of Elgin on the banks of the Moray Firth, a mere ten-minute flight from here. He is a loyal but sometimes troubled servant of the crown and will be more than happy to put us up for the night. Since he won't be in until the dawn, we should be able to sleep in relative safety."

Bee was too tired to question Pecky further, and Pecky seemed reluctant, for some unknown reason, to give her a straight answer, so she just sat back and tried to enjoy the flight to Elgin.

Beside her, Ian was thinking about his home in the valley of the two green mountains. It was the first time he longed for home, his family, and the comfort of his room and own bed. He thought about his mother reading his letter, and maybe the heartache the letter caused her. He knew someday he would be home again.

Doubt entered Ian's mind about going on this journey, but he realized if he stayed home, he might never have met Pecky or Bee. So far, everything had worked out. He needed to keep the faith that maybe it always would, at least if his friends were near.

Pecky announced that Lord Claridon's castle was on the horizon and that they should prepare themselves for landing.

The moon was moving below the horizon to the west. They could only see a large structure silhouetted by a large body of water sparkling in the fading moonlight. Bee guessed that the body of water was the Moray Firth that Pecky had mentioned earlier.

Ian felt an overwhelming coldness well up in his heart as they approached the castle. The building seemed dead, and all that remained was a shell. Bee and Ian turned to each other with understanding that needn't be spoken. They both felt the same blank feeling. Ian sensed that the empty feeling he had in his heart was the same feeling he had when he was at Sobeck's home. Something was causing a dead area to engulf the castle. It felt like he was traveling to a different time and place once they entered the property.

Pecky skillfully flew the sleigh right into the barn on the south side of the castle. He found a stall that was big enough to house the sleigh out of sight of anyone who might happen by, or who might care to examine a flying sleigh.

As the trio walked towards the front gate of the castle, Bee commented, "Pecky, it just dawned on me that there are no horses in the stable - in fact, it seems that there are no animals anywhere."

"I didn't want to alarm you," Pecky said, with a concerned look on his face, "but there is a curse on this castle that will allow not man nor beast, nor even you, my dear, any peace. Be cautious, but know that I wouldn't bring you anywhere that was beyond our abilities."

At this moment, Ian saw something out of the corner of his eye move fast on a hill to the west. He had a momentary vision of a beast with radiating green eyes and a black soul trapped in the body of a man.

Unaware of this, Pecky continued, "We will be quite safe inside the castle. for the night. You are not to wander the grounds until the sun shines on the Firth once again, agreed?"

Bee and Ian both let out a resounding, "Agreed!" They were exhausted and had no desire to go anywhere but bed. Ian wondered if he could sleep after seeing the—what? He did not know. The vision of the beast concerned him, and he tried vainly to erase it from his memory.

A thought, or rather a picture, filled his heart and mind of a black rose on the side of a distant shore. The black rose was one of many that covered the mountain in his vision. His visions came in short bursts, not unlike memories that he never had, or maybe had in another place or another life. Ian considered that perhaps he had other lives, and maybe there are many other places than what appears in front of his eyes.

On the other side of an old drawbridge, a towering open oak door greeted the travelers. Illuminated by warm yellow light from the hall was a tall, gaunt man in a traditional butler's suit, neatly ironed and black as the night with a bright white shirt but tattered and threadbare.

Pecky handed the man a folded paper with the seal of the Queen on it, saying, "We are here on the Queen's business. Please announce us to the Lord of the house."

With a stern expression, the butler opened the letter and glanced at it. He then said, "Of course, Mr. Peckerage, my name is Portman. Welcome to Claridon Castle. The Lord of the house is indisposed, but be assured he will be most pleased that you make his home your home. Please follow me and I will show you to your quarters."

As the trio walked through the grand entrance to the castle, Ian had an overwhelming feeling of floating. The feeling was not unlike what he felt when he traveled in a small airplane once. He felt grounded but not grounded at the same time.

They followed Portman through a massive lobby, a grand staircase, then a labyrinth of halls and chambers until they reached a set of three small cozy rooms on the south side of the castle. Each room had bright and cheery patterns of flowers, not unlike the home of Sobeck.

After they had each deposited their packs and bundles in their rooms, Portman brought them to a large room with a bright fire in the stone fireplace and food laid out, as if their arrival was expected and their host had long since prepared, so Ian asked, "Portman, did you know that we would be arriving tonight?

Portman replied, "Sir, there is little that happens in the Highlands that does not come to our attention."

Pecky interjected, "You didn't answer the question."

Portman replied, "Yes, exactly."

Pecky decided to leave it at that and indulge in the late-night goodies before him, which included Scottish delicacies like Finnan Haddie, Arbroath Toasties, and more Finnan Haddie in the Cullen Skink.

"Lots of fish here, isn't there?" Bee said, smiling at Pecky.

"Never too much fish, I say, " replied Pecky.

After their late supper, which Ian found surprisingly good, the three retired to their rooms for the evening. A cool breeze from the Firth rippled over the castle, and the Highlands and damp fog moved in over the hills. But the fireplaces in each room emanated warmth. On their beds traditional Scottish clothes were laid out for their breakfast in the morning with Lord Claridon.

Ian lay in bed and wondered what adventure tomorrow might bring. He thought about vacationing with his family on a sunny island in the Atlantic. Each summer, his family would rent a small house on Block Island. The highlands surrounding Claridon Castle reminded Ian of the island and brought back warm memories of his childhood, good enough to calm his mind so that he could fall asleep without thoughts of a beast moving about the highlands.

The howling that startled Ian out of a sound sleep was entirely different than the music of the bagpipes he heard a few hours earlier. He fumbled for his coat, quickly pulled out the watch the Queen had given him from the pocket, and turned the face towards the dying embers in the fireplace. The clock read exactly 3:33 a.m.

A tenseness filled the room. Everything became still, and even the cinders in the fireplace seemed not to move. Ian sensed that something was outside his bedroom window. The moon had dipped below the horizon, and outside his window, it was pitch black. He peered into the darkness beyond the win-

dow looking for some glimmer of light when to his shock a set of cold green
eyes looked back at him from the veil of night.

Ian started to move back from the window when whatever crouched on
the other side of the window let out a howl that shook the foundations of
Claridon Castle. The sound was not like a wolf but like a beast fighting for its
sanity. The din had a hollow sound like a man crying out in a deep dark cave.

Ian ran out to wake Pecky, but both Pecky and Bee were standing in the
common room carrying candles that lit their faces. There was a frightened
look on Bee's face, but Pecky seemed not to be worried. He was trying to
calm Bee down when Ian approached.

Ian walked up to Pecky and said, "You know what patrols outside of this
castle in the dark of night, don't you Pecky?"

Pecky hesitated a moment and then said, "Yes, I do know the beast."

With a look of pity that Ian had not seen before, Pecky continued, "It is
our benefactor Lord Claridon. Tonight, he is fighting for control of his soul,
as he has done every year at this time for the last thousand years."

Pecky's lack of alarm despite the woeful howling calmed Bee and Ian.
Bee remembered Pecky's remark that as long as they were in the castle, they
would be safe, and it went a long way to comfort her heart.

"Many feel that the actual transition of the year does not happen during
January, but it occurs during late October. It is as if one door closes, and another one opens. When the moon is full, and the world is between the two
cycles, we are most vulnerable to that part of ourselves that tries to control
our minds and hearts."

"What door are you talking about, Pecky?" Bee asked.

"Bee, as a child, you celebrated Halloween during October for a reason.
Many feel that the world around us is made up of many layers of energy that
come together or come closest during the autumn. You see, when someone
dies, they don't 'die' as we think of death, they transcend to another level of
consciousness. When we see a ghost, what we are seeing is a clearer vision of
that other side and those who occupy different levels of energy."

He turned to Ian. "Ian, what time was it when you looked at your watch?"

"It was 3:33 a.m. exactly."

"3:33 is another time during each day of the year that the two realities of
energy are close to each other. Many believe that the dead are around us all
the time; we don't see them during the natural course of our day. Unless you
are a pure heart, then, as you have mentioned, you start to see them out of
the corner of your eye."

Ian considered what Pecky said. "Is there a connection between Lord
Claridon and Sobeck?"

Pecky walked over to one of the big comfortable chairs near the fire and sat down. He replied, "Your heart is more sensitive than I had imagined. You have already made the connection between Lord Claridon and Sobeck. I am quite amazed.

"Yes, Ian, there is an old connection between the two. Sobeck was once a man like Lord Claridon. Sobeck is not merely hundreds of years old; he is many thousands of years old.

"Sobeck was once a guard for an Egyptian prince who ventured into the jungles of Africa to search for the City of Light. The City is so ancient it has many names that men have uttered for a millennium. It dates before the Druids built stone monuments in Europe. The Egyptian prince found the Ancient City, but Sobeck betrayed the prince to his death. Sobeck's heart is so greedy he couldn't allow any others to enter the City of Light. He stood guard for centuries at the path leading to the City.

"Sobeck didn't know it at the time, but he was bending to Legorian's will. Many have traveled to the City, but when they lose the battle with their souls, they end up becoming devotees of Legorian."

Bee and Ian sat down in the chairs by the fire. They knew that the time had come to learn information that had been flittering in the background since they began the trip.

"You see, the City was a gift of light to the world," Pecky continued, "but those who have no light in their souls twist what gifts the Ancient City offers into darkness, at least in their minds. They stand guard trying to keep the Ancient City from those it was intended to help. In time they go mad and transform into beasts.

"Legorian is the most ancient of all the travelers who have succumbed to their desires of power. As each creature loses its mind, it slowly falls under Legorian's control."

"What about Lord Claridon?" Bee asked.

"Lord Claridon was a Scottish prince who lived more than a thousand years ago. He traveled to the City of Light, because he saw his homeland was under siege from hunger and pain, and he thought that the City could heal the ills of his kin. He is not evil, but when he found the Ancient City, he decided to bring back one black rose, believing it would hold the same healing power over his land as it had done on the hills of the City of Light."

Pecky got up, grabbed a poker, and pushed the logs about to spark them up. "Claridon didn't understand that the force of the City is in its collective power, not in one rose. But by removing the rose, he cast himself and his land into darkness for the last millennium. The field of black roses lie on the outside of the Ancient City. The field of roses are ultimately not what power the Ancient City possesses."

Bee and Ian sat in silence, waiting for Pecky to continue. He was staring into the fire with his head down. Then he continued, "I have heard that to reach the City is to pass through many tests of your courage and, most of all, your ability to listen to your heart. Many, like Lord Claridon, don't meet the challenges set before them." He sighed and turned to the others. "Lord Claridon secured the rose in some ingenious way when he returned from the Ancient City. It has been in this castle for over a thousand years. I don't know what he did, but I imagine he will tell us in the morning."

A sliver of light flooded through the window, and they could see by the hands on the clock on the mantle that it was 5:03 a.m.

Pecky turned to Bee and Ian. "I believe it is quite safe to get a few more hours of sleep. I would counsel both of you to return to your rooms. We don't know what trials we will have to overcome today, but I'm sure we will need our rest."

With a renewed faith that everything would be okay, they returned to their beds and fell asleep with the comfort only wisdom can bestow on a restless mind.ⓒ🅢

ℭ

Chapter Eight
Hall of Mirrors

L ord Claridon slumped in his chair at the head of a long oak table set with gold-rimmed china and etched-glass goblets as Portman guided Pecky, Ian, and Bee into the main dining hall. The battle that had raged the night before between the weary man's mind and heart still showed on his face.

All three travelers wore Scottish kilts that had been laid out on their beds the night before. Lord Claridon required that all his guests wear Highland clothes, because it reminded him of his heritage and grander times in the region.

Lord Claridon motioned to the bagpiper standing like a statue near him. The bagpiper began playing as Lord Claridon stood up with a stagger. He grabbed the piper's arm and pushed him towards the far end of the room as he gripped his forehead. "Damn noise," he said, "but necessary." When the piper finished, he managed to salute the trio with a smart English salute, palm out. "Welcome to Claridon Castle, and God save the Queen," he said as he sat, and before the three sat down, they replied in chorus, "God save the Queen."

Throughout breakfast, Lord Claridon stared out the window and said not a word. His distance made the three uncomfortable as they dined. Pecky ate his breakfast of broiled tomato, beans, and tattie scones covered with honey and relish, but Ian and Bee felt the oppression of their host and merely nibbled at oatcakes with jam. The tea was comforting, and they filled their cups several times with the sweet milky brew.

After the breakfast dishes were taken away, Lord Claridon turned to the trio. "I apologize for my bluntness, but I sense that there is a true heart with you, Pecky."

Pecky replied somberly, "Yes, Lord Claridon, his name is Ian. He is my dear friend, so my heart would break if any harm comes to him."

"I promise you that I don't wish you any harm," Lord Claridon replied, looking at Pecky with sadness in his eyes, "but you see, I have been waiting for someone like Ian to enter the great halls of Claridon Castle for over a thousand years. Only he can free this land of the darkness I conferred upon it."

Portman entered the room, walked behind Lord Claridon, and bent slightly to whisper in his ear. Lord Claridon nodded, stood up, and said, "A warm fire awaits us in the library, so I would ask you all to follow me."

Lord Claridon led them through a long hallway to a comfortable library with thousands of books lining the floor-to-ceiling shelves. Opposite the door was a wall of frosted glass with rectangular outline of a door in its center.

Lord Claridon sat down by the fire in a large chair and said, "Please, make yourselves comfortable, and Portman will attend to your needs. I must confess that I'm not good at the light talk. I've been alive too many years, and as the centuries have passed, so does the need to conceal my purpose with idle chatter."

They barely settled into their chairs when Portman walked into the library laden with tea and scones on a massive silver platter. He placed a steaming tea kettle with Earl Grey tea in front of Pecky, who nodded slightly and smiled.

As Portman poured the tea, Lord Claridon continued, "I assume you know the story of the black rose I took from the field by the City of Light? It has been so many years since I took the flower, even I wonder if the story is made up or changed in some unforeseen way. One thing is certain, and that is the curse on this land."

He sighed and looked gravely at his guests. "Like many things in this world, even the best intentions can go awry. I traveled to the Ancient City to find a way to help my people, but I confess that once in the land, I became possessed with my own need for power. The feeling that rose in me while there was like none other I have experienced."

He dropped his head and was silent for a moment. Pecky stopped eating and watched him intently, and Bee rose slightly from her chair as if she would go to him, but stopped as Claridon continued, "Fear and doubt leave the mind, and there is a sense of bliss that I cannot explain. Only when I left that ancient land did fear and doubt once again enter my mind. When one enters the City, they are not only in a different place; they are in a different state of being— a different state of consciousness.

"I was warned not to take anything from the ancient land, but in my arrogance and stupidity, I would not return to my homeland with nothing in hand. I wanted that rose, and I took it.

"I knew once I returned to Claridon Castle that the beasts that guard the Ancient City would try to repossess the black rose, so I devised a trial that only one with a true heart could understand. I was such a person once," he groaned and slumped back in his chair, his face stony, "but the curse on this land has confused my heart. Now not even I could free the black rose from the hall of mirrors.

"For many centuries, I have hoped for one such as you to come and release the black rose," Lord Claridon said, looking at Ian, "You answered my prayers."

Ian leaned forward and asked, "What is the hall of mirrors?"

Lord Claridon gave Ian a wan smile. "The hall of mirrors, my dear young man, is what lies between you and the black rose."

He continued, "When I returned from the Ancient City, I imported the finest alabaster found in sacred places from around the world. Alabaster is a precious stone that is translucent when polished. From the alabaster, I constructed a labyrinth of mirrors in the courtyard of the castle. I put the black rose in the center of the labyrinth, and it has been there since.

"The black rose created a charm of light and dark on the reflection of each mirror in the labyrinth. As you walk through it, you will see different reflections of how you perceive yourself. Each mirror reflects a different illusion of the observer. For the observer with a kind heart, the right path leading to the black rose will be found. If the observer is not, well, one wrong turn and they will find themselves lost in the labyrinth forever."

Bee looked puzzled for a moment and asked, "Why don't you just tear down the labyrinth and return the black rose to the Ancient City?"

Lord Claridon looked distraught at the question and was silent. Finally, he replied, "The spell that the black rose is casting on the maze is a lot like the ancient land itself. Everything in the City of Light interconnects as a whole—if you disturb one part of the whole, everything is affected. Were I to tear down the labyrinth, the black rose would be lost in the reflection of the alabaster, and this land would forever be cursed.

"Legorian knows this, so he has stayed away. But be assured he knows that you are here and one of his devotees is waiting for an opportunity to take the black rose. I have seen Legorian's followers walking in the forests and along the mountain ridge that surrounds this castle. They are always waiting, never sleeping, but will not come close because of the curse."

"Then why don't you let Legorian bring back the black rose to the City of Light?" Ian asked.

Lord Claridon replied, "I have considered this, but you see, Legorian doesn't want to return the black rose to the City. Instead, he seeks to use the black rose to increase his demented power.

"Legorian has never been in the ancient land; he has always been guarding it against others. I don't think that Legorian can ever enter the City of Light. He connects to the City of Light in some unimaginable way or at least a way beyond my imagination.

"I suppose I should not talk about Legorian's need for power. My own need for power cast the land that I love into darkness. There is only one way to free the black rose and this land, and that is if one transverses the hall of mirrors, one with a true heart."

"If you guard your black rose, why is Sobeck's black rose in his front garden in plain view?" Bee asked him with concern.

"The false black rose that is in Sobeck's garden is a trap. Were you to try to take that black rose and brushed up against the other roses, even a little, you would become his meal. He keeps the real black rose in a safe place, and that is in the room he never leaves."

He looked at Ian. "We are at an impasse. I cannot force you to enter the hall of mirrors and free this land from darkness, nor would I want to. You have to enter the hall of mirrors with an open heart and an open mind."

Bee felt troubled by what she needed to disclose to Lord Claridon and conflict welled up in her heart. She hesitated for a moment but said, "Lord Claridon, we came here to take the black rose to Sobeck because he has the map to the Ancient City. He will only give the map to us if we give him the black rose."

"I appreciate your honesty, Bee, but there is one thing I know. Ian is here to free this land. Once you have the black rose, many things will take place to change the direction of your path back to Sobeck. I must keep faith that whatever happens, it is for good. I advise all of you to take time to consider what lies before you because once Ian enters the labyrinth, he cannot leave until he has reached the black rose. I have found," he said contemplatively, "that clearing my mind is the best way to hear what is in my heart."

The land surrounding Claridon Castle was grand in the light of day. Fields of heather lay to the south of the castle with majestic mountains jetting up in the distance. The jagged mountains reminded Pecky of his home in Penderby; he had told Bee before he returned to the still-full tea table, at least enough to bring a tear to his eye. Ian and Bee waved him off then followed the path into the woods near the Moray Firth.

As Ian entered the woods, out of the corner of his eye, he saw movement, a dark figure, and, in an instant, he had a vision of Legorian on his dark steed. The dark figure disappeared into the forest. Ian felt a wave of fear before he regained his composure. He knew that he could not show his fear as the shadow devotee of Legorian would exploit his feeling of dread.

Bee and Ian walked for several miles on the path through the woods without saying a word. As they turned to go back, Ian finally broke the silence. "Bee, I'm starting to feel like there is a bigger journey ahead of us than finding my father and the Ancient City—that even Pecky doesn't understand the nature of our adventure."

"Yes, I also feel that there is a reason you and I are here. We must work together to lift the curse from this land. I hope the black rose will never fall into Sobeck's hand."

As they reached the castle, Ian said, "Bee, I need to enter the labyrinth first, and then, for some reason, you also will have to enter. Knowing you will be there, that I will not be alone, will give me courage."

Bee replied, "Ian, you are never alone while I'm here."

In the library, Lord Claridon and Pecky were patiently waiting for them, and both stood up when Bee and Ian entered the room. Lord Claridon turned to Ian and asked, "Ian, have you found your path?"

With determination in his voice, Ian replied, "My path leads through the labyrinth to the black rose." Bee smiled at Ian, then said to Lord Claridon, "I, too, follow that path."

Lord Claridon raised his glass of port and said, "Here is to the end of darkness and the beginning of the light once again."

"You don't need to do this if you don't want to," Pecky said with a concerned look on his face. "We could go to Africa and find another way to the Ancient City, my dear boy." He glanced at Bee with some perplexity. He was seeing that there would be more to this adventure now that Bee was showing her resolve.

"I know that you are concerned about me," Ian replied, "but if I were to turn my back on this trial, I would have to come back another day to face what lies behind the glass door."

He turned to Lord Claridon and said, "Where do I begin?".

Lord Claridon looked at Ian with a steady eye, then turned and pointed to the glass door on the other side of the room. "You begin at the entrance to the labyrinth."

Ian walked over to the outline of the door and could see no apparent doorknob or handle. The door was perfectly fit into the wall. Ian could not see a crack between the wall and the door. The alabaster was much finer than glass and had a silky sheen.

He had paused before he pushed on the right side of the door. He knew if he waited too long, he might lose his courage. He glanced at Bee, who nodded at him, then pushed on the outline. The door swung inward, exposing a small hexagonal room with mirrored doors in five of its walls. Ian walked in, looking back at his friends, then let the door shut behind him.

When the door shut, it appeared to have no seam that marked the outline of the door. Ian pushed at where the door had been, but all that was left was a wall of dark glass. He turned around to face five mirrored doors. At first, he could see no reflection on any of the doors, but slowly each mirror started to pixelate and move. His image appeared in the mirrors, each one facing him and not moving.

Ian thought of what Lord Claridon had said, that each of the mirrors only cast an illusion and to keep listening to his heart.

A bold voice startled Ian from the door in front of him. Looking at the mirror, Ian saw his reflection staring back at him. It was such a clear image he had a hard time discerning if the figure in front of him was the reflection or he who was the mirror image. The figure mouthed something.

Ian asked his reflection, "What did you say?"

The reflection replied, "You are a fraud."

"What do you mean, I'm a fraud?"

"You might have Pecky fooled, but I know that you are not what he says you are. Maybe you should have told Pecky that he had the wrong person before you even started this sham of a journey. You may think you have what it takes. but if you question it at all, then perhaps you haven't deluded yourself as much as you think you have?"

This convoluted statement puzzled Ian. He stared at himself, but another voice started talking. He turned to his left and saw a reflection of himself that looked much younger than he was.

The reflection said, "You are special, Ian, but Pecky had no right to ask you to go on such a dangerous journey. You don't need to go on this venture to prove yourself. Pecky is not true to you, Ian. He has many secrets and will betray you in the end."

Before he could reply, his reflections in four of the five doors began talking to Ian, trying to persuade him of his foolishness. The clear reflection on the fifth door merely stood before Ian with a warm smile on his face, not unlike the smile Pecky had when bantering with Ian.

The four reflections were talking louder and louder until Ian thought he'd go mad. He could barely discern what they were saying, and he had a hard time hearing his own heart. He thought of the beautiful apple tree that stood by his home in the valley of the two green mountains. The image calmed him and focused his understanding.

He reflected on the fear and doubt that riddled his mind and wondered if he was a true heart. What even was a true heart? Pecky seemed to know and believe. He knew he needed to overcome his fear and doubt. He had to believe in himself and believe in his friend's wisdom.

He studied the mirrors. It seemed obvious that the reflection that said nothing would be the right way, but he felt it was a trap. He looked at the reflection in the first door that had reflected his fear and doubt and said, "I don't want you anymore." The room of mirrors became silent, and Ian opened the door.

He was in a dark hallway lined with another five mirrored doors, but these mirrors each reflected the black rose, and each of the five reflections seemed to be the same. As Ian walked to the end of the hall, a great sense of sadness welled up in his heart. He felt tired to his core. The black rose has brought such grief to this land, he thought, even though it was intended to bring only joy.

There was not a sound in this corridor of mirrors, and each reflection felt to Ian to be the right way. Ian sat down on the floor and considered the puzzle before him. He was so tired, and all he wanted to do was to fall asleep. He lay down on the floor and drifted away into his dreams.♋

ℭℨ

Chapter Nine
A Silent Voice

Ian was walking in his dream. He was conscious of himself dreaming yet knew that he was still asleep. As Ian slept, he reflected deep in his heart that if he were in a dream, and the dream was his, then he should be able to control the dream and create whatever he needed to protect himself. As he lay in his unconscious state, he remembered a dream in which he was on the edge of a tall building looking down, fearful of falling. In that dream, Ian was aware that he was dreaming, and he willed himself to fly. He controlled his actions in the dream and saved himself from falling.

The dream he was in now was dark with no apparent direction. There was a light haze all around him and a single dim spotlight overhead. He walked freely in the dream but felt he was going nowhere. He couldn't walk away from the spotlight that was casting a shadow below his feet.

He remembered lying down on the floor and going to sleep and tried to remember how long he had been asleep. He didn't know where to walk, and he surely didn't know how to wake up. He went back to his memories and remembered the labyrinth.

In the dimness, he heard a faint voice. He couldn't tell if the voice was in his head or the haze. He looked in the direction of the voice but couldn't make anything out.

Ian called out, "Is someone there? What was it you said?"

A voice in the distance replied, "I said, 'Are you lost?'"

Ian looked hard and started to make out a form in the haze, and then he replied, "How can I be lost in my dream?"

Ian watched as the form walked around him in the dark just out of his vision. He couldn't tell if the shape was male or female, and the voice didn't give any indication of gender.

The figure stopped on the edge of the haze and said, "We often find ourselves lost in this dimension or others."

The word "dimension" struck Ian as odd. "Is this not my dream, or am I somewhere else?"

The form continued to walk outside the dim circle. "This is surely your dream, but unlike any dream, you might have experienced before, not many return from this dream. This place is in between the light and the dark."

Ian felt a sinking feeling in his stomach at the thought of never returning from his dream. He looked directly at the form. "Who are you, and what are you doing in my dream?".

The shape walked towards him into the light haze. As Ian focused on the image, he began to make out a young man wearing a Scottish kilt and sporran. His shock of black hair, dark as the night sky, was partially covered by his hat, and his bright green eyes that shone even in the haze seemed familiar to Ian.

As Ian realized who he was, the man replied, "I am Llewellyn Murchadh Fingal Claridon, Lord of Claridon Castle, which sits on the shores of the Morey Firth in the Scottish Highlands. Who are you, laddie, and what are you doing in this place?"

Perhaps Lord Claridon was just a phantom in his dream, but then Ian reconsidered because Lord Claridon seemed so real. He asked Lord Claridon, "Don't you remember me?"

Lord Claridon stopped a few feet away from Ian, "Why should I remember you?"

"We just had a conversation in your library at Claridon Castle. Don't you remember?"

With a look of longing on his face, Lord Claridon replied, " I have been cut off from the man you had a conversation with for a long time. The man that resides in Claridon Castle is an empty shell eaten away, day by day, year by year, by the curse on the land."

"How can you be cut off from yourself?" replied Ian.

Lord Claridon looked sadly at Ian. "Ah, but you are lost from yourself the same way. As long as you are in this place, that part of yourself that brings love and hope to your life will fade away slowly. So slowly, you won't notice it until one day, all that is left is an emptiness in your heart."

The thought of being lost in such a place was frightening to Ian. "How can I find my way back?" he said urgently. "How can I wake up?"

Lord Claridon looked at Ian with an empty stare and said, "It has been so long I don't remember where I came from, nor where it is I was going. I do remember encasing the black rose in the labyrinth, but after that, the haze clouds my mind. You are the first one to come this far since I have been here." He paused, looked at Ian, then said abruptly, "The rose resides under the spotlight."

Ian looked around and saw nothing. "I don't see the black rose. How can it be under the spotlight?" In frustration, he cried, "You said there are others here. Where are they?"

"There are many others who have tried to take the rose and have found themselves here. I come across them from time to time wandering in the mist," replied Lord Claridon. "They are of such a black heart that they have become devotees to Legorian, losing all light in their minds and souls. They become mad with power, with a hunger to destroy those who are still alive."

"But how can the black rose be right in front of me, yet I can't see it?"

Lord Claridon looked bewildered. "I don't know; I don't know! But I do know that the black rose is under that spotlight. I just can't…" Lord Claridon turned around and walked away into the mist.

Now alone again, Ian became frightened. He ran after Lord Claridon, but he had vanished into the endless darkness, and Ian found himself standing under the hazy spotlight once again.

Ian told himself that he didn't need to be scared. He calmed his mind again with the image of the apple tree and sat down in the circle of the spotlight. Knowing that he was so close to the black rose helped cheer him. He focused all his attention on the spotlight.

Ian thought of how, in his dream, he was able to change the outcome. He felt deeply that this place was different but, in some way, the same as his dream.

Ian knew deep in his heart that he could change the outcome to his fate in this place. Something beckoned from his heart and mind, a thought that if he overcame this challenge, it would be presented to him again during his journey to the City of Light.

Ian thought of his friends waiting in the library. Time passed without measurement in the haze, without beginning or end. He wondered if it had been hours, days, or maybe even years since he entered the darkness. Unlike Lord Claridon, his mind was still clear, so he didn't feel that it had been that long.

A conversation popped into his mind that he had with Pecky during their flight to England when Pecky told him that the reason people couldn't see the sleigh was that they couldn't perceive that such a thing existed. People block out what they can't understand.

Maybe, Ian thought, he couldn't realize that a thing like the black rose existed in different dimensions, or that there were different dimensions of time and space.

A voice broke Ian's concentration. The voice seemed to be all around him in the haze. He couldn't make out what it said. It sounded a lot like being underwater and hearing someone yelling his name through the water.

He remembered his name, and that the voice was shouting it, "Ian!" The voice became louder and louder, "Ian, wake up, Ian wake up. Why won't you wake up?"

A distant light came towards him, and the haze around him brightened. From that place, in between, he moved back into the light.

He found himself lying on the floor of the labyrinth hallway, looking up at a face cast in yellow light with multiple colors radiating out. As his eyes cleared, he saw Bee looking down at him with bright blue eyes. A smile began on her beautiful face. "I thought I lost you," she said gently.

"I guess for a moment you had," replied Ian. He took a deep breath and continued, "How long have I been asleep?"

With surprise, Bee asked, "Don't you know?"

"No, I don't remember."

"You've been gone for almost three weeks!" exclaimed Bee.

The news that he had been asleep for many weeks didn't shock Ian because Lord Claridon warned him of time passing in that place in between. He did find it interesting that he wasn't hungry, nor was he thirsty.

"How did you find your way through the mirrors?" Ian asked Bee as he stood up and brushed himself off.

"If there is one thing that I'm sure about, it is how I feel about myself." Ian looked at Bee, bewildered. "How is that?"

"I will tell you someday when we know each other a little better." A half-smile came over Bee's face, then she continued, "So, what do we do now?"

"I saw Lord Claridon when I was asleep. It was a lost part of him. He told me that the rose lies under the spotlight."

Ian and Bee looked at the five mirrors in the doors. Each mirror had a perfect image of the rose, too perfect. How could the rose be on the other side of the mirrors, Ian thought, if the reflection showed inward? He looked at the spotlight overhead and wondered about what Lord Claridon had said. If the black rose resided under the spotlight, where was it, and why couldn't they see it?

Ian thought again about his conversation about perception with Pecky. Did he need to change his understanding of the black rose? He thought about the flower and what he considered it to be.

Ian sat down, hugging his knees to his chest. Bee settled in next to him. He closed his eyes, thinking of all he had learned about the black rose.

"You're not going to sleep, are you?" Bee said anxiously.

"No, but I've got to work this out. Why are there black roses in the mirrors?" Bee sat while Ian thought. He remembered what Lord Claridon said about the rose not existing inside the Ancient City but on the cliffs that surrounded it. He started to understand that the roses that surrounded the Ancient City created a barrier, not a doorway and that he would need to overcome the same obstacle if he were to see the City of Light.

He looked at Bee and slowly, talking out his jumbled thoughts, said, "Perhaps the black rose creates a higher energy level than most can see. Perhaps if I increase my energy, I could see the rose. Maybe the rose isn't evil at all. Maybe it becomes what people think of it. Maybe the rose creates the world that Lord Claridon thought would be best for his people?"

Bee looked at Ian as he spilled out his thoughts. She was trying to make sense of them and knew that he was right but didn't know how or why yet.

"Maybe the land wasn't cursed at all," Ian wondered. "Maybe time just stopped? Maybe Lord Claridon thought that if time stopped, then all the pain of his kinfolk would stop? Since the black rose existed in another time and space—the time and space it existed in must be what Lord Claridon created more than a thousand years ago. And, if the rose existed a thousand years ago, then it also existed now. I have to believe it or realize it at a higher level of consciousness."

Bee touched Ian's arm and said, "Are you okay?"

With love in his heart, he said, "I think I understand what power the black rose yields. It has no control other than the power of any person before it gives to it. It only creates what is in the heart of that person."

"I don't understand, Ian. If the black rose has only the power of who is before it, then how are we to find it?"

Ian thought for a moment, "Well, I don't know exactly how this works, but there is a time when everything changes hands, or in other words, there are cycles of time and space that make up the world around us."

He paused, then took a breath. "I know that it is time for the black rose to come with us. The rose is not needed here anymore. We have to believe it."

Bee and Ian regarded the mirror and its rose that was in front of them. "You see," Ian continued, "the flower is created based on cause and effect. The rose initially took on the purpose of Lord Claridon, which was to stop all the pain of his kin on this land, but he could never really stop all the pain of life without stopping life itself.

"The effect that the black rose created was to stop all the time for his people, but that creates a whole new experience of pain and suffering. I understand that the rose is only doing what Lord Claridon expects of it. Lord Claridon and his clan are not being held hostage by the rose. The black rose is being held hostage by Lord Claridon. The black rose needs to become part of a new cause for it to create a new effect. Our cause is to obtain the golden map from Sobeck, so we need to engage the black rose with our cause so that it redirects its impact on this land. Does this make any sense?"

Bee replied. "I think I understand what you mean. I once thought that the only way the world would be at peace would be if there were no people in the world. I realized that the effect of world peace would be much different than I could imagine or would hope for, so, yes, Ian, I think I understand."

Ian looked directly into Bee's bright blue eyes and said, "Do you believe?" Keeping her gaze steady on his, she replied, "I believe."

The two looked in the direction of the spotlight. The black rose slowly materialized in the center. It was in a simple crystal vase on top of an old wooden box. The two reached their hands out and together grasped the vessel. In an instant, the alabaster mirrors all around them began to crack and break under pressure, then shattered onto the floor. The sound of the alabaster collapsing was deafening, but not one splinter of glass landed on either Bee or Ian.

The two found themselves standing alone in the middle of a courtyard with the blue sky above them. They stood for a moment in disbelief. Ian considered what would have been if they had not freed the rose.

The library was open to the sky, and the frosted glass wall melted away. Pecky was standing by the fireplace with a tear in his eye when he saw his two friends suddenly standing in the courtyard. He ran to them with open flippers, and with a roar, he exclaimed, "Good God, you have done it!" The three embraced and stood under the bright blue sky, laughing and basking in the moment.

As they enjoyed the exhilaration of their reunion, they noticed that around them in the courtyard now stood those poor souls who had been in the labyrinth. There were more than fifty people of different ages, genders, and origins. They stood silently, looking at the three friends. Some had been in the hall of mirrors so long they didn't remember what brought them to this place or why they were here in the first place.

Ian looked at them and knew that one of them might have been he. He turned to Bee. "Thank you for coming to my rescue."

Bee interjected before Ian could finish and said, "Ian, I am so sorry that I waited so long to enter the labyrinth. I knew we made a deal to go in together, but I was fearful when you first didn't come out that I would be lost, too."

Ian replied, "Bee, not to worry, each one of us has to find our courage. We faced challenges far greater than we initially thought. Everything happens for a reason—you were to enter the labyrinth when you did, and I was supposed to meet Lord Claridon in the dark when I did.

"When I was in the dark, I felt a deep understanding that this task was more than just saving Lord Claridon and retrieving the flower. I realized that this challenge was an important experience that I would use down the road during our journey to the Ancient City. So, you see, you have no reason to feel bad. Ultimately you came to my rescue, and I learned what I needed to know."

Bee replied, "I think what I have learned, Ian, was that I didn't want to lose you. You've become more important to me than my self-preservation, and I know that the only way we can reach the entrance to the Ancient City is together."

As Pecky, Bee, and Ian stood in the courtyard, the spirits of the failed adventurers in the labyrinth faded and disappeared. Ian felt sadness for their lost cause. Looking in the library, they saw a withered man sitting in the chair near the fire. The old man looked vaguely like Lord Claridon. He motioned with his hands for Ian to come closer.

The three walked into the library to see if he was Lord Claridon, but they didn't need to ask because his crystal green eyes gave him away.

Ian leaned over the ancient man so that his ear was as close as possible to Lord Claridon's mouth.

In a low gravel voice that wheezed out of him, Lord Claridon said, "Thank you, laddie." Then the ancient man died with a smile on his face.ᙣ

C8

Chapter Ten
The Way is Hidden

Ian's vision was more than just a passing image in his mind's eye—his vision was a complete and captivating experience. He was no longer at Clarendon Castle, but on the North York Moors, watching a gruesome event take place.

From the ridge above Sobeck's home, a group of shadow devotees descended on Sobeck's home led by one dark entity. The mysterious being was clothed in a cloak, walking but not walking at the same time—he was almost gliding over the land towards the house.

Ian realized that this evil was Legorian, and he was witnessing the start of a battle—a clash between Sobeck and this small dark army. Ian tried to focus on Legorian's face but was unable to see anything other than a shadow.

A cry rent the night, "Ian, Ian snap out of it."

In an instant, Ian was back with his friends outside Claridon Castle in the Scottish Highlands. It took him a moment to regain his composure and remember where he was.

He shook the vision out of his head. "Sorry, Bee, I was somewhere else. It was so real. I was watching a battle unfold between an army and Sobeck."

Pecky flapped in agitation. "Ian, do you know if your vision is happening right now, or was it of the past or future?"

"I don't know, Pecky. I've never had such a strong vision in my life. Things I see are always a brief vision in my head, but this was different. I was there, there on the battlefield, watching the event unfold. It was strange. I knew that Legorian knew I was observing him. I think he felt more powerful knowing I was an observer to his horrid deed."

"We have to leave right now," Pecky commanded. "We might have already lost our opportunity."

The trio quickly secured themselves in the sleigh before abruptly ascending into the clouds. Pecky directed the sleigh, with an urgency and anxiety that they all felt, towards Sobeck's home in the North York Moors.

The black rose had been securely stowed away in the sleigh's oak cargo hold. Portman built a special strongbox, which no power could emanate from within its confines. The oak box was long and thin, with alabaster glass lining the inner walls. Portman assured Pecky that the alabaster would reflect the charm back on the rose.

Bee and Ian were surprised that the sleigh could move with such speed and grace. Up until now, Pecky flew the sleigh at the same sensibly moderate speed, like an old station wagon on a country road. Pecky's face showed urgency and determination. He was so focused on the land ahead he seemed even not to notice his fellow passengers.

The sun was rising in the east, casting a long shadow on Edinburgh Castle as it loomed on the horizon. Pecky flew the sleigh so close to the castle they could see the changing of the guard on the hour. The sound of the bagpipes soared over the high walls and spread out over the highlands.

The sleigh passed by the highest stone tower with such speed and so close that Ian thought they might collide. It troubled him enough to mention it to Pecky. Pecky just smiled at him and said, "Hold on."

Pecky looked at Ian again, but this time with concern in his eyes. Ian considered that Pecky knew something, that he had information that pushed him towards Sobeck's home.

Ian asked Pecky, "What do you know about Sobeck?"

Pecky looked at Ian and hesitated for only a moment, then said, "A Queen's messenger came to me early this morning and reported that shadow guards were marching on Sobeck's home in search of the map to the Ancient City. I fear that we might be too late."

"Pecky, how was it that I could see the battle so clearly, almost as if I was there on the field of battle?"

"Your experience in the hall of mirrors for many weeks," Pecky began, "has awakened one of your valuable gifts—the gift of sight. For most of your life, you have had just passing visions, but nothing as clear and concise as the one you just had.

"Ian, there are two kinds of memory. One is a recollection, and the other type is experiential memory. Recollection is in your mind, but experiential memory is somewhere else. All experiences in the universe are in an infinite reality, for all time.

"Because of your experience at Claridon Castle, you can access this infinite storehouse of knowledge. The experience you had in shadow has awakened that special gift of sight."

Thinking about what Pecky said, Ian said, "Pecky, there was something else. Legorian was leading the shadow army, and I knew he was aware of my presence."

With an anxious look, Pecky replied, "Ian, I was worried that might happen. You see, Ian, you existed in a land of shadow for weeks. Legorian commands that world of darkness.

"Now that you have awakened your gift of sight, you have become a deadly adversary for Legorian. He is now aware of your existence—and your power."

"There's Sobeck's home," Bee exclaimed, pointing ahead in the distance. "I can see the roof." They all strained to see Sobeck's house as they flew nearer. As they neared the grounds, they saw the first evidence of impending trouble. Below, walking around in shock, they saw two of what looked like Sobeck's reliable companions. They wore their bowties, but one had some of his formal jacket ripped off, and blood was splashed on their feathers.

"Maybe Sobeck was going to make a snack out of them, and they ran away," Bee surmised, but her heart was conflicted with this scenario. She knew that something more significant had happened. Bee didn't want to believe that Ian was right about Legorian. In some fashion, she didn't want to trust that Ian had a gift of sight that she didn't have, but her heart told her otherwise.

There was something different about Sobeck's house. The windows were dark, and animals were running around the property, through the gardens and past the white picket fence surrounding the house.

Pecky landed the sleigh a hundred yards from the front gate to determine what was going on. "I didn't want to take any unnecessary risks," he said crisply, "so Bee and Ian, you stay in the sleigh while I inspect the house."

Legorian's army had destroyed the garden in the front of the house and had burned all the plants to the ground. The false black rose that was in the center of the front yard was gone, and all that was left was scorched, smoking earth.

One of Sobeck's ostriches was walking around in a daze, muttering something. Pecky walked up to the chap, "My dear fellow, what happened here?"

The ostrich kept muttering, "The master is dead; the master is dead." Looking into the eyes of the ostrich, Pecky saw that something had terrified it so much that it had gone blind. He knew the fate of a blind ostrich on the North York Moors didn't look good but didn't quite know how to help the poor fellow.

Pecky motioned for the others to climb out of the sleigh and follow him into Sobeck's house. He could see that whatever had happened had long passed and that they would not be in any danger.

They cautiously walked through the halls of the house towards the main room, looking for other animals or anyone that might be able to help them discover what happened. The house was in shambles, with furniture and vases and lamps smashed on the once-beautiful wooden floors, now splintered and gouged. Someone had taken off all of Sobeck's pictures from his walls and sliced them open off the frames. Ian couldn't understand what they wanted. Why would it be on the back of pictures?

The drawers in the cabinets were torn out, and the floral wallpaper was ripped to shreds. The closer they got to the drawing-room, the stronger a stench permeated the halls of the house. The heavy smell seemed to wrap itself around the trio as they cautiously moved towards the center of the home.

A faint voice warbled something from behind them. All three of the travelers spun around to see one of Sobeck's servants standing in the hallway by a slashed portrait. The bird's beautiful coal-black eyes looked at the trio with despair. "They came in the morning mist. We had no warning."

"Who came in the morning mist?" Pecky asked gently, approaching the ostrich.

"Legorian, and they who walk beside him in shadow." A feather drifted to the ground. Bee felt she would cry, seeing the desolation of the once-proud bird.

"Did they find the map to the City of Light?" Pecky asked.

"The map is still in its secure place, but they did take the black rose," replied the ostrich mournfully.

Sobeck's most reliable companion hung its head, and large tears dropped to the floor. He looked up at Ian and slowly walked toward him, his nails clicking on the ruined floor. "Ian, my life was spared to give you a message from Legorian. He is now aware of you, and your intention to enter the City of Light. He wants you to know that he will do everything in his power to prevent you."

Ian felt immensely lost and alone for a moment as he heard this terrible message, but then something deep in his heart told him that Legorian had no power over him unless he gave it to him.

In an instant, the bird regained his cheerful nature, and the ostrich asked with a bright smile, "Can I make you all some breakfast?"

Pecky replied with surprise, "That would be nice, thank you."

The servant turned around and now, with purpose in his heart, click-clacked away into the kitchen.

Pecky looked at Ian and said, "Remember, Ian, Legorian aims to inflict fear and doubt in your heart. He cannot have power over you if you oppose him."

They continued slowly towards the study. Pecky reckoned that a battle had played out between Sobeck and Legorian and was concerned with what they would find in the crocodile's study.

Sobeck's body was lying on the floor in front of his chair. He wasn't moving, but the trio approached cautiously for fear that Sobeck was setting a trap. But when they neared the enormous crocodile, they knew he was dead. Sobeck's swelled stomach spread over the parlor floor. His bulk was even more impressive as they stood over him. He looked more like a prehistoric dinosaur now that he was dead, other than the animated character that had so recently greeted them.

Pecky examined Sobeck's body to try to determine what had killed the crocodile. All he could find was a small indentation at the base of the skull. He couldn't imagine that something so tiny could take down such an old leather-tough crocodile who had lived so many years. Pecky knew that Legorian had murdered Sobeck.

"They took the map!" Bee abruptly blurted. "The ostrich is wrong. They must have found the map to the Ancient City!"

Pecky stood up, shaking his head. "Most likely, they took the black rose because it existed in Sobeck's destroyed arboretum. But they don't have the map to the Ancient City."

"How do you know?" Bee demanded.

"Because the map to the City of Light is in a clever hiding spot," Pecky replied. He walked over to the fearsome crocodile and pried apart the crocodile's massive jaw, exposing its row of lethal teeth. There was a golden tooth near the front of his mouth. Pecky bent down and, with his beak, tapped at the gold tooth. The sight of Pecky with his head in the crocodile's deadly jaw unnerved Bee, and she gasped. Pecky looked up at her, smiled, then reached in with his flipper, dislodging a round golden sphere inside the tooth. He stood up and presented to Bee and Ian the map to the City of Light.

The golden sphere appeared perfectly round and smooth without any apparent markings. With closer examination, they saw a small indent on one side of the globe, and at the opposite side of the orb, there was another small indent. Each of them came to the same conclusion that the two indents represented the south and the north end of the globe.

"But what end is which end, and how do you use it?" asked Bee.

Pecky replied, "We won't find the answer to that until we are at the gate to the Ancient City. Just getting the map without any major mishap is the first step. Everything else will fall into place as we move along."

Bee had an overwhelming feeling of calmness that Pecky was right. A good heart needs to decide on what path they are walking, and the universe will direct the steps in the right direction. But she remembered her concern about giving Sobeck the black rose in exchange for the map to the Ancient City. She wondered if Legorian would be furious if he knew that he helped them get the map.

The ostrich walked into the study with a laden silver platter. They all thought it strange that the servant did not react to its master lying dead on the parlor floor. The ostrich went about his business as if nothing had happened.

The thought of eating breakfast so close to Sobeck's already decaying body didn't sit well with the three, so Ian asked the ostrich to wrap their meal for the journey ahead. Sobeck's most reliable companion cheerfully returned to the kitchen, where he carefully wrapped each breakfast, tying it with red and white string to keep it tidy. The good fellow filled a large thermos with hot tea and milk and then bagged up some gingersnaps, adding to the big basket he brought back to the study.

Ian wondered if the ostrich was so happy because his master was dead. The fear he most likely lived with daily was gone, thanks to Legorian. Pecky momentarily considered giving the old chap a proper burial, but he knew that the ostriches who were left would take care of all the details. His hope now was that with Sobeck dead, maybe his most reliable companions could get on with their lives.

They walked out of the house into the morning sun with the pleasant smell of biscuits wafting from the carefully wrapped packages the ostrich had prepared. Now that they had the map from Sobeck, things started looking up for the journey ahead.

As the three walked towards the sleigh, Bee asked, "How did you know the Ancient City map was in Sobeck's mouth, Pecky?"

Pecky looked tickled, and said, "When anyone lies, they give away clues to the lie. You might not have noticed, but when we were here last talking to Sobeck, he kept tapping his face with his scaly forefinger. He was tapping his finger right over his golden tooth, and when I asked him about the map to the Ancient City, he only tapped faster. I concluded that he was taunting me with the truth, and he felt smug that he had the map, and what good is it to be smug if no one knows about it?" Pecky guffawed, "If no one knows about it!"

They reached the sleigh without further interactions and climbed in.

"Now on to Spain," exclaimed Pecky.

"Spain? Why Spain?" asked Ian.

"Because that is where Ogden is, and if we are to travel to the darkest parts of Africa, then we will need him," replied Pecky.

"I thought the Queen said he was going to meet us at Hillary's watering hole in Cameroon. Is there something you're not telling us, Pecky?" asked Ian with concern.

Pecky turned to Ian. "I sometimes forget about your gifts, my dear young man. Well. Hmm. The Queen's messenger told me that Ogden is in a bit of a jam and needs our help. Ogden has abilities we will need if we are to make it to the Ancient City, and like any good friend, I need to help him."

"Of course, we will help Ogden," Bee assured him.

With one last look at Sobeck's house, Pecky gracefully lifted the sleigh off the North York Moors, turned it south towards Spain, and gently increased speed.

Bee looked down and noticed that the sun had cast the most beautiful clear light over the moors, highlighting the subtle green and gold shades that spread in every direction. She considered that there is beauty in every place, even what might seem to be the bleakest.

Pecky set the sleigh on autopilot, and all three happily dined on the scrambled eggs, buttermilk biscuits, and fried bacon the ostrich had packed for them.

Ian decided not to worry for the moment about what jam Ogden might be in, and whether they could be of any help. He sat back and enjoyed the company of friends who were becoming dear to his heart. And of course, his buttermilk biscuit, even though it wasn't as good as his mother's. ❧

ᘓ

Chapter Eleven
Energy Sprite

Dense fog and mist engulfed the sleigh like a hand trying to squeeze out whatever enthusiasm might be left in the trio for the journey ahead. The fog was so dense they couldn't see more than three feet in front of them, and from time to time, it would turn from a cold mist chilling their bones to a damp, humid haze that soaked through their clothes.

Pecky flew the sleigh only a hundred feet above the dark ocean below, to not take any chance of hitting a low-flying plane in the fog. The fog created an eerie feeling that made the sleigh seem like it was standing still, despite how fast Pecky accelerated.

They were flying over the Bay of Biscay, a large body of water that lay between the southwestern shore of France and the north bank of Spain. As the sleight passed over the peninsula, they could see the historic town of Brest, which jetted out on the northern part of the Bay of Biscay. It was the last landmass the trio would see before they moved into the emptiness of the fog.

The sun was almost at the peak of its ascent to noon and acted like a kaleidoscope bouncing the rays in an infinite number of directions. Every so often, a streak of light from the sun would penetrate the fog and find its way to the sleigh and into the eyes of its passengers.

Ian was sitting in the front with Pecky when he had another vision. A dark entity was standing in a large underground cave. The entity was not Legorian but in some ways, connected to the shadow lord. The cave was large, with a maze cut out of stone sprawling over the cave floor. In the middle of the labyrinth was a warm light. Ian heard a voice crying out for help, but, in an instant, the vision left him, and he was back on the sleigh next to Pecky once again. Ian thought about the revelation. He knew he could see his future, and it was unsettling.

He wondered if he would ever be able to control the visions and better understand what they were trying to tell him.

He noticed that he was sweating profusely and felt his damp forehead. He didn't know if the vision caused the cold sweat or was it the fog. He decided to put the image out of his mind and think of better things, like his home in the valley of the two green mountains.

Ian looked up at Pecky for a moment considering if he should mention his vision, but Pecky seemed lost in thought. He appeared to be contemplating something, so Ian didn't want to interrupt whatever was going on in Pecky's head.

It had been hours since Bee uttered a word. She had been bundled up on the last bench seat in the sleigh for most of the journey from Scotland. He could sense her melancholy but thought that it might be from the suffocating fog. Ian considered that maybe Bee needed a friend right now, so he made his way to the back of the sleigh.

Ian sat next to Bee. She was wrapped in the black and white striped blanket he used on the journey from New England over the Atlantic Ocean, which seemed like a million years ago. She was reading a book but looked so tense, Ian felt that there was more going on than what was apparent. Ian had little experience with women, except his mother, and didn't quite know what to say.

"What are you reading?" Ian asked.

Bee looked up at Ian with an expression that communicated she wanted to be left alone, and reluctantly replied, "Moby Dick."

Ian considered his next words with as much thought as possible and replied, "That's one of my favorites."

Bee didn't look up this time and replied, "I have to read it for my English class. I find it annoying."

Ian paused for only a moment, "Would you like to be left alone, or would you like a sympathetic ear?"

Bee looked at Ian with a blank, cold stare he had not seen from her, so he was about to turn around and move back to the front of the sleigh when Bee finally replied, "It's okay, Ian, I could use a friend right now."

Ian and Bee looked out into the fog. Bee draped half of the blanket over Ian, which helped him to feel a little closer to Bee, but the distance in her voice still made him feel a world apart from her.

"I've been thinking about my brother, Torin," Bee said with great sadness.

"Do you miss your brother?" asked Ian.

Bee looked at Ian with the blank, cold stare again. "I thought you knew."

"Knew what?"

"I thought because you had a gift for prophecy, you would know."

"Know what?' Ian asked again, feeling strangely stupid.

"That my brother died a year ago today," The quiver in her voice gave away that she was on the edge of tears.

"I'm sorry, Bee, I didn't know. I did feel something, but I didn't know what it was," replied Ian. "When I first met Pecky before our trip, he also was surprised that I didn't have a premonition of his arrival."

Bee sat back in the cushy red seat with resolve and said, "That's okay Ian, I have a hard time making sense of it myself. How can I ask someone else to have insight into something…" Bee stopped and sat back in her seat.

"Can I ask how he passed?" Ian asked.

"My family said he committed suicide. My brother did not die by his own hands," Bee said, with so much intensity it made Ian uneasy.

"Is that why you are going to the Ancient City?" asked Ian.

"Yes," replied Bee, "and no. I want to find out what killed my brother and see that he didn't die for nothing. I know deep down that I'm going for another reason. A reason I can't quite explain. I believe it is the same reason my brother went to the City. There is a longing for the City of Light that my whole family has felt. Each generation has been tied to the City of Light in such a way that until one of us completes the journey back, none of us can find peace again. Does that make any sense?"

"Yes," replied Ian, "and no. I have found myself doing things in my life that make absolutely no sense, only because I feel it deep in my heart."

"You're the first person I've found, except Pecky, who understands my rants—thanks," Bee said, with some warmth in her voice.

"What do you mean by going back?" asked Ian. "Were you at the Ancient City before?"

Bee looked at Ian with that stony blank stare again, "Did I say go back to the City?"

"Yes, you said your family couldn't find peace until one of you went back to the Ancient City."

Bee looked at Ian like she was looking through him. "I've never been there, but I feel as if I have always been, and I'm really out of place here. Like there has always been a little bit of myself missing, no matter how hard I have tried to fit in. I think in some ways, not being able to fit in is what caused my brother so much pain, and a broken heart. I'm a little scared of finally reaching the City because if I don't fit in there—I don't know where I would fit in."

Ian struggled to understand what Bee was saying but was distracted by Pecky, yelling from the front of the sleigh.

"Pecky, what did you say?" Ian yelled back.

Pecky pointed. "The coast of Spain is right ahead."

Ian and Bee looked out to see the coast of Spain rising out of the fog. Bee looked behind the sleigh and saw the fog that they had flown through like an impenetrable wall of nothing. Bee touched Ian's arm and said, "Thanks, Ian. I guess I did need a compassionate ear."

They moved to the front of the sleigh and noticed the big smile on Pecky's face. They both surmised that penguins don't like thick fog either.

"Pecky, where are we going?" asked Bee.

"Toledo, that is where we will find Ogden, and where his assignment was," replied Pecky.

"What assignment?" Ian asked.

Pecky looked down at Ian. "That's going to take a little bit of explaining, my dear young man. Maybe we will have time later."

Pecky slowed the sleigh. Ian looked down and saw beautiful green hills and valleys below. Then a feeling struck Ian with a force that he had never felt before. The feeling was like an exquisitely painful void in his heart.

Ian turned to Bee and Pecky. "Do you feel that emptiness?"

"I do, but not as much as you do," replied Pecky.

"I feel something, but I can't make out what it is," replied Bee.

Pecky slowed the sleigh down more, flying closer to the ground. He seemed to be hesitant about something, something unseen ahead, that made Pecky fearful. He slowly moved the sleigh ahead when suddenly the sleigh started to lose altitude, sinking to the ground like a rock in a pool of water, not fast but with force.

Pecky was able to maneuver the sleigh into the border of the forest below, next to the edge of a large, craggy cliff. The sleigh landed with a thud. Pecky instantly got out of the sleigh to assess if there was any damage.

Ian felt that they had passed through a door of some kind. He looked around and saw no difference visually between where they had been and where they were now, but the void in his heart told him differently. There wasn't any apparent difference, but the world around looked far away. Ian felt not connected.

"The sleigh has no damage, but we won't be able to fly again until we resolve what is going on here. I guess we are committed to the task," Pecky said, half talking to himself and wiping his fins on each other.

"What task?" asked Bee.

"The task at hand," replied Pecky with one of his non-answers.

Ian looked at Pecky with a critical eye and said, "You might as well tell us now, Pecky."

Pecky looked at Ian with concern. "I guess you are right, my dear young man, better to tell you now than later." Pecky sighed and continued. "You see,

Ogden Pearce is known in the trade as a 'Deux Ex Machina,' or better known as an Energy Sprite. Ogden was sent here by the Life Energy Consortium to resolve a conflict between two families at war for control of Toledo, Spain, but was unable to complete his task, so the conflict has caused an energy void to take hold. Now we need to find Ogden and help resolve the dispute, or we are going nowhere."

Ian and Bee looked at Pecky like they didn't know what question to ask first.

"Save your breath; I'll start with what an Energy Sprite is," Pecky said, as he sat down on the edge of the sleigh and grabbed the tea flask and the last butter biscuit prepared by the ostrich at Sobeck's home, or former home.

Pecky continued, "It's quite simple. In ancient Greece, they had theater running all the time, not unlike your ongoing television shows. These plays were ad-libbed, which means the cast made everything up as they went along. When a play developed a conflict or stalled in a way that the players were unable to resolve, they would lower another player on a rope seat from above the stage who would represent God, and that player would solve the conflict in the play.

"In other words, they would add something entirely new to take the show in another direction and start the whole process up once again. Ogden is a lot like the player who resolves the conflict, but in his case, his job is for real, and it is for the well-being of all. When a conflict starts to build between two influential individuals, families, or countries and is not resolved by the participants, then a pure heart like Ogden is sent by the Life Energy Consortium to change the dynamic, and the energy being built up is resolved."

"How does he resolve a conflict?" Bee asked.

Pecky took a sip of cold tea and then continued. "You see, my dear young woman, there is a fine layer of life energy that weaves through all things. It starts in the north and moves south throughout the world. In each area of the world, there is different energy. Everything around us has a different vibration of either positive or negative energy. Everything connects to everything else.

"The way Ogden resolves conflict is simple; he either takes away something that will redirect the energy, or he adds something. Sometimes it's as slight as dropping the right piece of paper to the right person so the whole event is redirected. Then the energy is resolved.

"Sometimes it's merely playing the right music to the right person at the right time, and that right person might drop their guard and open his or her heart just long enough for a resolution to take hold. What we have found is that it does not take much to change the course of history. A small event or series of events redirect the conflict."

"Ogden is a pure heart?" Ian asked.

"He is a pure heart," Pecky replied, "but is not a true heart. He still is troubled by many demons from his past, and those demons have blocked him from really knowing the depth of his being.

"An Energy Sprite is only one of many jobs for a pure heart. It suits Ogden, and he is good at it, but he is still young, and something went wrong here. Now let's hide the sleigh and look for a way to get to Toledo."

They covered the sleigh with branches. They were in dense forest, so Pecky didn't feel that there was much danger of someone coming across the sleigh. But with extra caution, he removed the golden lever, and the black rose from the sleigh and hid them nearby in a rocky crevice.

They had walked for more than an hour before they came to a village in a clearing on the edge of the forest. The town had just a few buildings made of plaster, and there were sheep everywhere.

The thought that it might be strange for the townsfolk to see a six-foot penguin crossed Ian's mind, so he asked Pecky, "Aren't you worried about people seeing you?"

"I'm never worried about people seeing me because most won't even notice. Remember, most adults can't imagine either a flying sleigh or a six-foot Emperor penguin walking around. Trust me, Ian, I have traveled a lot, and it has never been a problem," replied Pecky with certainty in his voice.

"Plus," Pecky continued, "the energy vacuum is starting to grow, and is causing a lot of havoc with everyone, even with those that don't believe in life energy."

"Is the energy vacuum the reason why the sleigh wasn't able to fly?" asked Bee.

"Good show, Bee," Pecky said, quite pleased with Bee's insight. "Yes, remember, the sleigh doesn't fly. The sleigh floats on positive energy, and when a void starts, it sucks all the positive energy out of the life energy field. I'm happy, but surprised that you figured that out so fast."

"It just popped into my head, I guess," replied Bee.

As the trio started to walk towards the village, Ian was worried. Pecky looked at Ian and asked, "Is something on your mind, Ian? Ian stopped, turned to face his friends, and said, "I did not know if I should tell you two, but I had another vision, and this revelation was dark."

"You need to tell us what you saw because your gift of sight will help us along our journey," Pecky said. "If you hold back, your abilities will take more time to grow."

Ian told his friends of his vision of the cave and the stone maze.

"I think, you are starting to build your gift of sight!" Bee pronounced.

"Was there anything else," Pecky asked, "that you can remember about your vision?'

"Well," Ian said thoughtfully, "there was a light in the center of the maze, and a voice crying out in the dark."

"The light is where Ogden is!" Pecky cried. " I feel in my heart!"

They started walking again, somewhat rejuvenated by the conversation, into the small town. It was deserted. ଔ

CR

Chapter Twelve
Dark Moon Rising

A single dark shape crouched on a grassy knoll high on the north side of the village. A beast was intently watching every move the trio made, looking for any sign that one of the three possessed what it was seeking. It watched for any weakness it could exploit.

Ian could feel something watching him, but when he turned around, it vanished before he got more than a glimpse of the dark shape. It disappeared so fast that he questioned himself if he saw anything. Ian wasn't even sure if he should mention it to his fellow companions. He decided to keep it to himself, at least for the moment.

Pecky, Bee, and Ian walked around the town knocking on doors, looking for any sign of life in the isolated village. The few shops that lined the dirt road through the center of town were open with lights still on. There was a radio on in the general store at the edge of a village, but it was playing just static.

Suddenly, Ian felt a wave of energy move through his heart once again. It lasted only a second, but the feeling created a sadness in his heart, and there was something else. When the wave of energy moved through his heart, Ian felt that there were people and animals around him that he could not see. At some level, the town was full of people that were moving about their day like any other day.

"There are others here!" exclaimed Ian.

"What do you mean?" asked Bee.

"I mean that there are other people and animals all around us that we cannot see. A wave of energy just moved through the town and my heart, and I felt other people around me. Why I feel this I do not know, but I know that we are not alone," replied Ian with a concerned look on his face.

"I believe you are right," Pecky said. "I also feel that others are here. When we walked into the town, I felt something, but I wasn't sure until the last energy surge passed through my heart. I believe the incident with Ogden created an energy void. Everyone here was cast into darkness when the void started. As I remember, we also will fall into darkness unless we reach Ogden in time."

"How much time?" asked Bee?

"I don't know exactly how much time is left, but there will be signs of our descent into darkness. First, we will see animals, and then we will see people, one by one, appear. The people we come across will reflect the darkness of their souls. We will first see them in torment; then, we might be part of their suffering if we don't watch our step. We may have as much as three days to finish our task."

A small voice spoke up behind Pecky, "Pecky, you made it."

The three travelers turned around to see standing behind them, a figure wearing a gray hood and cloak. He looked like a man, but he was as short as a boy and sturdily stout. His skin was pale and smooth like fine china, and he had the most beautiful piercing blue eyes, like blue water in a tropical paradise without any imperfections. Bee instantly felt that an enormous depth of wisdom flowed from those eyes.

Pecky looked surprised. "Samuel, it has been a long time. I guess I know why you are here."

Pecky and Samuel gave each other a warm embrace; then, Pecky turned to Ian and Bee. "I would like to introduce my old friend Samuel Dupuis. He is the commissioner of the Life Energy Consortium, and, I believe, our guide to Ogden."

Samuel nodded at Pecky and said in a subtle French Canadian accent, "Oui, you are a wise bird, Pecky." He turned to Ian and Bee and greeted both with an embrace and a kiss on each cheek. The expression on his face then became grave as he said, "We are not alone; Legorian has dispatched his devotees to the area. You and your companions are not safe in this village, so we need to move on before night."

Pecky considered this information for a moment, then earnestly said, "We need to get supplies for our journey to Toledo, so let's spread out and find what we can to sustain us for the next few days."

Pecky and Samuel quickly walked away from Ian and Bee towards the general store. They could tell from Pecky and Samuel's intense conversation that they were discussing something in great detail and needed time alone to work things out.

Bee and Ian decided to venture into the local diner to see what they could find in the way of food. The restaurant's façade was bright white stucco, a mixture of sand, lime, water, and cement, prevalent in the area. The inside of the building was not unlike the diner back in Ian's hometown. The same stainless-steel equipment and coffee maker decorated the restaurant, with red plastic covering all the seats.

"What is that smell?" asked Ian, breathing deeply.

Bee took a deep whiff of the spicy aroma that permeated the room and said, "I know that smell. I bet it's…" She walked over to a big stainless-steel pan on the back burner of the diner's large gas stove. She grabbed a nearby ladle and scooped out a little bit of the contents and then tasted it. A delighted expression came over her face. She handed the spoon to Ian and said, "Do you want to try something yummy?"

Ian smelled the contents of the ladle and then cautiously put it in his mouth. The same pleasing look came over his face. "Wow! What is this?"

"Paella. My mom used to make it before my father went off to war. Now she doesn't make it at all. Isn't it tasty?" replied Bee.

Ian didn't know if he should reply about the paella or the slight comment about Bee's father going off to war. Ian decided to ask about the later, "Your father went off to war?"

Bee looked at Ian like she didn't understand the question and then replied, "My dad has been gone for two years. All I know is that he was part of a special envoy to the Middle East. He's a Colonel in the Royal Marines. The military is not telling us what happened. Even the Queen doesn't seem to know what happened to my father, or at least she isn't telling us."

Ian stood looking at Bee, not knowing what to say when his heart brought forth a vision of Bee standing in the rain crying as her father boarded a plane. The image that passed through his mind was so real that it was if he had a moment of memory, but a memory of what happened to Bee.

The depth of Bee's sorrow touched Ian's heart. He stood looking at Bee's beautiful face, red hair, and blue eyes for a long time. Enough time to see her in a way that he had not seen before. She always seemed so strong, but at this moment, she appeared soft and vulnerable. He felt especially privileged to be so trusted.

"Loss is a hard thing, Bee," Ian said. "I know what you are going through, and I want you to know that I will always be your friend and willing to listen."

Bee regained her composure, saying, "Well, I guess we better get busy and pack up some food."

The two rushed around packing as much food as they could in containers and utensils that they found in the kitchen. They packed the paella, full of spicy sausage, in a large box, Bee adding extra mussels that she knew Pecky would enjoy. They packed fruit, a loaf of heavy, chewy bread, and some local sheep's-milk cheese. They also found two dusty bottles of Spanish amontillado, and a box of Piccadilly Earl Grey tea, which they knew would please Pecky.

As they left the diner in search of more supplies, something from a darkened corner of the diner opened its cold red eyes and peered at them as they walked away. The beast in the dark didn't follow them but lightly tapped its claws against the floor, considering its next move.

Once outside, Bee turned to Ian and asked, "Ian, did you feel the creature in the corner of the diner?"

"I felt it when we walked in, but I didn't want to alarm you. I'm surprised that you didn't give away that you knew."

"Weren't you scared?"

"No. I don't know why I wasn't scared, but I just knew that it wouldn't harm us. I felt it was looking for something, and since we didn't have whatever it was looking for, we were not in any danger. I felt sad for its soul."

"I felt the same thing. It's good that we are such good friends," said Bee with a sweet smile.

The two walked with bags of food and provisions slung over their shoulders in the direction they last saw Pecky and Samuel. They soon found them in the general store piling up supplies they would need for the expedition ahead.

"I can smell the paella from here!" cried Pecky, looking up happily as they entered the store.

"We can't think of food now. We have to pack up and move on before night falls," Samuel said sternly.

"What happens at nightfall?" asked Bee.

"We need to be far from this village and the beasts that follow Legorian because the night is when they are most powerful. There is a safe house just on the outskirts of Toledo that we can make before dark—that is, if we pack up now and leave," replied Samuel.

The travelers stuffed the backpacks they found in the general store with the provisions and set out of town just after noon. Pecky made sure that his pack contained the Porto and Earl Grey tea. He was happy and thankful for his friend's discovery.

The dense green forest lined the dirt road. "We will be safe as long as we don't wander off the road, and stay close to each other," advised Samuel.

Ian looked at Pecky with a nervous look on his face, and said, "Pecky, I have to tell you that Bee and I saw a creature in the diner. For some reason, we didn't feel it would harm us. It just stayed in a dark corner and watched us."

Pecky looked down at Ian and nodded. "Devotes of Legorian are no different than any bully. They will only attack when they see defenselessness. You both did what was needed—you showed no weakness."

The travelers all felt a great sense of relief as they left the village. As they moved a few miles away from the town, the scenery started to change. The terrain became like a desert with small trees and scrub brush lining the dirt road.

Late in the afternoon, the travelers took a break next to a stream running down from a spring on the side of a knoll. The banks of the creek had bleached-white sand with large rocks, and the water was so clear they could see fish moving about the bottom.

"Mr. Dupuis, how much farther to Toledo?" asked Ian.

Samuel turned to Ian with a smile on his face. "Now that we are good friends, Ian, you may call me Sam. Eh, oui, Toledo is only a couple miles away, and our safe house is just over the next hill. We should have no problem reaching our destination before dark."

"Sam, what was Ogden sent to do? What was his mission?" asked Ian.

Sam looked at Ian with a surprised look on his face and replied, "Ogden is an Energy Sprite. He was sent to Toledo to change the dynamic of energy. I thought Pecky had already explained the situation to you and Bee." Sam glanced at Pecky, who was striding ahead with Bee.

"He told us what an Energy Sprite was, but he didn't know what Ogden's assignment was, and why he didn't complete it," replied Ian.

Sam took a second to consider what to say. "Eh, oui, for more than two hundred years, there have been two families in Toledo vying for power and control of the region. The Pizarro family and the Salazar family. The Pizarro family has been the primary rulers of Toledo, wielding power and control through fear and intimidation. They control the central bank of Toledo, so all the commerce and money pass through their mighty grip. The Salazar family is made up of artisans and craftsmen that would like to see a rebirth in the city. The family has tried to free the hold the Pizarro family has over the city but have been unable to change the tide."

"Doesn't the city have a mayor and police that maintain order?" asked Ian.

A slight smile formed on Sam's face. He replied, "Ian, most power and control in this world lies below the surface of what most people see or want to know. Most governments are just facades that hide what struggles go on behind closed doors. There is always a battle in this world between light and dark, and we are all participants."

"How do we all participate?" asked Ian.

"Some of us participate by creating misery for others. Some of us participate by rising above our own needs and desires and creating good for others. Some of us participate by not participating at all. Apathy and indifference are the fuel that feeds the fire of darkness," replied Sam.

"So, Ogden was here to help the Salazar family gain control of Toledo?" asked Ian.

Sam considered how to clarify what he was trying to tell Ian and said, "Oui, his task was more than to help the Salazar family; he was sent to change the dynamic of energy."

"How can he do that?"

"Ian, as Pecky informed you, the world we all occupy is made up of energy. The energy ebbs and flows like a river through all things. There is permanent energy and temporary energy. When we are born, we take on the permanent energy of the place that is our home. Each place on this earth has a different vibration of permanent energy. That vibration or wavelength of energy travels through the core of our being no matter where we go."

"Yeah, I was learning about that in physics class. Pretty interesting."

"Eh, oui. As we move about in our lives, we build up temporary energy. Some of us call it emotional baggage, but temporary energy is just an opportunity to resolve issues in our lives. The temporary energy vibrates at a different frequency than our permanent energy, and if the temporary energy builds too much, it could tear away at the delicate fabric of our being."

"Yes, my father was telling me that would happen with ships moving about the world, and even the steel on boats is affected by the energy!" said Ian.

"Oui, oui. So, you understand this. Well, when powerful families conflict, like the battle between the Pizarros and the Salazars, it builds up temporary energy and affects not only the individual family members but also the entire inhabitants of the region connected to the outcome of the power struggle. The more powerful the person, the more pain many will feel, and the more souls will fall into darkness.

"Ogden was in Toledo to create a moment where the two families would find a balance with each other. Their perceptions of each other have hardened through the years. There has been little communication or understanding between them. In the last few years, there has been an opportunity to change the tide.

"The current patriarch of the Pizarro family, Miguel Pizarro, has a beautiful, loving daughter. The patriarch of the Salazar family, Alberto Salazar, has a compassionate son. Ogden was to create an opportunity for the two to open their hearts long enough to see each other in a different light."

"So, it's Romeo and Juliet all over again, and love will save the day," Ian joked.

"It could be. Oui. You see, Ian, as we go through this world if we hold onto our perceptions too long, temporary negative energy starts to build around what we believe to be true, and it starts to wear away at our souls. Truth is a fluid stream that continually feeds an open heart. Once we close our hearts to what is true, we close our hearts to what lies beyond the façade of the world around us."

Ian thought about what Sam said, and asked, "What was Ogden supposed to do to help open their hearts to each other?"

"That I don't know. A big part of what an Energy Sprite does is look for opportunities and possibilities to help resolve a situation. I can tell you that most cases resolve with little effort. Sometimes built-up negative energy can be dispersed with as little as an 'I'm sorry,'" replied Sam.

Pecky slowed down and walked back to Ian and Sam with an intent look on his face and said, "I believe we should be getting a move on, walk faster now. The sun is getting down in the sky, and I don't want to cut it too close before the darkness falls."

"Eh, oui, I believe you are right, my friend. I lost myself in discussion with Ian. He is a wise young man with many questions," replied Sam.

A crescent moon was already rising in the east before the sunset. The travelers noticed that the crescent moon was slightly blood red. Pecky and Sam knew that the blood-red moon was the first indicator of their descent into darkness.&

 beginning

Chapter Thirteen
A Shade Too Dark

Dark rain clouds moved in from the north just before the four reached their destination for the night. The drops of rain had a different weight than Ian had ever experienced. They felt thick and dense like Jell-O might feel just before it hardened in the fridge.

The world was shifting in subtle ways. Ian didn't know if the world was changing or was his perception of the world changing, and the world was reacting to his perception.

Ian laughed out loud, startling the others. They turned around, and in perfect synchronization, all asked Ian, "What is so funny?"

Ian looked amused at this and replied, "Pecky told me once that the world around me only reflects how I perceive myself. I started to contemplate how cut off I feel from myself. I began to think that maybe the world I see now is only reflecting how I feel. That the world is not cutting me off—I am cutting myself off from the world."

"Wow, that is funny," said Bee sarcastically, but she smiled and then laughed. Pecky smiled too and Sam stood looking at all of them with a raised eyebrow.

"Well, you know, I got so tangled with my thoughts, I found it funny."

"'If you can't laugh when contemplating quantum physics, then you don't understand quantum physics.'" Sam quoted Max Planck. "He was the theoretical physicist who discovered quantum physics, which is what you were discussing. So, Ian, you are in good company."

"Smarter than the average bear!" laughed Bee. Ian laughed, too—he was surprised that Yogi Bear could be in Bee's experience. There was much to learn about his companions, Ian mused.

Without another word, they continued their trek down the dirt road towards their destination. Pecky and Sam did not want to linger too long for fear of something yet unknown.

Ogden spotted the safe house on a small hill just south of a large golden field of wheat. The two-story blue farmhouse was built of wood and stone and was new compared to the other ancient structures dotted around the countryside. A dense forest backed the farmhouse, making it appear to be isolated from the world.

A single light illuminated a window near the front entrance of the house. The light was bright enough to be seen from the road and lit the porch that wrapped around the house.

The travelers moved cautiously towards the house. The rain was coming down harder, which motivated them to move faster, and hopefully, to a safe and dry sanctuary for the night.

Sam motioned for the others to stand their ground while he entered the house to make sure it was safe. A moment later, he came to the door and waved them in. He turned on the kitchen light as his companions entered the house. He didn't want to attract too much attention, so he asked them to keep the lights to a minimum.

Ian immediately noticed the stranger sitting in the living room. The stranger was rocking back and forth in a wooden rocker, his legs barely reaching the floor. Ian could hardly make out the stranger in the shadow of the dim light in the living room, but what he could see startled him. The stranger looked exactly like Sam.

Sam entered the living room, walked over to the rocker, and kicked the man's feet out from under the chair. The stranger shot out of the rocker, fists clenched and glaring at Sam for a moment, but then he laughed, and the two embraced and thumped each other on their backs. Sam turned to the others and said, "I want to introduce my brother, Dan."

Up close, Dan looked less like Sam but still had the same impish features. They were sturdy and stout and had large, strong hands. The main thing that stood out was their piercing eyes. Both brothers had a strong brow over their brilliant blue eyes that expressively showed when they were contemplating.

Dan approached. "Are you the one who only comes along once in a thousand years? Eh, I don't know if I necessarily believe that. I hope you can convince me of your gift because times are becoming dark, and we need a light to show the way."

"I'm still trying to convince myself," Ian replied, "I have no comfort at this time for you."

Dan laughed. "Eh, oui, fair enough, Ian, fair enough."

Sam, Dan, and Pecky went into another room to discuss the next day's plan of action, leaving Bee and Ian to settle in their rooms. Bee immediately called first dibs on the biggest bedroom, which was off the living room, and started unpacking her things.

Ian wandered upstairs to check out the rest of the bedrooms before he headed for the kitchen to scrounge up some food. The stairs leading up to the second floor were slightly crooked, and some of the wallpaper was peeling. The wallpaper pattern was covered with flowers, like the wallpaper in Sobeck's home on the North York Moors.

He could not imagine that the same wallpaper in both houses was a coincidence. Ian wondered if the floral wallpaper had some significance to his journey. He thought that maybe the flowers represented the hills leading up to the Ancient City.

Upstairs were four bedrooms and a small bathroom with a tiny shower that had a pull-down cord that let out water from a large bucket overhead. The shower was tiny, even for Ian. He didn't know how Pecky was going to use the bath. Pecky liked to take long, cold showers in the morning and would always leave the bathroom in shambles. Ian made a mental note to wake up early so he could beat Pecky to the bath.

Ian decided on the smallest of the four bedrooms, which faced east and had a big window to catch the morning light. He turned an old fashioned lamp on by the bed. The floral wallpaper covered the room on only one side. The other three walls had a scuffed yellow paint that showed its years. There was a small bookshelf that held a few volumes of books, all in Spanish.

There was no closet, but rather a large armoire for clothes. Men's clothing filled the armoire, which Ian thought was strange since there was no one in the home—at least no one he could see. The dresser emitted a strong smell of outdoors that reminded him of a little attic room in his home in Vermont. He remembered his mother nailing cedar siding on the walls in the room to keep bugs away from their seasonal clothing stored there.

A scream rose with piercing vibration. Ian instantly knew it was Bee. He dropped his pack on the bed and rushed down the stairs, almost tripping on the way down. He ran into Bee's room, finding all his companions huddled together and squeezed his way through them to find Bee sitting on a small chair rocking back and forth with a terrified look on her face.

Ian blurted out, "What happened?"

Pecky bent over and whispered to Ian, "Bee came across our first shade."

"What is a shade?"

"A shade, my dear boy, is someone lost in the dark."

"Where is this shade?" asked Ian.

Pecky held his breath for just a moment to consider if Ian was ready to see the poor soul in torment. He pointed to the mirror over the bureau and said, "He's in the mirror, but do not gaze at him for too long."

Ian walked over to the mirror and looked in. At first, he saw nothing, but after a few seconds, a slight image started to appear. The image looked like a reflection of his face but then began to take on a life of its own, a form that was ghostly.

The shade in the mirror was clearly in torment. Its mouth was open in a most grotesque fashion. At first, the shade looked to be smiling, but the grin took on a twisted feature. Ian could see that the soul in the mirror was trying to wash his face, but what he was doing was rubbing away at his skin. He must have been rubbing his face for a long time, not knowing he was shredding his flesh.

The image became more and more distinct until Ian had to turn away because he felt like he was falling into the mirror. He turned around again to take a last look, but the figure in the mirror was gone.

Ian walked over to Bee. "Bee, are you okay?"

Bee looked up with tears on her face, and a little bit of a smile. She wiped her face with her sleeve and said, "I'm hungry. How about some dinner?"

The group all broke out laughing.

"Let's go raid the kitchen!" Pecky chuckled.

Ian knew that Bee was trying to be tough, but he sensed that this experience shook her up, and fear and doubt were starting to seep into her heart. They were all going to find themselves in the dark if they didn't soon reach Ogden and resolve the void.

For a moment, Ian became agitated with Ogden, starting to get angry at him for not completing his task and for putting Ian's friends in harm's way. The more Ian thought of Ogden, the angrier he became until a voice deep in his heart broke through.

He started to wonder why he was becoming so mad. Then he thought that maybe the vacuum surrounding the house was causing him to descend into darkness and instantly snapped out of his anger. He understood now the importance of being on guard over his feelings, feelings that would no longer be his if he wasn't careful. He did not want to go down a road to insanity, where he could not return.

The rest of the evening was much lighter. The group went about preparing dinner; a meal fit for a king. Pecky insisted on the paella being the main dish. He took out the containers from the packs and dumped everything for the paella in one big pan. As the paella heated up, Pecky dropped in some more spices he found in the drawers and a dash of the amontillado. The heavenly smell started to take over the house and lighten the hearts of the travelers.

Dan cautioned Pecky not to add too many onions, reminding him of a journey they took once to Asia, then grumbling how Pecky always put too many onions in the food. "Thank you, Dan, I know exactly how many onions to add, and the group shall appreciate my culinary expertise, you will see." Pecky waved his fins at Dan, ushering him out of the kitchen.

Soon the kitchen table was filled with dishes of good food and good friends sitting all around laughing and telling great stories of heroics and times past. In the middle of the festivities, Ian thought that even in the darkest times, there could be light—that laughter is the best medicine.

The early evening turned into a late-night, and late-night turned into early morning. None of the companions at the table wanted this good companionship to end, so they moved into the living room with the crackers and sheep's-milk cheese, the remainder of the amontillado, and a pot of Pecky's Earl Grey tea. Both Bee and Ian sipped at the fortified wine of Spain, enjoying their inclusion with the older members of the group.

The rain was coming down in buckets outside, creating an unusual sound against the metal roof on the farmhouse. A dense sound, like thousands of hollow marshmallows thrown against a wall. It had a calming effect on the travelers.

Pecky found an old record player in the corner of the living room with some albums nearby. The record player was made of beautiful cherry wood with a distinct sweet smell. All the records were Spanish folk tunes that no one in the group had heard of before. Pecky found an album that looked promising and put it on the player. Although they couldn't tell what the musician was singing, Sam assured them that the song was about lost love.

Bee broke the mood with a question. "Are all lost people shades?"

Dan sat up, poured a splash of liquor into his glass, and replied, "Eh, oui. Shades are part of my expertise, so I guess I would be the best person to answer that question." He took a sip and continued, "The people lost are not shades. Each one of us has a darker side of our nature, living below our surface selves. This darker side of our nature is the devil on our shoulder, urging us to do that thing that will be most destructive. It's the voice in our heads that tells us to lie.

"The energy void is like a dark mirror that puts a spotlight on the shade in each one of us, although the shade works hard to conceal its presence from its host. When there is no light to hide behind, it's exposed for all of us to see.

"There is a darker angel of our nature," Sam cut in. "Eh oui, but there is also the better angel of our nature. We can't see the better people of this valley because they are lost in the dark and are wandering about without knowledge. Or, in other words, they are asleep, and the darker angels of their nature have taken over their being. Even if we found them and tried to convince them of their plight, they would only reject our knowledge because they would not believe they are lost.

"Oui, that is true," Dan said. "The man in the mirror who was rubbing his skin away must have always felt dirty. He must have experienced something in his childhood that sent him down this path. Harsh words from a parent can create a shade or no words at all about how precious their child is. It doesn't take much to give life to a shade. It always seemed to take much more effort to rid ourselves of them."

Sam and Dan were each nodding their heads, muttering "Oui, oui," as if they were one.

Ian interrupted them, saying, "When I was looking at the figure, I felt like I was falling into the mirror."

"Oui, you could have if you looked at the shade for too long," Dan replied. "Have you ever heard of the phrase, 'Misery loves company?'"

Ian and Bee both nodded yes, looking over at each other for just a moment to acknowledge the other. Sam was nodding, "Oui!"

Dan continued, "Each one of us has shades, but some of us, like the fellow in the mirror, have shades that are hungry for energy. They feed off those closest to them that wander into their trap. In many ways, a shade becomes alive by the misery it creates. It wants to pass on the void to others closest to them. The best way not to fall under their spell is to keep clear, and not look into their eyes."

The grandfather clock in the living room struck two chimes, making the group of friends aware of how many hours they had been talking. Pecky sighed and clapped his fins. "Well, we have an important day ahead of us."

A long pause in the conversation signaled the end of the conviviality for the night—in conversations energy shifts to indicate the end of one experience and the beginning of another. They could all feel the pull of sleep and knew if they continued the conversation now, it would just feel forced.

"Can the shades hurt us?" Bee asked as they started to move towards their rooms. Ian stopped walking at the question and turned around.

"Eh, no—no worry, this house is safe," Dan replied. "This house sits on a fault line between three energy patterns. It's the lightest energy in the area."

Bee paused in her doorway. "You mean that energy here is different than outside?"

"Eh, oui, Bee, have you heard of worm holes in the fabric of the universe?"

"Yes, I've heard of those in science class, but those are far away, right?"

"Yes and no," Dan replied, shaking his head back and forth slowly.

"Those worm holes are part of the universe where the fabric between our world and other worlds is thin and weak, but there are also energy patterns that are much sturdier. Those energy patterns are made up of light that is closer to an infinite light."

Ian moved closer to the conversation, and Bee glanced at him knowingly. Ian seemed to suck up this kind of information like a dying man drinking water in a desert. There was a need to understand all that he could, to work out the patterns and events that he was experiencing, and the feelings that were coming up.

"As you walk through this world," Dan continued, "you might not be able to see the difference, but I assure you there is a difference to the energy that surrounds you. Being a sensitive person comes in handy. You should be able to feel the differences as you develop your skills—you will understand those differences at a deeper level."

Bee was too tired to ask any more questions and thanked Dan before re-tiring for the night. Ian gave a little wave as he and Dan ascended the stairs.

Bee hesitantly entered her room to get ready for bed; she breathed a sigh of relief when she found that one of her friends had come to her room and removed the mirror. This thoughtful act made her feel much safer and more appreciative of her companions. ✿

CB

Chapter Fourteen
Labyrinth

The energy that passed through Ian's heart was emptier than he felt the day before. This void surge left him with a feeling of foreboding. It felt sinister. It felt like Legorian.

Ian was sitting on the edge of his bed, bent over from the emptiness he felt in his heart. The irritation that was growing in his mind was more painful than he had ever experienced. He felt cut off from a part of himself. A part of him that was now lost in the emptiness.

He tried to shake off the feeling and calm his mind. He thought about the old apple tree that protected his house in the valley of the two green mountains. This experience helped him remember where he was and what he needed to do. He knew Ogden was waiting in the shadows.

Ian heard the water going in the bathroom. He knew that he had missed his opportunity to shower. That Pecky was taking a long cold shower annoyed him. He sat in his bed, getting more and more irritated that Pecky was trashing the bathroom once again.

Bee knocked on Ian's door and asked, "Are you awake?"

Her voice calmed him, and he replied wearily, "Come on in."

Bee entered the room, holding a tray with crusty toasted bread, scrambled eggs, and thick hot chocolate made the Spanish way. Ian eyed the tray warily, not sure if he even wanted to eat. Bee sat next to him on the bed and asked, "Do you feel it? Do you feel the emptiness?"

Ian looked at Bee, almost feeling like crying. He leaned over and hugged Bee, and then said, "I'm glad I'm not alone in the dark."

The sound of the shower stopped, and Pecky walked out of the bathroom with three different colored towels wrapped around him. The towels left out for Bee and Ian. He noticed Bee and Ian sitting on the bed, and said, "You two look a little glum. Try not to lament. Remember, we have each other."

Pecky waddled off towards his room, leaving puddles of water everywhere. Bee and Ian looked at each other and started to laugh. The laughter lightened their mood.

Ian picked up his pocket watch on the nightstand. The face read 9:33 a.m. He hastily stood up with a frustrated look on his face. He looked down at Bee, and said, "We have to get to Ogden—why did Pecky let us sleep so long?"

Bee replied, "Calm down, Ian, it's okay. Sam and Dan went out early this morning to find Ogden. There is nothing we can do until they return."

Ian laid down on his bed and placed his face in his hands. "My heart and soul feel so empty."

"It isn't us, Ian. It's the void," Bee said, putting her arm around Ian.

The downstairs door slammed shut, and Bee and Ian heard Pecky greet Sam and Dan. The two got up and started towards the stairs. Ian grabbed his backpack on the way out of his room, hoping they would leave soon before it was too late to reach Ogden.

Sam's and Dan's faces communicated the severity of the situation before they even opened their mouths. Sam spoke first. "The journey to Ogden, unfortunately, is going to be fraught with fear and doubt. Many shades are starting to appear along our path."

Dan continued, "Eh, oui. We found out where Ogden is. He is in an old part of Toledo. There are caverns below the city, once used as dungeons and torture chambers. There is something else below the city, but we were unable to find out what. Ogden was caught holding a letter written by Isabel, the daughter of Miguel Pizarro. Our contact didn't know what was in the note, but for some reason, Ogden was put in the dungeons with the letter still in his possession."

Sam interjected, "The two families are falling into paranoia, and they are drawing battle lines. As the darkness engulfs all things, and without light to hide behind, it will become clear who supports the Pizarro family and who supports the Salazar family. There will soon be war if we don't reach Ogden."

Bee interrupted, "How will we know who is who?"

"Those who support the Pizarro family have hearts that are dark as ash, and those who support the Salazar family have clear hearts. The reality of this vacuum is that neither family nor their supporters can feel their hearts anymore," replied Sam.

Pecky noticed that Ian's backpack, which had been slung over the living room chair when he came down with Bee, was starting to glow.

Pecky stood up with excitement, and exclaimed, "Ian, I almost forgot about the map to the City of Light."

Ian grabbed his backpack, pulled out the golden orb, and said, "I saw it glow late last night, but I'd forgotten about it this morning. I was not thinking about anything."

"Eh, oui, it is bad energy here, taking our will." Sam grabbed the map from Ian and lifted it into the air. The orb started to glow and change the energy in the room. The dark energy left all the travelers' minds, and clarity once again filled what shadow once occupied.

Sam explained, "The map to the Ancient City holds a powerful energy. Pecky told me he placed the golden orb in Ian's backpack when they left the sleigh. I can't believe I forgot Ian still had it in his possession. The golden orb changes everything. Now we have a little more time to reach Ogden."

Ian, feeling much better, asked, "How does this globe change everything?"

Sam replied, "Ian, remember, woven through all things is life energy. In some places on the face of the earth, the energy is pure because dark energy hasn't polluted the area with fear and doubt.

"Legend tells that the map to the City of Light was created on Machu Picchu high in the mountains of Peru. Machu Picchu is the convergence of three primary high energy flows that balance out the world around us. Its high energy is so powerful that no dark energy can permeate it. The Incas knew this long ago. That is why they built the city on the mountain.

Dan interrupted, "We need to leave, and soon, but first, I need to remind all of you. The shades we will encounter on our way to Ogden don't know that they are in darkness. They're lost and do not know it. They feel great pain, but don't know from where. The shades might try to trick you into helping them. Know this one truth—you cannot assist them by falling into their grasp. You can only help them by finding Ogden and righting what is wrong."

Not more than a mile from the farmhouse, Toledo appeared on the horizon, sitting elegantly on a green knoll encircled by a beautiful green river. The spire of a magnificent Gothic cathedral and the turrets of an enormous castle looked over the ancient stone and brick buildings of the town. In better times Toledo would be magic to visit, Ian thought, but of course, these were dark times, and he had to keep focus.

The first shade the group came upon was a child of no more than three or four sitting in a puddle. His garments were tattered, and he had scars on his arms that were slowly bleeding. At closer observation, Ian could see, or smell, that the child was sitting in a pool of his waste. The scent became overpowering the closer Ian came to the child.

The group kept walking, but Ian knelt close but not too close and asked, "Where are your parents?"

The child looked up at Ian with a blank void. His eyes had no pupils, only a dark black covering. The boy looked at Ian and said, "I don't know. Can you help me find my parents?"

Sam's warning popped in Ian's heart. Ian stood up and walked away from the child. The child cried a horrific shriek. "Help me! Help me find my mama! My papa! Help me!" the boy pleaded to Ian. Ian backed away, while Sam and Dan motioned to him hurry away from the shade and catch up to them. Bee looked stricken and was walking fast, almost running. Ian reminded himself that the only way he could assist the child was to find Ogden. Ian kept saying to himself, "Find Ogden."

The shades along the travelers' route did nothing to hinder their journey. Sam told everyone, "Eh, this was not a good thing. The shades are deeply lost in shadow. The emptiness that has engulfed Toledo is moving faster than we initially estimated. We now have less time to reach Ogden. We must press on, faster."

Pecky felt the emptiness intensified by Legorian's devotees. They were creating conditions that only aided the darkness. He knew that there was more afoot than he thought earlier. Pecky considered that Legorian wanted something, but didn't know what, maybe the map to the Ancient City?

In no more than an hour, the group of travelers entered the old part of Toledo—a part of Toledo that held Ogden deep below the streets in a place that was darker than the world above.

A group of shades, still in military uniforms, huddled together around the entrance to the old town. The shades looked like they were playing a game, looking down and laughing —a revolting laugh, full of malevolence. They turned to expose their gruesome game as Pecky, and the others walked by. Their arms and legs were sliced and bloody. Each shade had cut themselves with their daggers. Their wounds dripped on the dirty cobblestone of the old street, leaving a thin cover of blood. The blood revealed a spectrum of oily colors in the light of day.

Sam whispered, "Each shade bears his guilt, and the scars are only the physical reflections of the pain they are in and the lives they have ended by murder."

One shade moved towards the travelers and said, "Are you here for the game? Are you here to play?"

Sam stepped forward. "Are you playing the game?"

The shade looked at Sam for a long time with his dark soulless eyes. Then he looked past Sam as if he didn't see Sam anymore.

Sam motioned the group to move swiftly past the shades. They found an empty storefront, a bakery, close to the center of the old part of Toledo. Sam and the others ducked in through the unlocked door and closed it fast behind them. The bakery had fresh bread lining the shelves. It had an old wood oven with the fire still burning underneath. There was no one in sight even though the shelves displayed baskets of fragrant bread, and the cups of coffee lining the counter were still emitting steam.

Bee sat down on the tiled floor with a heavy heart. She asked, "Sam, why did you ask the shade if he was playing the game?"

Sam sat down next to her on the cold floor and replied, "Eh, the only way to disarm a shade is to respond to their question with a question. They are conflicted, and if you refuse their pleas, it will only end with disaster. If you distract them with a question, they will soon forget about you. You need to remember that the shades don't know they are in the darkness. When someone is in the void, they feel alone. They are not aware that there are other entities than shades."

Ian sat down next to them as Sam continued, "We are only a reflection of them. The shades don't understand that we are separate from their pain. If you disagree with them, they will start to think we are causing their suffering, and then they will hate you, as they hate themselves."

All five companions sat on the floor with heavy hearts. They were quiet for a long time, not wanting to disrupt what little peace they had left in their minds and hearts.

Pecky finally broke the quiet. "We have to move forward. The golden orb is starting to fail us. It's just too dark for it to shine. We need to reach Ogden before we lose each other."

Ian blurted out, "Lose each other?"

"Yes," Pecky, with a somber note, replied. "If our hearts fall into the darkness, we will lose sight of each other."

Pecky pulled out the map to the City of Light and handed it to Ian. "Ian, you have the best chance to reach Ogden. If you lose sight of us, place the orb close to your heart, and it should help you stay clear for a bit longer, maybe just enough to reach Ogden."

The moment Pecky handed him the globe, Ian lost sight of his friends. A deep haze in his mind created a feeling of depression. He looked at the world through a fog. He felt like he was floating, and the world around him was far away, but close at the same time. He couldn't hear the voice of reason in his heart. For a moment, he considered giving up. He didn't know why he needed to move forward. He couldn't imagine anything making sense. All reason had left his mind.

The last words Pecky said drifted into his thoughts. He lifted the golden orb and put it next to his heart. Instantly, his mind found clarity once again. He remembered what it was that he needed to do. He looked around and saw his friends, but they were all lost. Shadow had covered their eyes, and they could not see him anymore.

He stood up and walked out into the street towards a small, old building standing in the center in the courtyard. Ian knew that Ogden was below the building waiting for him. But something else was waiting, too, something in the shadows that he could feel watching.

The shades in the courtyard didn't see Ian. Shades are in a darkness in which they could only see the torture they inflict on themselves. Ian didn't dare look at any of the shades. He just kept walking towards the building, trusting in his heart—hoping that all was not lost.

The tiny building was perfectly square and seemed ancient. It was dappled wood that Ian had never seen before. Dark ivy vines covered most of the walls. The plants lacked the green coloring ivy should have; they looked dead but were alive. The panes of the two windows on each side of the building were yellow opaque glass that looked a lot like the alabaster at Lord Claridon's castle. The bottoms of the glass panes were thicker compared to the top. It appeared that the alabaster had slowly dripped down over the centuries. The door was old brown wood with iron hinges and a large round iron knob in the middle.

Ian grabbed the knob and slowly opened the door. A wisp of air rushed out as the door creaked open, and a smell of rotting flesh and blood assaulted Ian from the depths of the damp stone staircase that opened before him. For a moment, he felt like he was going to be sick.

The thought of walking down into the darkness and stench terrified him. He stood at the entrance without the will to move forward. He considered turning back. He pictured himself walking out of the area, walking far away from all this emptiness. Fear and doubt started to seep into his heart and mind, and then he remembered his friends. He knew that there was only one way to save his friends and himself.

He stood at the front entrance to the staircase for several minutes, not wanting to move forward and not being able to go back. Time was ticking away, and every moment he did not descend into the dark portended woe for those he loved.

Ian mustered up all his courage, steeled his mind to the task before him, and placed his right foot on the first step of the staircase going down into the shadows. Each step was an effort. Each step was fear and doubt.

He slowly descended into the depths. The walls were closing in on him. He had a hard time breathing with the dank smell of water and rotting flesh. The darkness was constricting his heart.

As he descended the stairs, sides opened up and below he could see torches lining the walls that led to a room that was as big as what he remembered of Grand Central Station in New York City when he visited his aunt Hilary who lived in Manhattan. It was an awe-inspiring sight.

The large chamber was carved smooth and square out of black granite speckled with flecks of mica that glistened in the torchlight. Because of the sparkling stone flecks, Ian could see almost everything in the room.

On the stone stairs, still high over the ground floor of the chamber, Ian saw another awe-inspiring sight. A labyrinth filled the room, carved out of the black granite. The walls were ten feet tall, and in the dead center was one boxed room.

He knew that this was where Ogden was waiting for him. He remembered his vision a few days earlier that the light was waiting to shine once again in the depth of this cavern.

Ian descended the stairs to the ground floor of the chamber and walked to the entrance of the labyrinth. There he faced three shades. Two shades were guarding the entrance to the maze, and the third was sitting at an old wooden desk before the front of the entrance.

All three shades were motionless. Their eyes were pitch black, and their hearts felt like black ash to Ian. They almost looked like the black granite walls that they were guarding.

Something else caught Ian's eye.

Behind one of the shades at the entrance, a dark beast was whispering in the guard's ear, like the devotee of Legorian that Ian had seen at the edge of the forest days before. He couldn't make out the form, but the red eyes were the same. He again felt no fear of the beast, only compassion, and sorrow for its soul.

Ian could feel that the beast was there for ill will and was not going to let Ian pass into the maze without trying to inflict more fear and doubt. Even in the darkness, he knew this to be true. He held onto this knowledge like a light.

The guard at the table raised its boney hand and pointed at Ian. "Are you here to walk the labyrinth?" it shrilled.

Remembering what Sam said, Ian replied, "Are you the one who guards the maze?"

The guard stared at Ian with his black eyes for a long time. Finally, it said in a low voice, "There are two paths through the maze, but only one will take you to whom you seek. If you walk the wrong path, you and your friends will be in shadow forever."

Ian realized that these words were not coming from the guard, but from the beast that stood behind the sentries. He didn't feel terror, but compassion, a great sorrow in his heart for the monster.

Even in the darkness, he had faith his heart would take him to Ogden.

Even in the darkness, his heart spoke to him. Ian moved slowly past the guards to the entrance of the labyrinth. Two paths surrounded by tall, dark stone walls stood before him. He closed his eyes and focused all his attention deep down on his voice of reason.

In the darkness, a voice from his heart rose above all the fear and doubt. The voice in his heart was stronger than Ian had ever heard before. The voice in his heart was not sound but pure feeling.

It spoke to him of images and experiences. It communicated to him in a breath that was once only subtle, but now was a flood. He realized that the fear and doubt he felt released what only once was a whisper. In the darkness, a part of him was freed to help, to heal, and to find a way.଼

CR

Chapter Fifteen
One Simple Note

The smooth, dark stone glistened brightly in the dim torchlight of the cavern, and the three shades that guarded the labyrinth stood motionless. Legorian's devotee slipped into the darkness of the cave, out of sight, leaving without another word, taunt, or warning, which concerned Ian much more. A snake hidden in the shadows is much more of a threat than a snake in plain sight.

Ian stood at the two entrances to the labyrinth for such a long time that the dark stones started to look like they were blending into each other. He stood there in front of the entrance carrying the weight of his decision, knowing the dire consequences for his friends if he made the wrong decision. Then something occurred to him.

He remembered, a few years back, being at the lake near his house with a friend, who convinced him to take a ride in a boat. The small rowboat was not theirs, but his friend assured him that it would be okay. Ian knew in his heart that the friend was lying.

The fisherman who owned the boat was upset, not only that the boat was gone but for his missed morning of fishing. The experience soured the trip to the lake, and Ian regretted both that he had listened to his friend and that he had convinced himself to believe a lie.

The memory of the trip flashed in his mind only for a second, but its message was clear. He started to consider who told him he would be lost if he took the wrong path. Legorian's devotee would tell him exactly what would be most distressing, but not necessarily the truth.

This realization gave him hope once again that maybe he could do this. That maybe there was a path through the maze and that maybe it wasn't as hard as he had built up in his mind.

He thought hard about the trial before him and how, many times in his life, there had been tasks that seemed insurmountable, but somehow he was able to overcome them. He remembered that the mountain he and his father had climbed the year before demanded one step after another to ascend, but in the end, they found themselves on the top of Camels Hump Mountain.

Ian decided to take the first step into one of the paths. He was going to move forward, and whatever happened, he needed to trust that his heart would take him to Ogden. He looked at the two paths—the left path was just a tiny bit different in his heart than the right. The right path felt heavy, and the left path seemed light. So subtle was the difference that he might not have felt it if he focused merely on how they looked.

Ian stepped on the path. Instantly the dark stone walls on either side of him moved and sealed him in. He was now committed.

Now that he made his first decision, the substantial pain in his heart started to lift. The lightness of his heart surprised him because he hadn't been aware of his suffering. The pain, now gone, was so subtle and had built up so incrementally that he wasn't aware of its real weight before it lifted.

The darkness that troubled his mind was gone. The effects of the emptiness that engulfed Toledo seemed to have dissipated. He thought for a moment that it could be that he was lost and didn't know it, but his heart was clear, better than strong.

The walls of the maze moved once again, and before Ian were two new paths. He started to understand that the labyrinth didn't have two separate paths, but each step created another two ways to test his ability to listen to his heart. One path would take him away from Ogden, and the other path would bring him closer.

A funny thought rose in Ian's mind. He thought how absurd it was that a few months ago he was in his mother's kitchen eating butter biscuits, and now he was deep beneath the streets of Toledo. He didn't quite understand why this would make him laugh, but the foolishness of the situation amused him.

Ian suddenly thought of a dinner over a year earlier with his father at a local diner near his home. That night out with his dad had seemed like magic. He and his father had exchanged stupid jokes the entire evening.

"A penguin walks into a bar," Eli started, "and asks the bartender, 'Have you seen my brother?' 'I don't know,' the bartender answered, 'what's he looks like?'"

"What's the difference between a friend and a best friend?" Ian countered. "A friend will help you move, and a best friend will help you move a body!"

"'Eew! Okay, buddy, a priest, a rabbi, and a minister walk into a bar. The bartender looks at them and says, 'What is this, some kind of joke?'"

"Ha!" Ian laughed. "Oldie, but a goodie. What happened at a bar when the past, the present, and the future walked in? It got tense."

Ian's dad groaned and said, "That was bad! Why don't ants get sick? Because they have little anty-bodies."

"Knock, knock."

"Who's there?"

"Cows go."

"Cows go, who?"

"No, cows go moo!

"Alright," Eli said, "answer this. Knock, knock."

"Who's there?"

"Impatient cow."

"Impatient cow.."

"MOO!"

They both laughed and laughed, maybe not at the jokes, but because it felt so good to have time together.

Remembering this special evening with his dad, and the stupid jokes, Ian's heart started to lighten. The more he thought of good or fun times in his life, the easier it seemed to make the right choice through the labyrinth towards Ogden. Each door through the maze presented two new paths, one away from Ogden and one towards him. He could feel the way through the lightness in his heart. As he got closer to the center of the maze, the less the dark energy that permeated Toledo above affected him. He knew that he was getting to the cause of the void and closer to resolving it.

He started to whistle a simple tune. His mother loved Bob Marley's music and often played the song "Three Little Birds." Ian started singing the lyrics under his breath. He sang it over and over. The lightness of the song made his heart sing as well.

He now stood one step away from the center of the maze, the boxed room in front of him. There was no door, no window, but he could hear someone on the other side of the wall coughing. He knew that it was Ogden. His heart started to race with the anticipation he would finally meet Ogden.

"Ogden, are you there?" No reply came, just more coughing.

The wall that divided Ian from Ogden didn't move. The path that he had just come from didn't move as well. He started to doubt that he had come the right way, but his heart kept telling him to be patient. He decided to sit down and consider his options.

While Ian was sitting on the cold floor of the labyrinth, another memory popped into his mind. This memory was of his friend at school, breaking his arm on the monkey bars. It happened so fast. He and his friend were jumping off a bench that they dragged close to the monkey bar area. There was a three-foot area between the bench and the monkey bars that they had to jump over to grab hold of the bars. They would swing out and then back again, drop down, run to the bench and jump again. Ian's friend jumped, grabbed the bar, but slipped off, coming down to the ground on his left arm. The boy's distorted broken arm looked surreal, and Ian felt guilty because it was his idea to jump off the bench. Ian also wondered why his friend had to suffer for his stupidity and why he didn't get hurt instead.

Ian thought that the guilt he felt in his heart for his friend's broken arm might be a lot like the guilt Ogden might be feeling about abandoning his mission and letting Toledo fall into emptiness.

The memory of this intense guilt and its connection with Ogden helped move the last wall standing between Ian and his destination. The wall didn't move—the wall just dissolved into nothing.

Ian merely had to see the wall a little differently for it to disappear. Ian thought that maybe the wall was the guilt Ogden had been feeling, and maybe empathy that one has for another is what brings down walls.

Ian walked into the center chamber of the maze. He knew that only he could pass the stone walls, that the young man who stood before him was still in the stone cell of his making. The man, standing by his cot against the wall, was around nineteen or twenty years old. He had thick, spiky blonde hair that brushed his shoulders and deep-set, brown eyes in his broad face. His eyes were not empty and black, so Ian knew that he had found Ogden, as a good soul always shows through the eyes.

"I guess you're Ogden?"

Ogden looked at Ian, "I imagine you're Ian?

Ian was stunned for a second. "How do you know my name?"

"Legorian's devotee has been whispering in my ear, telling me that you are going to fail."

"How does Legorian's devotee know about me?"

Ogden grimaced. "Legorian learned about you at Claridon Castle. Those who live in shadow wouldn't admit it, but they are also connected—they are all one in their way."

Ian had spotted another person in a small cot in the corner of the cell when he entered the cell. At closer observation, Ian could tell that the other person was a young man around the same age as Ogden. The young man was slender and seemed tall, had olive skin, though not as dark as Ogden's, and prominent muscles, perhaps from working on a farm. Ian surmised, because he had the hands of a workman.

The clothes of both men were dirty and tattered. Ogden was wearing what had been a white pair of pants, and a dark blue shirt. The other young man wore a style of pants and a shirt that wasn't known to Ian.

Ian sat down on the cot next to where Ogden was standing and asked, "What happened?"

With his eyes watering up, Ogden sat down on the other end of the cot and turned to Ian. "Ian, you know when your parents warn you of the one thing that will cause them the most amount of pain?"

Ian sat back against the wall and replied, "Yeah, I know."

"When I trained as an energy sprite, Sam Dupuis told me that I could never get involved with my subjects. The slightest step off my path from my destination could alter the dynamics of the whole world. I don't think I ever really believed what he said until I screwed up here. I didn't just slightly step off my path—I dove into the wilderness.

"I don't understand, Ogden. What happened?"

Ogden took a long breath as if he was about to spill his guts. The kind of breath someone might take, hoping that another answer would come out before he started to speak.

Ogden dropped his head and said, "I fell in love with Isabella Pizarro, Miguel Pizarro's daughter. One of the people I was sent to Toledo to benefit."

Ian merely sighed, "Oh, I see."

Ogden stood up abruptly with a terrible scowl on his face, "How can you see, Ian? You have never seen a woman as beautiful as Isabella."

Ogden's movement startled Ian. He saw the anger in Ogden's face before he turned away, and it scared him for just a moment.

Ian stood up, too, and redirected the conversion to the person sleeping in the corner. "Ogden, who is that?"

Ogden turned around with a slight smile on his face and replied, "That, my friend, is the son of Alberto Salazar. He is Pietro Salazar, and he is one of the reasons I'm in this dark place, and Toledo is in shadow."

Pietro must have heard Ian and Ogden talking about him, because he awoke, wiped the sleep from his face, and abruptly sat up. He didn't say a word at first. He just sat in the corner, looking at the two others with his piercing brown eyes.

Ian walked over to Pietro, offered him his hand, and said, "Pietro, I'm here to help."

Pietro just looked at Ian's hand with scorn, and replied, "How can you help me—are you another energy sprite?"

Ian patted Pietro on the shoulder and replied, "No, that is not my profession, but I'm here to help none-the-less."

Pietro stood up and stretched out his legs, and mumbled, "Great, another so-called energy sprite, or whatever you are. All I know is that I'm here, and I can't find my way out."

Something occurred to Ian, and he turned to Ogden. "Ogden, why are we not affected by the emptiness that is taking over Toledo?"

Ogden sat back down and leaned against the stone wall of the cell before he replied, "We are at the center of the storm—or you might even say that we are the center of the storm."

"What happened, what was your mission?" Ian asked once again.

Ogden took a long breath and said, "I was merely here to make sure that Pietro here, and Isabella hooked up. Their two families have battled over Toledo for a long time, and war was imminent, maybe still is, I don't know, I've lost track of time down here. Anyway, they fell in love with each other and were planning to get married, but I intervened because, you see, Ian, I also fell in love with her."

Pietro walked over to Ogden and shouted, "How can you fall in love with Isabella, imbécil! You are but a ghost to Toledo, and a ghost to her."

"How does Pietro know about you being an energy sprite?" Ian asked Ogden as Pietro strode back to his cot.

"We've been here a long time, and I told him everything. Anyway, I was supposed to deliver a letter to Pietro. A letter that Isabella had entrusted to me, a letter that would explain her love, but I kept the letter, and the rest, you know. Toledo has fallen into darkness because their love would have created a renaissance in Spain."

A puzzled look came over Ian's face. "How can a simple letter do so much?"

"Ian, resolution is almost always simple. We tend to make things much more complicated than they need to be."

"So, what is it that we need to do to stop the desolation from taking over everything?"

Ogden lowered his head and replied, "I need to give the letter to Pietro."

Ian stepped back with shock on his face. "You just need to give him the note?"

"It's easier said than done, Ian. I love her, and I know that the moment I give that man the letter, I will lose her forever. I haven't been able to do it even though I am aware of the misery that is spreading." Ogden groaned, "I just can't lose her."

"Legorian's devotee left you with the letter," said Ian, trying to work it out. "That doesn't make sense."

Ogden pulled the letter out of his pocket and said, "It makes perfect sense. You see, Legorian loves nothing more than tormenting anyone who hasn't bowed to him, and nothing could torture me more than leaving it up to me to stop the emptiness."

Ian stood looking at Ogden and then at the white folded piece of paper in his hands, not knowing what to do next. He reached for the letter only to have Ogden jerk his hand back and quickly stick the letter in his pocket.

Suddenly Ian had another recollection. Ian remembered getting a Chinese finger trap in his Halloween bag once. When he put his two forefingers into the straw trap, he was unable to pull them out. He tried harder and harder, using force to wriggle free. His friend William found Ian's plight to be of great amusement and laughed wildly at Ian's expense.

When Ian stopped forcing his fingers apart, and instead pushed them together gently, the Chinese finger trap fell off without a fuss. The memory of the trap was not unlike the predicament he was in now. Ian apparently couldn't force Ogden to hand over the letter, but Ian could provide Ogden a solution to his dilemma.

He needed to present Ogden with another decision than the one he was conflicted with, a decision to give Ian the letter, not Pietro.

Ian turned to Ogden and said, "You have been in conflict with the decision to give the letter to Pietro, but maybe the only reason I'm here is for you to give the letter to me, and allow me to make the decision so that it can be out of your hands."

Ogden looked at Ian and smiled and then replied, "Ian, you're a pretty smart character."

Ogden took out the letter, gently stroked it, and then handed it to Ian. This simple act changed the energy in the cell, and the stone walls started to take on an almost transparent appearance. Ian opened the letter and tried to read it, but it was in Spanish, and he only knew a few words.

Holding the letter that would change everything gave Ian pause for a moment. He thought maybe this was a trick from Legorian. Maybe, Ian wondered, would handing the letter to Pietro only intensify the melancholy that is spreading over Toledo?

Something deep down told Ian to give the letter to Pietro—that everything would be okay. Ian snapped out of his daze, and he walked over to Pietro, knelt, and put the white letter in Pietro's lap.

Pietro looked at Ian with sad eyes. He looked different. Where he once looked angry and bitter, he now seemed like a gentle soul.

The walls of the labyrinth were fading away into particles of dust. Then the three were standing in the middle of a large cavern on a hard cold surface. Even the shade guards that stood at the entrance had disappeared into the brilliant granite of the chamber. ∝

C3

Chapter Sixteen
Lost and Found

The bounty of food displayed before Ian was a medley of bright colors and enticing smells. His whole group of friends was back at the taberna in the Spanish village on the edge of the vast forest. Where Pecky hid the sleigh, and Ian had his first delicious taste of paella.

The once-empty taberna had all sorts of characters eating small plates of tapas—specialty aged pork, grilled octopus, squid and shrimp dishes, fried potato and egg. Beautiful aromatic cheeses that overwhelmed the palate.

Ian couldn't believe how tasty the aged pork montadito was. A small sandwich with only meat and freshly baked Spanish bread—the combination was almost heaven.

It occurred to Ian looking around the dinner table that there are moments, even in the darkest of times, for a lightness of heart and laughter. Ian had a hard time shaking off the feeling that only a few hours earlier, the world around Toledo was on the edge of an abyss. But now everyone was sitting around the dinner table, creating merriment.

He saw the people he'd saved from the void, spending time with their friends and loved ones, and enjoying life. He wondered if they had any idea how close they came to fall into the darkness.

The group at the dinner table, consisting of Ogden, Sam, Dan, Pecky, Bee, and Ian, were having an early dinner before they all moved on to their next destination, which was still unclear to Ian and Bee.

Ian watched and listened as Pecky and his friends told great stories of adventure and conquest, of secret energy deals made in the dark, and of better days long gone.

Out of the corner of his eye, Ian noticed that Pecky was motioning to join him outside. Ian and Bee got up from the table and followed their good friend out the door of the taberna.

The sun was low in the western sky, moving towards Ian's home in Vermont. Ian thought of his mother in the tiny village nestled in the valley of the two green mountains looking up and viewing the same sun. This thought helped Ian to feel a great sense of peace.

Pecky pulled out his pipe and bag of tobacco, a dried cod mixture that Pecky loved to smoke after a good meal, but, being a considerate sort, usually did while alone. The smell was strong, and Bee and Ian found it to be most repugnant.

Pecky led the two to the side of the taberna, where someone had painted a large mural of the old world before the time of Christopher Columbus. The painting was a good representation of western Europe but lacked any detail beyond the Atlantic of the new world or east towards China.

Pecky pointed to a place on the map and said, "That, my friends, are where we are going next."

Bee and Ian moved closer to see where Pecky was pointing and noticed that his flipper lay on a small point of land at the end of a peninsula in the Greek Isles.

Bee had known Pecky long enough to understand that he liked to create drama along the way. Pecky never wished to disclose the whole opera before the fat lady sang. Bee thought that she had no other choice but to ask Pecky. She asked, "Okay, Pecky, I'll bite. Why are we going to what seems to be in the middle of nowhere?"

"I'm glad you asked," Pecky said while taking a long toke on his pipe. Sometimes prying information out of Pecky, Bee thought impatiently, was like pulling a rock out of the red mud at the bottom of the river back home.

Pecky sat down on a wooden milk crate below the mural. He relit his pipe while considering what he wanted to tell them, and what information he wanted to hold onto until a more appropriate time.

As frustrating as Pecky could be with imparting information, Ian knew in his heart that Pecky was only considering their well-being. Ian found that data being held back by Pecky often was handy at the time when Pecky finally disclosed the truth.

With a worried brow, Pecky looked at Bee and Ian and said, "Dan and Sam told me that an explorer has turned up at the holy Mount Athos monastery in Greece. This explorer was thought to be lost in the Amazon jungles of Brazil many years ago. He was looking for a lost city, which he called the lost City of Xingu.

"What is remarkable is that he was found in the foothills of Tibet two years ago. Although he was lost for many years, he has not aged at all. Many consider that he found the City of Light, but we won't know for sure unless we travel to the monastery."

"Pecky," Ian asked, "I thought the Ancient City is in the Congo. How can it be in other places?"

Pecky replied, "That is one of the questions we need to ask."

From the taberna, Ogden came over with a perplexed look on his face. He briskly walked up to where Ian, Bee, and Pecky were standing and said, "Okay, what's up?"

Pecky let out a laugh that filled the air with glee. Pecky had been expecting Ogden to come around the corner at any time and planned this little meeting to test Ogden's loyalty to the quest.

"We are discussing our next destination," replied Pecky.

Ogden looked at Pecky with a little bit of frustration on his face, and asked: "And where would our next destination be?"

Bee and Ian looked at Ogden with surprise, because this was the first time that they were aware of Ogden's intent to move forward with them. A little smile came over Bee's face. It seemed Bee was happy to spend more time with Ogden.

Ian turned to Ogden to explain Pecky's plan in the Greek Isles. Pecky still hadn't told them who this person was and why they needed to talk to him, but Ian knew that it was an essential key to their destination. Pecky interrupted him, saying to Ogden, "There was a reason that I wanted to talk with Bee and Ian first before I discuss our next destination with you."

Pecky paused, then hesitantly continued, "Unfortunately, the monastery we are about to visit does not allow women to enter. A woman has not set foot inside the monastery's walls for many centuries."

Pecky sat back to relight his pipe and waited for Bee's response, or at least the response Pecky expected from a woman of Beatrice's spirit.

Bee took only a moment to consider what was just told her, then, to Pecky's surprise and relief, said, "That's fine." But with a more determined look on her face, Bee continued, "It's fine that this archaic church won't let me enter, so I hope this person is worth the extra trouble, because if he is not..." Bee stopped herself from ranting and took a deep breath to calm down. She didn't want to fume in front of Ogden. She still didn't know him well enough.

Pecky quickly interjected before Bee could continue and said, "The explorer's name is Neils Stephan Van Den Berg. He is, perhaps, one of only a few to have entered the Ancient City and come back unaffected to tell the story."

Pecky pulled a file out of his briefcase. "Sam handed Van Den Berg's dossier to me early this morning. Having reviewed it, I would like to go over the report with you before we move forward."

"Who keeps a dossier on Neils Stephan Van Den Berg?" Bee asked.

Without a beat, Pecky responded, "The Life Energy Consortium keeps records on all of its people. I supposed there are files on all of us somewhere in the library stacks at the Life Energy Consortium." Bee and Ian looked at each other with astonishment.

Bee insisted, "If you have my dossier in that briefcase, you keep so close, and yes, Ian and I have seen you try to look through the briefcase without us noticing. Anyway, I would like to see my dossier if you don't mind."

Pecky looked at Bee over his eyeglasses and responded, "I'm sorry, my dear, but the dossiers are for Life Energy Consortium executive management only. You will have to submit a request form 1025.33, to the Life Energy Consortium hall of records when we get back to Britain—that is, if we ever do."

Pecky leafed through the folder and continued, "Yes, yes, let's see where to start. The first thing that I want all of you to be aware of is that Neils Stephan Van Den Berg did not have the sleigh or knowledgeable companions. He was alone during his journey.

"We did not even know that one could enter the City of Light in northeastern Brazil. We suspected other portals to the Lost City but never confirmed their existence until Van Den Berg re-emerged in Tibet. His travels should give you both a better respect for the dedication it will take to reach our goal.

"Ian, listen carefully, you most of all, need to know the history of Van Den Berg. You are going to be most affected by his knowledge. You might want to think of questions to ask him. I don't know how long we will have with him when we reach the monastery."

Ian said, "I have a thousand questions I would like to ask him."

Pecky again flipped through the folder, considering where to start and then said, "Well, yes, it's best to start at the beginning.

"Neils Stephan Van Den Berg. He was born in 1858 in the Netherlands. At nineteen, he joined the Dutch navy and rose through the ranks to become a chief navigator. After ten years in the service, he was commissioned by Dutch naval high command to chart a course through the Amazon river into the northwest basin. Dutch investors were interested in expanding their sugar holdings in South America. They wanted to expand sugar plantations into the Amazon jungle and needed a clear trading route through the different rivers that connect the Amazon.

"Before his expedition began, the then-secretary of the Life Energy Consortium, Robert Purcell, indicated to Van Den Berg that there might be more to his journey. He was to report back if he came across any signs of the City of Light or any Ancient City.

"A Life Energy Consortium chief energy sprite, Danial Klein, had often worked with Neils in his days with the navy and in his secret Life Energy Consortium work. Van Den Berg was not a pure heart, so he had to have an energy sprite work with him on all his adventures. Sometimes an energy sprite can save the day," Pecky looked at Ogden, "Right Ogden?"

Ogden sat up abruptly and replied, "Right you are Pecky."

Pecky stopped to fiddle with his pipe again, and the three listeners sat down in front of him. Bee was anticipating a long talk as she watched Pecky stuffing the dried cod and seaweed mix into his pipe.

"Van Den Berg saw the tragic life of the natives under the sugar plantation owners. The workers were treated like slaves. Neils considered it contrary to the purpose of the Life Energy Consortium. Ian, this is important, because the situation with large companies that are presently affecting Africa, especially in the central region, is not unlike what happened in South America during Van Den Berg's time.

"Van Den Berg believed that if you treated the natives with compassion, you would receive the same in return—the European industrialist saw it differently. They considered the natives to be sub-human. An energy sprite was dispatched to help Van Den Berg shift the energy so to divert war between the natives and the European plantation owners.

"During a trip up the Xingu River to find fertile land that the European industrialist could exploit, Neils had an opportunity to test his theory of compassion. Van Den Berg had been warned not to travel up the river because the tribes along it had a reputation taking the heads of Europeans. Ian, we won't be coming across many ancient tribes, but there are rebel forces in Africa.

"After three weeks on the Xingu river, Van Den Berg entered a region with known headhunters. The tribe of headhunters had a large encampment on the banks of the river and were not happy to see Van Den Berg's expedition move through their territory. They came out to meet Van Den Berg's boats with their traditional war paint on and enough warriors to wipe the intruders off the map.

"Van Den Berg tried to reach the natives with compassion, but it didn't work. A fellow traveler in Van Den Berg's boat started to play his violin. He played Beethoven's Violin Concerto. The chief of the tribe of headhunters put his hand up to stop the battle. He was mesmerized by the sound of the music, believing that Van Den Berg was a powerful being to be able to create such a sound out of wood. He offered Van Den Berg and his fellow travelers safe passage."

Bee smiled and said, "I play clarinet in my school band. I could always play our school song if we come across any ancient tribes or rebel forces."

Ogden looked at Bee with annoyance. Pecky motioned with his flippers to stop their bickering and said, "I want to emphasize that redirecting energy most times is a simple process. We must remember this when we are in dark times ahead. We might not be playing music if we come across militants, Bee, but they do respond to money or jewels quite well.

"During his trip to up the Xingu River to discover its source," Pecky went on, oblivious to any discomfort for his listeners, "Van Den Berg came across an area near the river that he described in his journal as otherworldly. He journaled that a region near the headwater of the river was perfectly round. When we explored this region, Neils concluded that it was precisely thirty-three kilometers in circumference. All the trees were slightly bent out with a ring of native flowers boarding the outer rim of the region. Van Den Berg did not recognize the type of flower.

"Van Den Berg and many of his companions had contracted malaria while they were in the jungle. But after they passed through the ring of native flowers, they were miraculously cured. They also found an abundant source of food in the region.

"Neils knew that the universe intervened and saved their lives. Soon after this event, the energy sprite returned to the Life Energy Consortium to chronicle the different serendipitous events that took place during their journey."

The sun had hit the horizon, and Ian could see the brightest star in the sky. He was in a place he had never dreamed he would be and listening to a tale of another far-off place. These adventures were to be savored, even if they were filled with uncertainty and danger. He knew each moment was precious and looked at his companions with a full heart.

"Van Den Berg returned to the Netherlands after five years charting the different rivers into the northwestern region of Brazil," Pecky continued, "When he returned to the Netherlands, he reported to his superiors at the naval high command what he found on the Xingu river. They discounted his findings as him being delirious with malaria. Also, on the return trip down the Xingu river, he was unable to find the region again. He even started to question if he found an Ancient City.

"When he reported to the Life Energy Consortium, he found that he was not the first to chronicle an area near the Xingu River that had healing powers. Another explorer in seventeen hundred came across the same region. The Life Energy Consortium concluded that the only way an explorer could witness this Ancient City was to increase their level of energy and that maybe it was another entrance to the City of Light.

Ten years later, in 1897, Van Den Berg mounted a private expedition to the Xingu river region. He became obsessed with the idea that the powerful Ancient City could help heal humankind. No official government organization would back Van Den Berg, because by this time they though him not sound of mind. They had no other evidence of an Ancient City in the middle of the Amazon basin and wanted nothing to do with Neils.

Van Den Berg financed his expedition with help from the Life Energy Consortium. An energy sprite that had been traveling with Van Den Berg's team was found years later, wandering the jungle. He was half-mad but did have a map to the City of Light. When the energy sprite came back to Europe, he told a story of Van Den Berg and an ancient tribe that guards the region. He also described shadow devotees of Legorian that were merciless with many who participated in Van Den Bergs expedition.

"It was the last anyone ever heard of the expedition. That was, until two years ago when Neils Stephen Van Den Berg was found living in a cave in the wilds of Tibet.

"Somehow, he made his way to Greece and then into the graces of the monks at the monastery. We don't know why he ended up at Mount Athos in seclusion, but hopefully, he will talk to us."

At this moment, Sam and Dan came around the corner, with a concerned look on their faces.

"Pecky," Dan exclaimed, "We feared that you had left without saying goodbye! But I see from the map on the wall you might be discussing your next destination."

"Yes, your news of Van Den Berg has sparked my interest, and we will be taking a little detour to Mount Athos."

"Good, then it's set," Sam chimed in. "Your group goes to Mount Athos."

"I would best be employed going with Pecky, Ian, and Bee to Mount Athos," Ogden declared. Pecky nodded his agreement.

The group agreed to the new arrangements. Dan and Sam, walked back towards the south, while the other party, now including Ogden, walked to the north towards the sleigh and the next step in their journey. ଓ

CR

Chapter Seventeen
Mount Athos

The early morning sun accentuated the clear green Aegean Sea below the keel of the creaky Grecian ferry, the Mount Athos. Because the sleigh represented a belief system that the monks did not recognize, the monks would not allow them to land the sleigh on the peninsula, so Ian and Pecky were taking the ferry to Mount Athos. Pecky knew that the energy surrounding the Mount Athos monasteries was so high that the sleigh would be hard to control.

Looking over the bow of the ferry, Ian could see the bright white sandy bottom as if no water at all separated the boat from the seafloor. The ship appeared to be floating in the air as it slowly moved away from the long beach of Ouranoupolis.

Colorful fish, jellies, and sea snakes seemed so close under the clear water of the boat that Ian could almost reach out and touch them. Some of the native fish were like those he and his father would catch off Gloucester, Massachusetts, on the Old Jezebel, a fishing boat owned by Ian's uncle Mike.

Mike only had seven fingers and one eye left from his fifty years of fishing. Ian asked him many times how he lost his appendages, but Mike would never discuss the details of his disastrous fishing trips. "My former wife took them when we divorced!" he would joke.

Ian surmised that not disclosing the details of adventures was a natural trait in his father's family because Ian's father never discussed his voyages either. It was only recently that Ian found out his father was more than a ship's captain.

He did not understand why his family settled on a farm in a valley of two green mountains in Vermont when most of his father's work was done out at sea. Ian suspected that there was something special about Vermont he hadn't discovered yet. He felt maybe this trip to the City of Light would turn up many answers to a whole lot of questions.

Ian slumped back into his deck chair as the stone tower on the small peninsula jutting out from the beach faded into the distance. He was exhausted from events that unfolded the night before.

Pecky insisted they make an overnight flight from Spain to Greece. The three passengers, Bee, Ogden, and Ian, didn't understand Pecky's big rush. They all just wanted to find a bed and sleep for two days.

Pecky seemed to have a timetable in his head he was trying to meet, but he was not communicating the reasons why to his companions. Ian had to trust that Pecky knew what he was doing and leave him to the task of delivering them to the entrance of the Ancient City. First, though, was this trip to Mount Athos.

Ian had found out much about Mount Athos. He knew that the peninsula was in the northeastern part of Greece but needed to brush up on the geography of the region, just below Bulgaria and to the west of Turkey.

As Pecky had told his fellow travelers, according to different Greek myths, the name of Mount Athos comes from the giant, Athos. Athos, who flung an enormous rock at Poseidon, which landed on the peninsula; or that Poseidon tossed a huge boulder at Athos, which crushed him at the place where the mountain stands.

An early Christian legend relates that the Virgin Mary and St John were on their way to meet Lazarus when a storm forced them to put in at the site now occupied by one of the Mount Athos monasteries. Mary loved Mount Athos so much that she asked Christ to make her a gift of the peninsula.

Early monastic life was hard. Most of the monks were hermits, living in improvised huts, eating the fruits of wild trees, and suffering the effects of frequent pirate raids. Over the centuries, the monks built monasteries, but the austere day-to-day life of a monk has not changed much in almost two thousand years.

Ian decided to walk around the ferry deck to see who else was making the journey. Ian could see the ascetic life in many of the pilgrims traveling to Mount Athos; some cloaked in traditional gray monk attire with only thin sandals on their dusty feet. Electronic devices such as cell phones, radios, or even digital wristwatches were not to be seen.

The face of one of the older monks had such crevices he looked like someone had chiseled his body out of stone. His long bright white beautiful hair reminded Ian of a sorcerer he once read of in a book. Ian thought that maybe the legend of a sorcerer came from those who are close to the Source. If this was true, then this individual truly was a sorcerer because Ian could sense the depth of love this man had for God. He could also sense a great peace in the wayfarer's heart.

Other than the monks, the main thing that stood out on the ferry was that there were no women. Even the small crew that ran the ship were all men, including the old fellow who sold food on the cafeteria deck. The only woman in Ian's life right now was missing—Bee was left on the shore with Ogden back at the ferry building in Ouranoupolis.

Ian was surprised that Bee didn't seem to mind being left behind with Ogden to roam the streets of the city while he and Pecky traveled to the monastery to meet Van Den Berg. Pecky had reminded the three, before the ferry boat left for Mount Athos, that the monks do not accept women in the monasteries—they are so devoted to their monastic life that they only see women as distractions. The only females they do receive are cats because they are good at catching the many mice infesting the peninsula; all the other animals are male.

Looking back to this morning, Ian reflected that Bee seemed pleased to stay onshore with Ogden. She wasn't upset at all. Maybe Bee was mesmerized by Ogden's good looks and, Ian thought, of course, Ogden was two years older than Bee.

Ian once heard from his friends that most girls like older men because they perceive them to be more mature than boys their same age. Ian considered this for only a moment, not wanting to believe Bee to be a regular girl with girlish thoughts.

Ian felt some new, interesting feelings for Bee. It might be that he was a little jealous that Bee seemed so captivated by Ogden. He quickly put these thoughts out of his head, but they kept creeping back, overshadowing the Van Den Berg meeting.

Ian thought that maybe he had been taking Bee for granted. She was always around, becoming a big part of his life. For the first time, he considered that he would miss her terribly if she were not around anymore. This thought made him feel a little queasy.

Pecky walked around the corner of the cabin and motioned him to the front of the ferry. Ian followed, wondering why no one on the boat seemed to be surprised that a six-foot-tall emperor penguin was aboard. Maybe he saw Pecky, in a way others didn't, or others saw Pecky in a way that he didn't. Ian did see the monks and others on the boat interacting with Pecky, so Pecky was not invisible, but they talked to him as if a talking penguin was an everyday event. Ian wondered what else there was in the world that he did not see.

Ian considered something he'd never thought of before—maybe the world outside will always deceive. Maybe seeing is not seeing at all. Maybe seeing is feeling what is in our hearts and only believing what is in our hearts to be true.

The ship's horn startled Ian as he and Pecky walked to the front of the ferry. The crew was preparing to dock at Mount Athos.

The trip from Ouranoupolis to the monastery docks at Mount Athos went faster than Ian expected. The scenery of the beautiful Aegean Sea had made the trip pass without time.

Nestled on the white stone cliffs, a few hundred feet above the water's edge, stood the Great Lavra monastery. The monastery looked as if the builders carved it out of the mountain. Ian could not imagine how artisans could build such a structure so precariously positioned on a cliff overlooking the Aegean Sea, especially with the primitive tools and equipment available centuries ago.

As the ferry positioned itself by the dock, Ian caught a glimpse of something. A single, almost transparent figure in the shape and height of a man appeared on the cliffs overlooking the main monastery. All Ian could see was a glimmer of light reflecting off the form.

Ian noticed that the dock area was quiet. Much quieter than when they left the dock at Ouranoupolis. The silence was almost unnerving to Ian because when they left the city dock, he could hear all the sounds of Greece, music, laughter, talking, and yelling. The Greek language was melodic and comforting, but near the monastery, people spoke in low tones, and the monks didn't speak at all. There were no cars or even animals in sight. It was as if the world Ian knew stopped, and he was transported back a thousand years to an ancient time.

As the dock workers moored the boat, Ian watched as more images started to appear all along the cliffs. If Ian looked directly at the silhouettes, he could not see anything. The shapes could only be seen through the corner of his eye. He felt a great peace in his heart as he considered the existence of these entities.

Ian wondered why Van Den Berg ended up in this place. Why didn't he come back to the modern world? He asked if the transparent figures had anything to do with Van Den Berg's decision.

Ian turned to Pecky and asked, "Do you see the radiant figures, Pecky?"

"Yes, Ian, I do. I'm a little surprised that you see them, but also I'm pleased."

"Do you know what or who they are, Pecky?"

Pecky walked over to a stone wall covered in green vines with little blue flowers and sat down. Ian noticed that the blue flowers carried a sweet smell, almost like jasmine.

Jasmine was not native to Vermont, but his mother kept a small amount it in a pot near a large southern facing window in their kitchen. Ian also remembered the sweet smell of jasmine from a vacation with his family in San Francisco.

Pecky always had a particular look on his face when he was considering his answer to a multifaceted question. Ian understood this and knew that Pecky was formulating an answer. He believed in Pecky's brilliance and understanding of complex concepts.

Ian realized, after spending time with Pecky, that penguins run on a different mental clock than humans. Most people he came across talked before they considered what it was, they were saying. Penguins don't speak until they know what needed to be said. Ian felt that maybe their shorter life dictated less waste in words, or perhaps they just don't need to talk as much as people. The more time Ian spent with Pecky, the more he saw how different he was from humans.

Pecky motioned Ian to sit next to him on the stone wall. Then with consideration, Pecky said, "Ian, many humans would consider the figures to be angels, but they are monks who have passed on, passed into another level of consciousness—a different degree of energy."

Ian thought about his conversation with Sam back in Spain about the different levels of energy that make up the world.

Pecky continued, "When we physically die, we don't die, we just pass onto another plane of consciousness, we transition into another level of energy.

"You may remember from your studies in physics that 'the law of conservation energy' was first formulated in the nineteenth century. This law states that the total amount of energy in a remote physical system or place, such as here on Mount Athos, remains constant over time.

"The total energy is said to be preserved over time. For a remote environment, this law means that energy is localized and can change its location within the setting. Energy can change within the system; for instance, chemical energy can become kinetic energy, but that energy can be neither created nor destroyed."

Pecky paused for a moment to make sure Ian was still following his logic. Ian was looking right at Pecky, which encouraged Pecky to continue.

"In other words, the reality that the now-deceased monks exist in, plus the world we are standing in, has a constant amount of energy that makes up both worlds together.

"Measurable elements that have rest form have equivalent amounts of energy. They are not conserved and can perish into forms of energy, including kinetic and potential energy, that lack rest quantity.

"An example of this energy phenomenon is the shades that you rescued back in Toledo. They transitioned from energy in motion to energy at rest, or in a state of rest, because of the depressed energy that was overcoming the area. The energy again was not destroyed but merely transitioned into another state of existence.

"In such a transformation process within a remote system, such as Toledo, neither the total mass nor the total energy changes over time, although the matter content may change. Therefore, conservation of energy, and conservation of mass, each still holds as a law."

Ian was nodding, but now looking up at the forms on the cliffs.

"The monks you see surrounding the monastery are a testament to these physical principles. One thing that I have always found interesting about most scientists is that they believe in this law of conservation energy. But at the same time, they believe that the energy which sustains people once they are physically dead is gone. Or that what we call our souls is not present anymore after we physically die. I've always wondered how they can believe that energy never dies, but our souls do.

"What I have learned is that the law of conservation energy goes beyond the world that we observe to other realities that exist in our universe at the same time—that the energy that occupies the infinite layers of consciousness around us cannot be destroyed.

"The angels surrounding the monastery have transitioned from physical beings existing in our world to spiritual beings living in a higher level of consciousness. The energy that makes up what we might call a soul can never be destroyed, only transitioned in other states of existence."

Ian was listening to Pecky's philosophy, now with his eyes closed. It was a lot to comprehend, but Ian saw the truth of it and felt the world expand as he listened.

"Many of the monks throughout the ages have continued to stay near Mount Athos because they protect this sacred land from Legorian. In many ways, they are a modern representation of angels because they protect us from the darkness."

"There are angels around us all the time. Most humans don't see them because most can't open their hearts to their love and grace. I'm surprised that you see them, but at the same time, I'm not surprised."

At this moment, a monk in a brown cloak walked towards Ian and Pecky. Ian could sense that this monk was different from the rest. He was more at peace than the others. He seemed to be closer in energy to the angels that surrounded the monastery.

The monk walked up to Pecky and said, "Mr. Peckerage Hornblaster, we have been anticipating your arrival. I am Father Isaiah."

The monk clasped his hands in a symbol of prayer and slightly bowed towards Pecky.

Pecky replied, "Please, Father, call me, Pecky."

The monk slightly bowed again and said, "Please follow me to wash up and eat breakfast before your audience with Neils Stephan Van Den Berg."

As the trio walked the steep and narrow stone walkway up to the monastery, Pecky had only one thought on his mind; he was hoping that they had fish on the menu. ☙

ß

Chapter Eighteen
Let Go Let God

An inscription on the base of the great wooden door leading into the monastery, read "Dimiserant, et Deus Faciat." Ian remembered a little bit of Latin from his tenth grade French teacher, who often taught the Latin roots of the French words, but the phrase on the base of the great wooden door did not ring any bells, other than Deus, "God."

Pecky and Ian were standing outside of the portico. They were waiting for permission from the Monsignor to offer them a haven from the world. The ceremony to provide pilgrims with food, comfort, and lodging went back a millennium and practiced many times a day. The monks of the Great Lavra Monastery consider the ceremony a sacred honor each time.

Father Isaiah mentioned that the Monsignor was on his way and for them to wait in silence. Remaining silent has never been a problem for Ian, but asking Pecky to be quiet was another thing.

In a quiet hum, Ian could hear Pecky chatter something. Ian surmised from his time with Pecky that standing still and quiet was not necessarily a natural strength for penguins. Maybe the severe cold of the Antarctic taught the Penguins to move continually and communicate.

Ian did want to ask Pecky what "Dimiserant, et Deus Faciat" meant, but was unwilling to break his silence until the Monsignor arrived.

At this moment, the wooden door of the monastery slowly opened, exposing an older man with a long white beard and simple black clothing. He wore a large cross and chain around his neck that reached almost down to his waist.

The elder monk stood on the other side of the entrance to the great hall of the monastery. He motioned for Ian and Pecky to move forward into the building through the portico—at the same time, asking them to enter the sanctuary by leaving a small part of the world behind.

Ian and Pecky respectfully stepped over the entrance and the inscription "Dimiserant, et Deus Faciat" into the monastery. Pecky and Ian were overwhelmed at first by the size and beauty of the room.

The enclosure was one hundred feet long and seventy feet high with ornate paintings and bright colors etched into stone and marble. Gold leaf depicting different events that took place in the Bible were everywhere in the hall, even on the floor.

There were tapestries similar to the ones Ian remembered seeing on the top floor of Buckingham Palace. Many of the scenes in the ornately decorated tapestries were of biblical pictures, but many had paintings not familiar to Ian.

The Monsignor and a group of five other monks, including Father Isaiah, approached Ian and Pecky. In unison, the group of monks all clasped their hands in prayer and bowed slightly before the pilgrims, chanting the Latin inscription Ian noticed on the base of the large wooden door.

Pecky motioned Ian to clasp his hands in prayer and slightly bow in response to the monks' gesture. Pecky thanked the Monsignor for sanctuary.

A smile came over the Monsignor's face as he approached Pecky. In perfect English, the Monsignor said, "Welcome old friend, I am most pleased to see you once again."

Pecky replied, "Yes, Bartholomew, it has been too many years. I am also happy to see you, my dear friend."

It crossed Ian's mind how Pecky knew the Monsignor, and how they were such great friends. Ian considered that maybe Pecky was older than he appeared.

Pecky and the Monsignor embraced each other. He then turned around and motioned for his monks to return to their duties.

The Monsignor turned to Ian and said, "Let Go Let God."

Ian was confused and replied, "I'm sorry, sir, I don't know what you mean."

The Monsignor continued, "You were wondering what "Dimiserant, et Deus Faciat" meant. Well, it means "Let Go Let God.""

Ian looked even more confused and replied, "How did you know I was wondering about the inscription on the front portico?"

Monsignor Bartholomew replied, "The angels that guard this house of worship told me your thoughts, young man."

Ian became a little undone with this news of the angels. He noticed that the transparent figures that he saw surrounding the outside of the monastery were not inside the hall.

Monsignor Bartholomew continued, "The angels tell me you are a true heart. I have been a monk in this monastery for many years, and I have never welcomed such a special person across the grand portico."

Ian replied, "The angels, sir—who, were they?"

Monsignor Bartholomew continued, "The angels were brothers who have passed on to another stage of their spiritual evolution. The angles now guard this monastery against dark powers."

"We who occupy this monastery have found some simple spiritual truths based on Let Go Let God.

"We are not physical beings having spiritual experiences; we are spiritual beings having physical experiences. We simply need to let go of our perceptions of who we think we are in this world, and we become more of who we truly are. Does this make any sense to you?"

Ian thought for a moment and replied, "Monsignor, in many ways, it makes perfect sense, but in other ways, it makes no sense at all."

Monsignor Bartholomew replied, "It's important that it makes some sense."

The Monsignor turned around briskly and motioned the travelers to follow him. He walked through a series of hallways that were less ornate than the great hall. The passages seemed more medieval than the entrance. Many of the halls were rough cut out of the stone from the mountain. Old tapestries were lining the hallways. Some of the tapestries looked to be old as a millennium with battles depicted with colored thread.

The trio finally entered another building with three long wooden tables. The tables were around sixty feet long with smooth surfaces, not from sanding, but from the many years of monks leaning on the tables. Ian could see indents in the table from monks praying before each meal.

Monsignor Bartholomew turned to Pecky and Ian and said in a quiet voice, "This is the hall where we eat our meals. Many of our brothers have taken a vow of silence. Please do not try to talk to any of them.

"A brother will come with a meal already prepared and put it down in front of you. We are a poor group of the Church of God; our food is simple but nourishing. I will return in an hour to show you to your rooms for the night and prepare you to meet Neils Van Den Berg."

Monsignor Bartholomew quietly motioned to the travelers to sit down at the table nearest to them, and then he turned and walked into one of the many passageways leading out of the room.

It wasn't more than five minutes when a monk appeared with two trays from the door leading into the monastery's general kitchen. The monk slowly and methodically walked over to Pecky and Ian and set the tray of food before them.

The monk leaned over and whispered, "Please partake of food provided to you and remember to thank God for such nourishment." The monk then quickly left the room.

Before Pecky and Ian were a meal of homemade bread, beans, cheese, water. To Pecky's surprise and delight a perfectly cooked filet of local fish. Pecky motioned to Ian to say a prayer before consuming the meal.

Pecky and Ian were so hungry that they became deeply involved with eating their meal, so much so that the monks coming and going around them didn't distract them from their task of consumption.

Ian and Pecky finally looked up as the last bite of Gopa, a local fish favorite, traveled down their gullets. The first thing they noticed was that they were alone. All the monks had left without a sound.

The second thing that Ian noticed was a beautiful fresco on the ceiling of the hall. The mural depicted an angel with flowing red and blue robes descending to earth surrounded by three white doves. One of the doves was carrying an olive branch in its mouth. The angel had a sword in its right hand and a mandolin on its left side.

This painting was the first real fresco Ian had ever seen. His art teacher back home had the book "World Art" that explained the process of painting a mural, but he knew now that a book could never communicate the beauty and depth of a fresco.

At this moment, Monsignor Bartholomew briskly walked toward Pecky and Ian. He stopped right in front of the pair, slightly bowed with his hands clasped in prayer, and said, "I hope you enjoyed your meal. I asked the kitchen to cook up our local fish favorite mainly because I know how much Pecky enjoys a good fish meal.

"If you two will follow me, I will take you to your rooms for the night." Monsignor turned around as briskly as he entered the room and walked towards an east door leading into another medieval-looking passageway. Pecky and Ian quickly got up and followed behind the Monsignor, leaving their dishes on the wooden table.

It crossed Ian's mind that Bee and Ogden would need to stay with the sleigh this evening because Pecky only left them with enough money to buy food for the day. Ian was happy that Ogden was with Bee because he would worry if she was left alone in a strange town, even though he knew that Bee could take care of herself in nearly any situation.

Monsignor Bartholomew guided Pecky and Ian to a courtyard at the back of the monastery. The courtyard was open to the blue sky above with a large water fountain in the center. Dotted around the fountain were small blocks of marble buried in the blue-green grass.

Ian could smell the sweet scent of jasmine permeate a garden that overlooked the ocean below. At closer observation, Ian could see that there was a sheer cliff on the other side of the garden leading down to the beach one hundred feet below.

Right in front of Pecky and Ian were five doors leading to five small rooms with beds made of wood and burlap. Each room had a single window, a washbasin, and a tiny cross hung on a wall depicting the crucifixion of Christ.

Monsignor Bartholomew motioned to two of the outer rooms for Pecky and Ian. He also motioned to an outhouse at the end of the row of apartments and then said. "It is getting late, please be our guests for the night, and in the morning you will be introduced to Neils Van Den Berg."

Pecky replied, "Bartholomew, we thank you for your gracious hospitality, but could you please tell us why we need to prepare to see Van Den Berg. We would also be interested in how he ended up in this monastery."

Monsignor Bartholomew considered what Pecky had asked for a moment and then motioned them to sit down on a marble bench next to the south side of the water fountain. Ian could tell that the Monsignor was gathering his thoughts.

The Monsignor leaned up against the edge of the water fountain and said, "Tibetan monks traveling to our doors from the east found Neils Van Den Berg in a cave deep in the foothills of the Himalayas.

"We don't know how long he had been living in the cave. He was illuminated when the monks found him. They were at first unable to communicate with him."

Pecky asked, "What do you mean by illuminated?"

The Monsignor continued, "You might consider someone living in a cave for any amount of time to have a long scraggly beard and maybe even be malnourished, but Neils was none of these things.

"He was perfectly fit, cleanly shaven, and generating an unusual amount of heat, even though it was the dead of winter when the monks discovered him."

Pecky asked, "How did the monks know to look in the cave?"

The Monsignor replied, "There is a small remote Tibetan village located at the base of the mountain, and over the years, a legend grew about a wise man living in a cave just above the village. The monks traveling from the east had also heard of the legend but discounted it as just something small village folk might make up."

"On one journey, the monks were asked by their senior monk to investigate the legend. They did so and found Neils Van Den Berg in a cave with no blanket, no apparent food source, or any earthly comforts."

Pecky asked again, "What do you mean by illuminated?"

The Monsignor replied, "As you will see tomorrow, Neils Van Den Berg is not of this world. He lives in both our world and in another reality. Not unlike the angels you have encountered outside this monastery.

"Neils has reached a state of grace that few in the world ever reach. He has come to higher consciousness. He is in this world but not of this world.

"It is hard for me to communicate what the monks found and how Van Den Berg ended up here, but we found him two years ago. He asked the monks to bring him here because he said one day, the Emperor of all Penguins and a true heart would need his help."

"So, you see, he came here for you. He knew before you even set out on your journey that you would need his help. He has a message for you and you alone. I have asked him many times where he had been and how he ended up in Tibet, but his only response has been to wait for your arrival."

Pecky interjected, "Why do we need to prepare for our meeting with Neils?"

The Monsignor continued, "You need to prepare because he exists at a higher level of consciousness. You and Ian need to let go of the world just enough to be able to heighten your levels of energy.

"This monastery exists at a higher degree of perception, so any traveler who comes here even for one day will rid themselves of lower darker energies they carry in the world.

"Also, Van Den Berg knew that the angels guard the monastery against dark powers, so he knew it would be safe to tell you what you need to know for you to continue your journey to the City of Light.

"My friends, more will be uncovered in the morning. Please feel free to walk about the monastery. Help yourself to anything in our kitchen if you get hungry during the night."

"We wake early for morning prayers and require that all our visitors follow the guidelines of the monastery. The Monsignor bowed to the travelers with clasped hands and quickly exited through a hallway.

Ian and Pecky sat for a long time watching the sun move towards the western horizon. In a short time, the sky started to radiate a brilliant red and orange as the sun touched the range of hills to the west of Mount Athos.

Ian asked Pecky, "I don't understand what Monsignor Bartholomew meant by 'Let Go Let God'?"

Pecky opened his smoking pouch and took out a pinch of dried herring to insert into his pipe. After a long time contemplating his reply, he said, "As most people travel through their lives, they believe that they can control their destiny, and those closest to them."

"A parent might try to control the lives of their children, or someone might try to control the destiny of their spouse or friend, for good or bad."

"Many feel that if they only become financially wealthy, they will be powerful, and then they can control their lives and those lives around them."

"Adolph Hitler was an excellent example of someone trying to control others by becoming what he believed to be powerful. His need to control caused a considerable amount of pain to the world.

"A famous quote from a British Historian in 1887, Lord Acton, states 'Power tends to corrupt, and absolute power corrupts absolutely. Great men are almost always bad men.'

"Many feel that if the world were only the way they think it should be, then the world would be a better place, and they would not suffer so much.

"The truth is that the belief one can control their destiny is an illusion. We will never be able to control our destinies no matter how powerful we think we are or how powerful we might become. Only the Infinite Being can write the story of our futures.

"The only control we have over our lives during our journey is to either go with the flow of our divine purpose or fight the current.

"The flow of time is like a river steadily moving towards the ocean. We can hold onto the rocks, or we can let go and have faith the river will take us where we need to go. If we choose to hang on, the river will only create more and more pressure on us.

"The only reason we might hold onto the rocks is that we are fearful of letting go and letting God take us.

"Do you understand what 'Let Go Let God' means now?"

Ian looked up at Pecky with a smile on his face and said, "Yes, Pecky, that makes much more sense. I feel in many ways that this whole journey is a testament to 'Letting Go Letting God.'"

Pecky and Ian sat for a long time after the sun dipped below the hills before they retired to their rooms for the night. They looked at each other for only a moment and without a word. They both felt that they were becoming good friends. ☙

CR

Chapter Nineteen
Self-Awareness

A loud knock on the door jarred Ian awake. He had been dreaming, standing in front of the old apple tree that towered above his home. It was early winter, the ground was just starting to freeze, and the apple tree was bare of leaves, glowing in translucent white light. Inside the light was an obscure figure standing without defined shape. Ian felt connected to the entity, but he didn't understand how.

In his dream, he remembered Claridon Castle and the haze, but this place was not dark, this place was the opposite of the dark. This place had a warm and brilliant light. He was feeling a deep sense of peace. With each step he took toward the tree, he felt a heightened sense of consciousness.

The undefined being wanted to communicate some information, but Ian could not hear what it was trying to say. The being was communicating in a language that was beyond words. Ian felt the entity was trying to communicate to him with pure consciousness. The language was outside his knowledge. No matter how hard he tried, he could not understand. That was when a faint voice from his heart said, "Trust."

It was the entity, Ian understood, telling him to trust. Ian was trying to understand with his mind, but this being was speaking in the language of the heart. He knew that the figure was trying to help him trust his own heart.

Another loud knock on Ian's cottage door jarred him wide awake. Ian looked out the small window next to the door and saw only pitch black. For a moment, Ian forgot where he was or what he was doing in such a strange place.

Then he remembered that he was a guest in the Lavra Monastery on the Mount Athos peninsula. He recalled Neils Stephan Van Den Berg and the purpose of his visit.

Another loud knock on the door, and then a voice behind the door softly said, "Ian, this is Father Isaiah, it is time for morning prayers."

"Father, please come in."

The door slowly opened, and Father Isaiah walked in with a warm smile on his face. "Good morning Ian, I hope you had a restful sleep."

"I feel much better. In fact, I haven't felt this at peace in a long time. I had the most interesting dream about someone trying to communicate with me without words. The entity, in my dream, wanted me to trust my own heart."

Father Isaiah replied, "Ian, it is vital to trust your heart, especially since many are relying on your gifts to keep the world from falling into darkness."

"I forget that I'm supposed to help save the world from Legorian. In my dream, I felt so far away from accepting what the form was trying to tell me. I don't know how I am the one to save the world from darkness."

Father Isaiah replied, "You heard the word trust in your dream. Many who travel challenging roads make things more complicated than they are. You were trying to listen to what you thought you needed to hear, but what you heard was a powerful word, trust.

"One thing you might consider as you continue on the rest of your journey; the language of the mind can become deluded and complicated, but the language of the heart is simple. That is why you will, in time, understand all languages because all words start in the heart.

"The language of the mind can become deceptive and dark, and that is why you must discern which language is of the mind and which language is of the heart.

"The other truth that one can know is that your heart will never lie to you. Your heart will always tell you what you need to know and tell you the truth."

Ian continued, "I had another interesting experience. I was sleeping but not sleeping. I feel rested but not in the same way that I would feel rested from sleeping back in Vermont. Does this make any sense?"

'You are feeling the heightened energy of this monastery," Father Isaiah replied, "Monks that stay in the monastery for any amount of time start to lose their need for sleep. Many of our brothers need no more than four hours of sleep.

"If you think about what sleep is, you might consider that sleeping is resting the mind, but if you are in a state of mental peace, how much sleep would someone need?

Ian thought about what was said. "What is next, Father?"

"We will need to attend morning prayers, and then breakfast before your audience with Neils Van Den Berg. You should find our meals to be bountiful and should carry you and Pecky for the rest of the day until dinner, or until you eat again."

"Father, what do you mean?"

"When a brother has visited Neils, he has often stayed longer than he thought he would. That is all I can tell you now."

"What time is it?" Ian asked.

"It is 5:00 a.m., just a few minutes before the sun rises. We will have our morning prayers on the terrace overlooking the ocean. The sun rising over the Aegean is beautiful. I look forward to it, the grandeur and peace of it, every morning."

"Is Pecky awake?"

Father Isaiah replied, "Yes, I woke him first. He will be along soon. I believe he is taking a long shower. I will leave you and return in twenty minutes." He smiled at Ian, then walked out the door. Ian slowly got out of bed, thinking of his dream, and felt the cool morning breeze coming off the Aegean Sea.

Ian wondered how Bee and Ogden were getting along. He had a feeling that they were having a pretty good time wandering the city. He thought it strange that he had done so much traveling in such a short period without seeing or enjoying much of the places he had visited.

Ian's life before he arrived at the monastery seemed to be a distant memory. It was as if he were looking back on his history as an observer rather than the participant.

Ian was excited to meet Neils and hear of his travels to the Ancient City. As he thought of Van Den Berg, he had a momentary vision of the undefined entity from his dream.

Father Isaiah returned to guide Ian and Pecky to morning prayers. As they reached the terrace overlooking the Aegean Sea, the monks were chanting, the most melodic sound Ian had ever heard.

Father Isaiah whispered to Ian, "The chant is in Latin. The universe vibrates at a constant key of C, and the monks primarily sing to God." Ian felt the sound of the chanting reach his soul.

The sun broke from the east and cast a great light over the blue-green Aegean Sea, illuminating the surrounding green and brown hills overlooking the monastery. The moment the warm sunlight reached the terrace, the monks stopped chanting. They stood up together, bowed towards the east with clasped hands, and then walked towards the main dining hall.

Ian and Pecky followed the monks with Father Isaiah. The monks were silent during breakfast, but this morning the dining room had been decorated with beautiful white flowers that were unknown to Pecky or Ian. The smell of the flowers reminded Ian of jasmine once again.

"Father, what are these beautiful flowers?" Ian asked. "The fragrance reminds me of jasmine I once smelled in San Francisco."

Father Isaiah replied, "They are local Greek flora that covers the island. They are called anemone. We decorate the dining hall each morning with flowers to honor our Virgin Mary.

"The jasmine fragrance is not from the flowers, however. What you smell are the spirits that guard this monastery. When saints pass on into another consciousness, their bodies become incorruptible. They have a faint floral smell, sometimes roses, at times the smell of jasmine, at times other flora."

"You said their bodies become incorruptible," Ian asked. "What does that mean?"

"What it means for a body to be incorruptible is that a body will not decay because the spirit who possessed the body during life was beyond the darkness."

"Remember the smell of angels because they do now always show themselves. During your journey to the City of Light, when the path becomes most dark, you may smell jasmine. The smell will remind you of the angels that silently guard you.

"I must leave you, but Monsignor Bartholomew will arrive to take you to Neils Van Den Berg after you finish your breakfast."

Ian and Pecky enjoyed a bountiful breakfast of brown bread, eggs, fried fish, and mushrooms and stewed tomatoes. Pecky had two portions of the fish.

Monsignor Bartholomew entered the dining hall as they finished their meal. "I hope you two have had a pleasant rest and a good breakfast. It's now time to meet Neils Stephan Van Den Berg"

Ian and Pecky looked at each other with relief. It was finally time to have many of the riddles answered by Van Den Berg.

Monsignor motioned for the two to follow him. Ian and Pecky dutifully followed behind Monsignor Bartholomew back to their bungalows overlooking the Aegean Sea.

Monsignor handed both Ian and Pecky a large bundle and said, "You will find white monk's clothing and sandals in these bundles. I would ask that you take all your worldly clothes off and put these simple garments on before you meet Van Den Berg. We need to rid you of any lower energy that is connected to the outside world so that your being will be as heightened as possible. I will return shortly to guide you to Neils."

"Why are the garments so bright white?" Pecky asked.

"White vibrates at the highest level of energy of any of the colors," Monsignor Bartholomew replied. "To reduce the lower energies, you need to be in white. White light is made up of all the colors, so there is unity in white as well." Monsignor Bartholomew walked briskly away through one of the many hallways leading to the west part of the monastery.

Ian turned to Pecky. "Pecky, I'm worried about what we might learn from Neils. I feel our journey will take a new path, a route that is much more dangerous. In many ways, I am more fearful of what lies ahead than what we have already overcome."

"Ian, try to remember that whatever road we take, for good or bad, the angels guide us. Always know that the universe is behind us one hundred percent because we are on our spiritual path. The Source wants us to find the Ancient City, and the Source wants us to heal the void.

"We are only following what is meant to be. If we end up traveling to dark and dangerous places, it is because that is the challenge we must meet to ascend to the Ancient City. The only choice we have is to either emotionally flow with our journey or emotionally fight our trip. In the end, we are going to find ourselves in the same place."

Ian nodded in agreement and returned to his cottage to put on the monk's clothing. Ian felt rejuvenated as he walked out of his bungalow in his simple clothing. He let out a guffaw of suppressed hilarity as he saw Pecky standing next to the fountain in his monk's attire. The sight of a six-foot-tall penguin in a white monk's tunic with a hood was a weird sight. Pecky did not see the humor in the situation.

Monsignor Bartholomew approached them, and said, "It is time for your audience with Van Den Berg. Please follow me." He motioned for the two to follow close behind. They walked through an endless series of passageways cut out of granite, then started to climb a long set of stairs leading into the mountain. The stairs went up and up, exhausting Pecky and Ian, but their elderly leader seemed unfazed.

After forty minutes, they entered an enormous cave, about one hundred and fifty feet high and two hundred feet long, covered with brilliant white and blue crystals. The crystals extended three or more feet out of the floor and ceiling of the cave. It reminded Ian of a trip he and his family took to the Luray Caverns in the Shenandoah Valley in Virginia. He felt a pang of homesickness and missed his mother.

There was a narrow path through the crystals, lit by candle lanterns that reflected off the stones. When they finally reached the far end of the cave, they could see a passageway. The outer columns of the ancient portico were carved with the Latin inscription "Intra re Intrepidus" that neither Ian nor Pecky recognized.

Monsignor Bartholomew stopped before the entrance and turned to his guests and said, "Unfortunately, my good friends, I must leave you here. At the end of this tunnel, you will find a smaller chamber where Sir Neils Stephan Van Den Berg resides.

"When you finish, I will meet you. Remember to 'Let Go Let God' when you are in the presence of Neils." Monsignor Bartholomew turned and quickly walked away.

Ian and Pecky turned to each other, and without a word, each motioned to the other to move forward. The passageway, hewn out of a massive, brilliant white stone vein in the mountain, was carved with angels, some battling demons. They slowly walked towards the chamber at the end of the passageway.

As they walked towards the chamber, Ian felt a lightness of being come over him. Ian's sense of time seemed to slow down. All his fears and doubts melted away with every step closer that he came to Van Den Berg.

At the end of the passageway, Pecky and Ian came to an old dark red oak door. The door was around seven feet tall by five feet wide with iron hinges holding it tight to the mountain cave.

A round iron knob projected from the middle of the door's cracked and splintered wood, worn away from the many years of use. Carved above the door was the same Latin inscription Ian had seen at the passageway entry, "Intra re Intrepidus."

Without any help from Ian or Pecky, the wooden door slowly opened, exposing a small room carved out of the same pure white marble. The room appeared to be a perfect circle, thirty or so feet in diameter. A man sat at the other end of the chamber in front of a fragrant fire that radiated blue flame.

Ian had an overwhelming vision of his dream that morning of the undefined being. Powerful energy moved from the top of his head down through his body.

He understood that the undefined figure in his dream was Neils Van Den Berg. He felt a connection with Neils that was beyond time and space. At this moment, Ian knew that he had taken this journey many times during his former lives. He felt that he had stood at this doorway many times before. He realized that each time he stood before the door to this chamber, he had to make the same decision—to continue the journey or to go home. ✆

CB

Chapter Twenty
Seven Portals

Ian and Pecky walked into the chamber, looking around with wonder. Seven mirrors polished out of white crystal were embedded into the chamber wall at Ian's eye level. The mirrors were about four feet high by two feet wide and equally positioned on the wall around the room. At the base of each mirror was a numerical inscription.

Ian and Pecky bowed to Neils Stephan Van Den Berg with clasped hands and then sat down on the other side of the blue-flamed fire.

Neils bowed back and said, "Enter without fear."

A little confused, Ian asked, "What do you mean, sir?"

Neils replied, "You were wondering what the Latin inscription meant that is etched about the entrance to this chamber, were you not?"

Ian replied, "Yes, I was."

"You have come to me for knowledge and wisdom. I hope that you understand what it means to enter without fear and doubt because if you carry any fear or doubt, you will never be able to enter the City of Light."

Pecky interjected, "Mr. Van Den Berg, you came to this monastery specifically to meet us and help us enter the Ancient City? You started your pilgrimage to this monastery two years before we even set out on our journey. How is this possible?"

"Yes, I knew that you were going to need my help. Everything has already happened in the realm of Shangri-La. We are just looking back on the residual effect of a cause. The reason I am here is to help heal the connection by the one who is a true heart. The true heart, of course, is you, Ian. You can refer to my Christian name, Neils, if you prefer?"

Ian and Pecky started to feel a heightened sense of energy traveling through their minds and bodies. They felt as if they were accelerating through time and space.

Pecky replied, "Neils, you talk of Shangri-La, but I thought that you entered the City of Light deep in the Amazon jungle?"

Neils contemplated before responding, "I'm sorry, my good friends, it has been many years since I talked to those who occupy this world.

"In the realm that I have existed in, communication goes beyond the spoken word. Communication encompasses our entire being—we who occupy that heightened sense, understand each other completely.

"Now that I occupy a linear reality, I feel that I must explain myself and the reason for my journey to this monastery in a direct historical manner. So, I will start from the beginning.

"I believe that you have knowledge of my journey that took me and my companions, deep into the Amazon.

"As you most likely know, my last communication with the physical world was in 1897. I discovered the outer edge of the Ancient City, and I knew that once I entered the forbidden region, all communication with the outside world would be lost. I remember telling the energy sprite to pass on what happened to the Life Energy Consortium.

"Unfortunately, the outside world would never know how successful I had been. Of course, perceptions create success. The success that I had found far outweighed my intended goal at the time.

"I had been to the jungle many times looking for the Ancient City. Unknown to most, even to my companions, I now had acquired a map to the City. I believe the same gold sphere you possess, Ian." His eyes pierced Ian, who put his hand into his pocket as if to find the orb there.

"How did you get the map to the City of Light?" Pecky interjected, looking worriedly at Ian.

"A colleague who worked as a curator at the British Museum came across the map hidden in an artifact brought back years earlier by a fellow explorer.

"My colleague discovered the directions to the Ancient City just days before I left on my last journey. At the time, I thought his discovery was just a coincidence, but now I know it was fate, just like I knew when Sobek took the map, it would find its way to you, my dear friend."

"You knew Sobek?" Ian exclaimed.

"Yes. For a millennium, anyone searching for the Ancient City would come across Sobek, for good or evil—well, mostly for ill. He initially helped me to find the Ancient City but tried to sabotage my journey in the end. Anyway, that is another story for another time.

"As soon as I saw the gold orb my colleague had found, I knew that it was the map. I knew I had found an essential part of the puzzle.

"The entrance to the City of Light starts with an obelisk. A three-sided structure precisely seven feet tall made from solid crystal.

"Directly below the obelisk is a chamber not unlike the one we now occupy. The difference is that the room is perfectly round like a ball. It's carved out of stone. The center of the chamber is another obelisk with a round hole for the golden sphere. The obelisk is a marker for the chamber, but the chamber is the actual entrance to the City of Light.

"I came across the obelisk many times during my search for the City of Light, but I could never move forward without the map. No matter what direction I would go, I would soon find myself and my companions lost in the jungle walking in circles.

"This all changed once I came back to the jungle with the map. The gold orb is more than just a map—it is a ticket and a key.

"When you find the obelisk at any of the entrances to the ancient City, you merely have to follow a single beam of light emitted from the golden orb map. The stream of light will take you to the entrance to the City of Light.

"The energy that surrounds the chamber to the City of Light will not allow you to insert anything but the gold orb you now possess. Once you enter the chamber of light, you will need to place the golden sphere in the obelisk. In only a moment, something magical will appear before your eyes.

Pecky interrupted and said, "Neils, I don't understand. You have indicated that there is more than one entrance to the Ancient City."

"Sorry, my dear friend, I am getting ahead of myself. There is one Ancient City but with many different names and at least seven separate entrances on this planet alone.

"Throughout time, humans have been searching for a way back to the Ancient City. At the beginning of the Christian Bible, it indicates that the original man and woman were cast out of paradise. The Bible says nothing about humankind regaining paradise because whoever resides in this plane of consciousness is still outcast.

"The Ancient City is what the Bible explains as heaven. The ancient City is also El Dorado, Shangri-La, Valhalla, Atlantis, Mount Olympus, the City of Light, and many more names. Some names remembered, and many forgotten—most considered only a legend or a myth."

He smiled and sighed. "Yes, the Ancient City is not a city at all but a higher state of being. We never lost the City; it's that humankind has forgotten how to find their way home.

"On the earth, there are seven destinations that lead to the entrance to the Ancient City.

"The seven objectives, inscribed below each of the mirrors that hang on the walls to this chamber are: one, North Pole, 90° North; two, Vermont, 43°

North/72º West; three, Kunlun Mountains, 36º North/84º East; four, India, 23º North/80º East; five, Congo, 0º South/15º East; six, South America, 5º South/54º West; and seven, South Pole, 90º South."

"Near each destination, there will be an obelisk marking the chamber below that will lead you to the City of Light. You merely put the gold orb map into the chamber obelisk and before you will appear the path to the City of Light.

"By each path to the Ancient City, you will find a village. The village exists at a slightly higher level of consciousness, but not nearly as high as the City of Light. If you did not have the gold orb and, by some miracle, you come across the village, you will not be able to move forward to the Ancient City.

"The golden orb represents a ticket because the people who occupy the village believe the sphere to be sacred, and anyone who possesses it is also considered holy. The shaman will help you find the entrance to the chamber that will take you to the entry of the City of Light.

"This is where the story becomes maybe confusing. Each leg of your journey towards the City of Light will challenge you.

"I was faced with seven different challenges that presented how I perceived myself in the world. I cannot tell you what my tasks were or how I overcame them. If I disclosed my challenges or how I overcame them, you would find yourself utilizing the same resolution. You would cause yourself harm. Your challenges will be different. The problems you face will reflect how you see yourself in this world.

"I can tell you that the path to the City of Light is like playing chess. You need to see the whole board and consider what your next seven moves might be. Above all things you might see or hear, you need to trust your heart. Knowing your own heart is, in fact, the only way you are going to make it to the City of Light.

"And know that Legorian controls each challenge." He sighed again, as if weary of the world, or sad, but Ian could not see those feelings in him. Perhaps it was a worry for Ian and his path?

"What I am telling you might seem confusing right now," Neils continued, "but it will make perfect sense once you enter the first part of your journey towards the City of Light."

Pecky interrupted, "Legorian guards the Ancient City?"

Neils glanced at Pecky. "No, Legorian and his devotees patrol the area just outside the region. Legorian has never known, nor will ever know, what the City of Light is, nor will he ever feel its level of consciousness. Legorian lives only in darkness made up of fear and doubt. You will find during your journey that Legorian's only purpose is to keep anyone from discovering the

City of Light, and he is good at it."

"Where did Legorian come from?" Ian asked.

"Ah, yes." Neils smiled at Ian, like a teacher whose favorite pupil once again rose to the occasion. "The level of reality we now occupy created Legorian, and if you travel the last distance to the City of Light, you will understand the nature of Legorian.

"I can't tell you what the Ancient City is—you need to go to the City to realize that you are not discovering anything at all. You just remember who you are and where you came from."

Pecky nodded and said, "Neils, you mentioned that the reason for your journey to this monastery was to help us find the City. So that Ian could heal the world's connection to the Source."

"Yes, the connection people had with the City of Light diminished so much that the world we now occupy is off-balanced with fear and doubt," Neils replied. "To heal the connection between humanity and the Source, a true heart is born during the darkest of times when humankind is farthest away from their relationship to the Source.

"A true heart is the only one that can heal the world of fear and doubt. If Ian fails to reach the City the world will fall into darkness."

Ian closed his eyes. Only a small burden, really, the future of the world, he thought. He smiled at how his mother would laugh at his dark humor and opened his eyes to see Neils smiling back at him as if Ian had said his thought out loud.

"I only have a few more important things I must tell you before you leave me," Neils continued, "and I will then travel back.

"On the wall of this cave are seven mirrors. Each mirror reflects our consciousness at a different level of energy.

"Ian, you will need to stand in front of each mirror and look for your reflection. Only one mirror on these walls will reflect your image. Ian," he said again, looking intently at the young man, "each one of us vibrates at a different level of energy. The one mirror that reflects your image will have an inscription at its base depicting the destination you will need to travel to reach the Ancient City.

"I know that you set out to reach the entrace to the City of Light in the Congo. We just need to make sure you are on the right path."

Ian stood up and walked over to the mirror nearest to the entrance of the cave. He stood in front of the mirror. One after another, Ian stood before a mirror without seeing his reflection until he stood before the fifth mirror.

That mirror reflected such a brilliant image of Ian that there was no mistaking his next destination. Engraved below the mirror was a simple set of numbers: 0° South/15° East.

Neils cleared his throat and quietly said, "The Congo."

A concerned look came over Pecky's face. "Neils, the Congo has been in the depths of civil war for more than thirty years. Is it safe for us to venture into such a war-torn region?"

Neils replied, "I am sorry, but the only way for Ian to enter the Ancient City is through the Congo. The civil war that is raging is caused by Legorian to keep out those who seek the path.

"You can reach your first destination in the Congo with the sleigh. After you reach your first destination, you will need to take a boat to travel down-river. The ship will take you to the village that surrounds the chamber."

"Neils," Ian said, "I find myself concerned about what lies before me despite what I feel in my heart. Can you share any wisdom that might help me along my journey?"

Neils contemplated Ian's question. "Ian, I will leave you with a story told to me by the shaman of the ancient village I encountered.

"This shaman told me that in the world, there is a great darkness, and this great darkness is made of fear and doubt. It's in the shadows of the dark woods, it's in the minds of men, and it awaits you in your dreams. This darkness will always be at your heels when you are in the wilderness and in your dreams when you are most tired.

"Balanced with this great darkness is a delicate veil of life energy that is woven through all things. This delicate veil of life energy is made up of love and hope and is balanced with the great darkness because without one—there couldn't be the other.

"On your journey through the wilderness, there will be a moment when all seems lost, and you will be empty of all things of the world. It will be at this time your life purpose will become apparent to you."

Pecky lay a large flipper on Ian's shoulder as they listened to Neils, who continued, "A simple truth will emerge as it has done for all who take this journey. This simple truth will be that if you can weave even one small strand of good in the veil of life energy, your life's purpose will be fulfilled."

Neils looked at Ian, the slight young man who stood in front of him with strength and compassion as he listened to the powerful message. "Ian, when you are confronted with fear and doubt along your journey, the only power you can have is not to want power. The only control you will have during your journey will be to let go of control and trust the Source—no matter what evil stands before you."

Neils stood up, bowed with clasped hands before Pecky and Ian. "My friends, I cannot tell you more, because any more information would only confuse and cause you harm along your journey."

He walked over to the seventh mirror and stood before it for only a moment before vanishing from sight. The moment Neils disappeared from the room, the fire in the pit changed from a blue flame to a red glow.

Pecky and Ian stood side by side for several moments, contemplating what Neils told them. Pecky knew that Ian was formulating a question that he would have to answer, even though he did not want to.

Ian finally turned to Pecky and said, "Pecky, I'm supposed to save the world?"

With a concerned eye, Pecky looked at Ian and replied, "Yes, Ian, you are on this journey to save the world. I didn't tell you this before because I didn't think you would have understood the quest we are on until you'd committed yourself to it."

With a sort of grimace, Ian said, "What happens if I fail?"

Pecky contemplated before replying. "The world will not be destroyed— humans will fall asleep and farther away from their connection to the Source.

"Ian, most people in this world feel that they are alone and cut off, but they are just asleep to who they are. Most don't know that they are part of an Infinite Being. The Source is in each one of us, and we all have the power to connect to this endless Source of energy, but over time and because of the illusion we see outside of ourselves we forget.

"Throughout time, we have had transitions of human consciousness that have accelerated the development of the world. True hearts caused these evolutions. A true heart named Cosimo De Medici sparked the great Renaissance that took place in Florence. Jesus of Nazareth, Buddha, Confucius were all true hearts, and they all brought a new evolution of consciousness to the world

"Looking back over time, most all transitions of human consciousness took place during the darkest of times and primarily because of one person."

He placed his fin on Ian's shoulder. "So, yes, Ian, you are tasked with saving the world by bringing a higher level of consciousness to humankind." ∞

CA

Chapter Twenty-One
Christmas in Greece

G ood to his word, Monsignor Bartholomew was serenely waiting for Ian and Pecky at the entrance to the cave. He had a warm smile on his face, but Ian sensed that he possessed some news he needed to disclose.

The heightened energy that Ian and Pecky felt in the presence of Neils began to dissipate as they walked out of the chamber. Ian still felt at peace with himself, but the finely tuned sense of time and space was slowly slipping away.

Monsignor Bartholomew greeted them, "Good morning, my good friends, you are just in time for breakfast."

With a surprised look on his face, Pecky responded, "Bartholomew, we just had breakfast not more than two hours ago. Don't you mean lunch?"

"No, Pecky, you have been in the presence of Neils for nine days. It is morning once again."

"How is this possible?" Pecky sputtered.

"The best explanation, I suppose," Monsignor Bartholomew said, "is that Einstein was right. Now, if you both follow me, we can have breakfast, and then I will point you in the right direction. The ferry is leaving soon, and we have much to do before you leave."

As they walked out of the cave, Ian turned to Pecky. "What did Monsignor Bartholomew mean by 'Einstein was right'?"

Pecky looked down at Ian with his pedagogic face, one Ian was becoming familiar with. He knew that Pecky had been going over the possibilities of this mystery in his mind, that he understood the reason and now would explain, in detail, everything. Ian smiled as he waited for the torrent of words that he knew was to come.

"You see, Ian," Pecky said, taking a deep breath, "Albert Einstein theorized that the closer we come to the speed of light, the slower time will move. He theorized that if an astronaut were to travel through space for five years moving at the speed of light, he or she would return to the Earth, having only aged five years. However, most everyone that they knew would be dead because more than fifty years would have passed on Earth.

Pecky continued, gesturing and talking with excitement—he obviously loved the subject. "One of my favorite examples of time slowing down the closer we come to the speed of light is when Albert Einstein rode a trolley one day. As the trolley began speeding up, each telephone pole would pass closer and closer to each other. Einstein envisioned a straight train track going on into infinity. The trolley is going faster and faster until it reached the speed of light. Then all that Einstein would see was one telephone pole standing completely still."

Monsignor Bartholomew, walking ahead of them but listening intently, suddenly stopped and turned to the other two. "Yes," he said excitedly, "Yes, exactly!"

Pecky smiled. "The notion states that infinite reality is standing still and encompasses all things everywhere. Many theorize that the world we live in is a world vibrating at a lower rate of speed than what we might experience moving at the speed of light, or in the state of infinite reality. If we were able to reach the speed of light, we would know what it felt like to be one with everything, not unlike the telephone pole is one with all the other telephone poles.

Monsignor Bartholomew clapped his hands and said, smiling, "Yes! Being one with everything!"

Ian looked at Pecky questioningly. "How do you know all this, Pecky?"

With a complacent look, Pecky said, "My undergraduate degree in physics from the University of Oxford opened my eyes to the vastness of knowledge in the universe, of which we are only beginning to comprehend. My knowledge of physics helped with my Doctor of Jurisprudence degree."

He continued, relishing his topic. "Einstein theorized that time was relative to any event in which each person was participating. The theory of relativity is complicated, but ultimately you and I just experienced a firsthand account of what Einstein meant."

"So, when we were in the presence of Neils," Ian cut in, "we were accelerating closer to the speed of light..."

"...hence the feeling of heightened energy we both experienced!" Pecky finished the sentence for him. They looked at each other and laughed. Monsignor Bartholomew nodded, then took Pecky's flipper to get him moving again.

"Yes," Pecky said, walking quickly behind the monk, "we thought we were experiencing the same time that our friends in the monastery were experiencing. In fact, time was slowing down for us. We were experiencing time-based on the effect caused by our interaction with Neils, not with those we left behind."

Ian considered what he experienced and what Pecky was explaining. He understood entirely and, at the same time, did not understand. During his tangle of thoughts, he remembered Bee and Ogden.

A dread came over him, and he yelled ahead to Monsignor Bartholomew, hurrying down the path. "Monsignor, our friends have been waiting for us for nine days. Do you know how they are doing?"

Monsignor Bartholomew turned his head, and with a warm smile on his face, he replied, "Don't worry, we got word to your friends on the first night you did not return. We sent Father Isaiah to set them up comfortably in a couple of rooms at a local hotel. I heard from Father Isaiah this morning that they were doing just fine. In fact, I heard they were enjoying the town and had a surprise for you and Pecky when you returned to Ouranoupolis."

At breakfast, Ian and Pecky only picked at their food. Both thought it strange that they had not eaten for nine days, but they were still a little full, from their first breakfast. They left the table with food on their plates. They rushed to their bungalows to change back into their street clothes. They hurried down to the docks to catch the morning ferry back to Ouranoupolis.

Monsignor Bartholomew and a few monks were waiting for Ian and Pecky on the dock to bid them farewell and wish them luck on the next leg of their journey.

Ian was thinking of Neils disappearing before their eyes. He asked Monsignor Bartholomew, "Monsignor, when we were with Neils, he mentioned that he was returning to the Ancient City. He stood in front of the seventh mirror and vanished before our eyes. What happened to him?"

"Neils exists at a high level of energy," Monsignor Bartholomew replied. "I did not follow you into the chamber because I would not be able to see him, and my energy might have lowered his energy. One of the reasons he arrived at our monastery long before your arrival was to lower his energy so that you would be able to see him. He is unable to maintain a lower level of energy for any amount of time.

"He conveyed to us his intention to pass his knowledge and wisdom on to you. He kept to the chamber away from anyone who would reverse his energy. His energy is higher than what our most enlightened monks can maintain for any amount of time. When you entered the chamber, Neils lowered his energy so that he could pass on information. He did not vanish when done, he just regained his heightened level of energy.

The horn from the ferry indicating the last call before departure jolted Monsignor Bartholomew. "What you have learned while you were here," he said quickly, scanning the dock, "is that much is happening around you. The world operates at multiple levels of energy."

Ian recalled that Pecky had told him that most wouldn't see a six-foot-tall penguin walking around because people don't always see what is right in front of their faces. He considered that maybe people were walking around at a different level of energy and didn't understand what they saw. It was perhaps not unlike the concept that many people are walking around knowing different languages. Most people perceive that others see the world the way they do, but much gets lost in translation.

The final call from the ferry and the revving of its engines awoke Ian out of his thoughts. Ian and Pecky bowed to the monks, thanked Monsignor Bartholomew for his generosity, and then quickly boarded the ferry bound for Ouranoupolis.

As the ship slowly moved away, Monsignor Bartholomew stood below them on the dock and yelled, "Ian, a monk in New York City went up to a hot dog vendor and asked, 'make me one with everything.'"

Ian and Pecky grinned at the monk's joke, then both started laughing at the absurdity of life.

The trip back to Ouranoupolis was a blur. The boat was almost empty of passengers. Many thoughts passed through Ian's mind as the ferry slowly moved back to the mainland. He stood in the windy prow with Pecky and thought of his friends waiting for him and what the surprise might be. He thought of what Neils said and how it all interrelated with everything he learned during his travels. He thought of why he started the journey. And how his perceptions had changed so drastically in such a short time.

Time itself was on his mind, and he wondered how long he had been gone from his home in the green mountains of Vermont. He left in fall, in late October after all the glorious color had left the trees brown and forlorn but was unable to figure out what day or even month it was now.

When he had left Vermont, he thought that the journey would be nothing but fun, and maybe he might end up being the hero for his father. But fear and doubt were starting to wear away at his determination. He wondered if he really was the right person, that maybe everyone was wrong about him. Perhaps he was a fraud. He asked how he would react to the inevitable challenges on their journey to the City of Light. He wondered if he should go home and let others better trained find his father and save the world from darkness.

At this point, Pecky looked over at Ian. He could see the struggle in Ian. "I can sense that much is on your mind, maybe more than most seventeen-year-old young men could handle. Ian, it is important not to lament. Not to let fear and doubt fill your mind."

"Pecky, am I the right person? Is this truly my destiny?"

Pecky looked at the waves churning past the boat, then replied, "Ian, a vital part of everyone's destiny is to overcome our fear and doubt. We need to find the faith that the universe is unfolding as it should, and most importantly, we need to find confidence in ourselves and our connection to the Source. Most of the trials and tribulations we encounter during our lives come down to building this faith. It is your destiny to find the Ancient City, help your father, and save the world from darkness.

He laid a flipper on Ian's arm and looked directly at Ian. "But more important than me, understanding your destiny is for you to realize your destiny. Faith is the most important thing you might gain along your path."

On the horizon, Ian could see the familiar Byzantine tower overlooking the beaches at Ouranoupolis. As the ferry came closer and closer to the mainland, he could see Bee and Ogden standing on the dock with Father Isaiah. They had big smiles on their faces. Ogden and Bee looked like typical tourists, both wearing tee shirts with Ouranoupolis written across the front.

Looking at his friends, Ian felt as if he had not seen them in years. He felt he had to readjust to his friends once again—especially after the silent world of the monastery.

The moment the ferry docked, Bee ran up the gangplank and jumped on board to embrace Ian. She held on to Ian for a long time and said, "Ian, I was so worried when you didn't return the first night. I was about to invade Mount Athos just before Father Isaiah arrived with word of your visit with Neils."

Ian looked at Bee as if he had to remember who she was. He had to remember what part she played in the drama that had been unfolding. But he was enjoying the embrace.

Close up, Bee saw something amazing around Ian. There was a warm light emanating from his body and face, and she noticed something was missing from Ian. His child-like features were gone; he seemed to have grown into a man over the last nine days.

Pecky raised his eyebrows over Bee's lack of welcome to him. "Well, Bee, I see you are not as worried about me as you were about Ian," he said huffily. But he smiled as he held out his flippers to her, and Bee smiled back as she gave Pecky a big hug. "Pecky, I don't worry about you because I know you can take care of yourself. I used to feel that Ian needed my help, but I look at him now and see a much stronger man standing before me than when I saw him last."

Ian smiled and said, "Bee, I always will need your help, no matter what."

Bee excitedly waved her hands as she said to Ian, "We, Father Isaiah, Ogden, and I, have put together a big surprise for you and Pecky. The Xenios Hotel found a… Well, you will just have to wait and see."

They walked off the boat together to meet Father Isaiah and Ogden, waiting on the dock. Ogden looked a little put out about all the fuss Bee made over Ian. Ian wondered what they had been doing while he was gone and thought about his feelings for Bee.

Ogden reached out to shake Ian's hand. "We missed you. I'm interested in your adventure to Mount Athos. I can sense something has changed about you, something brilliant."

Ian didn't feel any different other than everything around him seemed far away—as if he were just observing everything that was going on.

Bee grabbed Ian's hand and started to drag him toward a hotel across the street. She giggled with anticipation of the surprise awaiting them.

Ian was looking at Bee as if through new eyes. He saw her as a strong young woman, but with the heart of a sprite—a healthy and strong spirit, Ian thought to himself. Ian could almost feel the beating of Bee's heart. He had a sense of oneness with everything and everyone.

He considered that maybe more happened while he was in the presence of Neils than just the knowledge of their next destination. Perhaps some of the heightened energy he felt had stayed with him, and the way he felt looking at the world around him was what Neils said is wisdom.

Bee interrupted Ian's thoughts, "After we show you your surprise, we want to hear all about your travels to Mount Athos and what Van Den Berg had to say. Ian, we missed you, but I have to confess, Ogden and I had a wonderful time walking around Ouranoupolis. The town people are the nicest. They welcomed us with open arms, and many invited us to dine with them and their families.

"Yesterday, we went to a farm on the outskirts of town and dined with thirty people from the Katsavavakis family. We had wine, grilled goat meat, and we danced the night away. You know the dance where they all…" She started humming "ta da ta ta" and dancing a few steps as she held her arms in the air. The others were smiling at her joy in the retelling of her story. She stopped, smiled, and said, "I was irritated that I could not go to the monastery, but a few days of having fun in Ouranoupolis made me reconsider." Pecky smiled her exuberance and looked at Ian.

Ian wondered what surprise awaited him at the hotel. He could not even imagine what would be such a big deal.

When the group neared the hotel, Ian could hear strains of Christmas music. Christmas lights and decorations covered the hotel windows and the terrace overlooking the beach.

Bee put her hand over Ian's eyes and said, "Ian, don't look until I tell you." She guided Ian into the main lobby, and then with an exciting announcement, she uncovered Ian's eyes and said, "Ta Da! Merry Christmas, Ian!"

To Ian's astonishment, in the corner of the hotel lobby stood a small pine tree. It was decorated with Christmas lights, popcorn strands, and pomegranates rather than red glass balls. Underneath the Christmas tree were some wrapped presents. He noticed that there was a plate of cookies and a glass of milk on the fireplace mantle.

Bee spoke up, "The cookies are almond paste with pignolia nuts, and the milk is goat's milk—well, when in Rome, right? Or, in this case, Ouranoupolis."

Ian was overcome with emotion. "Is it Christmas already? Whatever happened to Thanksgiving or even Halloween? Have we been gone that long?"

Pecky replied, "Yes, we have been traveling for more than two months. How time flies when you are having, uh, adventures!"

Bee grabbed a present from underneath the small Christmas tree and said, "Ian, this is from me. I hope you like it." Ian slowly opened the gift to reveal a small locket with a picture of Bee inside. Inscribed on the back was the quote, "A friend is a treasure more precious than gold, for love shared is priceless and never grows old." Bee watched to see Ian's reaction. "We didn't have a lot of money to spend, but believe me when I say that the gift is from my heart."

Ian looked at the locket for a long time and started to feel grounded once again. He gave Bee a big hug and thanked her and Ogden for putting together a Christmas in this far-away place. The Christmas decorations made him feel homesick for Vermont. In another way, with no snow on the ground and seventy-five degrees outside, he didn't feel Christmas-y at all.

Pecky interrupted, "I believe it is time for us to have our lunch and maybe even take a little siesta before we leave for Africa." Both Bee and Ogden chimed in at the same time, "Africa?"

Pecky repeated, "Yes, my dear friends, our next destination is Africa—the Congo region of Africa to be exact." ଔ

CB

Chapter Twenty-Two
Gift of Healing

A dry blast of heat startled Ian from his thoughts. The sleigh was quickly moving in a straight line about three hundred feet off the ground. He glanced east toward the bright sun rising over a long and sloping yellow dune. Looking west and south, Ian took in a glorious sight he never thought he would see—the dunes of the Sahara Desert in all directions.

The massive dunes looked desolate, without trees or any green plant life. But as Ian gazed at the desert, he saw elegant long shadows, rocky bluffs, and subtle changes in the color of the sand that looked like a painting.

To the north, where they had departed many hours earlier, Ian could see dark rain clouds in the far distance. Every so often, thin bands of lightning spread out like a giant spider web filling the sky for a brief second.

Ian noticed the feeling of heightened energy had left him. He felt grounded and tired. His body creaked and ached as an old man might feel early in the morning. He looked at his companions, asleep in the cushy bench seats of the vehicle, snuggled under blankets. Pecky was snoring with his head tightly tucked under his right flipper. Everyone was tired from the Christmas festivities they enjoyed late into the evening.

Ian could almost taste the barbecued goat meat, Greek bread, and the feta cheese salad they'd eaten at the party. He had his first sip of strong alcohol, a locally bottled Greek ouzo, which was fermented from grapes then flavored with anise and other spices giving the liquor the taste of licorice with a punch. Everyone was still recovering from the ouzo as they slept.

As the sleigh moved swiftly to the south, Ian caught a glimpse of something on the horizon. He thought it might be a mirage, but as they flew closer, he could just make out a grove of palm trees, an oasis, with a few tents among the tall palms.

Ian decided that it would be wise to wake the others. He was a little tense. They were out in the middle of the desert without any way to call for help. Then he remembered all the other situations he had already overcome and felt a little more secure with his abilities to resolve challenges.

Ian gently nudged Pecky. Pecky always claimed that he didn't sleep well during his trips, but he seemed to sleep fine, at least from Ian's point of view. Ian nudged Pecky a little harder. First, one round black eye opened and then the other. Pecky looked down at Ian, grunted a bit, then said, "Good morning, Ian, have we arrived at the first oasis?"

"Yes, but there are tents around the oasis that alarm me a little."

Pecky snapped fully awake and looked around to gain his bearings. He could see the camp in the distance and tried to discern if there was danger ahead for the travelers. A calmness came over Pecky's face. He turned to Ian and said, "That, my friend, is Zayed Ruwallah."

"And is he also a friend?" Ian asked.

"I have done business with him. He is an acquaintance. He travels primarily from Morocco to Egypt, dealing in precious minerals and jewels. He is a Bedouin prince from the family Ruwallah. I am friends with his father, Abdullah. His father helped me once on a life energy case that staved off a war in the Sudan region of Eastern Africa."

"I think it best to wake the others before we arrive at the oasis, just in case there is more to the situation than what I can see from the air."

Ian woke Bee and Ogden, informing them of the situation ahead. They looked exhausted, but it took them only a moment to gain composure. Ogden quickly made his way to the front of the sleigh and with a worried look on his face, asked, "Whose tent is it, Pecky?"

"Don't worry, Ogden, it's not Yusuf. He wouldn't be in this part of the desert during this time of the year. It's Sheikh Ruwallah's son, Zayed."

Ogden hesitated, "Are we going to need... I mean, can he be trusted?"

"Yes, we can trust him—for the right price. I brought gold and silver for such an occasion. The bars are in the cargo hold. Pick out three silver and one gold bar. We won't need weapons."

With a confused look on his face, Ian asked Ogden, "Who is Yusuf."

With a slight smirk, Ogden replied, "Yusuf was a casualty of a life energy job I did a couple of years back. What you need to remember is that most times, when an energy sprite is dispatched, we try to create an environment where everyone wins, and the power is balanced out just right.

"Every so often, though, there is a situation where someone comes up short. When I was last in Syria, Yusuf Saud was on the short end of the energy stick, and I don't think he has forgiven me."

"I thought an energy sprite moved about without anyone knowing that they are intervening?"

"That is mostly correct," Ogden replied, "but Yusuf was the senior energy sprite on the case, and I was his apprentice during that assignment.

"During a life energy case, there is a moment when the power shifts from its present trajectory. Sometimes the change happens with a simple nudge. Still, other times there needs to be a turn of events greater than the total of the energy dispute. You may know the term 'the tail waging the dog'?

"This is when an energy sprite must make a hard decision between self-preservation and fulfilling the assignment. In the case of Yusuf, I faltered for only a moment, and he needed to take the fall. I have been avoiding him since."

A puzzled look came over Bee's face as she asked, "What fall did he take?"

"A dusty cell in a dark Syrian prison for six months."

Ian asked, "Do the Syrian police know that Yusuf is an energy sprite?"

"No, they saw him as just a simple man in the wrong place at the wrong time."

Bee looked amused and interjected, "I would be a little upset at you if I ended up in a dusty cell. I hope you learned from your mistake."

Ogden leaned back on the sleigh and replied, "Lesson learned."

Pecky slowed the sleigh down to the speed of a butterfly and informed the others, "We need to be cautious and stay together. Do not separate for even a moment. This family may be trusted, but they are opportunists who will exploit a situation in their favor. Let me do most of the talking, agreed?"

All three shook their heads in agreement as Pecky slowed the sleigh to prepare to land. As they got to the oasis, they could see that a battle had taken place recently.

There were clothes, food, and other debris scattered about the camp. Two camels lay dead, rotting in the already hot morning sun on a dune downwind from the oasis.

Bee pointed out a gathering of Bedouins in front of the main tent. About fifteen to twenty people were looking inside the tent at something. The travelers couldn't make out what was happening, but several of the women were crying.

Pecky landed the sleigh north of the camp on the other side of three large palm trees giving shade to the group. He pulled the ruby out of the golden lever and gave it to Ogden for safekeeping.

As the travelers approached the main tent on the edge of the miraculous spring that gave life to the oasis, a large Bedouin dressed in flowing robes walked towards them. The man motioned at the sleigh and said something to Pecky in his native tongue. Pecky replied in the same language. The Bedouin turned around and motioned for the group to follow close behind.

As they walked behind the man, Pecky said to his companions, "The Bedouin's name is Amir. He told me that at dawn, bandits from the north attacked, and he thought maybe we were more bandits. I assured him that I knew his prince well and that the prince would be most pleased to see us."

Ian listened to the language spoken and asked, "Pecky, I thought I would be able to understand all languages, yet I didn't understand a word that man said."

"Try to listen with your heart, Ian, not your perception," Pecky replied.

Amir motioned for the travelers to stay outside the main tent while he announced them to Prince Zayed. He said something to Pecky before he walked into the tent.

Bee asked, "What did he say to you?"

"I can tell you," Ogden said. "During the battle, Zayed's son was shot by bandits. They don't think he will make it through the night."

The four travelers sat under a palm tree by the spring of water. Bee dipped her feet in the pool to cool herself from the now-blistering hot morning sun.

Ian thought about what Pecky said to him. He was still confused about language and his ability to understand all words. He turned to Pecky. "Pecky, I don't understand what you meant about languages."

Pecky had put his feet in the cold pool of water under the palm tree. He was splashing about, enjoying the moment. After a moment of thought, he replied, "You need to think of language as a result of intention, and the purpose of language is conveying whatever the entity or person wants you to understand. Often the aim of the communication is based on truth or a lie; if it is a lie, then your heart will know that it is a lie. If it is the truth, then your heart will be aware that it is true. The mind may not understand the difference between a lie and truth, but the heart will."

Pecky splashed his feet in the water while he gathered his thoughts. Ian could see by his expression, pursed lips, and a faraway gaze, that Pecky was in his pedagogue mode, and would be giving Ian another lesson in physics or history or philosophy. He focused on Pecky and waited.

"Understanding the basis of all language," Pecky began, "is not unlike understanding the basis of all computer programming language. Behind all computer programming language is binary code. Binary code is made up of 1s and 0s, and represents a switch turning on or off—the 1s being the light on and 0s being the light off.

"Those who created binary code actually mirrored the basis of all languages—the basis of all languages is light and dark, a lie or truth.

"Behind the language is meaning, what is the intention of the programmer. When we listen to our hearts, we do not hear a word, we are listening to the objective of the person speaking. We are deciding the meanings with the help of our heart's inner wisdom.

"An example of listening to your heart is when you are interacting with your farm animals or your pets. When you are around your animals, do you know what they want?"

Ian thought about it. "Yes, I know what they want, but it takes me time to understand what their needs are. I've found that my chickens have a complex and diverse language, but my cats make it easy for me to understand their wants."

"Yes, yes, that's right!" Pecky continued, "And the reason you can understand your animals is that you trust their innocence and truth, and you have opened your heart to them, and they have opened their hearts to you. You just need to take this to the next level.

"When someone is talking, don't listen to the words. Listen with your heart to what is conveyed, and your heart will translate. You must be able to open your heart to even strangers to hear their intentions. You need not trust them, but ultimately you need to trust your own heart." Pecky raised his flipper and touched his chest, dripping water on the white feathers. He then touched Ian's chest and nodded.

"Yes, yes, " Pecky tutted, still nodding. "We will often trust others before we trust our inner self. Many times, we will discount that part of ourselves which is most wise and will never lie to us. We do this to believe in the illusion around us that is trying to deceive us."

Amir came around a palm tree and motioned for the travelers to follow him into the main tent. He had an anxious look on his face that communicated to Ian that things were dire with Zayed's son.

Ian thought for a moment what Pecky said and how he knew what Amir was feeling from just a moment of looking at his expression.

They followed Amir into the tent to where a group of Bedouin men were sitting on cushions on the ground. In the center was a young man, no older than Ogden. Ian could see that he was bleeding from his abdomen.

Prince Zayed began to speak in his native language, and Ian understood each word as if the words were in slow motion, moving across his heart and then speeding up. Ian could examine each word for intention, and his heart translated the meaning into pure consciousness.

Pecky nodded at Ian to acknowledge that a significant transition had just taken place in Ian—he had started to trust his own heart. Ian could see that the prince was trying to be strong for his son, but he could feel the pain in Zayed's heart, and the fear that he would lose his beloved only son.

Zayed looked up at them and said, "Pecky, I hope your arrival here is a sign from Allah. My son needs a healer."

Zayed's eyes were welling up with tears at the prospect of losing his son. As Ian stood looking down and the prince and his son, he began to feel the pain from Zayed's son. He could feel the gunshot wound in the young man's stomach. He could feel the bullet lodged in the side of his hip bone.

"Prince Zayed," Ian bowed his head to the prince and asked through a jaw clenched with the pain he felt, "what is your son's name?"

As the words came out of Ian's mouth, he knew that he was talking in the prince's language. He could almost see the words forming from his heart.

Prince Zayed looked surprised that the blond-haired westerner could speak his language. He replied to Ian, "My son's name is Hanif. How is it that you speak my mother's tongue?"

Pecky interjected, "Zayed, Ian is a true heart."

Zayed sat up, and an expression of hope glowed across his face. He looked at Ian and said, "I believe that it has been more than fifteen hundred years since a true heart, one of Allah's true children, has walked this desert."

Ian thought about the importance of his response. "Sir, I don't claim to be a prophet. I am just Ian, and all I can hope is that I might help your dying son."

Ian felt the pain growing in his stomach as Hanif's fever rose from his wounds. Pecky looked at Ian with tremendous compassion in his heart and said, "Ian, you have the gift of healing. It is one of your most meaningful gifts. I didn't know that you would have to use your gift so soon, but maybe Prince Zayed is right that Allah brought you here to heal this young man."

A heavy weight descended on Ian, but then a clear voice rose from his heart. Ian could visualize himself healing Hanif with a simple touch of his hands.

Ian knelt next to Hanif and placed his hands on the red gaping wound in his stomach. At first, he felt nothing but the pain in Hanif's abdomen. Then something happened, something miraculous. Ian felt a lightness of being like the heightened energy he felt during his experience with Neils Van Den Berg.

Bee blurted out, "Ian, there is a glow surrounding your body. It is the same light I saw when you returned from Mount Athos."

The light that surrounded Ian's body gently moved out to encompass the whole tent. Everyone in the tent and the people waiting on the outside became still. There was not a sound in the tent other than the low hum of Ian's heightened consciousness.

Then, in an instant, a flash of pure white light traveled from the top of Ian's head, though his body, and through his hands on Hanif's wound. Then the light receded, and the hum of heightened energy dimmed. Ian gently raised his hand from Hanif's stomach. The wound was gone. Ian could sense that the bullet lodged in Hanif's hip bone had vanished.

Ian stood up with a surprised look on his face. For a long time, no one spoke, just looked at Ian with astonishment. Then Hanif looked up at Ian with renewed strength and said, "Thank you for my life."

The prince bowed down in front of Ian, and the other Bedouins followed suit, saying, "Allah be praised! A true heart walks among us." ❧

CX

Chapter Twenty-Three
Zorkin

I an felt a substantial change had taken place. Not just change with his abilities but a significant shift in how his companions viewed him, that was, except for Pecky. Pecky interacted with Ian as if nothing had changed.

Ian appreciated that Pecky was the only one that believed that he had these gifts. Pecky always knew these gifts lay dormant, waiting for a chance to come to the surface of Ian's consciousness.

Ian understood that the only way that these gifts could rise to the surface of his awareness was a critical moment where he had no other choice but to embrace them.

Ian felt that maybe Bee never believed that he was a true heart, or that he would ultimately lead them to the City of Light.

Prince Ruwallah insisted that Pecky and his companions stay for traditional Bedouin festivities to bring in the New Year. The prince assured the travelers that the Bedouin house of Ruwallah is known from the Sea of Galilee to Marrakesh as excellent hosts looking after guests and making them feel welcomed.

He assured Ian that they will always consider him more than a guest. The house of Ruwallah will praise Ian's life for generations to come, and that he will always be considered a brother among brothers and a prince among princes.

The first night of celebrations reminded Ian of the movie "The Ten Commandments." Moses, who was played by actor Charlton Heston, was cast out into the desert by Rameses, the Egyptian Pharaoh. A Bedouin tribe found Moses after he wandered for many weeks in the wilderness.

Ian could not see much difference from the movie portrait of a Bedouin celebration three thousand years ago and how the Bedouins celebrate today.

Bee stared at Ian with a nervous look on her face throughout the festivities. Ian walked over and sat next to Bee to assure her that he had not changed, just her perception of him. Bee was thumbing through a small book. Ian asked, "Bee, what are you reading."

"I'm reading a children's book about life as a Bedouin, Aida Ruwallah gave me the book after I showed interest in their customs." Bee continued reading from the book, "The Bedouin family live, work, and celebrate as a tight-knit community. For generations going back beyond the Pharaohs, Bedouin people are known as excellent hosts that look after desert travelers."

"That's true," chimed in Ian.

Bee looked up at Ian, smiled, and then continued reading, "There is a celebrated Bedouin tea, made from tea leaf with sugar and desert herbs of Habak and Marmaraya. The desert herbs give the drink a distinctive flavor; Habak tastes like the herb sage. It's customary as soon as a guest arrives to get the tea on the fire while sharing stories and news.

"The Bedouin hospitality consists of traditional Bedouin food, which includes delicious Bedouin bread cooked on an open fire, rice, and either meat, fish or vegetable dish. The cooking is always from fresh produce grown or reared locally.

"The Bedouins serve meals on large trays shared by several people. All feast meals include wipe-it food, delicious rice, and vegetable Magluba dish, a traditional Matfuna dish - a whole stuffed chicken, home-made kebab, and side dishes. Bedouins take much pride in their cooking."

"I wondered what we were eating. I found out fast that you don't use your left hand to eat, only your right." Ian said.

"For many desert travelers, the sight of a Bedouin tent was equal to that of seeing an oasis. The custom is that food, water, and a place to sleep should be provided to all travelers and guests if needed for up to three days. After this time, the guest would be well and fit enough to continue onwards with their journey in the desert."

Bee looked over at Ian and asked, "Would you like me to continue?"

Ian replied, "I haven't changed, Bee, you don't have to be so nervous around me. I'm not going to do anything weird."

Bee put the book down and wrapped her arms around her legs, "I know, Ian, I just need some time to work out what you did for the prince in my head."

During the height of the merriment, Ian and Pecky were able to witness Ogden for the first time in a relaxed setting. Ian, Pecky, including the Bedouins, found Ogden to be funny. This was surprising because they never thought that someone with such an important job as an energy sprite would be hilarious.

As the evening rolled on, Ogden imitated famous actors and politicians so realistically that everyone in the main tent couldn't stop laughing. His humor was so irreverent Bee thought that he should do stand-up comedy instead of being an energy sprite as a profession.

Pecky thought that Ogden certainly had whatever it was that made someone funny. He didn't know what that something was, but Ogden had it.

Bee leaned over to Ian and said, "Now, you know why I was so happy to stay with Ogden when you and Pecky were at Mount Athos. My time with Ogden was a welcomed break from the heaviness of our journey."

Ian took a second to look around the tent at everyone enjoying the festivities and considered that this moment would be etched in his mind forever. This time under the stars will be a memory that he will remember many times.

This revelation about memory gave him a feeling of peace as if he was not experiencing the moment but looking back on his time in the desert as if it already happened.

Late into the evening, when the children were asleep in their tents, Prince Ruwallah told a story around the campfire of his father, Sheikh Ruwallah. He said, "My father battled with a mythical beast called a Zorkin. The Zorkin is an ancient evil that lives deep in the ground under pools of clear water.

"The Zorkin creates small islands in the middle of a lake where they can trap unsuspecting travelers. The Zorkin is one of the darkest and most brutal devotees of Legorian.

"When my father was a young man, he traveled through the desert on a pilgrimage He was ambushed in a remote part of the wilderness by who he thought were bandits. He escaped into a small lake next to a village. To flee his pursuers, he swam to a tiny island in the middle of the pond.

"My father thought that his pursuers gave up, but he would find out later that the village people made a bargain with the Zorkin. Their pact was to lure travelers to the small island so that the beast could feed, and if the villagers did so, the Zorkin would not kill them.

"Because of this shadowy bargain with an evil beast, the villagers descended into darkness—they in time started to feed on what the Zorkin did not finish.

"In the black of the new moon, my father confronted an entity crawling out of a trap door below the island. He could not see the beast other than many eyes of blazing red and hairy arms with terrible strength.

"My father pulled his sword from its sheath and thrust it into the eyes of the beast. The creature retreated into its den, and my father barely escaped under the dark of the night sky.

"He returned a week later to the village with my grandfather to find all the people slaughtered by the Zorkin except for one small boy who told the villagers' sorrowful tale. The island in the lake was gone, and so was the beast.

"The Zorkin is known to my people, but no one has ever seen one in the light of day. Many who have encountered a Zorkin do not return to tell the story. We only find out when we see the carnage left behind.

"Our spiritual elders know of the Zorkin and have told stories that the creature is not one solitary creature but many that are all part of the whole beast dedicated to Legorian and his pursuit of darkness. All the Zorkin throughout the world is of one mind—a mind of death and destruction."

Ian turned to Pecky and said, "My father told me stories while camping in the green mountains of a Zorkin he had encountered in the lake district of New Hampshire. On a small island out on a tiny lake, a beast that caused much misery for the town.

"My father told me that a Zorkin above all fears the light of day. The Zorkin's power is greatly reduced during the day and is most powerful at night. A gun has no effect on a Zorkin but relieving the monster of its head with a sharp sword will kill the beast."

Pecky looked down with a grave look on his face and replied, "Ian, there are monsters in the night. Your father was preparing you for what might cross your path.

"Many times, what we think are only fairy tales, are stories of real monsters. Most humans will never see or encounter these monsters. Still, as you travel through different levels of consciousness, you will come across both good and evil. Your father knew that it was important that you understood how to combat those entities before you encountered them"

Prince Ruwallah announced, "Friends, it is late, and we have many days of celebration ahead of us. Please, accept the tents we have provided for your rest. Remember, it is always wise to check for sand spiders before you retire."

A shiver ran down the spines of all four travelers. Bee considered that the story of the Zorkin only intensified the prospect of a hefty sand spider crawling in between bedding in the tents.

Bee reluctantly got up and walked to her tent with the other Ruwallah family members. They told her that Zayed plays that same trick on all travelers, and her tent is thoroughly inspected. Bee was guaranteed that she will find no sand spiders or any other desert creatures in her tent.

Ian stayed behind with Pecky and watched as the night sky became increasingly brilliant as the campfire decreased in strength. Pecky stayed behind because he knew that Ian had an important question to ask.

Ian turned to Pecky and asked, "How did I heal Hanif?"

Pecky replied to Ian with a simple two-word response, "You didn't."

The response from Pecky confused Ian more as he continued his search for the truth, "I don't understand, Pecky. I touched Hanif's wound, and it healed before my eyes. How is it that I did not heal him?"

Pecky continued, "Ian, it is a matter of faith. In every being on this planet, there is a deeper potential connection with the Source.

"The Source I speak of is the infinite being. Most humans on this planet feel alone and disconnected. They believe that they are separate from those they see in the world around them.

"The separation that people believe to exist is only an illusion. It is a fundamental cause and effect—the cause was when the infinite being had a concept of a separate reality. The effect created the world we perceive to exist outside of ourselves. Are you following me?"

Ian nodded his head and said, "Yes."

Pecky continued, "The only way we are separate is by our perceptions of ourselves. If we feel that we are cut-off from the Source, the world outside of us will support how we perceive ourselves.

"If we feel abandoned, worthless, and cut off from those around us, then the world will support that belief. Since we are part of the infinite being, we are so powerful that we can create the world around us by our perceptions.

"Each one of us has not only the potential to connect to the Source but is always connected.

"We all have the potential to remember our connection to the Source, but we all can't do it alone.

"In many ways, a true heart acts as a light for those in the dark. When you touched Hanif, you brought your light to the darkness. You helped him connect with his own heart because, in each one of us, there is the potential to heal ourselves.

"We are spiritual beings having a physical experience. Healing has a lot to do with knowing that we actually can never be sick and that death is a lie.

"When I said that you didn't heal him, what I was saying is that Hanif healed himself with your help. Do these concepts make sense?"

Ian listened carefully to what was being said by Pecky, so attentively, he started to have a heightened sense of energy. Ian felt he was not participating in the world but was only watching it from some point beyond his body. He thought that he was observing this moment from above.

Pecky continued, "I can sense, Ian, that you are in a place outside your body—a heightened sense of consciousness, not unlike what we experienced in the presence of Neils Van Den Berg."

Ian replied, "Yes, I feel like I'm watching the world around me, but not connected to the world in any direct way. I feel that I have a better understanding of my own experience by watching it from another perspective."

Pecky continues, "The Christian bible states that when any two people come together in the name of the Lord, he will be there. What that means is that when we speak the truth, we become closer to the Source, and the illusion of the world around us starts to disappear. We feel a heightened sense of consciousness.

"This is an unsettling moment for Legorian. You see, Ian, in each one of us we have both the Source and Legorian. The light balanced with the dark. One cannot exist without the other in this world of separation."

At this point, the heightened sense of consciousness Ian was experiencing was intensifying. The world around him not only started to dissipate, but the world became two-dimensional.

He asked Pecky, "Who is Legorian?"

Pecky continued, "Legorian was created by the infinite being when he created this world. Legorian's singular job is to convince us that we are separate from our true selves. Legorian's very existence depends on him keeping us in this reality of separation."

Ian asked, "Then why does Legorian want to destroy us and this world?"

Pecky thought for a moment and replied, "Legorian is ultimately insane. We are also insane when we believe this reality is real, and we feel cut off from the Source."

Ian thought for a second and asked, "If you know that you are only a spiritual being, then why are you still in this world?"

Pecky continued, "Actually, Ian, I am in the world but not totally of the world. What I mean is that we all chose to experience this life to know what it would feel like to be separated from the infinite. The only way we can truly experience this reality of separation is to commit to the process. Without total commitment, we would never experience feelings of abandonment, worthlessness, and loss of connection from ourselves."

The more Ian and Pecky continued the discussion, the more Ian's consciousness became heightened. In a moment of total realization of what Pecky was saying, Ian started to see his face in Pecky.

Ian looked around and saw the world only in a two-dimensional black and white projection of his perceptions. Ian had a second of infinite consciousness, an epiphany. Then the universe flattened totally, and a moment later, he was back in his body again with a three-dimensional world surrounding him.

Ian looked at Pecky for a long time and said, "Pecky, I saw my face in your face."

Pecky looked with a surprised grin and replied, "That is because we are all one. Whenever you are talking to those outside of yourself, you are just talking to yourself."

Ian and Pecky started to laugh, a laugh so deep and so intense that Ian thought he might split his sides if he didn't regain his composure.

As the two started to calm down, Pecky stated, "Remember, Ian, the truth is funny and absolute truth is hilarious."

The two friends sat under the stars for a long time, not saying a word. The stars above Ian's head were so bright that they reminded him of the fireworks he saw during New Year's Eve back home.

Without another word, both travelers stood up. They walked to their tents, not knowing if they would get any sleep after what they just experienced under the cosmic sky.

Before they entered their tents, they took one more look at each other with a knowing that Ian had never understood before, but now was part of him forever. ❦

CB

Chapter Twenty-Four
Taken

B ee lay in her soft bed for a long time after the sun rose to the east. She woke many times during the night with a cold breeze. It reminded her of Britain in the depth of winter. Bee felt a foreboding presence in the camp during the night.

Bee stayed in bed for a long time, mainly because it was January 1st, and she and her companions were going to move on to their next destination. She felt that maybe she could stall their departure if she refused to get out of her comfortable bed.

She never considered that the desert could get so cold at night, even though it radiated heat during the day. So severe that she could see her breath in the little candlelight of her tent. It crossed her mind that the threatening presence she felt during the night might have something to do with the severe cold.

During the height of the festivities over the last few days, she tried to forget where her ultimate destination was. When she did remember her objective, a shiver ran down her spine, and she considered that maybe she would just stay in the desert with her Bedouin friends.

Bee lay in bed and thought about Ian and Ogden, and how close they all have come in a short time. Bee never was able to make friends fast, and most of her life, she had the same few friends she made in her early school days.

She left on the quest with Pecky and Ian without a word to her friends. She knew that her friends would worry when she didn't show up for class. She pondered that she always had a small group of girlfriends to lean on, but on this trip, Bee was making friends with young men.

She considered that both of her men friends were handsome, and both were capable. Ian was introspective and thoughtful, and Ogden was gregarious and made her laugh.

The books she read back home would often read of the girl ending up with the hero at the end of the adventure. She wondered if that same storyline was in her future. Would she fall in love?

She considered maybe neither, because it was too early in the quest to tell, and perhaps another twist was right around the corner. She believed that maybe she would be the hero of this tale, and one of them would fall in love with her.

Pecky poked his head in Bee's tent and said, "Bee, it is time to get up and prepare ourselves for the next leg of our journey."

Bee replied, "I know, Pecky, I was hoping you would forget about me so that I could continue the festivities with our Bedouin friends."

Pecky looked perplexed and replied, "I'm sorry, Bee, but if I left you here, you would have a long walk home. Prince Ruwallah and his family are moving in another direction. I don't think that they would adopt you into their tribe."

Bee sat up in her bed and replied, "Pity."

Pecky replied, "Remember all good things come to an end; of course, on the flip side, all bad things come to an end as well."

Pecky walked away from Bee's tent, letting her have another few moments of peace before she got up and helped get ready for the trip to Cameroon.

When Bee finally emerged from her tent, she observed that Pecky was having a serious conversation with Prince Ruwallah. Pecky kept shaking his head, but the Prince seemed determined with whatever he was saying.

Ogden was loading the sleigh with provisions as Bee walked up and said, "Good morning Ogden. Do you know what all the fuss was about between Pecky and the Prince?"

With a grin on his face, Ogden replied, "Good morning, I was wondering when the fair lady of our tribe would show herself, or at least get her lazy butt out of bed and help."

Bee quickly replied with a big grin on her face, "Ogden, we ladies need a little more time to get ready than you scoundrels, plus I was hoping you all would leave me here with the Bedouins."

Ogden replied, "The Bedouins are moving on today, so at least you would have the place to yourself and the sand spiders, of course. Anyway, Pecky and the Prince had been discussing something, but I don't know what."

Pecky briskly walked up to his fellow travelers and said, "The Prince wants us to take his son Hanif and one of his best warriors along to Cameroon. I assured Prince Ruwallah that we would be perfectly safe, but he continued to insist. He said that it would be an insult to the Ruwallah family if they didn't at least protect us until we reached the outer edge of the desert.

"I told him that swords and guns did not affect Legorian. He assured me that swords and guns had a considerable effect on bandits."

Ogden asked, "What did you finally decide?"

Pecky replied, "That swords and guns do have a positive effect on bandits. Hanif and their best warrior Aasim will be traveling with us to our next destination."

Bee thought to herself that Hanif was handsome and brave, so again, she considered that the journey had many twists, and she should keep her options open.

Prince Hanif walked up with Aasim dressed in black Bedouin garb and said while bowing, "We are in your debt and will die if necessary, for your quest to be successful."

Pecky replied, "We appreciated it, Hanif, but I don't think a death oath is necessary. We do enjoy your company, though. Please stow your belongings in the last row of seats on the sleigh, and remember we wear seat belts in flight."

Pecky turned to Bee and Ogden and asked, "How are the provisions going?"

Ogden replied, "Prince Ruwallah has supplied us with enough food and water to fly around the earth twice. I don't think we will have to stop again until our next destination in Cameroon. By the way, Pecky, where in Cameroon are we going?"

Pecky looked puzzled, "We are meeting Hilary at his favorite watering hole in Cameroon."

Ogden, with an annoyed look on his face, replied, "Yes, Pecky, I remember that we were to meet Hilary, but where in Cameroon is his favorite watering hole? Prince Ruwallah gave me a map of Africa, and I would like to keep better track of our destinations."

Pecky leaned over and looked at the map and pointed, "That's the place; his favorite watering hole is on the eastern edge of Lake Legdo near Garoua."

It finally occurred to Bee that Ian was nowhere in sight, she asked, "Pecky, where is Ian?"

Pecky looked up from what he was doing and replied, "I don't know. He wasn't in his tent. I assumed he was taking care of his morning business. I asked Hanif's sister Aleah to find him and hurry him along."

A grim look came over Bee's face as she replied, "Pecky, I felt a menacing presence in the camp last night. I think we all should spread out and look for Ian."

Before they could start their search, a scream rang out near the tents on the eastern side of the oasis. When Pecky, Bee, and Ogden arrived, they found Prince Ruwallah and Hanif standing over two murdered guards.

Pecky and Prince Ruwallah looked at each other with a knowing eye.

Prince Ruwallah said with great sorrow, "Legorian and his devotees did this terrible act upon my family."

Bee asked, "How do you know that Legorian killed them?"

Pecky leaned down over the dead guards and pointed to a small wound on the back of each worrier's neck, and said, "It is the mark of Legorian that took this poor soul's life."

Bee replied, "Prince Ruwallah, I'm sorry for your loss. I hope our presence here did not cause this terrible deed?"

Prince Ruwallah looked at Bee with a warm smile and said, "My dear young lady, our life in the desert is dangerous, and we have accepted our fate. We live with death almost daily. These brave men had a great purpose and died with honor. No, your presence has only been a blessing to my tribe."

Bee looked down at the lifeless bodies baking in the early morning heat. She was concerned because she had no feeling for the death of these two brave men.

She had seen death before and felt no loss. Her mother told her that she was a stoic person, showing no weakness. She wondered if she had any feeling about death, or that she even believed in death.

She was taught from an early age that death was only a lie, and that ultimately energy cannot be destroyed. She did not fully understand this concept, but she felt the importance of the belief in her heart.

A Bedouin warrior ran up to Prince Ruwallah and whispered something in his ear. The Prince whispered something to the warrior. The warrior then sped off on a camel to the south while another two fighters galloped east and west.

Prince Ruwallah watched the three soldiers move fast into the distance, and then he said, "Legorian took Ian."

Bee stood for a long time watching the warriors move beyond the horizon. A sense of great sadness and fear welled up in her heart. She had never felt such a great sorrow, not even when her father went missing, or her brother died.

She realized that the loss of Ian meant everything to her. A great sense of hopelessness came over her as she sat down in the sand and started to weep.

Pecky leaned down and said, "Don't worry, we will find Ian. Legorian will not harm him. He is too valuable to Legorian. Legorian cannot kill a true heart."

Bee stood up and walked with the others to Prince Ruwallah's tent. She felt comforted by Pecky's assurance that Legorian wouldn't harm Ian.

Out of the early morning sun, and with tea in hand, Bee felt a calmness overcome her. She felt deep in her heart that everything will work out. She had an overwhelming feeling that the universe was unfolding as it should, and in the end, Ian will be returned the group and to her.

Bee asked, "Pecky, how do you know that Legorian took Ian and that he means him no harm?"

Pecky looked over at Bee with a concerned look and replied, "Legorian left many signs of his deed. First of all, the wounds on the back of the two dead guards are an indicator, because no other being on this planet has that kind of power to kill. Do you remember the last time we saw a wound like that?"

Bee thought for only a moment before she replied, "Sobeck, the wounds are the same that we saw on the back of his neck. You never explained how Legorian creates such a wound that kills."

Bee could see that Pecky was considering what to say next. Bee continued, "I'm okay, you can tell me."

Prince Ruwallah injected before Pecky could reply, "It is a mark of a powerful demon. We call it the mark of the beast."

With a confused look on her face, Bee responded, "What causes such a mark?"

Prince Ruwallah continued, "Unfortunately, the mark is caused by the demons we create during our journey through this life."

With more bewilderment on her mind, Bee replied, "I don't understand."

Pecky replied, "Bee, there are two worlds that we occupy. We occupy the world we see around us, and we occupy an infinite reality that is made up of love and hope.

"The two realities that we hold during our journey through this world are balanced by each other. Seven energy points on our bodies connect us to the two realities. Some call them chakras. Some call them Chi.

"The guards that Legorian killed were brave men, but because they were warriors, they have killed to protect their tribe. When anyone murders another, for good or evil, darkness wells up in their soul. This darkness often breeds guilt, hate, and fear.

"Legorian knows where to find this darkness in our hearts. He knows how to use our fear and guilt against us. He is part of the void, and those who are consumed by this darkness cannot hide from Legorian.

"Legorian used the guilt and fear the two guards kept hidden in their hearts against them. He cut them off from the light and love and hope. In simple terms, the guards died of a twisted soul.

"When we descend into darkness, the better angels of our nature reach out to us to bring us back into the light. Legorian cut that balance off from the guards and Sobeck. They found themselves lost in the dark forever.

"As the light in each one of us is infinite, Legorian is infinite in his connections to all things. He believes that he is separate. Since he lives in the emptiness, he does not know his being.

"Legorian took Ian because he thinks Ian is the key to enter the City of Light. He believes if he can enter the Ancient City and destroy it, he would be set free."

Ogden interjected, "Pecky, it seems to me that you are overly calm about losing Ian. Did you know that this might happen?"

"Yes, I thought it might, but I wasn't sure," replied Pecky.

Bee was startled by Pecky's candor and replied, "Why would you knowingly allow Legorian to take Ian? Why would you put Ian in a vulnerable position?"

"A few days ago, when we first arrived in the desert, Ian and I had a transcendental moment. Ian had a moment of pure awareness. In the Life Energy Consortium, we call it being extended.

"I talked earlier about how we are existing in two realities at once and are connected by seven energy points on our bodies. When a person becomes self-aware or self-realized what they are primarily doing is becoming aware of the two realities that they occupy. They are in the world but not of the world.

"The illusion we see outside of us that we call the world starts to dissipate. This state of being of pure consciousness is light.

"One of the most essential jobs Legorian does is to persuade us that we are cut-off from who we are. We are separate from the source of love and hope. Legorian wants to keep us in darkness, and he is excellent at his job.

"When someone starts to become self-realized, such as Ian, Legorian sees the light in the darkness that he exists in. The light that Ian emanated creates a painful beacon for Legorian. The closer we come to the truth, the harder Legorian works to keep us asleep, keep us in the dark.

Bee interjected, "Pecky, you still haven't explained why you allowed Legorian to take Ian."

Now with a tentative look on his face, Pecky replied, "We are coming to the last leg of our journey before we enter the Ancient City. Ian will be tasked with seven challenges. If he fails any of the seven trials, he will not be allowed to reach the City of Light.

"If Ian does not reach the Ancient City, the world will fall into darkness. Much is riding on Ian being the truest of hearts, and the only way Ian can truly know his mettle is by facing the beast that is tasked to stop him.

"Ian has built up Legorian in his mind. He has most likely made him much more significant than he is. Ian must know who Legorian is to pass all seven challenges.

Prince Ruwallah walked up to the travelers and said, "Pecky, our riders have returned. We now know where Legorian took Ian."

Pecky looked at the Prince with an assured smile and replied, "Is it where we thought he would take him?"

The Prince replied, "Yes, Legorian has him in the village near the city of Moundou on the edge of the desert in Chad."

Bee with a bewildered look on her face asked, "How did you know where Legorian would take Ian?

Pecky replied, "The small village near Moundou fell into darkness many years ago, and our energy sprite failed to change the flow of energy. It is the darkest of all the towns in the area, and if Legorian is anything, he is consistent. He wants us to know that he has Ian and where he has him."

Bee interjected, "Why would Legorian want us to know? I don't understand."

Prince Ruwallah replied, "Bee, power is attractive because one can never really have power unless others give the power to them.

"Most people who journey through this world do not need great power or great wealth. When someone achieves great power and great wealth, it is worth nothing unless others know about it. Legorian is not separate from the need to continually display his power."

Pecky proclaimed "Bee, you need to calm down and start listening to your heart. Ian needs us, and he needs us to be cool. There is a bigger reason why Legorian took Ian. It will make sense to you in the end, but for now, you need to have faith that the universe is unfolding as it should." ❧

CR

Chapter Twenty-Five
A Dark Twist of Fate

Ian slowly opened his eyes, vaguely making out a figure standing at the foot of his bed. As the haze started to clear from his mind, he felt something was wrong, something was different. Ian began to remember his tent at the oasis in the desert. Ian knew that he wasn't at the oasis anymore but could not remember how he arrived, wherever he was now.

The figure at the foot of Ian's bed started to come into focus. A young man around Ian's age stood before him with beautiful long black hair and a pale angelic face with piercing blue eyes.

Ian could tell that the young man who stood before him was not African or Arab. He wore long silk robes common to wealthy people in Africa, but his manner was different than Ian had yet encountered.

Something else occurred to Ian. He felt that he knew this person. That for some reason, he had encountered him once before, but he could not remember where or when.

Ian sat up in bed and asked, "Hello, do I know you?"

The young man came closer to Ian and replied, "I don't see how. We have never met. Maybe you remember me when my father and I found you walking in the desert, but you were delirious at the time?"

Ian instantly figured out the young man's thick accent, and asked, "Your French?"

The young man responded with a sense of pride, "Oui, my family is citizens of Chad, but oui, our heritage is French."

Ian sat up and put his feet firmly on the ground. "I'm still in Africa?"

The young man stood up straight as if he was a soldier about to salute, and responded, "You are a guest on my father's cotton plantation outside the southern Chad township of Moundou. My dad is Pierre Faisons, and my name is Leon Faisons."

Ian wobbled to his feet and put out his hand to shake Leon's hand and replied, "My name is Ian, and I am grateful for your hospitality. How is it that I was walking in the desert? I don't remember any of the events since I went to bed last night at the oasis."

A shocked look came over Leon's face as he replied, "My dear friend, you have been asleep in our home for seven days."

A chill ran down Ian's spine as he sat back down on the bed. He didn't know what to think or say. He just looked down, wondering how he lost so much time.

Leon patted Ian on the shoulder and said, "My friend, don't try to make sense of anything right now, just know that you are safe. When you are ready, you can come to the main hall and have a bit to eat. Your clothes are in the closet, washed and pressed. My father is eager to meet you and discuss your escape from the battle in the desert."

Ian looked up with a surprised look on his face and asked, "What battle?"

A concerned look came over Leon's face as he replied, "Don't worry about details right now, Ian, just rest until you are ready."

Leon turned and abruptly left the small room, closing the door behind him.

A cold, empty feeling flowed over Ian's heart as Leon left the room. Ian had felt this empty feeling a couple of times during his journey with Pecky and Bee.

Suddenly Ian remembered his friends. He sat up in his bed again, wondering what happened. He quickly moved over to the closet, retrieved his clothes, and put them on.

Ian rushed out of his room into the main hallway looking through each door as he went for signs of his friends, but all the rooms were empty.

Ian walked through the estate. He noticed that it was big and beautiful with high white stucco walls and pink and gray marble floors with thick dark wood beams overhead just below the bright white ceilings.

Scattered throughout the estate were furniture and artwork that were from some bygone French period. Ian started to notice that the land was a little rough around the edges. He could tell that a woman did not decorate this property. Nothing in the estate was feminine. The estate was masculine, more of a large hunting cabin for wealthy French men than a home.

Ian reached the kitchen on the far side of the estate. An African woman in her late fifties was bent over a stove, stirring a pot of stew. Without a word, she motioned for Ian to sit down at the small table near a large window overlooking a courtyard.

Dutifully Ian walked over to the table and took a seat. Smelling the stew reminded him of how hungry he was, and thirsty. He wondered how he made it seven days without food or water, or maybe someone fed him while he recovered.

The woman cooking the stew looked familiar to Ian. He thought that maybe he remembered her feeding him while he was fevered. He didn't remember being delirious, but he did feel as if he had been asleep for a long time.

The cook grabbed a plate out of the cupboard and plopped a large portion of stew over white rice with some fresh bread. She filled a large glass with milk. Ian watched the cook go through the motion with an interest only a hungry person could understand.

Ian couldn't remember being so hungry even after he worked on the farm all day in Vermont. All other concerns seemed to fade away as his hunger grew. He thought that maybe the anticipated food had heightened his appetite to a ravenous pitch.

Ian dove into the plate of food like a wild animal devouring its first fresh kill of the spring. The moment, the cook placed the food on the table in front of him.

The stew was more delicious than any he had ever eaten. It had subtle herbs and spices that he had never tasted before. The stew had chunks of tender meat of some kind. He considered that he was either eating sheep or goat. He hoped not a camel.

Halfway through his plate of food, Ian grabbed the glass of milk and took a long slow drink. Instantly he knew he was drinking goat's milk, which led him to believe that he was consuming goat meat.

He had goat's milk before in Vermont and remembered the distinctive tang. He remembered he didn't like the taste of goat's milk, but the milk now was like pure butter traveling down his gullet.

Ian hastily sopped up the last drop of stew with the bread the cook provided him and leaned back in the chair with a glow of contentment. Now that he was full, he looked up and realized the chef had left the kitchen, and Leon was standing in the doorway watching him hungrily down his food.

A look of embarrassment came over Ian's face as he sat up straight in his chair and said, "Leon, I'm so sorry to act like such a glutton, but I was hungry beyond anything that I had ever felt before. My mother would be unhappy with my manners in your home. I am sorry for my poor behavior."

Leon walked over and sat down across the table from Ian and replied, "My mother died when I was young. I don't think my father would consider your hunger as an insult to our family, so don't worry. After seven days, you have all the right to take care of yourself.

"Christabel looked after you during your recovery. She did try to feed you a simple chicken broth, but you would often just refuse."

Ian asked, while taking another drink of goat's milk, "Christabel is your cook—the African woman that was in here earlier?"

Leon replied, "Oui, she has been with us for most of her life. Her parents worked for my grandparents on the plantation. She has no husband or child. She treats my sister and me as her children."

With a warm smile, Ian said, "Sorry, you lost your mother."

Leon replied, "She died when I was a small child. I never really knew her. Christabel has always looked after us. I guess she would be the closest I will ever have to a mother."

Ian asked, "You said you have a sister?"

Leon replied, "Oui, but Suzanne is away at college in France. She is three years older than I am. Just my father and I occupy this home."

Ian replied, "It seems like a large estate for just three people."

Leon replied, "Oui, our family built this farm and cotton plantation in the early eighteen hundreds, and for more than a hundred years, our family farmed much of the area around Moundou. That was before a dark lord, and his devotees, took control of Moundou.

"Most of my uncles and aunts fled to other regions of Africa, and many family members, including my sister, returned to France. My father is a proud man and will not yield to the shadow forces that now occupy the region."

Ian exclaimed, "Is the dark lord's name Legorian?"

Leon thought for a long time and replied, "Oui, I think I have heard him called that name. We call him Malfaisant. I have never encountered him until we found you walking in the desert."

A loud sound in the courtyard surprised Ian and Leon. Ian could instantly tell that a group of riders on horses arrived near the south wall of the house.

Leon interjected, "I believe my father and his men have come back from their search for more survivors. My father will explain what happened."

A moment later, two men walked through the hallway leading out to the south entrance of the estate. The man leading the way looked like Leon. He had long black hair, pale skin, and piercing blue eyes.

His face looked as if it was carved right out of the marble that made up the floors of the estate. His hands and arms showed strength. He had the power of a farmer and a warrior's strength.

The man that trailed right behind him also looked to be carved out of granite. He was jet black with the green-set eyes and hands that showed a hard life in the fields and battle.

Leon's father whispered something to the other man. His father entered the kitchen while the other man went quickly off in another direction.

Leon's father walked up to Ian and held out his hand, "Young man, I am most pleased to see you back on your feet. I trust my son has taken care of you, and Christabel has fed you?"

Ian stood up with a snap and took Mr. Faison's hand, "Yes, sir, I have been taken care of well. Christabel's cooking is a great treat. By the way, my name is Ian."

Pierre Faisons replied with a warm smile, "It is a pleasure to meet you, Ian. Christabel does a great deal with the little we have. I trust that my son has informed you of your situation?

Ian sat back down in his chair and replied, "Yes, sir, everything except how I ended up here, and what battle took place in the desert, and where my friends are."

Pierre Faison took off his dark blue jacket, which looked to be military, and sat down at the table next to his son. He poured himself a glass of goat's milk out of the pitcher left on the table and looked at Ian with soulful eyes. Ian could tell he was considering what to say and how to say it.

Ian sat up in his chair with a determined look on his face, and declared, "Sir, you can tell me anything. I have already been through much. There is little that you can tell me that will surprise me."

Pierre Faison thought for a moment, laughed, and replied, "Oui, my dear young man I don't believe you are old enough to have encountered everything that might be disturbing, but I can see from your eyes that you are sincere, and I respect anyone with that much conviction."

Ian again asked, "Please, sir, I need to know what happened and also where my friends are, and if they are okay?"

Pierre Faison let out a long and soulful sigh and replied, "You see Ian— we are a proud people. Our family has farmed this valley for many decades. I refuse to let the darkness that now engulfs Moundou to take what is ours. I am willing to lay down our lives to fight for our way of life.

"Two weeks ago, we were informed that Malfaisant and his devotees were traveling outside of Moundou to an oasis in the desert near Bilma, Niger. The dark lord rarely leaves Moundou. Much of his power comes from the emptiness that he has created. His devotees who used to be the town folk are in darkness."

Ian thought to himself that maybe this dark lord was not Legorian. Legorian had shown up in many places over the last few months, never staying in one place for any amount of time.

Pierre Faison continued, "Thinking we had a chance to destroy Malfaisant, we put together a makeshift army of fifty other men in the region. We followed his tracks in the desert for three days.

"We caught up with him and his twenty devotees thirty miles south of a desert oasis. We waited until noonday when his power would be at its weakest, and we attacked his column.

"We slaughtered all his devotees, but when the battle ended, we didn't find Malfaisant. He had escaped undetected while the fight raged. One thing that we learned was that he is a coward that will abandon those who follow him.

"Unfortunately, we lost twelve good men during the battle. We were hoping to destroy the dark lord but were unsuccessful. We questioned what good the deaths our friends were if Malfaisant is still breathing."

Ian asked, "Did you find me with Malfaisant's devotees?"

Pierre Faison promptly replied, "No, we found you wandering in the desert, twenty miles south of the oasis. We didn't understand why the dark lord let you go or why he didn't kill you.

"You do have the mark of the dark lord on the back of your neck. We have encountered that mark before, but whoever has that mark has either fallen into darkness or is dead.

"How is it that you have the mark and are still among the living?"

Ian quickly felt the back of his neck to discover a round indentation mark. He instantly remembered Sobek and the mark on the back of his neck. He recalled that Sobek had a stamp that protruded out, not an indent.

Ian replied to Pierre Faison's question, "I don't know why I am still alive. I have come across those who have suffered the dark lord. All that I have encountered are dead or lost in darkness."

Ian thought that maybe it was because he was a true heart. Maybe Malfaisant or whoever this dark lord was cannot kill someone like him. Ian's inner voice told him not to disclose this information to Pierre Faison, at least not yet.

Pierre Faison looked at Ian for a long time with a concerned look on his face and continued, "After the battle, we decided to backtrack Malfaisant to the oasis. When we backtracked is when we found you walking in the desert. We knew that you had not been in the wilderness long because you didn't have any of the symptoms someone might have lost in the desert.

"You were delirious, but not for lack of water or food, and not because the sun had been beating down on you. You were almost in a state of bliss. We discerned that you were battling the mark of the dark lord.

"For some reason, when the dark lord inflicted his mark on your neck and your soul, you reacted in a much different way than anyone we have ever seen respond.

"You were coherent but not lucid at the same time. You seemed to be in a state far from where you were standing."

Ian asked, "What about the oasis and my friends?"

Pierre Faison again looked at Ian with a curious eye and continued, "We thought it best that we should send you back to our estate to recover from whatever fever was raging in your mind and soul. We have never come across someone who has survived the dark lord, so we didn't know how to treat you, other than rest."

Ian started to consider that Pierre Faison was stalling. He didn't want to disclose what happened at the oasis and to his friends. Ian proclaimed, "Please, sir, I need to know what happened to my friends."

Pierre Faison sat back in his chair, took another long drink of goat's milk, and considered for a long time what to tell Ian, "After we sent you back to the estate, the rest of us, who were still alive from the battle, moved on to the oasis.

"We started to see signs of the battle that took place a few miles from the camp. Bedouin soldiers were lying dead in the sand with the mark of Malfaisant.

"When we arrived at the camp, we found all slaughtered, including the camels. The tents and all the Bedouin's possessions were burned and destroyed."

Ian sat back in his chair with his eyes starting to tear up as he asked, "Did you see a six-foot-tall penguin, a young woman with red hair, and a young man with long blond hair?"

Pierre Faison leaned in and put his hand on Ian's shoulder and replied, "Yes, Ian. Unfortunately, I found your three friends slaughtered." ∝

CⳄ

Chapter Twenty-Six
Walk About

Ian's alarm clock on the stand next to his bed read 3:33 a.m. This was the third morning in a row since Ian heard the news about his friends that he woke covered in a cold sweat at precisely 3:33 a.m.

He suddenly became aware of a large black scorpion crawling on the wall next to the window in his room. He had killed four over the last few days. He found one under his sheets before he crawled into bed the other night. Leon told him that they wouldn't hurt him, but he crushed the one on the wall with his boot just in case.

After diligently checking for other such bugs, Ian flopped himself back on his bed and lay still for a long time looking at the ceiling. He felt numb from the news of his friends and concerned about his fate. He had many discussions over the last few days with Pierre and Leon about what direction he would need to go next.

Pierre kept asking why he was in the desert and what did the dark lord want with him. Ian wanted to trust Pierre and Leon with the details of his journey, but his heart kept telling him to keep the information secret. Pierre offered to take Ian to the airport in Chad's capital city of N'Djamena and put him on a plane for home.

Ian didn't know what to do or where to go because his heart was conflicted. Over the last few days, he has had no help from his connection with the Source. The one thing he could always rely on was cut off from him, he thought.

He was concerned because other than feeling numb be had no feeling about the loss of his friends. The friends that he grew to love and feel close too were gone, and he did not feel sad—he just felt in conflict.

Ian wanted to go home, but his heart told him that was not an option. His father had vanished near the City of Light, and he had to find him.

Ian was so in conflict with his heart that he started to doubt everything. Ian was supposed to reach the Ancient City and bring light back to the world. Why did Pecky, Bee, and Ogden die?

The Source of all creation is supposed to be behind him one hundred percent. He considered that the Source might have abandoned him, and he was never the one destined to reach the City of Light.

For three days he had been intently thinking about what to do and where to go with no resolution. Ian wondered why Pierre Faison was so interested in his destination.

A distant thought passed over Ian's heart that maybe Pierre and Leon were not what he thought them to be. Over the last few days, he had seen no other field hands or workers come to the estate other than Pierre, Leon, and Christabel. At the same time, the property seemed to be kept up, and the fields seemed adequately managed.

The subtle voice in Ian's heart started to grow louder. He began to think that maybe the conflict he has felt in his heart, is not about the death of his friends, but what Pierre told him about their demise.

Ian considered that he accepted the information that his friends were dead at face value, trusting that Pierre was telling him the truth. He didn't know Pierre or Leon. Why would he believe that they were telling him the truth?

This was when the voice deep down started to get even louder. Ian realized that the conflict in his heart was his consciousness, trying to reach him. He realized that he cut himself off from his heart because he trusted and embraced information that most likely was not true. He started to realize that maybe his friends were still alive.

Embracing the possibility of his friends being alive started to resolve the conflict in Ian's heart. He began to feel light of spirit again. He began to hear the inner voice speak out to him in the dark. He started to recognize that his heart was talking to him all along, he just had not been listening.

Ian sat up on his bed and looked around his room. Now that he was not in conflict anymore, his bedroom started to look different. Ian saw cracks in the stucco walls with chunks of plaster on the floor of his room. He saw ivy growing on the walls, where there was none. For a moment, Ian considered that he might be delusional again. Still, at the closer view, he could see the entire room changing in appearance.

The sheets on his bed now looked torn and worn, and his mattress had yellowed and became old. The bed frame became rusted and bent. The room looked abandoned.

He quietly opened his bedroom door to observe the hallway leading to the central part of the house, which also looked abandoned. He recognized that everything around him had been a lie, an illusion that he believed.

He started to comprehend that his fear and doubt brought on his false perceptions. He needed to feel safe, but now he knew that he was not safe. He started to wonder who Pierre and Leon Faison were. He understood that his safety would rely on him doing something fast, but he did not know what.

A powerful feeling moved down the spine of Ian's back. He had felt this feeling many times before when he felt a presence near him that he could not see. He felt it back in England on the top floor of Buckingham Palace and in Vermont when someone died and wanted to speak to him.

Ian abruptly stood up and said, "Hello, I know you are here, what is it that you want to tell me?"

Before Ian's eyes, two ghostly figures started to materialize. They were a thin transparent wisp of light. They became more and more apparent standing right in front of Ian.

Ian had experienced ghosts from an early age and was beyond fearing them. He knew that often people died and held onto their human connections. Many spirits didn't know that they were even dead. Many felt that they still had much to do and didn't want to move on.

A sinking feeling occurred in Ian's stomach as the two specters formed before Ian. He instantly realized that these two apparitions had been trying to reach him all along. He was just too much in conflict to see them. He was in the dark without sight.

The two ghosts were now clear as day, and Ian felt his greatest fear. The two spirits that stood before Ian were Pierre and Leon Faison. Ian knew that these two phantoms occupied this estate and that the others were something else, but what he did not understand.

The presence of Leon Faison came near to Ian and said, "We are glad that you have found the light once again. We have been waiting to talk with you for many days. We believe that you might have some questions to ask us."

Ian sat up on his bed and looked at the specters for a long time, and then replied, "How do I know that you are not an illusion?"

The ghost of Pierre Faison replied with great warmth and concern, "Ian, the only thing that you can trust is your heart. Your heart will never lie to you and will never hurt you. The only harm you can cause yourself is not following your heart, so what does your heart say?"

A smile came over Ian's face as he replied, "My heart tells me to trust you."

The ghost of Leon Faison said heartily, "Good, now let's get on with what you will need to know before you leave."

A concerned look came over Ian's face as he asked, "Where am I going?"

Leon's ghost replied, "Ian, now that you are awake again, you have to leave right away. Legorian will not allow you to leave once he finds out that you have found the light."

Ian asked, "So, Leon and Pierre were Legorian?"

Pierre Faison's apparition replied with great unrest, "No, and yes. You see, Ian, Legorian does not control us. He creates the illusion that we believe. Legorian was everyone and no-one during your stay here. He simply established a safe place for you, so you thought. You created the world around you by your perceptions of what would be safe. Does this make sense?"

"My friend Pecky once told me that the world outside is only a reflection of how we perceive ourselves. The illusion outside of us is individually and collectively created. Is this basically what you mean?"

The ghost of Leon exclaimed with great enthusiasm, "Oui, you are stronger than you can understand. You created the illusion you participated in over the last few days.

"Legorian supported what you needed to feel safe so that he could maintain control of you. Because you are a true heart, you broke free of the dark lord's control."

Ian interjected with great concern, "Do you know if my friends are still alive?"

Pierre Faison's ghost responded, "Oui, they were not harmed by Legorian."

Ian asked, "How do you know so much about my friends, and what happened to them?"

Pierre Faison's ghost sat on the bed next to Ian and replied, "We exist in another level of consciousness that has no boundaries. All information is part of an infinite reality that can be accessed if you only open your heart. You will, in time, be able to access any information and any memory."

Ian thought for a moment and asked, "Why are you here?"

Pierre Faison's spirit said, "Our family left this region before the darkness fell on Moundou. My son and I stayed thinking that we could avoid the evil that has taken over the area, but we were wrong. The energy that has cast this region into darkness traps us here for eternity, that is, unless you make it to the City of Light.

"How do you know that I was on the way to the Ancient City?"

Pierre Faison's ghost continued, "Ian, even in the darkness, your true heart shines with warmth and brightness that can be seen even in the evilest of places. My son and I woke up when you entered our home. Once you leave, we will fall back into the darkness and forget who we are. So, you see Ian for everyone's sake, including my son and me, you need to reach the Ancient City, even the cost of your own life."

For a moment, this revelation by Pierre Faison's ghost heightened Ian's fear, but only for the time being. Ian asked, "What do I do next?"

Leon Faison's spirit replied, "Ian, you need to leave right now, and travel to a village that borders Chad and Cameroon. In that village, you will find a shaman that will help you find your friends. The village is a day's walk directly west."

Pierre Faison's ghost said, "Oui, you need to leave right now. In our study, you will find a map, compass, and money enough for the trip in a secret drawer located on my desk next to the east wall."

Ian got out of bed and gathered all his belongings and quickly but quietly walked out of his room into the main hallway leading to Pierre Faison's study.

Ian walked through the estate. He noticed the walls had thick vines and large dense spider webs.

Ian wondered what he had been eating over the last few days. He wondered if he was eating anything at all, or did Legorian trick him. He noticed many black scorpions crawling all over the walls and floors of the estate.

Ian reached the door to Pierre Faison's study. He quietly opened the door to reveal a large room with many different animal heads lining the walls.

Ian considered that there would be many dangerous animals along his path to the village. He reached Pierre Faison's desk and searched for the secret drawer but found nothing.

Pierre Faison's ghost reappeared and said, "Ian, pull the bottom drawer entirely out, and behind you will find a cubby hole that contains the map, compass, and money. Legorian does not know about this."

Ian quickly pulled out the bottom drawer of the desk and searched for a secret cubby hole. He pulled out a small box and opened it. The box revealed an antique compass, a slightly yellowed and torn map of Chad, and ten gold pieces. That looked to be old with writing on them that he did not understand.

Ian asked Pierre Faison's ghost, "How long have you been in darkness?"

A depressing look came over Pierre Faison's ghost as he replied, "Unfortunately, we have been in darkness for more than 120 years. You see, Ian, how important it is to us that you succeed."

Ian thought for a moment and asked, "Pierre, what about the wild animals on the road to the village. Should I take a gun or some weapon?"

Pierre Faison's ghost responded, "No, Ian, you are a true heart. One of your greatest gifts is to walk among the beasts of the world. There is a sense of innocence in the most vicious animals that a true heart humbles.

"Legorian was right when he told you that the scorpions in this home would not harm you, because he knew that no animal of the world will hurt you. Still, there is one animal that you will need to stay clear of, and that is the jackal.

"You see, Ian, the jackal is not of this world. The jackal is a beast that feeds off the misery of others. It is born in the evilest corners of the world. It is a devotee of Legorian—a follower that greedily takes comfort in destroying those that are of good heart.

"I have not seen a jackal for more than a hundred years and felt that they will not be a threat to your journey to the village. If you do come across a jackal, it is best not to show them fear. They are great cowards that will not attack anyone or anything that they feel is more powerful than they are. They only feed off the weak."

Ian interjected, "Where is the village on the map?"

Pierre Faison's ghost pointed to a town next to a large lake near the border of Cameroon called Lere on Ian's map, and said, "You need to make it by nightfall.

"The village shaman's name is Kehfun. He is the spiritual leader of this clan. He will help you find your friends."

Ian thought for a moment and asked, "What will Legorian do when he finds out that I am gone? Will he know that you and your son helped me?"

Pierre Faison shook his head and replied, "Oui, Ian, he will be aware that my son and I helped you, and he will punish us, but you see, we will do anything to be free from this prison.

"Legorian will send his devotees to find you, but if you reach the village before nightfall, the shaman's power will protect you from the dark lord. Ian go, you have no time to waste. Walk due west along the road through the thicket."

Before Ian's eyes, Pierre Faison disappeared back into a wisp of light and then faded.

Ian grabbed a bag on the desk and hastily put in all his belongings with the map, compass, and ten gold pieces. Ian looked around the room for anything that might help him, and he spied an old walking stick with the head of an eagle on the top. A further examination found that the walking stick held a sword in its case.

Ian grabbed the walking stick and quickly but quietly walked towards the west entrance to the house. The door leading out into the west courtyard had long been torn down by age.

Ian made his way out into the abandoned cotton fields and then into the thicket. Ian turned around and took a long look at the house he occupied for many days.

The bright white stucco walls still stood firm after one hundred and twenty years. Much debris and decay surrounded the outer walls with thick vines and other plant life attempting to overtake the estate but having a slow go of it.

The sky was still pitch black with an array of stars brightly shining in the heavens. Ian turned around with confidence and continued his walk into the wilderness, knowing that it might mean his life.

He truly understood for the first time during his journey to the Ancient City what was really at risk, and he knew failure was not an option. ൠ

C3

Chapter Twenty-Seven
Darkness Fades

The vapor coming out of the nostrils of the thirty-eight black Arabia stallions that stood along the dune outside of a small village rose quickly in the early morning mist. The town bordered the Faison plantation a few miles from Moundou, Chad.

Bedouin warriors from the Ruwallah tribe rode each horse, and each horse and rider had been tested in many battles and was restless for the slaughter.

The horses strained to breathe, and impatient hooves were attacking the sand, creating a sound that was deafening. The Bedouin warriors sat still. They were all waiting for the decision to move on the African village from their Prince.

Embedded in the column of horses next to Prince Zayed sat Pecky on a black gelding. The harsh look of a warrior king replaced his usually cheerful expression.

Pecky sat in armor and helmet with a long sword and scabbard tightly attached to his saddle. The sword had sentimental value for Pecky; it belonged to his father. His dad used it in the Penguin's great battle with the leopard seals.

Bedouin trackers had traced Legorian's movement with Ian to the little village on the edge of Moundou in Chad. Prince Zayed was waiting for the two scouts he sent into the town to return with news of Ian before he had his Bedouin warriors move in.

Pecky was restless, feeling as if he was on the edge of a knife. Patience was not exactly his forte, mainly because he knew the journey to the City of Light would fail if he lost Ian. Ian had become his good friend, and it would break his heart.

"Are you sure the village is where Legorian took Ian?" asked Pecky.

Prince Zayed quickly respondid to Pecky, "Yes, my friend. I knew that the village near Moundou would be Legorian's destination before my trackers confirmed my suspicion."

Pecky asked with a confused look, "How did you know this town would be our destination?"

Prince Zayed slowly moved his hand over his horse's throat to calm his stallion. He warily looked out over the desert towards the village. He then replied to Pecky, "You see, my friend, Chad's history is one of sadness. It has seen many colonial forces, civil wars, and much death. It is known as the dead center of Africa, landlocked by all sides by many other countries continually consumed with conflict, fear, and doubt.

"This village is one of the darkest spots in a country fighting for its survival. Legorian feeds off suffering, hatred, indifference, and apathy. His being is supported by dark energies. This town would feed his need for misery like no other place in the region. It is known that the people of this village made a pact with a Zorkin."

Pecky interjected, "A Zorkin?"

Prince Zayed looked a Pecky with a surprised eye and replied, "My friend, I thought you knew that a Zorkin resides here? This particular Zorkin is an ancient beast that is one of Legorian's first and foremost devotees. Where it came from, few know, but this Zorkin is from an early age.

"Because of the pact with Legorian, the Zorkin became something else. It moves into dark places and makes deals with the village folk not to harm them if they lure others into its trap. Slowly, the people of the village fall into emptiness and start to feed off the flesh and bone of those that wander into the Zorkin's clutches."

In the distance, Pecky and Prince Zayed could see one rider move quickly in their direction over the sand. The hooves of his stallion picked up the early morning dew, still covering the dunes. The closer the rider came, the more they could see the fear on his face.

Prince Zayed looked at Pecky with caution in his eyes, "It is rare my friend to see the fear on the face of a Bedouin warrior. Be cautious when he approaches. Be ready with your sword if necessary."

Pecky braced himself for what might happen if the rider had fallen into darkness. He readied his sword for what might come.

The rider reached the column of Bedouin warriors and quickly dismounted from his stallion. His face was pale white with a look of insanity in his eyes. He sat down in the sand and curled up, murmuring something inaudible on the edge of his lips.

Prince Zayed's captain dismounted and approached the scout with trepidation. He slowly put his hand on his shoulder, asking what happened to the other scout that went into the village. The captain insisted that the man calm down and regain his strength.

After a moment, the scout started to calm down. He slowly looked up with an expression of fear on his face, and said, "My apologies, my captain, for a moment, the void was beckoning to me."

The scout stood up and brushed the sand off his clothing and continued. "Our brother was lost to the Zorkin. I was able to escape or set loose by those who are devotees of Legorian so that I could bring back a warning of what awaits us in the village."

Pecky injected with irritation, "Is Ian in the village? Is he still alive?"

"Yes, Pecky, Ian is in a plantation house on the edge of the village near Moundou. He has no idea what happened or what brought him to the village," replied the scout with determination.

Pecky asked, "How do you know so much when you were in the village for only a short amount of time?"

The scout replied, "The villagers told me. They seem to take joy in the fact that they have such a prominent guest under their control. They did not hide the fact that Legorian controlled the village and that we would fall if we attacked."

Pecky turned to Prince Zayed and asked, "What say you, Prince?"

Prince Zayed looked down at the scout and his captain with a thoughtful look that showed he was calculating all options.

He turned his gaze to Pecky and replied, "Pecky, my friend, I sense that the village is a trap, but I believe we have no other alternative than to attack.

"If Ian is in the village, we both know that it doesn't matter what happens to us. If he doesn't fulfill his destiny and reach the City of Light, we will lose everything. Legorian knows this—that is why he is baiting us."

Pecky looked at Prince Zayed with an understanding eye and replied, "You're right, my dear friend. We have no other choice."

Prince Zayed looked around at his column of warriors with pride in his heart. He said with a loud and patience voice, "My countrymen, my friends, my companions, we move on to the village. Remember that the town has fallen under Legorian's control.

"Legorian will try to deceive us. He will try to cast us into the same darkness as the people of the town. Believe your hearts, not your eyes.

"We move in to destroy everyone—no one shall be left alive. If you find the Zorkin cut its head off. Only dispatching the Zorkin will release the village from its curse."

The column of Bedouin warriors slowly moved towards the town. With each step of their stallions, a darker and darker energy engulfed the fighters.

The closer they came to the village, the faster the horses picked up speed until all were in a gallop, swords drawn with determination to slaughter all dark souls.

In the distance, the village outside of Moundou appeared on the horizon surrounded by patches of green and scrub brush and mountains in the range with rivers framing the outer edges.

When the column of warriors approaches the center of the village, the rising sun to the east cast light on a deserted town. Prince Zayed and Pecky looked in every direction but only saw empty streets and buildings.

"How can this be?" cried out Pecky.

Prince Zayed calmed his stallion in the center of the village, but he felt his heart still racing. His heart was telling him that he has walked into a trap—that his men and Ian are doomed if he doesn't act fast.

To his right, a warrior screams out and then disappears into the backdrop of the village. Another soldier to his left and three behind him scream out, all vanishing, all gone before his eyes.

"It's a trap," shouts Pecky.

Prince Zayed acknowledges Pecky's concern and then tries to calm his heart. He knows that his only hope is to hear his inner voice. In the desert, he knew his heart was trying to communicate, but he didn't want to believe what it was telling him.

In an instant, Prince Zayed pulled out his sword from its sheath and, with one mighty stroke, slices off the head of the scout that returned. His warriors and captain all look in horror at their Prince.

His captain yells out, "Have you lost your mind?"

A feeling of peace descended over the village before anyone can consider what had just happened. Little by little, people started to appear on the streets of the town. All around them, life began to return to the township.

Then to everyone's repulsion, a dark beast lay on the ground just below Prince Zayed's stallion bleeding dark green blood.

Prince Zayed, Pecky, and the captain all dismounted and with trepidation walked closer to the dying beast.

"What is it?" Pecky asked.

Prince Zayed knelt down closer to the beast and replied, "I believe that this weak monster is the Zorkin, even though I have never seen one."

It is a Zorkin," Said a voice from behind the trio.

All three turn around to spy a tall, thin black man with glistening skin and ragged clothes moving towards them with an elegant but cautious stride.

Prince Zayed quickly stood up and held his sword towards the stranger and said, "Come no closer, or I will dispatch your head. Who are you, and what business do you have with us?"

"My name is Hassan, and I was the mayor of this village before we all fell. You have freed us from suffering," replied the stranger.

"Is this another trick?" interjected Pecky.

For a long time, Prince Zayed looked at the stranger standing before him. He was again not relying on what he saw outside of himself, but what he knew in his heart.

He looked back at Pecky and answered, "No, my friend, this not a trick. The Zorkin that lay before us cast everyone in an illusion—we are now waking. I believe we will receive our answers to where Ian is and what has happened to him. Do I speak the truth, Hassan?"

"Yes, Prince, you talk the truth," Replied Hassan.

The people of the village started to appear all around the warriors. The surrounding area became vibrant, and the mountains became grand.

As the people of the village started to appear. The beast lying in the sand started to disappear into the dirt that it once was spawned from. Prince Zayed knelt down to touch the Zorkin, but the creature became sand between his fingers. He couldn't remember what the Zorkin looked like. The beast left a haze in his mind.

The disappearance of the Zorkin confused Pecky but did not surprise him. "Hassan, I thought that your people helped the Zorkin. I heard that you participated in the flesh and bones of others."

Hassan looked down at where the beast once lay. "Yes, many of my people did participate in the Zorkin's nefarious acts, but those people will stay in darkness forever.

"My people that now surround us never would bow to the Zorkin. The Zorkin cast us into a purgatory that was neither in darkness nor light. We all have been wandering in a haze for many years."

"What about Ian?" interjected Prince Zayed.

"You speak of the true heart?" replied Hassan.

"Yes, his name is Ian, he is why we are here," replied Pecky.

Hassan looked at Pecky and Prince Zayed with concern and continued, "The dark lord brought him into the village a week ago. Legorian traveled with many dark riders and devotees.

"Legorian met with the Zorkin for many hours and then left Ian at a plantation that borders the village."

Pecky interjected, "How do you know Ian was a true heart?"

A tear fell down Hassan's cheek as he replied, "Even in the shadows, we could see his light. His heart shone like a beacon reminding us of hope and faith that we had long forgotten.

"There was something we saw in the shadows. We saw Legorian fearful of Ian. Legorian has visited the village many times, but this was the first time we saw him concerned about his control."

Prince Zayed hastily mounted his stallion and asked with determination, "Take us to Ian."

Hassan was helped up by the prince's captain onto the back of his stallion. He pointed in a direction, and the prince, Pecky, and his captain all rode towards the plantation. The prince left instructions for his warriors to stay and help the people in any way they could.

The plantation was not more than five miles on the western edge of the village. The riders quickly found a road leading up to the south side of the main house.

The energy that was released when the prince killed the Zorkin was just starting the reach the plantation. Flowers, birds, animals, and insects were fast returning, bringing life again to the area.

The riders rode up to the house with caution and dismounted, leaving their horses to graze on the green grass surrounding the main house.

The main entrance to the home was partly ajar, hanging on one hinge.

"Legorian slaughtered the family many years ago. He used the plantation for desperate acts of cruelty and torture. Even in the shadows, my people could see the deeds committed upon others in this place."

Prince Zayed, Pecky, and Hassan slowly entered the abode, leaving the captain to tend the horses and keep a watch for any raiders that might attack them.

The three noticed the scorpions crawling everywhere. The crunch of the bugs under their boots echoed throughout the halls of the home.

All three called out for Ian, but only a faint echo returned.

Then in the mist that hung over the main hallway, the three started to see an apparition appear. The specter was faint at first, then in an instant, two forms began to take shape in a grey haze. One ghost was a man in his late forties and the other a young man in his teens.

Hassan spoke out, "They are the ghosts of the remaining family that once occupied this plantation. Most of their kin left long before Legorian cast the village into obscurity."

"You seek the true heart?" the specter asked with great sincerity.

Pecky replied, "Yes, have you seen him? Is he still here?

"He was here but is gone." replied the young phantom.

Pecky asked with concern for his friend, "Gone where?"

"He escaped Legorian into the wilderness." replied the phantom.

Prince Zayed interjected, "Spirit, tell us what happened here, and where we can find Ian."

The elder ghost beckoned the three to follow him to a back bedroom. They all entered the quarters that Ian once occupied. The walls were covered with vines and scorpions.

The spirit in a faint voice continued, "A many days ago, Legorian brought the true heart you call Ian to this room and cast a spell over him. Ian thought that he was being hosted by my son and me when we were still alive and were masters of this plantation.

"Legorian let Ian believe that he was taken care of and safe. He led Ian to believe that all his friends were dead, and he was alone in Africa."

Prince Zayed interjected, "Why didn't Legorian just kill Ian?"

The specter replied, "Legorian wants Ian to enter the City of Light and destroy it for good—even though destroying the Ancient City would surely destroy Legorian.

"That is why we are now ghosts in our own home. We would never bow to Legorian lest our souls be lost forever. We have found that Legorian has weaknesses. His desire to destroy all creation and all good in the world is his greatest weakness."

Pecky interjected, "Why does that make him weak?"

The specter replied with great sorrow, "Because he can never be at peace in this world when this world is at peace. He has to find a way to destroy the world even though it would ultimately destroy him."

Prince Zayed asked, "What happened to Ian?"

The ghost continued, "What Legorian didn't understand was that a true heart cannot long be fooled. Ian woke up from the dream Legorian cast on him and saw the truth.

"He could see us and hear the truth. Early yesterday morning, he left the plantation and walked into the wilderness. He is going to a village in Cameroon called Lere to meet a shaman named Kehfun."

Pecky exclaimed, "He is going to meet Kehfun. He has decided to see the journey through to the end, no matter what." ଔ

CB

Chapter Twenty-Eight
The Wilderness

T
he morning sun beat down on Ian's brow. The heat did not create the misery that Ian would have assumed. The warmth was more like a gentle kiss on his forehead, forming a layer of sweat that comforted him.

Ian wrapped his body in the Bedouin clothing given to him by Prince Ruwallah. He once read that the people of the desert survived by creating a thin layer of sweat under layers of clothing that keep their bodies cool in the heat of the day.

Most desert travelers move in the dark and rest during the afternoon sun. Ian knew that he had to reach his destination, or he would be alone at night. The thought of being alone in the wilderness of Africa at night did not comfort him.

Ian walked through a land covered in green thick scrub grass with bushes and small trees dotting the landscape. There were stretches of dry, cracked land with small ponds surrounded by flora that he did not recognize.

The estate of Pierre and Leon Faison faded over the eastern horizon. The more Ian traveled away from Moundou, the more he could again hear his inner voice. He knew for sure that he was on the right path because the conflict in his heart was gone. A feeling of serenity moved over his body like a cool breeze on a summer afternoon in the green mountains. Even though he was walking into the wilderness, he felt no fear.

Ian walked through tiny, desolate villages with huts made from the same scrub brush dotting the landscape. He peeked in the shelters to find nothing but tattered blankets and broken clay pots—the buildings long abandoned.

The air smelled sweet with the rain that came down the night before. Ian felt lucky that he was walking in the desert during the rainy season. He considered that maybe the animals wouldn't see him as a food source with many other prospects.

Ian did not see any animals, but as he moved beyond the range of Moundou, he heard large animals moving through the underbrush. He listened to the familiar roar of lions in the distance. The sound of the lions was familiar from his travels to the Boston zoo and from television.

The more Ian walked into the wilderness, the more the western plains of Chad took on an almost spiritual feel. The highlands of west Chad seemed to expand out endlessly in every direction with plateaus reaching up to the bright blue heavens.

The sky covering the high plains changed drastically in whatever direction Ian looked. He could see dark storm clouds to the east, drenching a spot on the landscape. To the north, clear blue skies with delicate high-altitude clouds covering a mountain range. To the south, big cotton candy clouds moved gracefully close to the flat prairie. To the west, a thin haze was rising off the hot, dry land, creating a mystical feeling.

Something occurred to Ian that stopped him in his tracks. In his heart, he had a vision of Pecky and Prince Ruwallah on horseback with many Bedouin warriors. They were attacking the village near Moundou—he knew they were looking for him.

Ian considered turning back. He decided to continue because he needed to reach his destination by nightfall. He knew that it would be folly to turn back. He knew that his friends would find him.

This vision of his future startled him because he had never had such a clear picture of events to come. This vision also comforted him because he knew what must take place. His revelation showed that he would, in fact, reach his destination. He was aware that if he didn't follow his heart, the future might change in some way that would damage the fate of everyone.

Then he considered that maybe he wasn't seeing the future but observing his past. That perhaps he had already reached the Ancient City many times. Maybe he was reliving or looking back on what has already happened. This thought ran a chill down his spine. He considered for a moment that if everything is already written, then what place does free will take in this reality?

The realization that time is circular and that he had been in this same situation maybe a thousand lifetimes created a strong feeling of déjà vu.

A transformation took place narrowing the gap between Ian's consciousness and the reality he now occupied. The wilderness that was once vast seemed to almost compress into a single bubble of perception.

He felt outside his body, watching himself walk through the desert. He considered that the entity watching Ian was his true self. His body was a façade holding the essence of what makes up his spirit—his connection to the Source.

His true self was the voice he heard in his heart; his spirit was the true nature of his being and the existence that he could trust.

The closer he came to his true self, the more at peace he felt. The place he now existed in felt like being back at his home in the valley of the two green mountains.

A loud noise brought him back to his body. He didn't know what the commotion was until he looked around at his feet. He had walked into a dry riverbed with many snakes slithering around his feet. He stopped in his tracks with terror.

Ian noticed a large animal sitting in a tree that spread out over the dry riverbed. At closer observation, the animal looked to be a leopard. The big cat looked at Ian with intensity but made no move towards him. His fear quickly dissipated as he realized that the animals around him meant him no hard. He felt that they were just curious about who was moving through their territory.

Ian looked down at his watch. He realized that he had been walking in a state of spirit for more than seven hours. What seemed like only a few minutes of walking took him more than halfway to his destination—at least he hoped he was close.

He evoked what Pierre and Leon Faison told him about the animals along his path. They said that animals would not harm him. He decided that he had no other choice than to put his faith to the test.

He picked up one foot and moved it slowly forward and then the other foot. The snakes slithered away as he walked down the path towards the other side of the dry riverbed. The leopard was content to stay in the tree, shaded from the afternoon sun.

Ian knew that if any of these animals decided to strike him, he would die fast. Then he remembered his vision, and his fate was not to die in this land alone but to move forward and reunite with his friends.

When Ian reached the other side of the dry riverbed, he turned and looked down at many hundreds of snakes moving about looking for any water left in cracks and fissures of the dry mud.

Not one snake moved towards him or showed him any concern. The leopard just yawned and went back to his afternoon nap.

Ian did sense that the animals were aware of his presence, but they did not fear him or consider him a threat in any way. He knew that a snake or any animal would attack when threatened. This experience was a profound illustration of his true heart. He felt that love in his heart connected him with all things great and small.

He felt that maybe this experience with the snakes was more for his benefit.

He didn't remember how he came to be among so many deadly animals. He recalled observing his body from afar. He thought that maybe his spirit guided him into a place of danger to show that there was no threat in the first place. Perhaps he was testing his faith in his ability to move beyond the physical reality to the spiritual realm. Ian felt deeply that his spirit was preparing him for what lay ahead.

Ian had a hard time getting his head around the time lost. He had been walking through the desert for many hours without a sense of distance, time, or space. A strange thought entered his mind. He thought that maybe the shortest distance between two points was an infinite line of consciousness that shows that there is no distance between two points.

This thought amused Ian to the point of laughing out loud. He found himself in the middle of the wilderness with a feeling of pure truth, which produced for him a big belly laugh.

Ian remembered a quote by Max Planck, the physicist, "If one does not laugh while contemplating quantum physics, then one does not understand quantum physics."

He suddenly realized that not only had he been considering quantum physics, but he had been playing with many of the parts, considering that quantum physics represented an infinite stage where he played all the roles, including the director and producer.

Ian noticed a change in the weather. The dry heat that he felt through most of his journey to Cameroon started to change. The air around him became heavy with moisture, and the sun began to beat down on his brow with a different intensity.

Ian noticed a substantial change in the landscape to the west. The green scrub grass was becoming thicker, and minor hills started to rise on the horizon.

The dirt leading into the valley was not brown but a light-yellow hue with streaks of red clay.

It occurred to Ian that he did not know where he was or how far he still had to travel. He left the estate near Moundou so abruptly that he didn't have any time to plan his journey. Ian sat down next to what seemed to him to be a palm tree of some sort.

He laid out the map and compass he found in the study. The compass read slightly to the northwest. The map was old but accurate, still showing Moundou and his destination of Lake Lagdo located in northern Cameroon. He measured ten-mile increments with his fingers from the plantation to the lake and worked out around fifty miles.

Ian wondered how he was going to travel fifty miles on foot in one day. In between the plantation and his destination was wilderness. There was nothing on the map about a village near the lake.

Ian's dilemma became amusing to him, and he again started to laugh out loud. He realized that unless a miracle transpired in front of him, he was in big trouble because nightfall was a couple hours away.

He ran through the little bit of food he took with him from the estate. Fortunately, there was an abundance of water around him. He considered eating the flora but was unsure of its safety. There were plenty of small animals and bugs but was unsure how he would capture them. He regretted dropping out of Boy Scouts.

Ian stood up, brushed himself off, and started to walk again to the west. He had no other choice but to follow the path that lay before him. Ian thought of his friends and traveling great distances in the sleigh. He told himself that if he found his friends again, he would never take them or the sleigh for granted.

The mist rising off the land to the east started to get darker as the sun came closer to the horizon. The animal noises that he heard in the distance earlier seemed to grow in intensity and diversity as the sun started to set. He knew he was in for a long night.

Just before the sunset, Ian decided that his best bet was to build a fire and stick it out where he was. He felt that moving about in the dark would increase his likelihood of injury or worse coming upon a wild animal that may feel threatened.

Ian picked a clearing next to palm trees around a pond. He had no flashlight or matches, but he remembered how to start a fire with his father teaching him during one of their many camping trips.

Ian collected a few pieces of wood and dry shrubbery. He used a two-foot stick to create friction and blew on the hot spot to give the flame enough air. A spark started a blaze that rapidly grew. The fire surprised Ian because he was unable to start one the last time he went camping.

There was plenty of dry wood around the clearing for Ian to create a sustainable fire for the night. Stopping for the evening reminded him that he had not eaten for some time.

Ian decided to trust the pond. The water to Ian's surprise tasted fresh. He thought that maybe the lake was fed by a spring. Ian did not see any sign of rain in the last few days. Everything around him seemed to be bone dry.

The last of the sunlight dipped below the horizon. For a moment, everything seemed to be dark, but in just a few minutes, something incredible happened. The stars came out in the night sky with an intensity Ian had never witnessed.

Ian had camped in the Vermont woods many times, but he had never been in the wilderness without a town nearby.

He looked up at the Milky Way Galaxy. He did not know the night sky could be so brilliant.

In the east, a waxing gibbous moon rose to cast a spotlight on the tops of mountains surrounding the valley to the west. The moon was bright enough for Ian to see figures. He thought most likely animals were looking for an evening meal.

Ian sat under the palm tree, looking into the flames crackling up in the star-studded sky. He thought about his home in the green mountains, and his family and friends he left behind. He thought a lot about his new friends and if they were looking for him—were they as sure of their destiny as he was of his, now that he had a vision?

He thought mostly about his mother's cooking. Every summer, his parents had a lobster feast with his family. The lobsters were brought up by his father from Point Judith, Rhode Island. He would buy them right off the lobster boats.

The summer feast would have plenty of Cohog clams, shrimp, shad from the Connecticut coast, salt, and butter corn, but most of all, the delicious fresh lobster with hot butter. Ian could almost taste the juicy lobster meat dipped in warm butter sliding down his throat.

The memory was so real that Ian could smell the warm bread his mother would bake for the feast. At this moment, he realized that a single figure was standing in the shadows on the other side of the fire between two palm trees.

At first, the man startled him, but then he quickly regained his composure. He felt that this person would not harm him. Ian believed that this man had come to help him.

The figure moved out of the shadows into the light of the fire. Standing before Ian was a short man with jet black skin wearing brightly colored tribal clothing. He had a brilliantly painted face, and he wore a large necklace with colorful beads. The light of the fire showed his muscle tone. Ian could readily tell that this man lived a hard life.

He held a staff adorned with some unknown animal skull and feathers in his left hand. In his right hand, he was holding a small basket woven from the same scrub brushes lining the valley. He wore no shoes other than thin wood covering the bottoms of his feet held on by only a few strips of what looked to be cowhide.

The man walked over to Ian and offered him the basket. Ian cautiously took the basket and looked inside. A smile came over Ian's face instantly as he realized that the basket contained the baked bread he had smelled earlier. It was also filled with fruit and vegetables.

Ian looked up at the man and thanked him for the food and pulled out a hunk of bread and started to devour it without a moment's hesitation. Ian felt that he had never tasted something so good.

Ian could tell that the baked bread was fresh and that they layered it with butter or lard or something delicious. Ian pulled out the fruit and vegetables and devoured them with the same intensity. After eating half the contents of the basket, Ian regained his composure and asked the man to sit down. The man stood motionless while Ian devoured the contents of the basket. It wasn't until Ian offered the man his hospitality, did he move.

The warmth of the fire and the excellent food helped to make Ian content, at least calm enough to consider the man's purpose. He asked, "What is your name, and why are you traveling in the wilderness?"

The man stood up and said in perfect English, "My name is Kehfun, and I am not wandering in the wilderness, you are."

Ian replied with a puzzled look, "I don't understand. Is this not the desert?"

Kehfun smiled with delight showing his bright teeth and said, "No, Ian, this is not the wilderness. You are only two kilometers from my village."

Ian was startled to know the man knew his name. He quickly asked, "How do you know my name?"

Kehfun replied, "Pierre and Leon Faison came to me in my dreams and told me of your plight. I am Kehfun Paridima, the shaman of my tribe. I am who you were to find, and it is I who you have found." ∞

CR

Chapter Twenty-Nine
Shaman

The crackling of the fire spewed hot flakes of scrub brush into the evening sky. An awkward pause filled the night. Ian was speechless for a moment while he considered what Kehfun had just told him. Ian asked, "How is it that you speak such perfect English?"

Kehfun sat down near Ian and pulled out two pieces of dried beef from a small pouch hanging from his waist sash. He handed one piece to Ian and bit into the other. He chewed on the meat for a moment then swallowed.

He looked at Ian with a broad smile and replied, "Christians came to my village when I was young. I attended their school and excelled at my studies, so much so, that I went to the University of Oxford and obtained a law degree. Oxford is where I first met your benefactor, Peckerage Hornblaster."

Ian sat up with relief on his face, and asked, "You know Pecky?"

Kehfun pulled out another two pieces of dried beef and handed one to Ian and devoured the other. He laid back on the palm tree, and continued, "Yes, I know Pecky. He and I became friends at Oxford. Elizabeth was among our group, as was Dan and Sam."

With an excited look on his face, Ian asked, "Do Pecky and my friends know that I'm here?"

"Yes, I've sent a messenger out this evening after I received word from Pierre and Leon Faison. Pecky and your friends should be showing up sometime tomorrow night. I believe he still has that old sleigh, right?"

Ian sat back with new comfort and replied, "Yes, the sleigh is how we came to Africa. I didn't totally appreciate the sleigh until I had to walk many miles through the wilderness. Kehfun, I don't understand how you could have talked with Pierre and Leon Faison when they are held prisoner?"

"I see that you still have much to learn. I thought that you would have had a better understanding of your potential. Pierre and Leon Faison exist in a place where there is no time or distance."

Ian asked, "Pecky has talked of different levels of energy all around us at the same time. Are Pierre and Leon residing in another level of energy?"

"Good, Ian. Yes, that is correct. Pierre and Leon Faison exist in another level of energy that we connect with through energy points.

"There are spiritual beings all around us in other realities. Ultimately, we are spiritual beings having a physical experience. Pierre and Leon Faison's home is not their prison, the void is their prison."

Ian scratched his head with a puzzled look on his face and asked, "Shouldn't we make our way to your village?"

Kehfun replied, "I think it would be best that we wait until morning. You most likely did not know this, but a pack of jackals had been on your trail since Moundou."

A stark look came over Ian's face as he considered jackals attacking him. "How did they know I was traveling in the desert. Are we safe?"

"Yes, we are safe. The jackals won't bother us if we are together and near a fire. Most bullies in life are fearful of any resistance, and they are no different.

"Legorian knew that you had left Moundou, so he sent his devotees to intercept you. What they might have done with you is still uncertain, because even the dark lord doesn't want you dead."

Ian asked, "If Legorian knew that I left Moundou, then why did he not stop me?"

"He can't prevent you from following your path. Legorian can only try to deceive you into making the wrong decision.

"Legorian is a bigger picture than just freedom of personal choice. I thought that Pecky would have already had this discussion with you, especially before you traveled in the wilderness."

Ian contemplated his next question carefully before asking. He wondered if he wanted to know the nature of Legorian, but asked anyway, "What is the nature of Legorian?"

Kehfun looked at Ian with his piercing eyes and asked, "Do you want to know the nature of Legorian?"

Ian thought long and hard and said, "Yes, I do."

"I feel privileged to tell you the story of the Infinite Father.

"You must know that the nature of our Infinite Father can never actually be communicated in this reality. Our Infinite Father lies inside everything that is living in this world.

"I can tell you a story that has been handed down from one shaman in my tribe to another. The story that I am about to convey is a metaphor for our existence in this world.

"In the beginning, our Infinite Father was confused about the nature of himself. Our Infinite Father wanted to know his self. He is endless, he cannot be separate from himself to gaze upon himself.

"The Infinite Father is creation, so he had an idea of creating himself so that he could gaze upon himself and know himself. The idea from our Infinite Father was so powerful that it created the beginning of our universe and every other universe that exists in this reality.

"What our Infinite Father created was an idea. Our Infinite Father created a world that was exactly opposite from whom he is. Our Infinite Father created a world of separation—where everything that existed in this world is not infinite but separate.

"He knew the world he observed, outside of his infinite self, was, in fact, the exact opposite of who he was.

"Our Infinite Father observed this world of separation through the eyes of every perceivable experience. He understood that everything in this world was the opposite of who he truly is.

"Through this process, he understood his true nature. By knowing what he is not, he could understand what he is.

"Ian, we are all part of our Infinite Father, having a collective experience in this world of separation. By knowing who we are not, we can start to realize who we are."

Kehfun sat back against the palm tree and observed Ian.

Ian sat back and looked up at the brilliant sky. For a long time, Kehfun and Ian did not speak. Ian contemplated the story with great reverence.

Ian looked at Kehfun and said, "In this story of our Infinite Father, I am him, experiencing the world outside of myself?"

Kehfun nodded his head in agreement.

Ian continued, "So, my purpose is to know myself by realizing who I am not? That the world I see outside of myself is only my perception of the world, but based on what?"

Kehfun moved closer to Ian and said, "If you feel cut off from the Infinite Father, the world will reflect your belief and support what you perceive.

"The world outside of us is only an illusion created by the Infinite Father to know himself.

"We are only separated by our perceptions. We all have different perceptions of the world outside of us. We might consider that others have the same belief in the world, but we will never know what others believe."

Ian replied, "Then if the world created our beliefs of how we perceive ourselves, then others are part of our perception, correct?

Kehfun sat up and started to laugh. He replied, "Yes, because those outside of us are an illusion. They are all part of us."

Ian started to laugh and said, "Then you are I, and I am you, and we are all together."

The epiphany about the world created a moment in Ian's life. He and Kehfun started to both laugh under the brilliant canopy of light.

Above them, the Milky Way galaxy took on a other worldly feel with many comets streaking across the night sky.

For a long time, Ian said nothing until another question arose, and he asked, "Then what part does Legorian play in this concept of our Infinite Father?

"If everyone outside of me is part of me, then am I not part of Legorian, and is he not part of me?"

Kehfun replied, "Everyone in this world is part of the Infinite Father. When the Infinite Father created this world, he created infinite experiences. Our Infinite Father is living these experiences through us. Each life is a spectrum of experiences that come close to the Infinite Father and move farthest away.

"Legorian is a being in this world that the Infinite Father created. Legorian is the exact opposite of the Infinite Father. Legorian is the keeper of this world. He perceives himself separate from the Infinite Father.

"The Infinite Father knew that the only way he could lose himself in this world was to go to sleep, forget that he is infinite.

"He created Legorian to help himself forget that he is infinite. Legorian's only job is to convince the Infinite Being that he is separate from himself."

Ian considered this and replied, "Then why does Legorian want to destroy me?"

"Ian, Legorian does not want to kill you. Legorian intends to destroy this world. Legorian believes by possessing you, he can enter the City of Light and destroy it."

Ian asked, "How does the City of Light fit in this story?"

"The Ancient City is closest to the Infinite Father. It is Eden. It is the paradise we lost when we wanted knowledge."

An epiphany came over Ian, and he exclaimed, "If Legorian intends to destroy this world that was created by the Infinite Father, would he not also end his own existence?"

"Correct, Ian. That concept often escapes others. You see, Legorian is insane."

Ian replied quickly, "Then are not we all insane?"

"Yes, Ian, we are all insane but to different degrees. We believe that this world is real. We believe that we are living lives, but we are only living an illusion.

"The closer we come to the Infinite Father, the less insane we become. The further we move away from the Infinite Father, the crazier we become. Legorian is the farthest away from the Infinite Father, so he is the most insane being in this world."

Ian noticed a heightened sense of being flowing over his mind and body. He started to feel separate from himself again, observing himself from someplace far away.

Ian asked, "Do you feel separate from your body right now?"

Kehfun laughed, "Yes, what you are feeling is called extended. Whenever you contemplate the truth or speak the truth with others, you become extended. It is a state of being when you occupy your true self, not your ego.

"The world is made up of dualities. There are our spiritual selves and our ego-self. We are both of those entities at the same time. The more we speak the truth and live the truth, the closer we come to our spiritual selves. The more we deceive, the closer we come to our ego selves, the part of us that is Legorian."

Ian's head started to spin. He thought of his home in the valley of the two green mountains. He thought about his friends and family. He considered everything in his life to be an illusion created by him. It made total sense and no sense at all. He felt that maybe even his beliefs were part of a duality.

He thought about Kehfun and wondered why a man with such wisdom is living in the wilderness of Africa. He considered that the world would be better off with Kehfun speaking the truth to millions, not just his village. `

Ian sat up and asked, "Why are you living in a village in the middle of the wilderness?"

Kehfun laughed, showing his bright white teeth and responded, "Ian, this is not the desert. Where I lived for twenty years was the wasteland.

"In my youth, I was arrogant. I excelled at school and felt better than the people in my village. I would often make my mother and father cry with my conceit. You see I was part of a lineage of shamans that went back thousands of years. My father wanted me to become the village shaman. As I learned about the outside world, I felt that I was more significant than my tribe. I was bigger than my heritage.

"The Christians at the school saw my ambition and genius and helped me make the transition to the modern world. When I graduated from the Christian school, the University of Oxford accepted me as a student.

"When I left the village, I swore that I would never return and would do everything in my power to wipe away my past. I became embarrassed by my life in the village and by my family.

"I found myself in England wearing trendy clothing and living a modern life. After I graduated from Oxford, I obtained a position at a major law firm in New York City. I quickly rose to an executive position as a defense litigator. I bought a beautiful apartment near Central Park. I went on vacations all around the world, and I met a woman that was from a prominent New York family.

"Everything about my life fed my conceit. I felt that I had achieved everything that I set out to do, but something started to happen after twenty years in the city. Emptiness began to swell up in my heart. I began to have visions of terrible things, and I started to slip into darkness. I started to hear voices and see things that only disturbed me. The sounds were from my homeland in Africa, calling me back.

"At first, I started to drink alcohol and do drugs to silence the voices. The more I tried to forget, the more I became content to slide into darkness.

"My work suffered because I started to see all my clients as liars. I began to see my marriage as a lie because she was only interested in me for my wealth.

"The wealthier I became, the more isolated I was from the natural world. Soon I found myself in a penthouse office far above the world isolated from even those in my firm. I found myself sitting in front of my computer with a headset on, lying with every breath I took.

"Then something wonderful happened. The voices of my ancestors started to reach me. I began to hear the music of my homeland once again.

"When I was young, my father told me that each shaman in the family goes through a transformation. A shaman lives in the world and then is given a choice to let go of the world. To basically be in the world but not of the world.

"Each shaman is given a chance to serve the people to 'Let Go and Let God.'

"When I heard my calling, I could not deny it anymore. At forty-eight, I left my possessions, my wife, my job, and New York City and came back to my people.

"When I arrived, I was greeted first by my father, the shaman of our village. He said our ancestors have been calling you. It is time you become a shaman.

"That was ten years ago, and I have never regretted once leaving the emptiness that is New York City. I do wonder about my wife, but she found out where I had gone and decided to take another path.

"Ian, we were not meant to live in cubicles and offices that are far from the natural world. We were supposed to embrace our natural mother and feel the dirt between our toes and in our souls."

Kehfun looked at Ian with loving eyes and gave him a blanket that he had brought with him. He patted Ian on the back and said, "It is late, and we have discussed much. Things will become clearer in the light of day."

Ian looked up at Kehfun and said, "We are safe?"

"Yes, Ian, we are safe. You can sleep knowing that everything is right with the world." ❧

ଔ

Chapter Thirty
The Oath

The night spent in the wilderness around the fire with Kehfun had enlightened Ian to another way of thinking. The fear he had of Legorian had dissipated. He saw Legorian's part in the drama unfolding with new eyes.

The people of Kehfun's village were kind and generous to Ian the minute he arrived. The women of the town already had a traditional tribal breakfast prepared of young cassava leaves with the juice of palm nuts, marrow puree cooked with plantain leaves, and parcels of meat enclosed in plantain leaves.

The vibrant colors and enticing smells of the food added to Ian's hunger. He made every effort not to glom his meal. He was amazed at how delicious everything was.

The tiny village overlooked a ravine that led down to a large muddy river. Ian could see the beautiful blue Lake Lagdo in the distance. Surrounding the lake were similar green shrubs and trees he noticed back in Moundou, but the energy of the lake was different. He could sense the region was abundant with life.

Kehfun's village was simple. The settlement consisted of a dozen homes made from white clay with roofs made of palm branches. Many of the huts had no windows or doors, just openings.

A few homes were near the river to the west, but most were close to the center. The village common had lush, thick green grass with rocks around the edges, apparently acting as a wall to keep herd animals in check.

Some of the outlying buildings had rusted metal roofs and wooden doors but looked to be for storage, not homes. It was apparent that a close community was critical in the village, Ian, surmised for mutual survival.

Chickens and goats walked freely around the village, which led Ian to believe he either ate chicken or goat during his breakfast. He considered that he might have eaten a snake or fruit bat. There was a plentiful supply slithering and flying around the area.

He never knew how big a fruit bat was until a few came close to his head on his way to the village.

Ian had a new respect for the way of life in the village after his discussion with Kehfun. He might have felt in the past that the villagers were missing out on the modern world, but after their talk, Ian realized that they were missing out on nothing, only stress, anxiety, and confusion.

After breakfast, Ian walked around the village for most of the day talking to the tribal elders. He felt it strange that all the people of the community spoke perfect English. He mentioned his surprise of the villagers' knowledge of the English language to Kehfun, but he just smiled a big grin and laughed.

The day went by fast, with much hard work done by the tribe. Fishermen showed up late in the afternoon with an abundant catch for the evening meal. The closer it came to sundown the more Ian became impatient and nervous for his friends to arrive as promised.

The evening flicker, just before the sun submerged below the horizon, showed a familiar sight in the far distance. Coming fast and growing from the east was a tiny object.

A chill ran down Ian's spine as he recognized the sleigh. Ian looked at the sleigh with bewilderment because it felt that he had not seen the sleigh in a millennium.

When he was in the wilderness, he sometimes forgot about the sleigh and his friends. He felt his trek through the wilds had changed him in some unforeseen way.

Pecky, in his usual cautious fashion, slowed the sleight a few hundred feet from Kehfun's village. Once he received the okay from Kehfun, he moved forward and landed the sleigh just outside of the village common.

Only a few days earlier, Ian thought that he most likely would never see his friends again. He wondered if his friends would notice any difference in him, the distinction he felt in his heart and soul.

Bee came running towards Ian with open arms. She flung herself onto him with an embrace that was uncommon for Bee. She had tears in her eyes and said, "We thought you were dead."

Ogden and Pecky soon followed. Ogden patted Ian on the back, and Pecky embraced Ian with his flippers, and said, "Well done, Ian. I see Legorian didn't get the best of you?"

Ian noticed a tear in Pecky's eye, which he worked hard not to show. Ian felt a great compassion from Pecky. He also looked different. Pecky looked dangerous, more like a warrior.

Pecky looked over at Kehfun, and said, "Thanks for finding our good friend. By the way, is it time for dinner? I'm famished."

Kehfun gave a warm pat on Pecky's flipper and informed the travelers a feast was ready, including traditional tribal music.

Bee turned to Ian and asked, "Ian, you have said nothing on our arrival. Does the cat have your tongue?"

Ian realized that he had been observing the arrival of his friends and had not thanked them for coming to his rescue. Ian said, "Sorry, but it is so strange to see all of you again after what I went through. I can't believe that I'm here talking to my good friends."

Ogden and Bee all looked at Ian with a puzzled expression. Bee walked up to Ian and asked, "Ian, what are you saying? What gibberish are you speaking?"

Ian withdrew with a stark look on his face and said, "What do you mean gibberish? I'm just thanking all of you for your efforts."

Kehfun intervened and explained to the group, "Ian is not speaking nonsense, he is speaking the native language of my tribe, Bakousi. He has been speaking my language with perfect dialect since I found him in the wilderness."

A powerful energy flowed through Ian that he had not felt before. It seemed like a realization. He knew why he was able to comprehend everyone in the village. He grasped that Kehfun's people were not speaking perfect English. He was speaking their language.

Bee drew back in bewilderment at the knowledge of Ian's transformation. She asked Kehfun, "How is it that Ian learned your language?"

Pecky and Kehfun answered Bee in unison, "He is a true heart."

A smile came over Pecky's face as he continued to answer Bee's question, "I had almost forgotten, but one of the transformations a true heart goes through is a connection with all languages.

"He, in other words, is jacked into the Infinite Source of knowledge. All experience, knowledge, and memory are held forever in the life energy field."

Bee interjected, "I still don't understand."

Pecky continued, "Everyone in the world has seven energy points. The points start with our feet and go up to our heads. They connect us to the Source and the world outside. These seven energy connections dictate our understanding and actions in this world.

Kehfun interjected, "I believe our friend Ian had unblocked his fifth energy point when he journeyed through the wilderness. The fifth energy point has a connection to this world through communication."

Bee asked, "How can unblocking an energy point help Ian learn a language?"

Kehfun responded, "He hasn't learned my tribal tongue. He has remembered it. All knowledge is in an infinite library. This library is part of our Infinite Father, who experiences everything in this reality through us.

"Our journey through this reality has already happened. We are only looking back on an idea that our Infinite Father created to know himself, or herself in your case, Bee.

Pecky interjected, "So, our Infinite Father created this reality to know what it would be like to be separate from himself to identify himself. We are all part of our Infinite Father having a collective experience in a world of separation."

Pecky continued, "As Ian unblocks all his energy points connecting his spiritual self with his physical self, he will be able to access all knowledge in the life energy field. Ian is looking back on the residual experience that already happened and remembering. He is obtaining language like a radio tuning into a frequency of the music."

Ian asked, "I would like to speak English to my friends. How do I change my language?"

Kehfun smiled and laughed once again, "You already have Ian. Now that you realize your connection to the Source, you are going to be able to access knowledge freely by knowing that you can."

Ogden voiced to the group what was on everyone's mind, "I still don't truly understand how an energy point can tap into this infinite library that you speak of."

Kehfun replied, "Of course, my dear friend Ogden, because if you understood, then you would be a true heart, and a true heart like Ian only comes along every thousand years.

"In time, you will have a deeper understanding of your connection to the Source, but none of us will ever during this life have the connection Ian will have."

Pecky patted his belly with his flipper and said, "All this talk of infinity has made me infinitely hungry. Let's eat."

Kehfun guided the travelers to a large tent made from spun goat hair near the center of the village. The women in the town had already set up the tent with beautiful rugs and pillows, carpets of spun goat hair and horse skin. A cool breeze flowing up from the lake moved through the tent keeping the temperature quite comfortable for dinner.

Villagers brought in colorful platters of food as soon as the travelers and the village elders settled in the feast tent. The women positioned one large plate in the middle of the tent with yellow maize topped with many kinds of meat and local fish. Spices filled the tent with smells that Bee had never encountered before.

Soon tribal musicians started playing local songs that spoke of deeds done by brave souls. Ian found that he was able to understand the words the musicians sang. The instruments were homemade with great love and care, and many of them passed down from one generation to another.

The festivities went long into the night with much merriment among the villagers and their guests. Just after sunset, the evening sky started to show the Milky Way galaxy with intensity. It created an almost surreal experience for the group.

Ian could feel a heightened sense of energy was moving through the camp. He considered that this might be the last time he and his friends could truly relax before they entered the Congo.

Little by little most everyone in the village went off to their huts for the night, including Pecky and Kehfun.

The women of the village cleared all the food and plates in the large tent and brought in cushions and more pillows for Ian and Ogden.

Bee went to a tent with other single women. Ian and Ogden were left alone in the large tent to fend for their selves.

After midnight an almost full moon rose in the east and cast a bright light down on the village. Ian and Ogden could see Lake Lagdo in the distance. They were wide awake even though most of the villagers were in their huts asleep.

The two sat in chairs outside the tent and watched the evening sky slowly move overhead. A set of stars rose in the east that Ian knew were three of the fifty-seven stars that were navigable by sailors.

Ian looked up and said to Ogden, "Growing up, I thought my father was a simple sailor. Pecky told me back in Vermont that he was part of a world that I would have never imagined. Now, I am in the middle of that world, with many relying on the better angels of my nature.

"Not one of my friends has asked me about my time with Legorian or my journey through the wilderness. I thought for sure that Bee would have drilled me for information, but she kept her distance the whole night."

Ogden replied, "She's scared, Ian. It is not her responsibility to comfort you; it is your job to comfort her. She is looking for signs of the Ian she knew only weeks ago. She knows that something has changed about you. She knows that her feelings towards you have changed, and maybe that frightens her most of all."

"What feelings?"

"For a true heart, you are oblivious. Bee has affection for you.

"Of course, a woman's feelings are complicated. Especially since her feelings for you are mixed up with the knowledge that you are a true heart and are the only person that can help us enter the City of Light."

"She has feelings for me? I thought for sure she was interested in you. She seemed to buzz around you. I've considered myself a third wheel whenever you are around."

"I told you that women have complicated feelings for men. She has been "buzzing" around me to push you away because she doesn't understand her feelings yet and wants to put distance between her and you.

"Ian, I might not be a true heart, but my heart is still sensitive enough to the feelings Bee has for you. I think most of all, she considers her feelings might be a burden you don't need."

"I do have feelings for Bee, but feel conflicted. I know I must focus on the task before me. I know how many people are relying on me.

"Ogden, I was terrified in the wilderness. I didn't know what to do other than continue alone. Legorian deceived me during my stay at the plantation near Moundou. I didn't know if the dark lord continued to deceive me. I still don't understand why he just let me leave."

The moon started to move below the western sky, creating a long shadow over the village. Ian and Ogden heard a group of animals in the distance that sounded like a lion's roar.

Ogden patted Ian on the back and said, "I know, Ian, that it is not easy taking on your responsibilities. I battle with being an energy sprite every day. I haven't seen my family or have been home in more than four years. The commitment each of us has to make to the task is more than most would make."

Ian asked, "How did you become an energy sprite-was your family involved with the Life Energy Consortium?"

"My parents still don't know what I do or where I am. They think I am away at college in Europe. I send them postcards and letters every so often.

"My story is long and complicated, and many times, like you, I have a hard time realizing that I am doing this job. Sam Dupuis approached me four years ago. Somehow the Life Energy Consortium keeps records of possible energy sprites and others who can help the world.

"I felt different from the others in my family and my town. I considered that I was supposed to leave and do something extraordinary. So, after high school, when Dan offered me an adventure, I left and went to Italy to train for a year. At first I considered it might be like the Peace Corps but, boy was I wrong.

"Spain was only my second energy sprite job without senior sprite help. When I accepted the group's offer, I didn't consider that I would not be able to have relationships outside the order. They don't tell you that at first.

"I have a brother and three sisters back in California that I have never felt close to, but still miss. I might never see them again. I don't quite know how I feel about that, but for the moment, I am accepting my fate. I know how important our job is and how many people we affect. Ian, do you have any siblings?"

"No, I am an only child. My mother and I are close. My father has been gone a lot during my life. I always envied my friends who had older brothers, even the ones who tormented them."

"Well, Ian, consider me your brother. We might not be the same flesh, but we are of the same spirit. We will make a blood oath that, if necessary, we will forfeit our lives to the quest."

Ogden stood up and took out a large bowie knife and passed it over his palm, creating a small cut from his pinky to thumb. Ian stood up and did the same. Under the brilliant early morning sky, Ian and Ogden committed themselves to their oath and their journey to the City of Light. ☸

CB

Chapter Thirty-One
Jackals in the Mist

The same animal roar that Ian and Ogden heard the night before was outside the village. The sound was so deafening that it woke everyone. Pecky, Kehfun, and many of the warriors in the community came running out of their tents.

On the ridge just to the west of the village moved a pack of ten or eleven jackals slightly hidden in shadow.

The jackals appeared to be almost transparent as the sun rose in the east. The roar was gruesome, more a sound of death.

Pecky turned to Kehfun and said, "Legorian knows that we're here. Your village is in danger, so, unfortunately, it is time for us to leave."

When the sun broke away from the horizon and rose into the sky, the jackals disappeared entirely. Kehfun told Pecky that these jackals were not made of flesh and blood but made up of the dark energy of Legorian. They only had power in the shadows. In the light of day, they cease to exist. Pecky had until sundown to find sanctuary.

Pecky knew he needed to get to Hilary before nightfall to secure the travelers with their next destination. He knew he needed to move fast.

Pecky moved quickly from tent to tent rousting his traveling companions from their sleep. Ian and Ogden had fallen asleep three hours earlier and were hard to wake.

Bee walked out of her tent with a warm smile on her face. With her came Kehfun's youngest daughter. A bright-faced eight year old, draped in a beautifully decorated garment made up of vibrant green, brown, and gold tribal designs.

Ian and Ogden staggered out of the huts with drool still on their chins and gunk in their eyes. They looked at each with a warm smile. They knew that their relationship has changed in a significant way.

Pecky commented, "Maybe you two will go to sleep earlier next time, knowing we have to move on the next day. Well, youth has its advantages, I guess, which includes being able to stay up all night and function the next day."

Ian and Ogden both let out a loud groan as they stretched their arms towards the sky. Ogden asked, "What is the big hurry? I was hoping to sleep in and have a late breakfast."

Pecky replied with a bit of irritation, "We are not on vacation, Ogden. There is a task at hand that we must pursue with all haste. We spotted a pack of Legorian's jackals on a ridge outside of the village. If the jackals know we're here, so does Legorian.

"Ian might have escaped Legorian, but he has no use for the rest of us. I don't feel like fending off jackals this evening. Hilary has been waiting much longer at the watering hole than I initially expected him to stay."

Ian interjected, "I had almost forgotten about Hilary. Pecky, how is Hilary going to help us enter the Congo?"

"Hilary has a particular set of skills and experience that we will find invaluable. He grew up in the Congo, not far from the entrance to the City of Light. He can take us directly to the chamber."

After a quick breakfast, Pecky and the rest of the travelers loaded the sleigh with food and supplies generously donated by Kehfun's people. Kehfun offered his eldest son, Teddy, to help the group travel to their next destination.

Teddy, named after Theodore Roosevelt, was in line to become the next shaman of his tribe. He wanted to experience the world outside of the village before he took on the duties of the shaman.

Teddy looked resistant to step aboard the sleigh. Pecky assured him that the sleigh was safe, and no harm would come to him. Teddy didn't look convinced but hopped on board anyway.

Kehfun hugged Pecky, Ian, Bee, and Ogden and then spoke a traditional prayer for each one. He assured Pecky that Teddy knew the way to Hilary's favorite watering hole and would be safe to return to the village on his own.

Kehfun was preparing his son to take a walkabout. It is a custom in the tribe for a young warrior to take a year traveling in the wilderness. In Kehfun's tribe, the modern world is the wilderness. Teddy will have an option to experience the contemporary world before he assumes his role as shaman.

The villagers came out to see the travelers along their way. There were many gifts and hugs given to the group. Ian thought to himself that these people have little but are among the kindest and most generous he had encountered.

The villagers do have what most people want, a community that works together with an appreciation and love for each other.

Pecky assumed his position as a pilot and skillfully lifted the sleigh into the air. The crowd of onlookers gave out a single gasp as the green light that surrounded the sleigh lifted it into the sky.

It was still unclear to Bee how a craft such as a sleigh can fly. She understood the concept of life energy and how it surrounds us, penetrates us, and holds the universe together. She was confused about how an object as heavy as the sleigh could float on energy. She laughed out loud at the thought of Star Wars, and maybe the force is real.

Teddy pointed in a direction to the southwest of his village. Pecky dutifully pointed the sleigh in the same direction. The sleigh sped off with the ground one hundred feet below them.

Pecky turned to the others and said, "We are moving into an area with civil war, and many of the tribes along our way will not be as kind as Kehfun's people. We will have to be extra careful now that we are getting close to the Congo."

The landscape below moved with a blur as the sleigh flew in the direction of the travelers' next destination, and hopefully, the last companion needed to complete their quest.

Ian considered for a moment all the new friends he made since he started this journey. He wondered what would have come of him if Pecky didn't come knocking on his door many months ago. He realized that the friends he made have become as vital to him as fulfilling his promise of finding the Ancient City.

The long green and brown sloping hills of northern Cameroon blended from one into another. The closer the sleigh came to Lake Lagdo, the lusher and greener the flora.

To the north, two giraffes nibbled on some low-hanging leaves. To the south, a small herd of African elephants sluggishly walked along an old trail beaten down by the animals that live in the area. A herd of gazelles dashed in all directions as the sleigh moved overhead.

The group could hear the familiar sound of lions growling in the distance but could not see the pride in the dense underbrush and trees. Ian knew how lucky he was to be in the sleigh instead of moving through the bush on foot.

He valued his time in the wilderness, but he found it much more enjoyable to watch the African landscape from a few hundred feet.

He realized that his time in the desert had committed him to the task more than ever. After his experience, he understood the haste that Pecky has been pushing—to move forward, always forward.

A light mist started to rise as the sleigh glided gracefully over the brilliant blue waters of Lake Lagdo. Surrounding Lake Lago were dense green and brown brush with sweeping low-lying hills on all sides. Every so often, a small village with cut-out boats and people walking about appeared below the travelers, but most of the lake was wild.

Ian remembered that the group was meeting Hilary at some watering hole. He considered that there must be some town or fort out in the wilderness that had a bar or a pub. This thought of entering a bar in the middle of this rough country gave Ian a bad feeling. He couldn't imagine a bar in the wilderness that would not be tough, and maybe a little too harsh for their safety.

Teddy pointed to another location on the lake, and Pecky guided the sleigh in the new direction. Ian felt that Teddy was uneasy with his position as a guide. He wondered if Kehfun forced his son to serve the travelers, or maybe Teddy was just anxious with everything outside of his village—the only world he has known.

Ian reflected that Teddy might not be able to take over the family responsibility of shaman. If Teddy does enter the modern world, his perception of his world will change dynamically, for good or bad.

Teddy stood up in the sleigh and pointed to a hidden cove to the southwest. Pecky nodded in acknowledgment. He turned the fast-moving sleigh towards the encampment that outlined the shore. Just outside the town, a dense green forest rose, expanding out in all directions and farther to the southwest.

The closer the travelers came to the town, the more they could see that it was old and abandoned. Most of the structures were made from wood from the surrounding forest. Most huts burned long ago, and the rest decayed over time. There was no sign of life in the village. Scattered throughout the town were fishing nets and broken boats left to rot in the hot African sun.

Pecky turned around and mentioned, "The humidity and heat in this area break down what humankind had made quickly. Please prepare for landing, make sure all your belongings are stored, and you have your seat belts tightly secure, and of course, no smoking in the lavatories."

A small laugh came out of Pecky's mouth with this quip. Pecky's three companions did not find it funny, and Teddy didn't understand the reference.

It crossed Bee's mind that Pecky would have had to fly on a commercial airliner to tell that joke, but when would have Pecky traveled anywhere in public? She shook the notion off as ridiculous.

Pecky slowed the sleigh outside the village to make sure that no unexpected events would befall the explorers. As soon as Pecky considered the area safe, he slowly moved forward.

The structure must have been a meeting hall or church because the wood was made from modern supplies. Pecky skillfully positioned the sleigh inside the remains of the building, hiding it from outside view.

Ian looked around for a pub but saw none. He turned to Pecky and asked, "Pecky, are we too late to meet Hilary? I don't see anyone or any watering hole in sight."

"Not to worry, Ian, Hilary is a short walk from here. The village is abandoned for more than a hundred years. I just wanted a safe place that we could leave the sleigh.

"This village is cursed, and the other tribes will not enter this area. A Zorkin once reigned here and kept the villagers souls imprisoned for five hundred years. The Zorkin moved on but left lasting dark energy that keeps all others out. The sleigh will be safe, I guarantee it."

Teddy pointed down a path that led into the dense forest to the south. The travelers collected their packs with food and supplies, not knowing where the road would lead them or how long they will be gone.

Ian made sure he had extra water and food just in case. He remembered when he was in the wilderness and was short of rations.

The forest came upon the group fast and with a massive force of energy. Ian felt that the woods were ancient. Many of the trees had strong bases holding up a large canopy covering the forest floor with darkness.

Pecky reiterated that they were all to stay close. No one was to wander away from the group. He assured them that he might not come after them if they don't heed his warning.

All the travelers let out a laugh, knowing that Pecky would never leave any of them behind. Ian, Bee, and Ogden had come to know Pecky's false threats and take them with a grain of salt.

The travelers with Teddy, leading the way, moved deeper into the forest.

Bee walked up on Ian and Ogden, asking, "I heard you two were up late talking last night. What were you talking about, or maybe it is just boys' talk?"

Ian and Ogden looked at each other with questioning eyes and started to laugh. Ogden replied, "You are mistaken if you think we were talking about you, my lady."

Bee replied with an irritated tone, "You're such a snot sometimes, Ogden. I wasn't thinking you were talking about me. I was thinking you might be talking about something important, but of course, you most likely were discussing something stupid."

Bee stomped off towards Teddy and Pecky. Ian and Ogden breathed in the dust she kicked up around them.

It occurred to Ian that the relationship he had with Bee has changed into something different. Something he didn't know how to navigate. It seemed the more they liked each other, the less they were willing to talk about anything.

The forest rising around the group was not a jungle but a dry forest with twisted branches creating a feeling of claustrophobia. A host of bugs and snakes seemed to be the only occupants except for monkeys moving high in the canopy.

The path moved through a long tunnel of trees. In the distance, Ian could see sunlight coming through the canopy above. He could see that there was some clearing.

Ian walked up to Pecky and asked, "I thought you said that we were to meet Hilary at his favorite watering hole. Is there some kind of fort or village ahead of us with a pub?"

"Ian, why did you think Hilary would be at some pub? We are to meet him at his favorite watering hole, which is a spring in the middle of this forest."

"Sorry, Pecky, I thought we were to meet Hilary at some rough bar. You see, back home in Vermont, a watering hole is a pub where dangerous men hang out."

"Ian, I think it is best that when things are not clear, you should ask, so not to confuse the situation."

The closer the group got to the clearing, the more sunlight shone through the dense canopy. It wasn't until the last tree was behind them could the travelers see the size and breadth of the clearing.

The clearing was a deep canyon cut right out of the limestone that lined the walls. The canyon was the size of two or three football fields with a bright blue pond right in the center. There were animals all around the lake drinking from the pool.

Pecky exclaimed, "This is not Ian's rough bar, but this place can be dangerous because it has all types come to drink from these waters. So be careful and don't wander away from the group."

The group moved to the edge of the south end of the pond. Ian looked down into the crystal-clear water and could not see any bottom. To the north, a pride of lions came out of the forest to drink from the pond. They just gave the travelers an inquiring eye but did not move towards them.

Pecky mentioned, "This spring is prehistoric and has a bottom that goes down more than a thousand feet. The local tribes feel that these waters are spiritual because animals come here to drink but do not attack each other.

"The elephants have been coming here for thousands of years. They bury their kin in shallow graves surrounding the spring. An elephant graveyard is a sacred place."

Bee asked, "I don't see anyone in the canyon. Do you think Hilary is still in the area?"

"Yes, Teddy has assured me that Hilary will show up soon. He must be foraging in the forest," replied Pecky.

Ogden asked, "What kind of man forages in the forest?"

Pecky replied, "Hilary is not a man. I'm sorry to have misled you."

Bee interjected, "Well, if Hilary is not a man, what is he?"

At this moment, the ground started to rumble. Something big was moving towards the group through the western edge of the forest.

A moment later, a large animal came bounding out of the woods towards the group. The long stride of the animal was graceful and mesmerizing. Instead of running, the travelers just watched as this huge and muscular beast came towards them.

As fast as he moved, he stopped a few feet away. The creature stood on his hind legs and said, "Pecky, I thought you would never make it."

Pecky smiled and replied to Bee's question, "You see Hilary is not a man. He is a silverback gorilla." ✄

CʒƐ

Chapter Thirty-Two
Sir Hilary?

Ian sensed that Pecky was a bit scared of his friend Hilary. This was the first time Ian had seen any fear in Pecky's eyes or felt fear in his heart. This gave Ian a little bit of comfort knowing that Pecky was, well not human, but close.

"I'm sorry, my good friend. I never thought that it would take us this long to reach Cameroon," explained Pecky with a worried look.

Hilary's presence fascinated everyone. On his hind legs, Hilary was over six feet tall with bristling black and gray hair covering his body. His muscular form ebbed and flowed like the tide every time he moved. What was most striking about Hilary was his powerful jet-black eyes. He seemed to scrutinize each person's soul, on whoever he directed his commanding gaze.

Hilary bounded over to Ian and responded in a deep husky voice, "So this human is what all this fuss is about, huh, Pecky? Do you think you can enter the City of Light?

Ian became nervous, with Hilary standing so close. The last time Ian saw a live silverback gorilla was when he was nine with his father at the National Zoo in Washington, D.C. The gorilla was behind a glass barrier.

"Ian, you do not have to fear me. I mean you no harm. I'm just a little annoyed that I have been waiting for so long. I assure you that your journey to the Ancient City is paramount to my interests, and of my homeland trapped in the wake of Legorian's wrath."

Ian took a step back and responded, "I'm sorry, I'm just a little surprised by your presence. Pecky didn't explain to us that you are a silverback gorilla. All he said is that you can lead us to the entrance to the City of Light. I assumed that you were human. To answer your question, yes, I feel that I am ready for the task at hand."

Hilary looked at Pecky and laughed, "Peckerage, I see you are still up to your old tricks. Pecky likes to keep information close at hand. I believe he loves creating a little bit of drama."

Pecky responded, "Hilary, my friend, I just didn't want Ian to worry about the validity of my plans to enter the Congo."

Hilary spun around to the group with force, and said, "So, I guess I will introduce myself. I am Sir Hilary Edmonton, king of the gorillas, living in the valley of the seven moons, and guardian to the City of Light in the Congo. What is your name, young lady?"

Pecky stepped up with renewed confidence, and replied, "This is Beatrice, but you can call her Bee, this is Kundu's son Teddy, and of course you already know Ogden."

Hilary leaped over to Bee and held out his enormous hand with powerful fingers. Bee gingerly placed her hand in Hilary's. He gently patted Bee's hand and said, "It is so good to meet you, my dear, I know we will become good friends."

Hilary turned to Teddy and said, "I've known your father for many years, Teddy, I hope you are as good a man as he."

Teddy replied, "So do I, sir."

Hilary replied, "Hilary, son, you can call me Hilary." Hilary abruptly turned to Ogden and said, "Yes, Ogden and I are good old friends, aren't we Ogden?"

Ogden sheepishly replied, "It was my first mission, Hilary. You can't still be upset?"

Hilary delicately patted Ogden on his back and said, "No, Ogden, I am not mad at you. My hope is that Ian will make everything right again."

Bee interjected, "What happened between you and Ogden?"

"Nothing happened between Hilary and me, it was just a mission that went awry. Remember what Robert Burns wrote, "The best-laid plans of mice and men often go awry.""" Replied Ogden uncomfortably.

Hilary gave Ogden a quick irritated look and continue. "Well, Bee, a few years ago, Legorian's devotees entered the valley that my kin has called home for more than ten thousand years.

"As I said before, my troop are the guardians of a secret portal to the City of Light. Legorian did not know about this portal until a few years ago. Legorian cannot enter the Ancient City, but he did infest the area with his dark energy and create a malaise that holds everyone prisoner.

"Ogden was sent to help heal the energy and free my wife and three children, but something went wrong."

Ogden interjected with sorrow, "When I arrived, Legorian did not hold the area yet. To shift the energy back to the light, I needed to get Hilary's wife and children out. During the confusion, another tribe of gorillas entered the valley and captured his family. I just got out with my life."

Ian interjected, "How can removing Hilary's family change the energy back to the light?"

Hilary sat up and replied, "Because Legorian knows that I would never challenge the other gorilla tribe as long as they have my family. It wasn't Ogden's fault. It was mine. I should have made my family my top priority. I was on the other side of the world, attending to another task.

"When we sent Ogden to recover my family, we thought that it would be a simple extraction. I didn't know about the other gorillas, or that Legorian put in place one of his nastiest devotees, a Zorkin known as Dark Angel. I believe Dark Angel is different from the other Zorkins. I think it is one of the heads of the snake, as you might say."

Bee chimed in, "So, Ogden, three energy spirt assignments went awry, Africa, Spain, and what was the other one? How many have succeeded?"

Ogden rolled his eyes and replied, "Plenty, my lady, plenty. I'm batting around four hundred if you must know."

Hilary pulled a tasty branch of leaves off a nearby bush and continued, "You see, the odds are against us for a full assault. The only way I can free my family is by having Ian open the City of Light. This act will set my tribe free. Many times, the less violent and simplest plan is the right one."

"Where are we going, and where is the portal to the City of Light?" Bee asked.

Hilary took a bit of leaf, chewed a second, and then replied, "On the banks of the Congo River below the Yangambi Research Station, the library, to be specific."

Bee interjected, "Who would build a research station in the middle of the dense jungle?"

Hilary continued, "The Station is the former Belgian headquarters for all the primary research in the Congo going back to around 1930."

"How big is the research station? Will we be able to find it in the dense jungle?" asked Ian.

Hilary kept munching on a nearby bush. "We will have no problem finding the research station. It covers around 33 km right next to the Congo River. It contains I believe more than 200 buildings, including the library.

"An ancient human tribe and shaman maintain and guard the entrance to the area. They keep the research station immaculate. It is quite interesting to walk the grounds. The Station is more 1,000 miles from any other man-made city.

"Legorian can't step one foot, if he has one, near the research station. The human tribe that maintains it live in peace."

"Are there still Belgians working at the research station? If there are, how are we to navigate to the entrance to the Ancient City? asked Bee.

"No, the Belgians all left the area back in early 1960 with Congolese independence. It seemed like only a second ago when I was young, well, younger. There used to be hundreds of scientists and other workers continually building and keeping the jungle back."

Bee asked with a worried look on her face, "Is it safe to enter the Congo?"

"It is a little bit of a story, but you should know that you are walking into a civil war," replied Hilary.

"What civil war?" Ian asked.

"Well, not one civil war but many. Many other countries have tried to conquer the Congo through persuasions of power and money and brutal acts.

"It really started with King Leopold II of Belgium. He wanted what most powerful men wish for—more power.

"King Leopolds wanted unrestricted access to the rejuvenating powers of the plants and minerals that are found nowhere else on the earth.

"These plants and minerals are most potent near and around the portal to the City of Light. My tribe has been blessed with long life and advanced intellect since we have been the guardians of the Ancient City. We have been butchered because of our responsibility, especially during King Leopold's reign of terror."

"How old are you, Hilary," asked Bee.

"Well, Bee, I feel like thirty-five, but I am around one hundred and twenty years old. I actually have lost track of my age after one hundred."

Ian interjected, "Hilary, did you know King Leopold?"

"No, I don't think he ever ventured into the Congo, but I did know some of his henchmen. King Leopold had many bullies doing unspeakable acts toward Congolese humans and my kind."

"How did a small country like Belgium take over such a large area in Africa?" Asked Ian.

Hilary continued, "Leopold created a Congolese colony with support from some other influential evil people. Leopold created the Congo Free State in, I believe, 1885. It was anything but free for the native population. This was one of the bloodiest times in my tribe's history

"Many white immigrants who moved to the Congo after the end of World War II were treated as superior to native black Congolese and, of course, to animals that occupied the area.

"By 1960, the Congo achieved independence, becoming the Republic of Congo under Patrice Lumumba and Joseph Kasa-Vubu.

"The Congo has continually been in one civil war after another with other

militant groups trying to take control of part of the Congo. I believe the
jungle and the massive size of the Congo have kept it from totally falling
into darkness.

"The Congo is one of the most precious gifts given to us by the Source,
and humankind has continually defecated all over the country."

Bee interrupted, "You did not answer my question, Hilary. Where is the
portal to the City of Light?"

Hilary wrinkled his brow and replied, "I'm sorry, sometimes I get distracted by my story. The hidden portal to the Ancient City is in a chamber
deep below the research center. Only a few know the exact location of the
entrance and how to access the chamber.'"

Ian interjected, "How do you know so much about the history of the Congo?"

Hilary kept munching on leaves and answered, "When the Belgians left,
they left all the books and research information in the library. Anyone can
read what happened. Funny thing is the Belgians recorded their own atrocities.
I guess they considered that the library was too remote for anyone to cause
them any pain.

"As I was saying, we will need to enter the country at Queso. There we
can safely stow the sleigh and move down the Congo River undetected."

Pecky interjected, "Why can't we just fly the sleigh all the way to Yangambi?"

Hilary knelt down on the ground and started to draw out a map with his
forefinger and replied, "We are about to enter one of the most dangerous regions in the world. As I said, civil war has been raging in the Congo for years,
and anyone trying to fly into the country will be shot down.

"There is a small concern that the dark energy Legorian unleased near
the research station has spread out. I'm not sure because I have not been back
in a few years."

"I feel our chances are greater if we move on the back roads of the country made mainly by my kind. We must stay away from other humans. Most
people are weak, and for a price, will expose us to Legorian and his devotees.
We have surprise on our side, and I don't want to announce our arrival to the
area with the sleigh."

Pecky interrupted with a confused look on his face, "Hilary, I don't know
if we have the upper hand. A pack of Legorian's jackals chased us out of
Kundu's village. The dark lord knows we are here, but he might not know
where we are going."

Hilary replied, "I guess we have no other choice than to move forward
and hope we can beat Legorian to Yangambi."

Pecky sighed and said, "Of course, it's not going to be easy. So, Hilary,
what do you recommend?"

Hilary roughly drew a map of northern Congo with different rivers intersecting each other and replied, "We make haste for a settlement just outside Queso. The village is a black-market supply depot of goods moving into the Congo, and of minerals being funneled out to less than reputable dealers.

"The transfer station is run by Reginald Smyth. Pecky, do you remember Reggie from Oxford?"

Pecky looked puzzled for a second and then replied, "Yes, Reggie. The red-haired Englishman that worked in the campus store. How did he end up in the Congo?"

"I got him a position with an exporter/importer that I knew who was setting up a business just outside of Queso. Anyway, Reggie will help us move into the Congo and hook us up with a boat traveling down the Sangha River.

"The ship will be full of black-market suppliers, so we will be most likely shot if captured. Don't worry, these men make this voyage many times a week, and it is in their best interest to keep us and their dealings under the radar of the local warlords and militants.

"We will work our way down the Sangha River to just before the entrance to the Congo River. At the point where the Sangha River meets the mighty Congo is a region called Mossaka. I know for a fact that Legorian has set spies in Mossaka.

"We will have to disembark from the cargo ship ten kilometers upriver from Mossaka. There is a town on the eastern shore of the river. It is protected from Legorian and his devotees by a powerful shaman. We can rest there for a day before moving on into the jungle."

Pecky interjected, "Can you trust that this shaman still has power in the area?"

Hilary looked at Pecky with his piercing black eyes and said, "I do get information coming out of the area. As far as I know, this village will be safe, but if it is not, then we will need to escape directly into the jungle with fewer supplies. I can eat almost anything in the jungle. I'm more concerned with our human guests and what they need to survive."

Hilary pointed back to the map he made in the dirt and said, "If we make it to the Congo River, we can hitch a ride on another cargo boat I know that runs in that area." Hilary then swept the map with his large hand and said, "There it is our present plan of action. Remember this is Africa, things change fast, and we may need to change with them. Any questions?"

A dark shadow moved over the group as the sun started to make progress below the tree line to the west. No one had any questions, but the knowledge of what lay ahead gave the travelers much to think about.

Teddy spoke up and said, "The sun will set in three hours, and I must set out for home if I am to beat the night. I wish you the best in your journey. I would come with you if my journey were not in another direction." Teddy shook hands with everyone and moved away through the brush in the direction of his village.

Pecky interjected just after Teddy left, "I fear that Teddy will never live up to his father's level of wisdom. Or be the man that his village will need to take over as shaman."

Hilary laughed and replied, "Actually, I knew Kundu before he entered Oxford, and he was much different than he is today. I think Teddy will do fine if he takes his walkabout. Most humans need a different perspective on life to see the bigger picture. Don't you agree, Ian?"

Ian looked at Hilary, wondering if he knew about his adventure in the wilderness and replied, "I agree whole-heartily."

Ogden injected, "We need to make plans before night falls. I'm still concerned about the jackals. They most likely have had time to catch up and might be upon us anytime soon."

Hilary replied, "I believe that it would be best to fly to Queso tonight. We should make it by daybreak. Pecky, I assume the sleigh is close by?"

Pecky replied, "Yes, hidden in the abandoned village on the edge of the lake."

Hilary sat up and replied, "Well, let's go."

The group of travelers moved through the brush back to the abandoned lake village, where the sleigh sat waiting for the next dangerous leg of their journey. In the dense dark brush, many sets of eyes watched as the group moved away.

Legorian's jackals would not take on such a massive silverback gorilla. Hilary knew this because before he left, he looked back in the direction of the jackals with pure hatred. Hatred for those who have separated him from those he loved most. ∞

CR

Chapter Thirty-Three
Heart of Darkness

The ten-hour night flight from Lake Lagdo outside Queso was supposed to give the group some rest before their journey into the Congo. Each member bundled up in a blanket in a different corner of the sleigh with the hope of sleep, but no one slept.

Hilary and Pecky kept a watchful eye discussing their plans late into the night. Ian thought it strange that Pecky did not sleep. He has not seen a situation yet that Pecky would not grab some sleep. He knew the conditions they were flying into were dangerous just from the difference in Pecky's habits.

Hilary was still a mystery. Ian could feel that Hilary was a being of light and hope and held little fear in his heart. His tendencies were the mystery.

Hilary, a new member of the group, brought to light how everyone has started to work together. Hilary's inclinations stood out like a sore thumb. Ian hoped that Hilary would gel with the others before they moved into the jungle.

The closer the sleigh moved to their next destination the heavier Ian's heart became. He could feel a darkness that was not made up of light or the absence of light. This dark energy was thick and more intense than the energy he felt in Spain.

The void was empty of hope and love. The desolation gave Ian a feeling of what might be ahead, which was death and destruction.

The energy reminded Ian of a time when he sailed with his father in the doldrums, a place in-between, a place waiting for something, anything to come along and change the conditions—a place that felt like purgatory.

Ian could feel the animals and people of the Congo were waiting for the light to return. He could feel their need for hope and love to return. He considered that the people of the Congo were stuck in limbo, not knowing what direction they needed to go. They were just waiting, maybe waiting for someone to open the City of Light, perhaps they were waiting for Ian.

The closer the sleigh came to the Ancient City, the more it became real for Ian. The energy was so thick he could almost smell the City of Light or at least the beasts that guarded its gate. He remembered Sobeck and wondered if other such monsters were waiting for him. Or maybe creatures that were even blacker of heart.

Most of the flight, Ian sat alone in the back of the sleigh, looking out on the endless dark jungle. Ian thought of his mother and home in Vermont. He thought about Bee.

His experiences challenged his concept of reality, especially in the wilderness. He didn't know if his connection with Bee was real or just made up in his mind.

The canopy of the jungle below the sleigh became the field by which the tapestry of memories started to pour out into Ian's mindfulness. He recalled his experience with the Queen of England and the ghosts in the palace. Sobeck and his comfy but deadly home, and the different labyrinths he overcame. He remembered the monks and angels in Greece, and the Christmas party Bee and Ogden arranged.

He started to consider that all his memories, even the ones before he met Pecky, were connected in some unforeseen way. The purpose of his life had been leading up to this point in the Congo.

With success or failure, Ian's life might be over after this journey. He had never considered that the journey might be his demise. If he is connected in some unforeseen way to Legorian, and the dark lord is destroyed when Ian reaches the City of Light—won't Ian also be destroyed?

Ian thought about Sam Dupuis's explanation of reality. The world we see outside of ourselves is an illusion. That we are all one, and the only way that we are separate from each other is through our perceptions.

Ian thought that if this was true, then what does this say about the nature of his journey? If the world is a hologram, then why does he have to go on this trip?

Then a more profound concept moved up from his heart into his mind. He thought that maybe since the world outside of him was just a fantasy, the journey is not to save the world but to change how he sees the world.

Ian considered that the only way he can transform the world is by changing his perception. That one person could change the world, but only by changing how they perceived the world. Ian let out a laugh at this thought, which confirmed that he was speaking the truth.

A loud thud coming from the bottom of the sleigh woke everyone out of their stupors. The sleigh hit the top of a tree poking out of the endless green canopy. Pecky tried to raise the sleigh higher, but it became unresponsive.

The sleigh started to sputter in the air, not unlike it did when the travelers arrived in Spain. Ian knew that the negative energy was causing the sleigh to slip and soon would not be able to move forward with the group. They would have to secure other transportation to make it to their next destination.

Pecky realized what was causing the sleigh to falter. He desperately looked around for a clearing in the dense jungle. A small clearing with a pond appeared to the west. Pecky directed the sleigh to the clearing.

Hilary asked Pecky, "Pecky, why don't you go away from this dark energy? We can land it in a clearing I saw a couple of kilometers behind us."

Pecky responded, "Unfortunately, Hilary, the sleigh is sluggish. I could not turn it around if I wanted to. The best we can do is try to land it in that clearing to the west."

The sleigh was losing altitude rapidly the closer they came to the clearing. Pecky was able to navigate the sleigh through a column of trees before hitting a knoll bordering a small pond.

Luckily the clearing was dense with leaves and other flora to break the fall of the sleigh. They struck the ground with force, causing everyone in the sleigh to jolt forward. The tail end of the sleigh slowly landed on the forest floor with a thud.

Once the sleigh was still, Pecky tried to raise the sleigh but to no avail. The sleigh wasn't moving until the energy lifted, and everyone knew it. A malaise ran over the passengers. The situation at hand started to sink in that they would have to walk through the dense jungle.

Pecky asked, "Is everyone okay. Did anyone get hurt?"

Other than stiff necks, everyone was not harmed. Hilary jumped out of the sleigh and, with a slight smirk, said, "Even the best-laid plans of gorillas, penguins, and people begin to go awry."

Pecky replied with a less than pleased look, "Hilary, your literary sarcasm is not helping our situation. How far from Queso do you think we are? Did you get a chance to see the village before we descended?"

Hilary responded, "No, Pecky, I was not paying attention. I will climb up to the top of the canopy and look."

Hilary quickly climbed up the nearest tree, gracefully moving towards the top of the canopy. His quick and determined movement looked unreal to Ian.

Hilary peeked out of the top of the jungle canopy and could see the dim light of the morning sun glowing to the east, and he could barely see Queso to the south.

Hilary looked around for any sign of the militia or rebel forces in the area. He could see a faint path made by elephants on the jungle floor. He knew that this way was safe because men do not walk these paths.

Hilary's steady and elegant descent was just as graceful as his ascent. His muscular frame stretched and tightened, as he moves down to the jungle floor with ease. His beautiful black and gray hair sparkled with every move.

Hilary leaped from the last limb of the tree towards the travelers and announced with great enthusiasm, "There is good news and bad news. What story would you prefer first?"

Ian started to realize that Hilary was a bit of a showman. He liked to increase the exhilaration. Hilary reminded Ian of a carnival barker from his childhood. Everything the showman said was with tense and heightened deliberation. Ian considered that Hilary could call people to lunch with intense fervor.

Pecky turned to Hilary with a frustrated look and asked, "The good news first, Hilary."

Hilary sat down and grabbed a stalk of leaves and devoured the whole lot in one big bite. "The good news is that we are around twenty kilometers from our destination. I can see the faint lights of Queso in the distance."

Pecky interjected with a frustrated look, "And the bad news, please?"

Hilary smirked a little before answering, "There is dense and dangerous jungle between us and the camp with only an old elephant path to walk.

"There are tigers, snakes, spiders, and other nasty things crawling along the forest floor, including my least favorite, leeches. I can make my way through the trees, but I fear if we come upon anything on the jungle floor, something might happen fast before I can get to anyone. I will keep a close eye on everyone as we make our way to the black market camp.

"Another good news is that the sun is coming up. The bad news is that the light of the sun will be little help in the dense jungle."

Ogden interjected with a grin on his face, "I'll just stay here and wait for you all to return."

Pecky replied with great haste, "Unfortunately, Ogden, we all must move forward, so let's get to it. We need to unload the sleigh with our provisions. Ian, you oversee carrying the black rose and the map to the City of Light. We won't be back until the end of this affair. We will need to bring everything with us. Please leave the rose in its container."

Hilary sat up with a concerned look and said, "You carry a black rose with you?"

Bee interjected, "Yes, we recovered it while in Scotland. Sobeck had one, but we lost that one to Legorian."

A cheerful look came over Hilary's face as he responded, "Good, a black rose will help us along our trip. No animal in the forest will bother us if you have that rose in your possession. It carries powerful mojo."

"Sobeck, I haven't heard that name in a long time. He was a guard at the Ancient City until he went rogue and started to work against Legorian, or at least Sobeck began to work for himself. How is Sobeck, is he still causing mayhem?"

Pecky responded, "Sobeck is dead. Legorian killed him in his own home on the North York Moors."

Hilary responded, "Poor fool, he couldn't even get out of his own way. You know I kind of liked that old crocodile for some reason, pity he is dead."

Pecky responded, "Poor fool? He tried to eat Ian."

Hilary replied, "Well, it is just his nature."

Bee asked, "Hilary, I don't understand why this black rose contains such power, and why we have carried it so long to return it to the Ancient City. Are there not many black roses growing in the City of Light?"

Hilary looked puzzled at Bee and answered, "It is not the black rose that has the power. It is the mineral that contains energy.

"The power is the mineral that is abundant around the City of Light; humans call it Coltan. Many are dying and are in misery because of the desire to obtain the ore. The Congolese people are both blessed and cursed with this crystal.

"Humans use it for your electronic devices, but you have yet to discover the real power of the crystal. The mineral contains energy beyond the need of this world. Your kind has yet to understand or even come close to unlocking its potential. Humans will not know the power as long as your kind fight for possession instead of working together."

Ogden asked with a concerned look, "How do you know so much about this mineral?"

Hilary moved towards Ogden and replied, "All gorillas are intelligent, but my kin who have guarded the City of Light for a millennium are gifted in awareness primarily because of this crystal. Animals are not unlike humans, some are ignorant, some are bright, and some are brilliant.

"My kin are intelligent but have high awareness. You can have intelligence but not awareness. Awareness comes with your connection to the Source. Many brilliant people are working in mining companies that are destroying the Congo and other beautiful places in the world. We have seen both animals and people use intelligence for good and bad.

"The key to healing the world and the Congo is to change human awareness. Collecting the bounty of the earth is not bad. It's only bad if you do it by destroying the world instead of realizing that the same ends can be achieved with care.

"If Ian reaches the City of Light, this one deed will help to change the awareness of the planet. He will unlock the power of the crystal that surrounds the City of Light, and the Congo will be released from purgatory.

"The mineral is alive. It contains the power of consciousness. That is its power, and anyone can take that conscious energy and use it for whatever ends desired, good or evil."

Bee asked, "How can a rock contain consciousness?"

Hilary let out a huge belly laugh and replied, "My dear young woman, all things hold consciousness. The world we see outside of our selves is the light we see through the filters of our perceptions.

"The crystal contains a pure form of consciousness because it is so close to the City of Light, and the City is pure creation.

"The mineral was what the Belgium government was trying to study at Yangambi. They knew that they were close to an energy source that could change the world, but time ran out as it often does in the jungle. Especially when Legorian showed up and changed the whole area into darkness."

Pecky spoke up with haste in his voice, "Speaking of time running out, we need to gather our things and move on to the black market camp. As dangerous as the jungle is in daylight, it will be much more deadly at night."

Hilary replied, "Pecky's right, there will be plenty of time to discuss what we will encounter once we reach the entrance to the City of Light."

The bright sun shined its light above the tree line, bringing life and sounds back to the jungle. The sun brought back warmth and a little concern that anyone flying overhead might see the group in the clearing.

Hilary exclaimed, "We need to hide the sleigh from sight, because rebel forces often fly missions over this area, and we do not want the sleigh to fall into the hands of the militia. They will surely use the sleigh for ill deeds."

The travelers instantly went into action, covering the sleigh with large leaves and other foliage. They filled backpacks with food and other supplies. Pecky hid the key to the sleigh nearby in a small underwater cave.

Hilary was impressed by the precision of the group to work together. He found comfort in the travelers' ability to resolve a task. He knew that they would need to band together even tighter if they were to survive the trip through the Congo.

Ogden asked Pecky, "Pecky, why don't you keep the key to the sleigh with you?"

Pecky looked at Ogden with a grim look and replied, "Because if we are caught or killed by militia or rebel forces, they would have the key. I would rather the sleigh become dust in the jungle than passed into their hands."

In a short time, the group was ready to move into the jungle. Pecky, Ogden, Bee, and Ian all stood before a wall of green, wondering if they would make the twenty kilometers alive.

Hilary pointed to an elephant path leading away from the clearing, and said, "Never get off the road and stay together. If you must take care of any personal business during the trip, please let everyone know, that includes you, Bee."

One by one, the travelers moved into the thick and dark jungle with Pecky taking up the rear. Just before Pecky walked into the bush, he turned around, looked at the sleigh covered by leaves one more time, and said, "Goodbye, my friend, I appreciate you getting us here. I hope to see you again soon, but of course, we will never see you again if we are not successful." **ଓ**

CR

Chapter Thirty-Four
Old Friends

I an stepped into the dense jungle, and something wonderful happened. His fear left, and a sensation of life energy started to fill his heart. He investigated the depths of the dark green bush and began to see the illusionary curtain of reality fade away.

The jungle became alive with light. A sense of well-being and knowing overcame Ian's mind and soul.

He knew that they were going to be alright. Ian had a vision of the City of Light. He was aware that the entrance to the City of Light was his destiny-what happened beyond the opening he could not see.

Bee grabbed Ian's arm and said, "Ian, are you okay? Where are you?"

Bee's voice seemed far away from where Ian stood, but soon the darkness of the jungle took hold. The light that was all around him began to diminish. Ian turned to Bee and asked, "Do you see it?"

Bee responded with a concerned look, "See what?"

Ian looked straight at Bee without seeing her. He was looking past her into the jungle and said, "The light, the light that is all around us?"

Bee looked around and replied, "No, all I see is the dense green jungle and the elephant path."

Ian began to see the forest, but behind the jungle he could still feel an energy that made up all living things. The energy vibrated at a much higher level.

He felt the life energy field through the darkness. The life energy and dark energy were balanced. Ian knew that both powers occupy the same space—without one, the other could not exist. The dark energy did not extinguish the life energy field—the field was just not in balance.

Pecky stopped waddling through the jungle and turned to Ian and asked, "Ian, you see the life energy field?"

Ian replied, "Yes, I see a field of light that is at the base of all things do you see it?"

Pecky shook his head and replied, "I have only seen it in flashes. Only a true heart can see beyond the illusion. To enter the City of Light, you will have to see the entrance, and it vibrates at a high level of energy."

Hilary dropped out of a tree and approached the travelers and asked, "What is the holdup? We need to reach our objective before nightfall. We do not want to be in the jungle at night. The evening is when the most vicious predators come alive, including your jackals, Pecky."

Pecky replied, "Ian has seen the life energy field that makes up all living things—this news is exciting."

A broad grin came over Hilary's face as he replied, "That is wonderful news. I was wondering if he would find his sight, but we have to move on."

A loud sound echoed above the group. At first, it sounded like a giant insect, but the closer it came, the more apparent it was a small two-engine plane flying close over the canopy.

Pecky said with great concern, "Someone is looking for us. Foe or friend, we cannot let our position be known. I hope they do not discover the sleigh."

The group all looked at each other with concern, except Ian. Ian had seen the vision of his destiny, and he knew that he would make it to the entrance to the Ancient City, but a concern did entered his mind. He saw himself in the vision, but he did not see his friends.

The group started to move south along the elephant path. All around them were sounds of animals, birds, and insects deep in the bush. Everything seemed to stay away from the travelers, or maybe the jungle was too dense to see just one animal.

The intense light that overcame Ian was gone, but the life in the jungle still filled Ian's heart with love. He always considered the jungle to be a terrifying place. Especially in his early years watching documentaries about the different tropical jungles of the world. He was concerned about spiders and snakes.

Now that he was in the jungle, he mused that you cannot fear reality, you can only fear anticipation. Ian laughed out loud, startling the others.

Ogden looked back at Ian and asked, "What's so funny?"

Ian looked at Ogden in a daze, and replied, "I was just thinking how scared I used to be of entering a tropical jungle. Now that I am here, it doesn't seem so scary."

"I don't know, Ian. The thought of walking through this jungle still terrifies me," replied Ogden.

The group started to move in sync with each other. There was a precision to how each member worked with the whole, walking through the jungle. Kilometer after kilometer, the group moved swiftly through the dense forest, always keeping to the path.

Ogden spotted a large snake basking on a rock in the little sun that was beaming down through the canopy. He yelled out to the others, "Snake on the rock to the left. It looks like a king cobra." The snake did not move or show any sign of interest in the travelers.

Pecky whispered, "Be quiet, there is something noisy ahead. Hilary is checking it out."

Hilary moved silently through the canopy to see what was on the path. He looked down and saw a family of seven elephants moving slowly towards a watering hole to the west. They were led by an old female elephant. Hilary instantly recognized the matriarch. He knew her to be wise, kind, and friendly to his kin. Her name was Sabella.

Hilary jumped down on a limb just above the heads of the elephants. They stopped their trek through the jungle and looked up at Hilary.

In a slow movement, the matriarch turned around and confronted Hilary. Her large eyes moved over Hilary's body, slowly examining him and remembering. A calm expression came over the face of the matriarch. In a deliberate voice, she said, "It has been a long time, my friend."

Hilary moved closer and replied, "Yes, too long, my dear friend."

The matriarch looked again at Hilary and said, "I thought you were exiled, and your family held hostage?"

"Yes, my family is imprisoned, but I have returned with a true heart," replied Hilary with great enthusiasm. Hilary continued, "We are bound for the black market camp near Queso. My friend Reggie is expecting us. Can you help us?"

The matriarch replied, "I have heard that a true heart had been born. Legend tells us that this human will change the world. There is darkness here, and we welcome any hope of light."

Hilary asked, "So, will you help us?"

A concerned look came over the matriarch's face as she replied, "We will take you close but not all the way. Those who live in the camp are not friends of my kind. They hunt us for our tusks, so we must be careful.

"There is a crossing one kilometer from the camp, but no further or our lives may be in danger."

Hilary replied, "You are kind, my friend. I will retrieve the others."

Hilary quickly moved through the trees back to the explorers to give them the good news. Since Ian was in the group, Hilary felt more hope. The elephants would not help just any human, because of the terror their kind has been inflicted on by humans.

Hilary bounded out of the dense jungle.

Pecky asked, "Is it safe to move forward?"

Hilary dropped down onto the jungle floor, grabbed a few leaves from a nearby bush, and said, "Not only is it safe, but I have secured transportation."

A puzzled look came over everyone as Hilary started to laugh a great belly laugh. He pointed to the trail ahead and replied, "I have found an old friend. She and her family are waiting to take us close to the camp."

Hilary had an interesting thought. He first considered finding his friend on the trail to be coincidental. Then Hilary wondered if the universe was helping them out or if Ian's presence was creating the coincidence.

Hilary then considered whatever the reason he would take full advantage. He announced, "My friend Sabella, an old matriarch of elephants, has agreed to deliver us near the camp. I have estimated that we are fifteen kilometers from the camp, but I need to warn all of you.

"This herd of elephants has suffered under the hands of humankind, especially white men. They are helping us because we are with a true heart. I expect all of you to be on your best and most respectful behavior. This includes you, Ogden."

"What did I do?" replied Ogden with irritation on his face.

Hilary patted Ogden on the back and replied, "You just sometimes react without thinking. Better safe than sorry, I always say."

The group moved through the path towards the waiting elephants. The closer they came to the elephants, the more impressive the herd looked standing in the jungle.

Ian could sense the great hearts that beat in these magnificent animals. They felt different than the elephants he saw at the zoo.

They had high spirits, and the elephants in the zoos seemed a little run down and detached from their surroundings. The zoo animals felt almost dead inside.

Hilary stood before the enormous pachyderms and said, "These are my friends, Pecky, Bee, and Ogden, and of course, Ian. We appreciate your help."

The two groups looked at each other with a perplexed look. Bee considered that this moment would make a great picture, but she did not have her camera.

One by one, the pachyderms moved towards the travelers. They lowered their heads so that each person could take their place on their backs. The matriarch walked towards Ian and lowered her head.

Ian bowed to Sabella and said, "I thank you for your assistance with my friends and me. You might have even saved our lives."

Sabella reared back and looked at Ian with surprise and replied, "I have never had a conversation with a human. Our voice is beyond the abilities of any person. How is it that you speak my language?"

Ian was taken aback back with surprise "Honestly, Sabella, I did not know I was speaking your language. I considered it would be appropriate. I still don't understand my linguistic abilities."

Bee interrupted, "What are you doing, Ian? You are making almost undistinguishable sounds."

Ian replied, "I am thanking our hostess for assisting us on our journey."

Bee replied with a smirk, "Don't tell me that you speak elephant."

Ian shrugged his shoulders and replied, "I guess I do."

Sabella again lowered her head and said, "Ian, you and your kind are welcomed. Please secure yourself on my back."

Ian gently climbed onto the back of the great beast and positioned himself right behind Sabella's neck. All the travelers except Hilary sat on the back of their newfound friends.

Hilary motioned for the group to move forward through the jungle. Hilary then moved up into the canopy to scout the path ahead.

The elephants moved in line behind the matriarch with military precision. The elephants walked through the jungle with slow and steady movement. The group felt extreme motion with each step.

The travelers started to relax now. They were off the forest floor, moving like clouds through the bush. They began to see creatures coming and going. In the distance, they heard the roar of a leopard and the sounds of other elephants moving through the jungle. The forest became alive.

Bee considered the terrible life-threatening journey through the jungle just became an enjoyable experience. The only hazard was low tree limbs or creatures hitting them in the head.

The kilometers started to pass swiftly below their friends' feet. The sun overhead moved to the west. The end of the road came quickly for the travelers. The elephants all stopped at once near a watering hole that was at a crossing.

The watering hole was tiny but looked to be deep. No other animals were around. The elephant matriarch lowered her head to let Ian disembark.

Ian stood before the family of pachyderms and said, "We appreciate your help and hope that whatever we do in this quest will help your kind."

Sabella looked lovingly at Ian and replied, "Knowing that a true heart has come to this darkened land has given us hope. I will pass along to the others who travel these paths that you are moving towards the City of Light. Goodbye, for now, Ian, I hope to hear of great deeds done for divine purpose." Slowly the herd of seven moved towards the west in the direction of a nearby mountain. The dark jungle hid them fast from view but not from memory.

Pecky was the first to speak up, "Where to now, Hilary?"

Hilary sat down and picked a few leaves off a nearby bush and then contemplated their next move. He drew a map of Queso and the black market camp and pointed out that the group was about a kilometer from their objective.

Hilary thought for a moment and said, "I sent Reggie a message of our intent last week, when I was waiting for you. I am not sure that Reggie is in the camp right now. He moves back and forth from Queso and a camp near the Congo River. I believe it is our best bet to get close to the compound without letting our presence be known. I will move into the camp from above and see if I can spot Reggie."

Out of nowhere, three men stepped from the bush into the clearing, surprising the group. One of the men exclaimed, "You don't need to look hard for Reggie. I have been waiting two days for your arrival."

Hilary looked up with surprise and with a grin on his face. He replied, "Reggie, you old rascal. You have found us, another coincidence, I suppose?"

Reggie looked at the group with a smug expression. He replied, "What coincidence? Kehfun sent a messenger a few days ago that you were traveling in our direction. Also, the Life Energy Consortium secured your passage.."

Pecky said, "It's been a long time, Reggie. I never considered I would see you again, especially in the depths of the Congo jungle."

Reggie patted Pecky on the back and said, "I was a different bloke back at Oxford. I should be in London following my father's footsteps, but politics was never my strong suit. I just had too much life in me to die a thousand deaths in Parliament."

Hilary interjected, "It's getting late, Reggie. Is the camp safe for our guests?"

Reggie laughed and replied, "As safe as any camp full of cutthroats and black marketers."

Reggie then turned to Ian and said, "Young man, your journey has become common knowledge. Many want you to succeed, but many don't.

"When we move into the camp, you are not to discuss who you are or why you are traveling through the Congo. The only people you can trust are me and my two captains, Pierre and Cullen."

Pierre and Cullen moved forward and offered their commitment to Ian and his journey. Reggie pointed in the direction of the black market camp and said, "Shall we?" ✠

CʒƷ

Chapter Thirty-Five
A Cup Half Empty

The sun was below the horizon when Reggie smuggled the group into the black market base camp. A low rising crescent moon kept the travelers' movement hidden. They made their way near the docks and to a large old English military canvas tent. Reggie prepared the shelter for them a few days before they arrived.

The compound was a hodgepodge of tin and wood buildings with makeshift tents near an abandoned military airfield. The concrete on the airport buckled enough to deter a large aircraft from landing, but not enough to prevent the black marketers from taking off and landing their small planes.

The one road that led out of the camp had long been taken back by the jungle. Vines, bushes, and trees covered most of the decaying blacktop. The only way out was by water, small aircraft, or by foot on the elephant paths.

Reggie mentioned that the camp was perfect for their business interests. It was impossible to sneak police through the jungle and onto their doorsteps without warning calls from the howling monkeys.

He mentioned that everyone in the camp could leave on a moment's notice, without a business loss comparable to time in a regional jail. He assured all his new friends that this experience would not be pleasant.

Ian noticed that the tent had a strong smell of mildew like everything else that was organic in the jungle. This included all his fellow travelers.

He considered that it was a bonding experience that they all stank, and not just of mildew. They did not have an opportunity to wash their clothes or bodies since they left Greece.

Another thing was clear to Ian. His companions were exhausted. He felt depleted more than any other time in his life. He was a little concerned that if he let himself fall asleep, he might not be able to wake up. He tried not to doze off.

Reggie served the travelers a simple dinner of steamed millet, chickpeas, tomatoes, and some kind of meat. Ian was hoping that the meat was pork or some other non-exotic animal. He could not tell from the sinew and fat content what he was eating. He trusted Reggie enough to know he would not die or get sick from the meal.

Ian and his friends feasted on the food with no apparent concern for manners. Even Bee and Ogden were shoveling food into their mouths as fast they could.

After what seemed like ten minutes of gorging on dinner, the travelers all lay back in their army racks. Before getting into their sleeping bags, they all opened them up, looking for some snake or spider that might have entered unnoticed.

Outside the tent, Ian could hear a storm move in fast from the west. A moment later, he listened to a sharp sound of thunder overhead and then a torrential downpour. Hilary assured the group that these storms move in fast and leave just as quickly.

Ian thanked the Source that he and his friends did not get caught out in the rain. He was exhausted and thankful that he was not drenched to the bone as well. The only positive thing with getting caught in the rain is their clothes might get cleaned.

When he left on his great adventure, he never considered that he would be filthy dirty for such extended periods. It was moments like that when he was thankful for the little things, like a clean private toilet, a hot shower, and of course, toilet paper.

Suddenly the tent's large door flap was pulled back. A single bright light from the front of a jeep, with the engine still running, blinded the travelers for just a second.

In walked Reggie with his two henchmen. At least that was the name Bee used when describing the men Reggie relied so heavily upon.

Reggie's number one henchman Pierre, looked to be sixty but was probably only in his early forties. He had tattoos all over his forearms and poking out of the neck of his dirty black tee shirt. Ian and Bee could not make out the tattoos. Bee surmised that Pierre either did time in jail or the French Foreign Legion, or both.

Ian asked Bee how she knew such things. she exclaimed, "Ian, I know a lot of things. You might think you know me, but maybe you don't know me as much as you might think."

Ian realized a long time ago that Bee liked to be in control and a little bit mysterious. He still hadn't made up his mind if he liked that about her.

Pierre had an unshaven face with thick stubble. Pierre's face was so dark from living under the sun in the Congo that it would not have made any difference if Pierre shaved every day. His leather-thick skin would still look unshaven.

Reggie's number two henchman Cullen, was a mystery. Cullen looked to be all of twenty-six with smooth white skin, freckles blanketing his face, and a shock of poorly cut bright red hair flowing down his back. Cullen looked more to be a Catholic choir boy than a hoodlum working in the Congo.

Ian sensed that he could trust Pierre more than Cullen. As angelic as Cullen looked on the outside, Ian felt a twisted black heart.

Reggie sat down on an old wooden chair near the entrance while his henchmen stood just behind him. Reggie pulled out a hand-made cigarette without a filter and lite it up. He said, "My intel tells me that all of you have made it here without anyone in the region, including Legorian's devotees, knowing your whereabouts. I have found out that the rebels to the east know that a true heart has entered the territory. They don't know that you are safe and sound under my care.

"I'll make this short and sweet. You all look like you need as much sleep as possible before we leave. We made all preparations to transport you down the Sangha River into the Congo River. We have fitted an old black market ferry boat with all the supplies we will need to make it to the Congo River, and on to Yangambi without delay, hopefully."

Pecky interjected, "What is our timeline?"

Reggie took a puff of his rapidly smoldering cigarette. He replied, "It is around 320 kilometers down the Sangha River to the entrance of the Congo River. Then around 1,000 kilometers to Yangambi. We will make the trip in about three weeks. We can't go any faster because anything out of the ordinary will attract unwanted attention."

Hilary asked, "Reggie, what about my plan that we discussed earlier?"

Reggie replied, "Good plan, Hilary, but our plan takes us directly to the research station without any fuss over land. Let's keep your plan on hand if things go sideways.

"Plus, Hilary, our ferry boat has traveled these waters for many years. Our movement shouldn't cause anyone to get their knickers in a twist."

Hilary laughed out loud and asked, "Who will be traveling with us?"

Reggie put out his cigarette on the bare dirt floor and replied, "It will be just me, Pierre, and Cullen. I trust these men with my life. Since I value my life more than I value your lives, I trust them with your lives.

"We will be picking up some cargo along the way to make our trip seem ordinary to those that might have an interest. We might as well make a couple of quid."

Hilary asked with a concerned look, "What cargo?"

Reggie looked at Hilary with a little bit of irritation, "Nothing dangerous, and nothing you should be concerned about." Reggie took out another handmade cigarette lite it up and continued, "That's it for now. I suggest you all get some rest. I will be waking you up before dawn to set sail.

"And, ah yes, I might add the ferry has a fully functioning shower onboard, with a small laundry. I suggest that all of you utilize the ship services. You all stink, and I don't think I could make the trip with the stench of all of you wafting about."

As abruptly as Reggie entered the tent, he left and sped off in his jeep. Pierre and Cullen were ordered to stay with the group. They sat on the outside near the entrance with machetes and automatic rifles.

An hour had passed since Reggie outlined the groups' next plan of action, and Ian was still awake lying in his rack, a concerned look painted on his face.

Most everyone, including Hilary, who said he might stay up to stand guard, was asleep. Hilary was not only asleep; he was snoring loudly. Ian never considered that gorillas snore, but he never envisioned a talking gorilla either.

Pecky was the only one that was still awake. He was looking over maps that Reggie dropped off. He wanted to know the path they were taking and where they might be dropped off so as not to alert Legorian or his devotees.

Pecky looked over and saw that Ian was still awake. He walked over and sat on the end of Ian's cot and asked, "Anything wrong, my friend?"

Ian replied, "I don't know."

Pecky patted Ian on the shoulder, and said, "Ian, we haven't had an opportunity to talk since your walk through the wilderness. I wanted to reach out to you. I felt that it was best you worked things out for yourself. I know that the time spent with Legorian was confusing. I bet you wondered why he did not kill you."

Ian replied, "Yes, I have wondered that a lot. Lately, a thought has been taking hold. I feel more and more that Legorian is connected to me in some way. He couldn't kill me because he would risk his own existence."

"Yes, good show, Ian. That is what I was talking about. I needed you to make the connection between your path and Legorian's path. I knew if I told you, you might not have believed me."

"Pecky, I think what is concerning me is that we are only three weeks from the entrance to the City of Light. I have no idea how to defeat Legorian and his devotees. I wonder if we should be getting weapons of some sort.

"Pecky, I have read many stories of heroic deeds and wars against dark lords. Those stories have always concluded with great battles, swords, and weapons. Highly skilled warriors would finally dispatch the bad guys.

"I am not a trained warrior and feel unprepared to meet Legorian on a battlefield. How is it that I enter the City of Light without killing the dark lord and his devotees?"

"Ian, you won't have to kill Legorian."

"I won't?"

"You see, Ian, Legorian is already dead. You couldn't kill him if you wanted. If you destroyed Legorian, you would destroy yourself," replied Pecky with a heavy heart.

"I don't understand," replied Ian.

"I have to be honest with you, Ian. After the Prince and his forces invaded the small village outside Moundou, we knew you were walking through the wilderness. I knew I had to have faith that you would find your path on your own. You had to empty yourself of what you thought you knew. You will not be able to enter the Ancient City with a full cup."

"A full cup? "replied Ian.

Pecky replied, "Let me tell you a story that might help."

Pecky continued, "A man of knowledge traveled into the mountains to meet a wise man. The man of intellect was told that the wise man knew the secrets to the universe. After seeking for many months, he reached the humble home of the wise man on the peak of a high mountain. He entered the home with the gracious permission of the wise man.

"The wise man asked the man with knowledge to sit, so that he could serve him tea, which is part of his custom. The man of knowledge sat and received the tea from the wise man. As the wise man poured the drink, he kept pouring even after the cup was filled. He said to the man of knowledge, "A cup that is filled cannot hold any more."

"When you walked through the wilderness, you needed to empty yourself of what you think you know. Only a cup that can be filled with wisdom can enter the Ancient City."

"Pecky, how I see the world has changed. I am still in the process of letting go. The more I let go, the more I feel connected to Legorian. How is that possible?"

"Ian, the world is a duality. All of us are made up of light and dark and good and evil. There is a natural balance to all things in the universe. Legorian lives in each one of us. He is the voice in the dark, creating fear and doubt. The Source is the voice in our hearts that speaks of love and hope.

"Legorian is a part of all of us except for a true heart. When a true heart is born, they are love and hope. When a true heart enters the world, Legorian takes on a physical form. The power of the true heart gives life to Legorian. The universe will always balance out the equation. Legorian has lived for many millennia as spirit.

"When you were born, he was released into the world and has taken a physical form. As he has done before when other true hearts have been born.

"The more aware and powerful the true heart becomes, the more powerful Legorian becomes. The dark lord's existence connects to the true heart. Do you understand what I speak of?"

"Pecky, I understand what you mean. Legorian's connection is the knowledge that has been growing in my mind and heart since I left the wilderness. I started to surmise that Legorian didn't kill me because his being connects to me. The only thing he could do is try to deceive me into not trusting my own heart."

Pecky said, "Remember, Legorian is insane. He both hates this world and loves this world. He thinks if you, under his control, enter the Ancient City, he will be able to destroy the City of Light.

"He is not aware that his existence connects to you. He only desires to control you or have power over you.

"To answer your earlier question. No, you do not need to be a warrior to meet Legorian on the field of battle. You need to be aware that Legorian's power only exists if you allow it to control you.

"Unfortunately, your awareness can only be tested during your seven trials created by Legorian before you reach the City of Light. His purpose is to keep you from entering the Ancient City free of his will."

Ian replied, "I have to trust my own heart above all things, is that it?"

"Yes, Legorian will do everything he can to distract you from trusting your own heart. The closer you come to the City of Light, the more he will work to deceive you. You must remember that the world outside is an illusion. It is created by how you perceive yourself in this reality."

Ian laughed out loud and replied, "I understand. A part of me sees what you are saying. The other part does not."

"Yes, Ian, this is part of the emptying process you need to go through before we reach the first entrance. Many call this process of emptying the dark night of the soul." Pecky announced with great enthusiasm.

Ian replied, "How does a dark night of the soul work?"

Pecky responded, "Just like the intelligent man trying to know the secrets of the universe. You need to be open so that you can change your perceptions of the world. A dark night of the soul can become painful because it tests everything you thought you knew about yourself and the world."

Ian slumped down in his bed and replied, "The part of me that does not understand is tired and is ready for sleep. The other part of me has much to consider but fears the future a little less."

Pecky zipped up Ian's sleeping bag and looked at him with warm and loving eyes, "That is enough wisdom for now. We must wake in a few hours. You will have plenty of time on the ship to contemplate."

In the distance, a loud noise of animals howling broke the night calm. Pecky considered for a moment that Legorian's jackals had found the group. After another round of wailing, he recognized the sound as wild dogs on their nightly hunt. ᕫ

Cଓ

Chapter Thirty-Six
Breakfast with Crocodiles

The last few weeks traveling on the Sangha and Congo River brought a sense of peace that the group did not expect. They all felt safe the moment the ship left the dock back at the black market compound.

To Reggie's knowledge, no one at the camp questioned the ship leaving before dawn. The vessel moved purposely away from the dock and then kept a steady speed of twelve knots down the center of the Sangha river. The world around the ship passed methodically. The engines were clunking along like clockwork. Every so often a strong smell of diesel fuel drifted topside.

Ian and Bee would sit for hours on the ship's forecastle and watch the green water pass below the vessel. Everyone was asleep when the ship made the transition from the Sangha River into the Congo River. The Congo was much larger than the Sangha but had the same green water under the boat.

The ship would pass by large pods of hippos or basks of crocodiles. The group caught glimpses of large animals moving through the dense jungle. Bee thought she saw a leopard sitting on a tree near the edge of the river, but lost sight of the animal.

The monkeys that lived on the river's edge would jump onto the ship any chance they could. They pilfered scraps of food rotting in the hot sun in garbage cans kept on the stern of the vessel.

Hilary was most disgusted by the monkeys. He considered them having no sense of dignity or shame. He felt that they would do anything for a handout.

The primary concern was the millions of mosquitoes that would come out to dine on the travelers during dusk. The group learned to stay in their cabin until the sun was down, and the moon was high in the sky.

Late into the evening, Bee, Ian, and Ogden would lay on the flying bridge and explore the brilliant night sky. Bee had never witnessed such bright stars. Bee had spent most of her life in London. She never knew that the haze of London kept a celestial secret that was now revealed.

One late evening without the moon, they could see the Milky Way galaxy travel across the sky with billions of stars piercing through the night canopy. Often Bee, Ian, and Ogden would talk late into the evening and then sleep late into the day.

Of all the travelers, Ogden luxuriated the most in the ability to sleep as late as he desired. It had been many months or even years since he had the opportunity to relax and not be responsible for an energy sprite transaction.

Every few days, the ship would make port in a small village. Reggie and his henchmen, good to his word, would deliver cargo in unmarked crates and barrels, then take on other freight that they would hastily stow in the cargo hold deep in the bowels of the vessel.

The ship would never stay long at any port. Just enough time to transfer the booty and take on more stores. The village elders would always meet the boat with enthusiasm and with whatever food was traditional to their village.

The travelers found the Congolese people to possess a kind and loving nature, even though they lived in an environment of such conflict and uncertainty.

Ian, Bee, and Ogden would always be cautious when the ship made port. Sometimes, they would have to eat something that would not sit well with their stomachs.

It would be considered an insult if they didn't accept the hospitality of the village elders. Along the Congo, travelers can still get their heads handed to them for a simple lack of etiquette.

Pecky spent most of his time in his cabin going over maps and old documents that he had carried on the sleigh. He wanted to be ready for whatever lay ahead. He knew that time was growing short, and after Ian moved beyond the first portal to the City of Light, he would not have the option or luxury to study information about the journey.

Pecky stayed in his cabin. He knew that tribal elders and shamans would understand that a six-foot-tall emperor penguin would most likely be traveling with a unique person. He could not trust that their traveling plans would not find its way to a devotee of Legorian.

At face value, the river was a calm and peaceful place for travelers. Ian could still sense the emptiness that engulfed the region. The same void that brought down the sleigh increased in his heart, the closer he came to the steps of the Ancient City.

Early morning a feeling of anxiety started to build in Ian's heart. He could not put his finger on the reason of the emotion except that he considered it a forewarning.

The feeling he had was about something on the river, or maybe somebody already on the boat, who would cause harm to the group.

Ian traveled down to the berthing area located forward of the engine room to find Pecky to discuss his feeling of anxiety. Pecky was lying on his cot reading 'Heart of Darkness' by Joseph Conrad. A smile came over Pecky's face as Ian entered his berthing area. Pecky put down his book and sat up in his rack.

Pecky asked, "I haven't seen you much, my friend, during this voyage. What brings you to me now?"

Ian picked up Pecky's book and replied, "You're reading 'Heart of Darkness'? I had to read this in 10th grade. I found the book hard to read. Not in my wildest dreams would I have predicted that I would be traveling the Congo River on a boat to a dark place. Pecky, I would consider that reading this book on the Congo would be a little too much, even for you."

Pecky replied, "I like overindulgence. I had the opportunity once to read the entire collection of C.S. Foster's Horatio Hornblower books on a voyage I made below Cuba in the Caribbean and British West Indies. What can I do for you, Ian?"

Ian sat close to Pecky and replied in a low voice, "I have had a strong feeling that something is not right. That something or someone on the ship might do us harm. I started feeling this early this morning, and the sensation has only heightened."

Pecky leaned close and replied, "Do you know what the forewarning means, or who it might be about?"

Ian replied, "When I focus, Cullen comes to mind. I have no proof of ill deeds or to betrayal, just an intense feeling."

"Ian, I trust your heart more than my eyes."

"So, what do we do?"

"Nothing." Replied Pecky with a stern voice. Pecky continued, "We are less than a week from Yangambi. We will have to disembark earlier and make our way to the entrance to the Ancient City on foot.

"If Cullen is going to betray us, then he will wait. He is going to wait until we are close to the research station. It is important to remember that we can trust our friends. We can't trust Cullen, Pierre, or even Reggie. Reggie has always made Reggie his number one priority. That was true at Oxford, and that is true now.

"Reggie is not taking us to the research station out of the goodness of his heart, or because he believes in our purpose. He is taking us because the

Life Energy Consortium has paid him a tidy fortune in gold and silver."

"Pecky, I don't feel Pierre or Reggie are privy to Cullen's plan. I believe something happened during our last port of call two days ago. I think something of value changed hands and plans hatched. How I know this, I am not sure, but I do know it."

Pecky smiled and replied, "Knowing is important. You see, Ian, some of us transition from belief to faith, but few make it to knowing."

A loud knock on Pecky's berthing area's door startled the two. Bee walked in with a frown on her face. She leaned up against the bulkhead and asked, "You two look like you are up to something. Ian, I have been looking everywhere for you. Reggie wants all of us on the mess deck, for some important news."

Bee walked out with her usual determined stride. She looked back briefly to make sure that Pecky and Ian were in tow.

Reggie, Hilary, and Ogden were already talking when Bee, Ian, and Pecky reached the mess deck. Ian surmised that Pierre and Cullen were probably on the bridge steering the ship.

Reggie looked relieved as the trio moved onto the mess deck. As is his usual manner, he got right to business, "We need to discuss our next move before we reach Yangambi."

Pecky asked, "How far are we from the research station?"

Reggie replied, "We are around three days out. At our present rate, we will reach Yangambi late Thursday evening."

Pecky, with a low voice, said, "Ian has some insight that the rest of you need to know about."

Ian, with a surprised look on his face, replied, "I thought we were going to keep my insight secret?"

Pecky replied, "Ian, we need to continue to trust our friends. I believe that Reggie needs to know, especially now that we are close to Yangambi."

Bee asked, "Ian, what insight are we discussing?"

Ogden added, "Yes, Ian, what insight, let's share with the group?"

Ian leaned in close to the others and replied, "This morning, I woke with high anxiety about someone of something that might have damaged or tried to harm our journey. When I focus on this feeling of anxiety, Cullen keeps coming up in my mind. By the way, Reggie, where is Cullen right now?"

Reggie replied, "What exactly do you think Cullen might have done to damage your journey?"

Ian continued, "Something was exchanged at our last stop, two days ago. I don't know what, but it might have been information for money or something to that effect."

A calm look came over Reggie's face as he replied, "You know, Ian, I didn't believe that you were a true heart. I've never met one, but I am starting to become a believer. Your insight is a little scary."

Pecky asked, suspecting something transpired without his knowledge, "Reggie, where is Cullen?"

Reggie replied with a whimsical look on his face, "Cullen is indisposed at the moment. You see, he had early breakfast arraignments with a clutch of crocodiles."

A startled look came over everyone's face. Bee finally asked, "Reggie, are you saying that you murdered Cullen by throwing him the middle of a group of crocodiles?"

Reggie responded, "Bee, murder is such a dreadful word. Let's just say that I had to fire Cullen for actions that were contrary to my business concerns."

Pecky asked with horror on his face, "You fed Cullen to Congo crocodiles?"

Reggie responded with great enthusiasm, "Pierre and I didn't feed him to the crocodiles. We just coated him with chicken blood and fat and dropped him off near the crocodiles. We gave him a fighting chance to swim to shore.

"Look, if you are going to cry for Cullen, I think you all should know that Ian was correct. Cullen had made a deal with a black market trader, who is in the pocket of Legorian. I have spies working for me in almost every port of call along the Congo.

"You see, dispatching Cullen was a sound business move. I was in a bit of a sticky wicket. Cullen has been with me long enough to know my business secrets. I couldn't let him go to the competition, and I couldn't keep him around. As much as you might think that we are all scallywags, we are serious businessmen.

"If my customers found out that one of my employees was divulging critical information about my business. I would be out of business quick, including joining Cullen at the crocodile breakfast table.

"You see, my friends, I had to make a difficult choice. I was fond of the lad. He was a nephew twice removed on my mother's side of the family. He just never understood how serious I was about keeping my reputation."

Ogden asked, "What does this all mean?"

Reggie replied with great gusto, "It doesn't mean anything. Oh, don't worry, Ogden, I'm not going to throw you overboard. In this scenario, you are part of my cargo. As you can understand, I take my task of delivering my cargo seriously. What we have to be concerned about is if Legorian knows where you are."

Ian exclaimed, "Legorian doesn't know where we are yet. Whatever transpired at our last port of call with Cullen has not reached Legorian."

Bee responded, "How would you know what Legorian knows?"

Pecky replied, "Ian has realized his connection to Legorian. Legorian is the darker angel of Ian. Where Ian might know what Legorian knows, Legorian might not be aware of his connection to Ian. We have to hope that Legorian would not find out before we reach Yangambi."

Reggie continued, "We do have to recognize that this vessel might be under scrutiny and that the word about our friend might reach bad people before our arrival.

"This news has put a bit of a crack in our original plans. We might have to improvise with a new strategy where no one will know that you all have disembarked before the research station."

Ogden spoke up, "How are you going to pull that off?"

Reggie laughed and replied, "Yes, Ogden, maybe I will have to throw you overboard. Or, better yet, there is a new moon on Wednesday night. We could put you overboard on a dinghy and have you row to the entry point to another elephant path I know.

"The path will lead you to the research station. No one should be able to see you disembark, and they would consider you still aboard. We can even make decoys sitting on the deck of the ship."

Bee asked, "Won't that be dangerous?"

Reggie looks at Bee with an agitated brow and then laughed out loud. He replied, "My dear Bee, this is the Congo. Everything will kill you. It is a miracle that you all have made it this far without dying."

The realization that they were all in the Congo and still alive moved through the ranks of the travelers where everyone started to laugh uncontrollably. Even Hilary began to laugh with gusto.

Ian considered for the first time that maybe he does have an angel watching out for him. With all his experiences over the last few months, he didn't know how he made it this far.

After regaining his composure, Reggie said with great urgency, "So, let's get to it. We have cotton bales in the hold that could be molded with your clothes to fool those who are watching.

"Pecky, your decoy is going to be a little tricky to pull off, but I might have an idea on how we could construct a six-foot-tall penguin. Hilary, I don't know about you."

Ogden interrupted with a little bit of concern, "I hope that you will at least stop the ship when you offload us onto the skiff?"

Reggie looked at Ogden with concern, "Sorry old boy. I won't be able to stop, but I can slow down a bit. Anyone observing a change in our route or speed might get wind of your departure.

"Trust me, Ogden, I seriously take delivering my cargo safe. You have nothing to worry about, except being in the Congo jungle. That is when my obligation comes to an end. I have fulfilled my contract with the Life Energy Consortium. I'm sure Hilary will be able to guide you in the right direction after you take leave of my company, right, Hilary?"

Hilary looked at Reggie with a sharp look and replied, "Reggie, you are a humanitarian."

Reggie responded with resolve, "No, Hilary, I am a good businessman. So let's get to it, we have no time to waste." ଔ

ℭ𝔅

Chapter Thirty-Seven
A True Believer

"Now, I know what they mean when they say, 'No turning back,'" Ian declared with an unhappy expression.

"What do you mean?" asked Ogden.

Ian sat down on a nearby rock next to where they just came ashore. He looked up through the dense green canopy of trees at the stars. He replied, "I've read many epic novels. The main characters come to a point in the story where they realize there is no turning back.

"In most stories, the characters don't say out loud that there is no turning back. They just realize it, and so do the readers. I've just recognized that there is no turning back."

Ogden replied, "I don't know, Ian. You can always make other choices. Options are my profession as an energy sprite."

Ian looked at Ogden with a smile, and replied, "Yes, we could just stay right here. We could build a house out of this tree and eat whatever there is to consume."

Ogden laughed and replied, "I don't know for sure, but I think that we always have choices even in the darkest of places. Maybe the feeling of depression is a reaction to the belief that we do not have any choices when darkness descends."

Ian replied, "Dan Dupuis told me that the universe is unfolding as it should. The only option we have is to go along with the flow or fight it. Either way, we are going to end up in the same place.

"I have to move forward, or everything that we worked so hard for will be forfeited. Maybe Legorian is hoping for my misstep. So, that he can claim victory without even a fight?"

"What else would you do if you had the choice?" asked Ogden.

Ian replied, "Well, of course, in every story, I might say that I wish I had never even started. Pecky didn't give me an indication of what I was getting myself into. Of course, all travelers feel this way at this point in the journey.

"Taking stock of my present situation, which consists of being off-loaded from the only transportation we presently know, and watching it move beyond sight. We are left in one of the most dangerous jungles on the face of the earth. With one narrow elephant path to lead us to a region full of demons and devotees in hopes of finding the entrance to the City of Light. When I arrive, alive, if I do, I will have to overcome seven obstacles. That I have no reference point to understand to free myself, my friends, and this world from darkness."

Ogden laughed when he replied, "Well, at least you are at the beginning of the end, instead of the end of the beginning. For what it is worth, I'm happy that you took the leap of faith and decided to make this journey.

"I now have a good friend that understands the world of energy. The only young male friend I have that knows what an energy sprite does. I can talk to you about my life with the Life Energy Consortium. Someday when this is over we can sit down over a beer and have a good laugh."

"Yes, your'e right, Ogden. I think in the long run I'm happy as well. Even if this journey turns out to be a disaster. I have the best friends I've ever had backing me up." Ian said with a slightly resolute look on his face.

Hilary jumped down out of the green canopy above. He had a sardonic grin on his face as he asked, "What are you two girls talking about?"

Ogden took a step backward as his heart started to race, "Hilary, you scared the hell out of me." Ogden took a moment to compose himself and continued, "Ian was just wondering if it is too late to go home."

Hilary sat down near Ian and grabbed a handful of young green leaves. He replied, "Ian, it's not too late at all as long as you go home via the City of Light."

Ian replied, "I was worried that's what you might say. By the way, where were you when Reggie and Pierre were shoving all of us in that little skiff?"

Hilary took another bite from his found leaves. He answered, "Luckily, Ian, we gorillas have strength and agility. I jumped onto a limb jutting out into the river a kilometer back. Believe me, I was watching all of you as you paddled your way to shore. I was ready at a moment's notice to jump into the river and save you."

Ogden replied, "Right."

Hilary continued, "I did not mean I would save your sorry soul, Ogden. You, I would let the hippos eat."

Ogden rolled his eyes and replied, "Ha, Ha Hilary. I will remember this the next time you need an energy sprite to save your hinny."

Pecky walked up with a stern look on his face and said, "I believe that it is still three hours till dawn. We better get our plan of action together. I don't trust that there are not devotees or dark guards patrolling the jungle this close to the research center."

Ogden asked, "How close are we to our destination?"

Pecky looked over at Hilary. He asked, "Hilary, you know this area better than I do. How far is it to the entrance to the Ancient City?"

Hilary replied, "To be precise, there isn't an entrance to the Ancient City. There is a three-sided obelisk standing over a cavern that was found right under the Yangambi research center library. We must make it to the library without being detected and make our way through a false door.

"I'd say that we have nine kilometers to the library door. What happens after we reach that pedestal in the cavern, I have no idea. No one I have ever heard of has made it beyond that point in the cavern. I don't even know if the cavern is human-made or natural because the walls are perfectly round with another smaller obelisk positioned in the center of the chamber.

"The heart of the Yangambi research center, particularly its library, was built directly over that cavern because that was where the energy was most potent. I have heard that there is a key that opens the first portal. I have no idea where that key might be. I considered that the key is hidden in the library. The librarian might know where to look."

Pecky said in a low voice, "We have the key."

Ian put his hand in his backpack and pulled out the gold orb. He held it up. The sphere started to emit a low vibration of sound. Hilary covered his ears and asked Ian to put the globe back in his pack.

Ian positioned the orb back in his backpack. Hilary replied, "That's a relief. I was wondering what we were going to do if we could not find the key."

Pecky looked at Hilary with a little bit of irritation. He asked, "Hilary, didn't it occur to you that you should have mentioned your concern about the key when you first met us back at the watering hole?"

Hilary replied, "Pecky, you asked me to take you to the entrance to the City of Light, not resolve all your problems."

Pecky sat back on a rock near Ogden. He replied, "Okay, look, everyone is a little stressed out and tired. Let's not work on each other's nerves.

"We need a plan to enter the research station and make it in unnoticed. By the way, has anyone seen Bee since we made it to shore?"

At this moment, Bee came barreling out of the jungle. She bent over, trying to regain her breath, as she announced, "Dark beasts are coming from the east."

Hilary instantly grabbed Ian and dragged him up into the canopy, leaving him on a large abandoned bird's nest one hundred feet above the jungle floor. Hilary repeated his lightning-fast feat with the other travelers, Ogden being the last to make it to safety.

Hilary put his finger over his mouth and motioned to the others to be quiet. He then moved to a lower branch to get a better view of what was traveling through the jungle.

A few minutes passed and nothing. Then in the distance, a howling that sounded eerily familiar to Bee, Ian, and Pecky.

Bee looked over at Ian with dismay and said, "That sound is so familiar. It's like I am remembering it from a dream."

Pecky whispered, "My dear, that sound is not from a dream. It is the same sound that Lord Claridon made when he was transformed into a beast. The night we arrived at Claridon Castle. Most likely, the poor souls who are weeping that terrible noise are also lost in the dark."

A moment passed, and then three dark creatures moved into the clearing once occupied by the travelers. The three mysterious creatures with gleaming green eyes and six-inch claws sniffed around the camp, looking for any evidence of intruders.

The travelers high in the tree above could hear the beasts' claws clicking on the hard jungle floor below. The sound was methodical and terrifying at the same time.

The beasts stood silent, listening for anything in the jungle that would give them a reason to attack.

The travelers high in the canopy held their breaths to the point where Ogden felt he was going to pass out.

Suddenly, Ian remembered his backpack and the golden orb and black rose. He whispered to Pecky, "Hilary grabbed me so fast that I forgot my pack. It is just on the outside of the clearing."

A fearful look came over Pecky's face as he replied, "Ian, I don't think that there is anything we can do. I believe our lives are in danger if they find us, even up in this tree. I can't take the chance of warning Hilary."

The beasts one hundred feet below the travelers started to move again. They traveled in unison like they were tethered together in some unforeseen way. A moment passed, then one of the beasts stopped and held its head up, sniffing the air.

Pecky and Ian knew that it discovered Ian's backpack sticking out of the bushes. The red flap on the bag glistened in the glare of the beast's green eyes.

The dark creature slowly moved towards the pack, not knowing what it was or whom it belonged to.

Pecky knew he had no other choice but to yell down, "Hilary, its got the backpack. You have to get it back."

The pure terror of what happened next surprised everyone. In a blink of the eye, Hilary jumped down on the beast closest to the backpack with such strength and intensity he instantly broke the monster's back. Dark red blood, muscle, and ligament were oozing out of the beast. It didn't even have time to cry out in pain before it was dead.

The other two beasts hesitated for a second, shocked by Hilary's presence. Then both creatures lunged at Hilary.

One monster pierced Hilary's lower back with its six-inch claws. Hilary let out a shriek of pain that sent shivers up Bee's spine. Hilary instantly turned towards the beast and grabbed its jaw with such power that he split the animal wide open from the jaw down to the throat. Hilary threw the creature onto the ground with only gurgling sounds coming out of what was left of its mouth.

The last beast slowly backed away from Hilary, the brute feeling less potent now that his two brothers were viciously slaughtered.

Hilary stood his ground, preparing himself for the thrust from the remaining creature. The two animals stood facing each other for what seemed to the travelers an eternity. Then the creature turned and ran back into the jungle. He disappeared as his coarse black fur blended into the night.

Hilary immediately followed the creature leaving the group stranded one hundred feet into the canopy. He was soon swallowed up by the jungle.

Ogden let out a sigh and said, "Now what are we going to do?"

Pecky replied with hope in his voice, "We are going to wait until sunrise, and then we are all going to make our way out of this tree. We are going to pray that our friend will return unharmed."

Bee spoke, "Why did he follow that creature into the jungle?"

Ogden replied, "Hilary could not let that beast get to Legorian or other dark guards that patrol this area. Our plans to enter Yangambi unnoticed would be at risk. Who knows how many monsters are out there."

Pecky said, "Right you are, Ogden. The only good we can do now is wait and hope. Maybe take this time to rest before we must trek through the jungle. It's fairly comfortable in this bird's nest."

An hour passed before the travelers heard a loud rustle of bushes. A moment later, out of the thicket walked Hilary with one of his legs severely injured. His lower back was bleeding profusely.

Hilary looked up at the group and yelled, "Is everyone okay?"

Ogden replied, "Don't worry about us, Hilary. You did all the fighting. By the way, can you get us down?"

Hilary sighed and replied, "Right."

Hilary climbed the one hundred feet to the bird's nest with little effort. He used his massive arms and one good leg. One by one, Hilary brought the travelers down to the clearing.

Bee hugged Hilary once she was on the ground. She said, "Hilary, we were worried about you."

Hilary replied with a smile, "Don't worry sweetie, I have been in tighter situations."

Bee kneeled next to Hilary and examined his wounds. She felt the gash on his back and said, "Pecky, his back is badly injured. We have to get him to a doctor."

Hilary reached around and felt his wound pulling his hand away with blood sticking to the dense fur on his arm. He laid down on the ground and said, "I know a shaman that can help in a village to the north. It would add a day to our journey. I can't make it to Yangambi in this condition."

Pecky asked, "What happened to the other beast, Hilary?"

Hilary looked up at Pecky with a hard look on his face. He replied, "I killed it."

Pecky ran a finger across his chin as he thought long and hard about what to do. The blood on Hilary's back was congealing. He was unsure of how much blood Hilary lost. He was concerned that the beast carried poison in its claws. Pecky knew he couldn't move Hilary. He was too heavy.

Pecky looked down at Hilary with concern. He asked, "Do you feel any poison moving in your body. Do you think the beast infected you?"

Hilary replied, "I don't know, my friend. I am feeling tired and just want to lie down and go to sleep."

Bee sat up with a smile on her face. She announced, "Ian can help. Ian can heal Hilary."

Pecky replied, "Right, we have the most powerful shamans in our ranks. What do you say, Ian, do you want to give it a try?"

Ian looked at Pecky and Bee with a tentative look on his face. He replied: "I'll do my best, but I don't know how I healed the warrior back in the desert."

Ian walked, cautiously over to Hilary, who was passed out on the jungle floor. Bee, Ogden, and Pecky all worked to turn Hilary over on his stomach, so that Ian could get a good look at Hilary's wound.

The gash on Hilary's back was full of blood, dirt, and pus. Ian slowly rubbed his hands together and placed them directly on Hilary's wound.

Ian focused all his thoughts on healing the slash. A moment went by, then a bright green light started to emanate from Ian's hands.

Ian felt like time was slowing down. He felt as if he was observing everything from outside his body again. He could see the jungle and all his friends close by watching what was transpiring.

Instantly, Ian felt back in his body. He pulled his hands away from the wound. The gash was gone; not even a scar remained.

A slight depression came over his mind and soul as he looked down at Hilary. Hilary was looking up at Ian with an expression of pure love in his eyes.

Hilary sat up and patted Ian on the back. He said, "I don't think I ever really believed you were a true heart. I also didn't believe that you could enter the City of Light. Ian, you have made me a true believer." ✿

CS

Chapter Thirty-Eight
Deja-Vu

The smell of roses was overwhelming. The group stepped out of the jungle into a field with thousands of white roses. The meadow of roses was as thick as a football field and curved in each direction, almost as if the area of roses went in a belted circle around some unseen center.

The white roses reminded Bee of the book, *"The Wizard of Oz."* She remembered a part in the book where Dorothy and her companions went to sleep in a field of flowers poisoned by the Wicked Witch of the West.

It crossed Bee's mind that maybe this was a trap, and Legorian poisoned the white roses. But as she and her friends walked through the field of roses, nothing seemed to happen.

Ian said, "I feel that we are near the entrance to the City of Light. I was expecting to see black roses that supposedly grow near the entrance, but all I see are white roses."

Pecky stopped looked around at the roses for a long time. He replied, "Ian, please pull out the wooden box holding the black rose in your backpack."

Ian knelt and opened his pack. He pulled out the wooden box and put it on the ground.

Pecky continued, "Ian, open the box, and let's see the black rose."

"Pecky, if I open the box, the black rose will put a curse on us."

"I don't think it will. Please open the box."

Ian slowly unfastened the three latches that held the box tightly closed. He then delicately opened the box to expose the rose.

Everyone gasped as they looked down on a pure white rose.

Ian pulled the rose out of its box and set it on the ground. The rose instantly faded away into the other white roses.

"Pecky, do you understand what just happened?"

Pecky replied, "The rose does not create the energy around the entrance

to the Ancient City. The rose is a result of the energy generated by the portal to
the City of Light. I surmise the rose turns black when taken beyond this area.

"The City of Light is pure creation. The rose is a residual effect of creation.
The rose is not a curse. It is a delivery tool of creation to anyone who possesses
one. Only a true heart can wield such power. Your heart is not corrupt.

"Even a slightly corrupted heart will turn the rose black. A corrupted
heart will create the world on personal desire and greed. Lord Claridon stole
the rose to free his people from misery. What the rose did was stop time.
Everyone living in the world will feel grief at one moment or another. Only
interrupting time will keep people from the misery of the world.

"There is a famous saying, 'When the Gods want to punish us, they give
us what we desire.'"

Pecky asked Hilary, "Hilary, you have been here before. Why didn't you
tell us about the white roses?"

Hilary replied, "You didn't ask."

The group stood in the middle of the field of white roses for a long time,
not knowing what to do next. On the other side of the area was a dirt road
leading to the Yangambi research station. At the end of the path there was a
group of large red brick buildings. Hilary specified that the main building was
the library.

Bee asked, "Do you think it is a trap?"

Hilary looked at Ian and asked, "Ian, what do you feel in your heart?"

Ian replied, "My inner voice is telling me that there is no danger."

"What does your inner voice sound like?"

"When my inner voice speaks to me, it isn't a voice. My inner voice speaks
to me in visions, flashes of experiences, and allegories.

"I knew the research station was not a threat because my inner voice kept
showing me the eye of a hurricane. The center is calm and not dangerous.
The storm rages around the eye.

"I was once told that there are two kinds of memories. One type of memory is experiential, and the other is recollection. Recollection is when you recall
a phone number or someone's name. When you experience a memory, you
are reliving the memory. All five senses engage during the process of remembering an experience. Does that make any sense?"

Hilary replied, "Actually, no, but I believe you understand, and that comforts me."

Pecky asked, "So, what do we do?"

Hilary looked at Pecky with a grin and replied, "Well, this journey is all
about a true heart. So, we trust our friend's heart and move on to the library."

A single figure came out of the library building and stood in silence as the travelers walked the three hundred yards. Ian felt that this person knew they were going to reach the station precisely at that time.

The closer they came, the more it became apparent that this person was a Congolese man in his late fifties. He couldn't be more than five feet tall with black weather-worn skin and with a little hair on his bald head. He stood motionless as the travelers moved cautiously in his direction.

Ian stopped in his tracks. He was jolted by the feeling that he had been at this place many times before. He felt that he knew the stranger.

Bee asked, "What's wrong, Ian? Do you feel something?"

"I just had an overwhelming feeling of deja-vu."

The closer the group came to the man, the more Ian felt that he had traveled to this place many times before. Ten feet from the stranger, the travelers all stopped with military precision.

A smile came over the Congolese stranger as he stepped forward and said, "Welcome, Ian, it is so nice to see you again. You might not remember me, but my name is Kasunga Berta. I am the director, librarian, and keeper of the sacred portal to the City of Light."

Pecky, Hilary, Bee, and Ogden all looked over at Ian with a look of pure disbelief. Hilary asked, "Ian, how is it that this person knows you."

Kasunga pressed his hands together in a comforting manner and replied, "Hilary, I know all of you. A thousand times before you all stood before me with the same questions, and of course, I have had to give you the same answers, repeatedly.

"Most times, we stand here and clear everything up. This time I want to proceed to the dining hall and have a bit to eat and drink. How does that sound?"

Kasunga turned and moved towards another building to the south of the library. He motioned for the travelers to follow him. The group all dutifully followed Kasunga without a word.

Throughout the compound, Congolese men, women, and children appeared as the travelers made their way to the dining hall. They came out of buildings and from behind bushes and trees.

Kasunga asserted that the people in the research station meant the travelers no harm. They hid so as not to dissuade the group from moving forward.

The Congolese people gave the travelers a sense that nothing, not Legorian or the rebels fighting in the Congo, had ever entered the research station. Everyone in the area seemed well-fed and happy, with big smiles on their faces.

Ian felt something more profound in his heart. He felt as if the people were old, even the children. When he connected with their energy, he felt a depth of spirit he had not felt before. They felt prehistoric.

When the group entered the main dining hall at the research station, food and drink were waiting for them. Three more elders from the camp were waiting to welcome the group, especially Ian.

It appeared to travelers that the food glowed in a way that concerned them, but not enough to avoid consumption.

It crossed Ogden's mind that this might be an elaborate trap set by Legorian. But his heart communicated that this was something else, something wonderful.

The day quickly moved into the evening as the visitors enjoyed the Congolese hospitality. Pecky was the first to broach the subject of their arrival.

Pecky sat down at the table next to Kasunga. He asked, "Kasunga, you mentioned that we had been here many times before. Can you clarify what you mean?"

Kasunga laughed and replied, "Pecky, I was wondering when one of you would pursue an explanation."

Ian asserted, "Kasunga, I feel that I know you. I believe that you are ancient."

Kasunga looked at Ian with tears in his eyes. He replied, "Ian, that is the first time that you have had that insight. You seem to be able to hear your heart."

Pecky asked, "Please explain how you know so much about us?"

Kasunga wiped the tears out of his eyes. He continued, "It is always best to start at the beginning.

"More than ten thousand years ago, the people you see in this village, including myself, lived in a region of the Congo not far from here. Anyone traveling in this area would disappear and never return. This legend kept most from venturing here.

Hilary asked, "You're saying that you and the people in this village are more than ten thousand years old?"

"Kasunga, I have been here many times in the past, and I have never heard this story. Most times, the research station looked abandoned. I look around now, and it looks almost new. I don't understand."

Kasunga continued, "I can't tell you how many times you have asked that same question. I would believe by now that you would just understand.

"Yes, Hilary, we are older than we look. How long we have been in this area is complicated. My people have been trapped in this energy vortex for more than a thousand lifetimes.

"When you entered the research station years ago, there was one big difference, you did not have a true heart with you. Ian's energy has heightened your energy, and you see the research station in a new light."

Kasunga paused for a second to take a drink of tea. He continued, "A devastating earthquake and then a flood took our village, forcing us to move into this region. We were at war with other tribes, and this was the only area where my people felt safe.

"When we wandered here, we found that everything grew in abundance. We can plant a seed in the ground, and a plant will grow within a week delivering a great wealth of fruits or vegetables. Wild game is abundant. Predators will not move beyond the white roses that surround the region.

"The soil is fertile with minerals including diamonds, gold, and silver. The air is fresh. The sun warms us but is not destructive with heat.

"Our people felt that we had found a paradise. You might call a Garden of Eden. But there was one catch, we can't leave or physically pass on until a true heart opens the portal to the City of Light.

"We discovered that the energy vortex that makes up the research station area is exactly thirty-three miles in a perfect diameter.

Bee asked, "What happens if you leave?"

Kasunga replied, "If you leave within the next few days, you will be okay, but you will have aged one year.

"My tribe is so connected to this world that if any of us leave, we will die a terrible death. We will then find ourselves right back here. Many of my people have tried to go, and they find themselves right back here once again."

Ogden asked, "How was it that the Europeans built this research station?"

Kasunga answered, "Many lifetimes ago, I can't quite remember how many, we found the center of the energy vortex. We found the chamber under a seven foot obelisk made out of pure crystal. We discovered that the chamber is the entrance to the City of Light.

"A second ago, relative to our life experience, the Europeans came because of the wealth of minerals. The Europeans considered that this area might be the lost Solomon mines written about in the Christian Bible. Of course, we knew better, but the Europeans viewed us as less than human.

"We knew that the Europeans would come and go in an instant. Because of their inability to see beyond their ignorance.

"At first they suffered once they were here for any length of time and tried to leave. One scientist figured out a way to come and go without the acceleration of age. They discovered that the roses would slow down time.

"The Europeans would carry the roses with them at all times. They found over time that the roses only delayed the process of aging, it did not stop it. Their greed for the minerals was insatiable, and finally, their downfall.

"They built the library over the chamber without knowing what lay deep in the ground just under their feet."

Ian asked, "How am I involved with this place?"

Kasunga took a sip of tea and continued, "This place is not only old, but it is part of reality that is infinite. That is why Legorian or his devotees dare not enter this place. Their whole existence is made up of time and space. They would cease to exist if they took one step beyond the white roses.

"You arrived at the research station a thousand lifetimes ago. You have walked up to me at the same time and the same place with the same companions, repeatedly. The world outside this energy vortex changed, we did not.

"We comprehended after many lifetimes our fate was tied to yours. Each time you took the journey, you became a little more self-realized. We felt that sooner or later, you would finally enter the City of Light and set us free."

Ian replied, "If what you are saying is correct, and my heart tells me your words are true, I have attempted to enter the City of Light many times but have failed every time."

Kasunga looked at Ian with amazement, "Yes, Ian, that's correct. That is the first time you have understood that concept.

"There are seven challenges that you must overcome to open the final portal to the City of Light. Once you open the first entrance, you cannot turn back. You live out your life in the illusion you have created and then return to try once again."

"Seven portals lead to the Ancient City. Each portal has a different level of illusion that you must overcome. Each illusion is relative to how you perceive yourself in this world."

Hilary asked, "How do you know this if you have never taken the journey to the City of Light?"

Kasunga laughed and started to reply but was interrupted by Ian, "He knows this because he is supposed to know it. He is the keeper of the entrance to the City of Light. His purpose is to tell me what I need to know."

Kasunga looked at Ian with love in his eyes. He replied, "Yes, Ian, that is correct. That is the first time that you understood that insight. This gives me hope that you might make it all the way."

"Your father tried to open the gate to the City of Light but failed along the way. He's lost in an illusion. He exists somewhere between this world and the final portal to the Ancient City."

Ian queried, "My father was here?"

Kasunga continued, "Yes, your father is a pure heart, but not a true heart. I tried to dissuade your dad, but he had a key with him and was determined to try."

Ian asked, "I thought there was only one golden orb key to the Ancient City."

Kasunga replied, "No, there are seven. There is a golden key for each of the portals."

Pecky asked, "When do we start the journey to the Ancient City?"

Kasunga replied, "Pecky, only Ian can enter the first portal to the City of Light. The journey is his burden alone. You cannot help or guide him anymore. Your trek with Ian is over.

"Ian must trust his heart to complete his journey. You are not a true heart and would only confuse him."

Pecky said, "Ian, we do have a choice to turn back. If we do, Legorian will continue to spread his darkness in the world."

Ian thought long and hard about his next move. He replied, "I feel deep in my heart that my purpose is to succeed or fail to open the final portal. If I turn away now, I will deny the purpose of my existence, and many would suffer. ☙

ଓଃ

Chapter Thirty-Nine
Unaided but Not Alone

For the first time in many weeks, or maybe months, Ian, Bee, and Ogden felt safe. Safe enough to take leisurely walks along the edge of the research station just inside the ring of white roses.

They could see dark figures moving about in the jungle but knew a devotee of Legorian would never dare to step foot into the heightened energy field, with fear of death.

Kasunga informed Ian that he must absorb the higher energy inside the research station for three days before he would be able to enter the first chamber on his way to the City of Light.

Kasunga warned the group every day they were in the heightened energy. They will feel depleted and depressed for a week after they leave. Bee, Ogden, and Pecky decided to take the risk and stay with Ian until the last possible moment.

Hilary decided to move back into the jungle. He needed to reach his tribe in the western part of the Congo near the Atlantic Ocean. They had been living there since Legorian forced them out. Hilary wanted to be ready to move back into the area if Ian was successful. He desperately wanted to save his family.

Hilary gave Ian a goodbye pat on the back with a tear streaming down his face. He assured Ian that he was always welcomed in his tribe. He thanked Ian for his life and then disappeared into the dense jungle.

Reggie will arrive at the docks the morning before Ian had to enter the chamber. Kasunga requested his presence earlier, but Reggie was resolving a business deal, and with Reggie, business always comes first.

Bee, Ian, and Ogden explored the thirty-three square miles as much as possible. The weather inside the research center was always like a spring day in New England, no matter what was going on outside the area.

Bee decided to have a picknic, so she put together some local food in a wicker basket she found and dragged Ogden and Ian to a large grassy area near the library.

She spread a large blanket on the ground and distributed plates, cutlery, and glasses. She then distributed the food on each plate, making sure everyone received equal portions.

Ogden asked, "Bee, I bet you used to like to play tea with your friends?"

Bee replied, "Yes, Ogden, I most liked to play tea with, Elizabeth, Queen of England. Of course, I also used to play trucks and GI Joe with my brother, and get into fights that I would win."

Ian asked, "Wasn't your brother older than you?"

Bee replied, "I have a younger brother, too."

Ogden replied, "It's funny, we have been traveling together for what seems like a long time. We profoundly know each other, but we do not know each other. Our past life, I mean."

Ian asked, "Well, what was it like growing up in California, Ogden?"

"I left when I was nineteen. Looking back, I was lucky to grow up in Monterey. At the time, Monterey was a small city on a bay next to the Pacific Ocean. It has been many years since I have been back. I hear it has become a pristine tourist destination. It was a sleepy little town when I grew up there. Of course, most of the time, my friends and I were bored. I used to hang out with my friend Danny at the Seven Eleven. The highlight of our day was to get microwaved burritos." Ogden replied. "How about you, Ian, what is it like to live in Vermont? I have never been there, but I did watch the movie 'White Christmas' each year with my family."

"That movie wasn't made in Vermont. I have watched the video, and there are large California evergreen trees in the background. Vermont has mostly maples and other hardwood trees.

"Vermont is paradise, especially now that I have been away from home for so long. Vermont has magnificent forests and lakes. I don't even mind the winters. I end up snow skiing."

Ian asked, "Bee, do you miss your friends back in Britain?"

Bee stopped fussing with the food and sat up with a startled look. She replied, "Oh my God, I forgot about my friends. I left so fast I didn't tell Beverly or Eleanor where I was going or when I would be back."

Ogden added, "I'm sure Elizabeth will cover for you."

Bee replied, Yes, I bet she did, but my friends will still be pissed at me when I return home. They will see right through any made-up story."

Bee put down the food, sat up, and displayed a stern look. She continued, "As much as it would be good to know each other's past. I feel that it is much more important to help our friend Ian prepare for what lies ahead, don't you agree, Ogden?"

Ogden looked a Bee with a big smile and replied, "Yes, your'e right, as usual."

Bee continued, "So, Ian, let's see what you have learned during your journey. There is one thing that is still troubling me. I don't understand the fundamental nature of the City of Light?"

Ian replied, "What I have come to understand is the City of Light is a pure state of consciousness. It is the infinite idea that created the world you see outside of yourself."

Ogden asked, "If the City of Light is endless, why must you enter it, and if the world around us is an illusion, then why must you save it?"

Ian laughed a big belly laugh. He then replied, "I don't know if you understand how big that question is, and how important it was that you asked it."

Ian thought for a moment on how he might explain the Ancient City. He continued, "You might consider that the City of Light is the Garden of Eden. In the Bible, the original humans Adam and Eve were cast out of Eden because they ate an apple from the tree of knowledge.

"They were cast out into a wasteland. The desert that the Bible speaks of is the world we see around us. The world is an empty dream that is filled with our perceptions. Eden is a place where we were connected entirely to the Source, or what the Bible calls Jehovah.

Bee asked, "So, I understand from what Kasunga has told us, that if you make it to the City of Light, you will not remember anything about the world we now occupy or your friends?"

Ian looked at Bee with a sadness in his eyes, "Bee, I'm just telling what I know about the City of Light. I'm not telling you I like it."

Ogden asked once again, "So, why do you need to save the world if it is only an illusion?"

Ian replied, "I believe the answer to that question is the evolution of the collective soul. You see, both realities do exist in one state or another.

"To put it in simpler terms, the infinite reality is occupied by an entity who is infinite. The world of separation is occupied by entities who are separate from each other, by our perceptions.

"The infinite being could only know itself by knowing what it is not. Once it created this reality of separation, it had to process through the entire reality to once again become infinite.

Bee sat up, laughed, and announced, "Mind blown!"

Ian replied, "Basically, I enhance the evolution of human souls if I enter the Ancient City."

Ogden replied, "Because a true heart is a link between the infinite reality and the reality of separation, is that correct?"

"Well, Darwin was correct. Everything evolves, including our souls. The Source is experiencing everything in this reality through all of us. By making a connection between the two states of being, all humankind will become more aware. Most of us will start to hear our inner voice.

"Scientists have been looking for the missing link between our ancient past and our present for a long time. A true heart is a missing link. Over the thousands of years of human history, a true heart has shifted the consciousness of humankind just enough to come closer and closer to remembering who we are."

Bee asked, "What part does Legorian play in this cosmic drama?"

Ian replied, "What I have come to understand is Legorian is a creation of the Source. The Source needed to un-know its true infinite self — the infinite being had to go to sleep so it could experience this reality of separation.

"Legorian only exists in the world of separation. His only purpose is to convince us that the world we see around us is real.

"Legorian was created by the infinite being to keep us here in this reality, and Legorian is good at his job. He is relentless. The more we wake up, the more he will work to keep us asleep."

Ogden asked, "How is it that you understand this? Since you know it, why can't you transcend the world?"

Ian replied, "I understand these concepts intellectually. I need to know this on another level to transcend the world.

"I have found that there are giant leaps between believing, faith, and knowing. The only one who knows can enter the City of Light and transcend the world to a higher level of consciousness."

Kasunga walked up to the group and said, "Ian, your friends will have to leave soon. Over the next few hours, I will prepare you for your journey to the City of Light."

Bee asked, "Why can't we wait just a little bit longer, or just stay and wait for Ian to return from the City of Light?"

"Every second you linger in this energy vortex, your lives outside this place will continue to fade. Ian's journey towards the City of Light could take days, months, years, and even lifetimes. Even if Ian reaches the City of Light, he will most likely not return here.

"Ian, If your friends leave soon, they will only suffer for a few weeks."

"I have sent word to Reggie on his ship to be at the research station docks earlier this evening instead of tomorrow morning.

"Ian, Reggie has been well compensated for delivering your friends back to the world and civilization.

"Pecky will be delivered back to where the sleigh is hidden and airlifted out of the negative energy by a helicopter pilot, Reggie knows. The dark energy will not expand beyond the Congo if you move forward towards the City of Light."

"Kasunga, I don't know if I'm ready to move forward without my friends," replied Ian.

Kasunga continued, "I don't feel that you will ever totally be ready to move on alone. I don't think any true heart can be so confident in their awareness that they would not feel that they need support.

"It is the seven tests that transform a true heart. The only purpose for Pecky and the others was to get you here."

Ian added, "Kasunga, I need to discuss a few things with Pecky. I promise it won't take long."

Ian walked with Bee and Ogden, looking for Pecky. The warmth of the afternoon sun setting over the research station hit Ian as he and his friends moved about the campus. The villagers all stopped what they were doing and looked over at Ian.

Ian could feel that the villagers were waiting for Ian to release them from their self-imposed prison. Ian spotted Pecky, sitting next to a garden nestled between two research buildings. He was smoking his favorite dried fish.

Beautiful blue and yellow flowers were growing in abundance next to Pecky. The flowers had the same heightened energy that Ian observed with other flora in the research station. The light effect was like looking through a magnifying glass at the flowers. Ian walked up to Pecky and said, "Pecky, you brought me here under false pretense."

Pecky sat back against a white stucco wall baked by the sun. He replied, "Not false pretense, my dear young man, just without an explanation that you would not have understood.

"If I knocked on your door and told you that you would have to travel a dangerous road alone, would you have come?"

"Most likely not," replied Ian.

Pecky took a long toke from his pipe and continued, "You see, my dear friend, most journeys start with one view and end with a different one. If everyone who sets out on such a journey would already have a clear understanding of the events that would unfold, then what purpose would the journey be in the first place?"

Bee asked, "What about Ian's father, my father, and brother, and Hilary's family?"

Pecky sat up with a stern look on his face, "They will all be free if Ian makes it to the City of Light. I know that this might not seem fair, but this journey was always about getting Ian to the entrance to the Ancient City."

Pecky continued, "We have little time to quarrel, so everyone listens up. Kasunga informed me earlier that Reggie is arriving soon to take us back to the sleigh and, hopefully, home. So, I would say your goodbyes to Ian."

Ian turned and looked at his friends with sadness in his heart. He said, "I think I always knew deep down in my heart that I needed to travel the last part of this journey alone. Though, I know I will never be alone with friends like you."

Bee hugged Ian and started to weep. She replied, "I'm sorry that my fate is tied so closely to your success. I thought that I would be able to enter the City of Light. You know I would go with you to the end of all things. Having to turn around after all that we have been through conflicts with everything I believe."

Ian returned a big hug to Bee and replied, "I can't imagine moving on without you. I think I became content in the belief that all of you would be with me to the end."

Ogden added, "Ian, remember our blood oath, brothers for life. Hopefully, after all is done, we can go on another adventure together?"

Ian replied, "Blood oath, right."

Pecky responded with hope in his eyes, "All you need right now is to have faith. Doubt will be stripped away as you move through the seven trials. You will know the truth, the closer you come to the City of Light. The best that you can do right now is just believe that you know."

Ian sat down on a tree stump surrounded by the blue and yellow flowers and asked, "If I do make it to the City of Light, what will happen to me—or should I ask what will happen to the person I perceive myself to be?"

Pecky replied, "We don't know."

Ian replied, "You don't know?"

Pecky continued, "We don't know what will happen to you because only those who have entered the City of Light understand what happens.

"Even when a traveler who has entered the Ancient City has returned, they have a hard time describing the process. What is certain is that they enhance the consciousness of the world, sometimes just slightly."

Ogden asked, "Why have I not heard of these people?"

Pecky replied, "Many you have never heard of, but many you have, such as Jesus of Nazareth, Prince Siddhartha, to name only a few. Many who have made the trip understand that satisfying their egos is not important. It is the journey itself and the effect on the world that is important."

Suddenly in the distance, the group heard a loud ship whistle. Pecky turned to the travelers and declared, "I believe that is Reggie. It is time for all of us to leave."

The group's movement down to the research station docks was slow and labored. No one said it, but most held hope that Ian would ask them to stay.

Just as Ogden, Pecky, and Bee reached the docks, Reggie on his ship came around a bend in the river blowing its horn.

No goodbyes or fond farewells. Ian's friends left with many things unsaid because they all believe that this was not goodbye. They were waiting for the inevitable moment when they would see each other again. Bee did give Ian a hug and peck on the cheek, but she would not say goodbye. ✂

CB

Chapter Forty
Transcendent

Ian felt alone but not lonely since the ship moved out of sight. When Ian's friends left, it was like turning off a light in his heart, and then something incredible happened, he felt a new light that was all around him. He recognized that his feeling of not being lonely was his connection to the Source. Since he could not rely on his friends, he looked to his inner support.

As time passed in the research center, the connection between Ian and the Source became stronger. A warm light-filled his heart. Ian felt love for all things as he did as a child standing before the apple tree back in Vermont. He and Kasunga spoke little since Ian's friends left. Kasunga wanted Ian to absorb the energy emanating from the chamber of light. Ian needed to heighten his energy before he entered the first portal. Kasunga assured Ian that nothing he would say before he increased his energy would make any sense.

Ian was to enter the first portal exactly at 3:33 a.m. This time at night has a thin layer of energy between the physical world and the spiritual world. Kasunga warned Ian that he had a small window of opportunity. If he waited too long, then his energy would change, and he would not be able to transcend the hold of the research station.

Since Ian had entered the area beyond the white roses, he almost needed no sleep. He was wide awake when he walked over to the library to meet Kasunga at 2:30 a.m. The closer Ian came to Kasunga, the more he could see a transcendent light emanating from his body. The dark night helped Ian see the light emitting from Kasunga with intensity.

The waves of light surrounding Kasunga moved similar to how water moves around a rock in a river. The waves of light shimmered in different colors. Ian has been aware of light surrounding people for a long time, but this was the first time that he saw the light with such clarity.

Kasunga sat on a bench near the entrance to the library. Kasunga sat back and smiled a big grin. He asked, "You see the light?"

Ian was taken aback by Kasuga's revelation. He replied, "Yes, I see the flow of light around your body. I can see it around the flowers, buildings, and the others in the area. How is it that you know I see the light?"

Kasunga replied, "It is because we all are one. The closer you come to the City of Light, the more you will know your connection to all things."

Ian sat down on a stump in front of Kasunga. He asked, "I have one important question that has been on my mind that I have not been able to move beyond. Even though I have asked this same question of Pecky, Dan, and Sam."

Kasunga asked, "Is the question why?"

Ian replied, "Yes, the question is why? I cannot make sense of the paradox. I logically understand that the world around me is an illusion. I understand this illusion created by an infinite being wanted to know itself. I realize that I am not a body. All things are connected to me. Since this is true, and I recognize it to be true, then what is the purpose to continue towards the City of Light? In all rights, I am already in the City of Light."

Kasunga replied, "Your being, your soul, exists in an infinite reality and a world of separation at the same time—of course, this is the paradox. Not unlike the paradox between Einstein's unified field theory and Planck's quantum theory. If you remember the conflict in the two theories from your high school physics class?

"To exist only in an infinite reality, you need to know 100% that you are infinite. If you knew 99.999%, you still would also be in a world of separation. Remember, the Source created this reality to understand itself. The Source can only know itself 100%, and because you asked the question why, you still don't know yourself 100%.

Ian asked, "Are you saying that I am the infinite being, the Source?"

Kasunga replied, "Yes, you are the infinite being. The Source is experiencing the reality of separation through all of us, equally."

"Kasunga, If I'm the infinite being, then I am only talking to myself. If I am the Source, then nothing can be outside of myself."

"Yes, Ian, you are only talking to yourself. Maybe a more straightforward way of looking at your journey in the physical world is to consider it an amusement park for your consciousness.

"When you had the thought to know yourself, you created an amusement park based on a world of separation. Once you entered the park, you could not leave until you rode all the rides. You needed to go through the process of knowing yourself 100% by experiencing what you are not.

"Similar to the amusement park, you still need to process through the experience of being separate from who you are. The most crucial aspect of transcending the amusement park is letting go of your desire for the world. You need to let go 100% of your desire to know yourself because you know yourself 100%. It is the purpose of knowing yourself that has kept you here. The primary desire for all who exist in this physical world is to understand who we are."

"Kasunga, my inner voice tells me that I will not lose the love of my family when I enter the City of Light. Their love will become my love."

"Yes, Ian, when we go home, we go towards those who we love. One of the most challenging concepts in this world to transcend is that there is no outside love. Most in this physical reality pursue external love and acceptance, but love comes only from within our hearts. We cannot receive love from those external to us because the world outside of us is an illusion.

"Ian, it is getting late, and we could discuss existence all night long, but we need to move on to the chamber of light. Are you ready to receive the information about the seven challenges?"

"Kasunga, I'm ready to understand the seven trials."

"Good, Ian." Kasunga motioned for Ian to follow him into the library. They moved through a labyrinth of bookshelves toward the center of the library, to what seemed to Ian was a conference room with a single large oak table surrounded by chairs. Ian could sense that below his feet was a powerful energy surging in all directions. He felt as if the power was connected directly to his heart.

Kasunga motioned for Ian to sit at the head of the table. A moment later, one of the Congolese men working in the library brought in local tea with English style biscuits and left it on the table.

Ian said, "Kasunga, I cannot get over that we have been in this same place at this same time for a thousand lifetimes. I feel it in my heart, but my mind has a hard timing processing the information."

Kasunga chewed on the biscuits while he gathered his thoughts. He continued, "Yes, Ian, you would think by now I would know what to tell you, but after you leave me, you are on your own. I always try to consider what I might not have told you or what I should have said instead. I wonder if a bit of knowledge I supplied you made you think twice about the correct path in the chamber."

Ian asked, "Why don't you just start from the beginning?"

"Right, you are, Ian. The beginning is always the best place to start. First, the world you are about to enter is controlled by Legorian. Pecky told me that you already understand that Legorian is a part of you.

"Legorian is a phantom, a shadow in the world, but he is in control of the challenges you will need to overcome. In other words, you will need to beat Legorian at his game. Legorian's purpose is to keep you from reaching the City of Light. He has been doing it for a long time and is good at it.

"A few words of wisdom that you might carry with you—the only way to control others is not to want control. The most powerful people are those who do not desire power. The best way to beat Legorian at his own game is not to want to play, understand?"

Ian replied, "No."

Kasunga laughed and continued, "You will understand when it comes time. As you already know, there are seven trials that you will need to overcome. Each test represents a level of energy. Everything in the universe, earth, plants, animals, and humankind are connected to the Source by seven points of flowing energy. You may have heard of them as chakras or Chi.

"These points of energy flow back and forth between the physical world and the spiritual world. Part of us resides in the world of separation, and part of us exists in the infinite reality. Each point of energy, or chakra, represents a different connection that you need to overcome. Most everyone in the world have blocks to prevent a perfect flow between the two realities. Only a true heart can clear all the blocks and create a perfect flow between the infinite reality and the physical world. Since we are all connected, your success will help the world transcend to a higher level of consciousness.

"The chamber of light is not a door to the City of Light. The exact nature of the chamber of light is impossible to communicate. Only those who enter comprehend what the chamber of light does.

"The chamber of light is a life energy accelerator or a superconductor. If you remember in your high school physics class how electricity works, you may consider that the chamber works similarly. Electrons removed from an atom sent through a copper wire, and when you turn on the switch, the particles go back home. During our journey through this reality we are basically electrons looking for our spiritual home. The chamber of light acts as a superconductor accelerating the process."

Ian interjected, "Yes, I remember my physics teacher explaining how lighting works. The clouds move across the surface of the earth, picking up electrons, and when enough moisture builds in the air, the particles go back home to the atoms."

Kasunga continued, "Yes, Ian, that is correct. You cannot transcend each level of energy unless you have a perfect flow between the world of separation and the infinite reality. I cannot tell how to create this perfect flow of energy. Each challenge is created by how you perceive yourself in the physical world. Because our perceptions separate us, I can never know how you see the world.

Your inner voice will guide you through challenges. You just need to listen to your heart."

Ian laughed and asked, "So, basically, what you are saying is that I am hearing what you are saying based on my perceptions, not yours?"

Kasunga also laughed and exclaimed, "Yes, crazy stuff, again, it is a paradox." Kasunga continued, "When you enter the chamber, your first energy point that you need to transcend is the root point or first chakra. This point in the physical world is located at the base of your spine. In the spiritual realm, the red energy of the root point will manifest as a perfect sphere of light outside your being.

"As I stated before, Legorian is in control of the test that you need to overcome to reach the City of Light. What is important to remember is that Legorian will have less and less control of the trials as you achieve a high level of energy. Legorian will be most potent during the first test with your root chakra. The first chakra is grounded to the physical world and in our primal need for safety in a tribe. Also, the root energy point represents your primary ambition and need to succeed. Masculine sexual energy is predominant in the first energy point. The root, or first point of energy, will manifest itself by a red stream of light in the chamber."

Ian exclaimed, "I guess the root energy explains what happens when two armies fight each other on a battlefield. I have often wondered why one group of men follow a leader and another group of men follow another leader, at the cost of their lives. It doesn't make any sense to follow one leader over the other, do you know what I mean?"

Kasunga answered, "Yes, Ian, at our base root energy point, we attach ourselves to a tribe, family, country, kingdom, beyond our own needs. We often blindly follow a leader into a situation where our lives and moral compass are compromised. Persuasive people know this and have used poor souls to follow false doctrine blindly.

"The second point of energy is in your lower stomach. Feminine sexuality energy, creativity, and self-worth are predominant with this energy point. Emotional freedom and sexuality will blossom when you balance this second energy point. The second energy will manifest itself by an orange stream of light in the chamber.

"This energy point explains why someone in an abusive relationship will stay no matter how bad it becomes. Our need for intimacy connects to this energy point, which becomes more significant than someone's own self-interest or belief system.

"The third point is described as the solar plexus energy point. It is in your upper stomach area. Personal power, ego, anger, and strength are central to this energy point. The third energy will manifest itself by a yellow stream of light in the chamber.

"It is important to remember that as you transcend from one energy point to another, Legorian will have less control over what you encounter. legorian's reduced power will peculiarly be true after you move beyond the third energy point. The first three energy points are of the physical world, and the last four are transcendent energy points.

"The heart energy is the fourth point. Love, compassion, and spirituality are central to this fourth energy point. The fourth will manifest itself by a green stream of light in the chamber.

"The throat energy point is the fifth. Communications and innovation are central to this energy point. Healing and transformation are in this point. The fifth energy point will manifest itself by a blue stream of light in the chamber.

"The third eye, right above your physical eyes in the center of your fore-head, is the sixth energy point. Psychic ability, higher intuition, is central to this energy point. The sixth energy will manifest itself by a purple stream of light in the chamber.

"The crown energy point is the seventh and final challenge. The seventh energy point resided just behind the top of your skull. Spirituality and en-lightenment are central to this point. The seventh energy will manifest itself by a white stream of light in the chamber.

"Remember, Ian, your main purpose is to release all the blocks between all seven of these energy points. Doing so will change your consciousness and the consciousness of the world."

Ian asked, "Do you know what the trials will look like?"

"No, Ian, unfortunately, each test will reflect how you perceive yourself in the physical world. I can tell you that the seven tests represent your past lives. Your perceptions have changed each life you have lived.

"As I have done a thousand lifetimes, I contemplate how much I should tell you and how much is too much. You see, Ian, once you enter the chamber of light, all the knowledge that you acquired during your journey to the re-search station and what we have just discussed will only be a faint voice in your heart. It is getting close to 3:33. Are you ready?"

Ian sat back and contemplated, for a long time. He replied, "No, but I am ready as I will ever be."

Kasunga led Ian down a stairway into the lower bowels of the library. In the middle of a cavernous basement floor was a round seal with ancient writing.

Kasunga stood over the seal and said, "Below this seal is the cavern that will open the first portal to the City of Light. The European builders of this research station tried to open this seal many times and were unsuccessful. They sought to cover the seal up with cement. Within one day, the cement would disappear, and the seal would be visible again. Ian, do you have the key to the City of Light?"

"Yes, I have it in my backpack."

"Good, then this is goodbye. In the next stage of your journey, you go alone.

"Hold the key out and stand on the outer edge of the seal. The seal will move down into a cavern below. A seven-foot crystal obelisk will move up through the center of the seal. In the center of the obelisk, you will find a perfectly round hole. Place the golden orb key in the obelisk.

"On the walls surrounding the center of the cavern are seven dots. Each dot is colored, representing the different energy points, the first point of energy being red. When you place the orb in the obelisk, the key will emit seven streams of color. Align the red color light with the correct color on the wall. This process will open the first portal to the City of Light."

Ian asked, "What should I do next?"

Kasunga laughed and replied, "Hold on for a wild ride."

They embraced each other with nothing else said. Kasunga only turned around and walked back up the stairs.

Ian did as Kasunga instructed, and as he foretold, the seal started to move down into a cavern. The cavern looked to be perfectly round except for a flat floor where the seal came to rest. A three-sided obelisk moved up through the center of the seal.

Ian placed the golden key in the center of the obelisk, and instantly the golden orb started to emit seven streaming colors. Ian positioned the red color light in line with the red-colored dot on the cavern wall. A warm light emanated from the center of the cavern and expanded to encompass the entire cavern. Suddenly a blinding light burst from the golden orb, and Ian vanished. ⁌

ભ

Chapter Forty-One
My Family, My Tribe

"Cosimo, you got to get up babe, Gus is early," said a squirrely redheaded woman in her twenties moving around a bedroom opening drapes.

Ian slowly opened his eyes. He lifted his head and looked around the dimly lit room and replied, "I'm sorry, who is Cosimo, and where am I?"

The young woman stopped and looked at Ian for a long time. She replied, "You must have laid one on last night. You're Cosimo, Cosimo Cricchio, and this is our humble hole of a home in Providence, Rhode Island. Now, do you remember?"

Ian slowly sat up in bed, hanging his legs over the edge. He kept rubbing his head, which seemed different to him. He looked over at the woman who was wearing a short black skirt, high heels, and a freshly ironed white blouse, and asked, "Who are you?"

The woman stopped applying her makeup. She looked over at Ian with irritation and replied, "Cosimo, I don't have time to play this game. I'm already late for work. I'm your girlfriend Carena, Carena Sanpaolo. Look, sweetie, I laid out your best suit. Gus is in the kitchen. I am out of here."

Carena rushed around the room, putting her coat on and then came over and kissed Ian's forehead and said, "Good luck today, sweetie." She then quickly moved out of the room. Ian soon heard the front door shut with a loud thud.

Ian slowly stood up. He was dizzy at first. His body felt old and tired. He had a headache and could smell whiskey on his breath.

He walked over to the mirror, fixed to a dresser against the wall of the bedroom. When he looked in the mirror, a stranger was looking back.

Ian saw a man in his late twenties with black curly hair and large dark eyebrows. He had thick beard stubble on his face. He was wearing a white sleeveless tee-shirt with light gray boxer shorts. His arms were muscular. He stood about six foot one inches.

"Bada Bing, let's go, buddy, what's the holdup?" Said a voice from behind Ian.

Ian looked around and saw a man in his late twenties leaning up against the door jamb. He was around five foot eight and stocky. He appeared to be Italian with dark hair, and his skin had an olive oil complexion.

Ian looked back in the mirror and realized that he was the person looking back. He also seemed to be Italian.

Ian's head started to clear up, and he remembered that he lived the life of a man named Cosimo Cricchio. He also remembered his life as Ian, or was Ian's life just a dream, he thought?

He turned around and said, "I'll take a quick shower and be out."

Gus looked at Ian with a big grin and replied, "Hurry up, buddy, today is a big day. I want to go to the diner before we do that thing."

Gus walked out into the living room. Ian took his shower and dressed in his suit, not knowing what was going on or if he was Cosimo or Ian.

He did start to remember from Cosimo's life that he could not trust anyone, even the guy in his living room. He had to keep his dream of Ian's life close and play it safe.

Ian walked out of his tenant apartment into the sun of an early spring day. He looked around and saw rows of homes and apartments lined up on both sides of the street. Some of the buildings were brick, and others had white clapboard siding. Many of the houses looked in disrepair with paint peeling and with missing shingles on the roofs.

Gus smacked Ian on the back and said, "You seem a little distant chief, you up for this thing we have to do?"

Ian replied, "I'm ready to go."

Ian started to transition to his life as Cosimo. His experience as Ian became a distant memory, or was it just a dream? Cosimo couldn't remember. He remembered the Congo in his dream. He vaguely remembered friends and a penguin for some reason.

Cosimo and Gus got into a golden brown 1970 Cadillac Eldorado with a bright white interior. The engine started with a roar, and they sped off.

Gus asked, "You're a little quiet chief, is something wrong?"

Cosimo replied, "I have a lot on my mind."

"I bet you do" replied Gus

Cosimo started to feel that the life of Ian was only a dream. He just didn't remember ever having such a dream or being so disturbed by a dream.

The buildings in Providence, Rhode Island, grew as Gus drove the car downtown.

Cosimo remembered that he grew up in Providence, and he had lived there his whole life. He could not shake the feeling that he had been in another life.

Cosimo started to remember that this was a big day for him. He began to remember that he was supposed to whack two Irish wise guys from Boston. He recalled that he was a button man, a soldier for the Manaudo crime family in Providence.

He started to recollect that Gus Aiello was his best friend, and he had known Gus since his early days in grade school. His memory of his life as Cosimo was now coming back in floods. He still could not shake the feeling that he lived another life as someone named Ian.

Gus pulled up into a parking lot just outside Angelo's Diner in downtown Providence. The outside of the building was stainless steel with large windows.

Cosimo had a warm feeling for the place. He knew he had many good times in this place, with many good fellows busting each other's balls.

Gus opened his door and turned to Cosimo and exclaimed, "Come on, skipper, let's get something to eat before we do that thing."

Cosimo knew that the thing they were going to do was murder a couple of Irish wise guys that moved in on their family's turf. This hit was going to make Cosimo a made-man. He was to become a full member of the Manaudo crime family. Like his father and his grandfather.

Gus and Cosimo walked in the diner with a sense of bravado. A large grim looking Italian man was behind the counter and nodded as the two entered the restaurant. A black haired woman in her late forties was behind the grill working diligently.

Gus looked over at the counterman and said, "Hey Luca, how is it hanging?"

The counterman replied back, "You know I don't like being called Luca. My name is Ratzamo."

A smirk came over Gus's face as he replied, "I call you Luca because you look like Luca Brazi from the Godfather."

Ratzamo replied, "I know, but I still don't like it."

Three men seated in the back corner motioned Cosimo and Gus over to their table. All three were wearing dark silk suits with wide lapels.

When Cosimo came close to the table, he could see that the older Italian man sitting between the other two men looked familiar. Not as someone from Cosimo's life but someone from Ian's life. He thought to himself that this is crazy, Ian's life was just a dream.

He knew the man as Vito Cricchio, a captain in the Manaudo crime family. He knew him as his father. He also knew him as Ian's dad in his dream.

Vito motioned for Gus and Cosimo to lean in. He said in a low voice, "You're taking care of that thing today?

Gus leaned in and said quietly in Vito's ear, "All will be right."

"Good," replied Vito. He stood up and kissed Cosimo on both cheeks and continued, "This thing you do is only the beginning. This will make your bones. Of course, if you screw it up, you might be bones, capiche?"

"No problems," replied Cosimo.

Cosimo never called his father papa or any other endearment. Even as a kid, he called his father, sir, or Vito. Vito wanted his children to know his standing in the family, not his own family, but the one he made a blood oath with. The family he expected his son to be part of for life.

Gus tapped Cosimo on the shoulder and said, "Let's get something to eat."

The two walked to the other side of the diner and sat down. Without ordering, a waitress walked up and put down two coffees and two plates with eggs, ham, and toast with one side of hash browns.

Gus looked up at the waitress and said, "Thanks, Cesca, you're a doll."

"Yeah, right, so, when are you going to ask me out?" replied the young waitress.

"When I get around to it," replied Gus.

The waitress walked away with an irritated look on her face. She then turned around and gave Gus her middle finger.

Gus laughed and then turned to Cosimo and said, "Nice Italian girl, huh Cosimo? Just a little too young. Plus, her ass is just a little too small. You know I like girls with a nice big ass."

Cosimo just looked at Gus with a concerned look on his face. He could not shake the feeling that he lived another life as someone named Ian. And the life Ian lived was beyond his understanding.

Gus looked at Cosimo for a long time. He then asked, "Okay brother, what is the problem, you have had your head up your ass since I picked you up. It can't be the drinking from last night. I have seen you drunker and you still pick yourself up the next day. Are you scared of this thing you have to do?"

Cosimo looked at Gus, wondering if he could trust him with his dream. He needed to trust someone.

Gus asked again, "Okay, what is bothering you, skipper?"

Cosimo looked down towards his father sitting with the other men and replied, "I had this crazy dream last night that I was living an entirely different life. I was some seventeen-year-old kid named Ian."

Gus replied, "So?"

Cosimo continued, "So, I haven't been able to shake this dream. I have a strong feeling that this day, especially the thing I have to do, is a test of some kind."

"You're friggin right. It is a test" relied Gus with a frown on his face.

Gus continued, "This thing of ours is a test of your loyalty to the family, to your tribe, capiche?"

Cosimo sat up with a shiver down his back and replied, "That's what I was told in the dream. I would have to make a decision about my tribe."

Gus, taking a sip of coffee, asked, "What decision?"

Cosimo replied, "This chief or shaman in my dream told me that I would have to break out of this reality I am in right now. I would break out by not fulfilling my tribal duty. If I complete my tribal obligation, I would be stuck here forever."

Gus asked, "Stuck, where?"

"Here with you, with the family, with my tribe," replied Cosimo.

Gus motioned the waitress for more coffee. He sat back in the leather booth and spread out his arms and asked, "I don't know what it is you are saying, Cosimo. Are you talking about not fulfilling your family obligation? If that is true, you know the consequences? You know what will happen? You have been waiting for this day for a long time. Are you going to let a dream screw you up?"

Cosimo rubbed his head with both hands. He replied, "Your'e right Gus, it was just a dream."

Gus leaned in close to Cosimo and, in a whisper, said, "If the feds are bugging us right now, they are going to have something to use against us. Let's go out to the car and just get to what needs to be done, done."

Gus stood up and waved to the waitress and left a hundred dollar bill on the table. Cosimo grabbed his coat and walked out of the diner with Gus trailing behind.

Gus and Cosimo sped away towards East Providence through Blackstone Park. Cosimo looked out the window as the city passed by, wondering what to do. He was conflicted for the first time about his duty to his family and his tribe.

Gus interjected, "Cosimo, you know what you have to do."

Cosimo looked over at Gus for a long time. He replied, "I can't do it. I can't clip these guys."

Gus punched the dashboard of the car with his right hand. He replied, "Cosimo, if you do this thing, you will be upped. You could be the next captain. Top of the food chain. Wiseguys will be earning for you. One job, and you're a made-man. You want to give all that up for a dream?"

Cosimo looked out the window and replied, "It's not about the dream. It is about what I know in my heart. I don't believe anything that is going on around me. I just know that if I do this thing, then I will be lost, even at the cost of my own life."

Gus didn't reply. He just looked at Cosimo with disdain and continued driving. A few minutes later, they arrived on Vincent Avenue, East Providence. Gus parked the car around the corner on Dodge Street.

Cosimo thought how strange it was that he was forced to murder. He could see kids playing at Silver Spring playground. The kids didn't know what evil he had to do. They were unaware of him and his world, at least until they grew up.

Gus turned around, grabbed a bundle from the back of the car, and slowly unwrapped it, exposing a nine-millimeter pistol. He then placed the gun on Cosimo's lap and said, "Don't worry, buddy, the gun is untraceable. I filed off the serial numbers and taped the handle and trigger, just like in The Godfather. You remember, what fat Clemenza did for Michael?"

Cosimo looked down at the pistol and then picked it up. He looked in the chamber to make sure it was loaded and then looked over at Gus. He exclaimed, "Your'e right, it was only a dream."

Gus replied, "Good buddy, the two potato heads are in the yellow house. After you clip them, drop the gun, and grab the money and the booking slips. We want to know what other family members are doing business with these guys."

Cosimo asked, "Are they alone?"

Gus replied, "Yeah, my snitch told me that they are alone when they count the take, and today is the day. They think we do not know about this place. We only have an hour before the others show up to take the money to Boston."

Cosimo stuffed the nine millimeters in his coat pocket and opened the door to the car. He turned around, looked at Gus, and said, "Are you coming?"

Gus replied, "No, buddy, this is your thing. I will be right outside the door keeping an eye."

Cosimo knew that Gus was supposed to keep an out for anyone showing up unexpectedly and keeping an eye on him. Gus was there to make sure he completed his obligation to the family.

Gus was his best friend from childhood. He was the guy that would have to kill him if he failed his family. Cosimo knew that was how this thing worked. It was always your best friend that walked up behind you and whacked you.

The two walked across the street and down an alley behind the little unassuming yellow cape. Gus motioned for Cosimo to proceed into the home.

Gus was holding another nine-millimeter pistol next to his thigh. Gus said, "Remember, two in the torso and one in the head."

Cosimo stood at the back entrance of the house for what seemed like a long time. He kept hearing a voice in his heart telling him not to go through with it at any cost. He wondered if the voice was the kid in his dream.

He then shook his head, wondering if he was going crazy. He used a key to open the door given to him by Gus. He assumed Gus's snitch delivered.

He pulled out his nine-millimeter pistol and slowly walked into the kitchen. He overheard talking in a bedroom just on the other side of the wall. He held his gun in position and kicked in the door to the bedroom.

Two men reached for their pistols on a table. Cosimo cocked his weapon and said, "Don't move, or I will blow your heads off."

The two men stopped and sat back in their chairs. The room had two large tables. On one table were stacks of cash and two assault rifles. The other table had financial ledgers.

Cosimo looked at the two men he was supposed to kill. The gangsters just kept staring back without making a move.

A relaxed expression came over one of the men. He asked, "So, what are we going to do?"

Cosimo replied, "You going to shut up as I decide if you are going to be clipped."

The man on the couch who Cosimo assumed was the boss started to talk again to his friend on the chair, "Kevin, I don't think this ginny can do it. I believe that this wop is smart and maybe wants a little bit of the action. I mean, what's the point of killing us, if we earn for him?"

Cosimo pointed the gun at the man on the couch and said, "I said shut up. I don't care what you think."

Cosimo stood there frozen, not knowing what to do. This hit was not the first time he killed for the family. He just could not do what his heart was telling him not to do. He knew if he didn't kill these two blokes, he would be dead meat.

He started to whisper to himself, "It was only a dream, it was only a dream."

The man on the couch looked at Cosimo for a long time. He asked, "Your Vito's son Cosimo, right? Look, my name is Colin. This whole thing is a mess. I got permission from your father to do our business in your town.

"I pay your father a percentage. You don't have to do this. We just need a sit down with your father. Your father is pissed because we are just a little late on the vig."

At that moment, Gus burst into the room. Gus shot both Irish gangsters in the head. He then walked up to both bodies and fired two more bullets in each torso. He suddenly grabbed a bank bag on the table and stuffed all the money and financial ledgers into the container.

Cosimo looked over at the two gangsters and said to Gus, "I couldn't do it, Gus. I just could not do it against my heart. I guess I'm dead now?"

Gus looked at his longtime friend. He replied, "You're not dead. I think your father will understand. I can't clip my best friend. I don't believe that it is the first time in our family someone froze. Who is going to take care of that girlfriend of yours?"

Gus quickly moved around the house, looking for any other money or evidence of the business. He stuffed everything in the bank bags and said to Cosimo, "Let's go, chief, we can divide this stuff later. We can decide to tell Vito how much we got.

Cosimo put his gun back in his pocket and started to walk through the living room when Gus came up behind him and shot him once in the head behind the ear. Cosimo instantly collapsed to the floor. Gus then fired two more bullets in Cosimo's back.

Gus slowly walked out of the house looking around for anyone that might see him, and then got into his car and drove away. ❧

CB

Chapter Forty-Two
White Wedding

The sound of the bullet was still ringing in Ian's ear as he materialized back in the chamber of light. Ian felt the back of his neck for a bullet hole but found nothing. He could still feel the pressure and the terror when Gus shot him.

He looked around the chamber and noticed that the walls were not made of stone anymore. The chamber had become a perfect circle of light. The entrance above him had vanished, and now he stood on a pedestal in the center of the chamber. The stand seemed fixed to the center of the sphere of light, with no apparent connection to the chamber.

The red light that made up the chamber's walls shimmered with movement. Ian focused on the red light that surrounded him and made out images shifting back and forth.

His inner voice told him that the images were his perceptions. The images were the residual effect of lives he had lived tied to his tribal realities.

At first, this made no sense to him. He still felt as if he was dreaming, and maybe he was still Cosimo. Soon the remembrance of Cosimo became the dream. He recalled all that happened. He remembered what Kasunga had told him about the chamber.

Kasunga said seven trials would challenge him, relating to how he perceived himself in the world. Each test would connect to a different energy point on his being. The energy point of red would represent his relationship with his tribal needs, his need to follow his tribe instead of listening to his heart.

In the walls of light that surrounded him, the images started to take on an almost movie-like reflection. His memories of other lives and his life in Vermont kept moving across the screen. He began to have a deeper understanding of the events before his eyes. He started to understand that the red light connected to his being and that the chamber was showing him the true nature of his world.

The golden orb was now floating in front of him. The obelisk that housed the golden globe was gone.

The orb was glowing a bright gold color. The key still had a ray of red light moving directly into the red channel on the wall.

Ian understood that each trial presented would be a reality that he might or might not realize was an illusion. Ian's ability to listen to his inner voice will be challenged by whatever might be presented to him in the dream.

Ian laughed out loud at the absurdity of the thought that each life he lived was just an illusion trapping him with his ego.

Ian noticed that he felt a little more peaceful. He felt giddy with the red energy processing through his being. He could feel the energy surge between the reality he could see outside of himself and his infinite existence.

Ian knew that he had overcome the first step on the path towards the City of Light. He needed to move the key's energy in line with the next energy point on the wall of the chamber. The next energy point was orange, and as he remembered, it had something to do with his connection to intimacy.

He wanted to remember who he was and why he was processing through the next challenge. He kept saying to himself, "I am Ian, I am Ian."

Ian slowly moved the orb in the direction of the second orange energy point on the wall. A moment later, he vanished.

• • •

"Jane, how do you feel?" said a blonde woman in her fifties. Ian looked around and found himself in a bedroom of some sort. The woman who was talking was sitting down on a leather cushioned chair next to a set of mirrors. When Ian studied the mirrors, he saw a young blond woman. She was wearing a white wedding dress. Ian instantly knew he was the woman he saw in the mirrors.

He was standing on a seamstress pedestal having last-minute fittings. Ian remembered the chamber of light and knew that this was another test. But, instantly his memory of himself started to fade.

Ian tried hard to keep his memory, but little by little, his new reality began to take over his mind. Soon Ian forgot who he had been. He was now a young woman named Jane.

"Jane, Jane, how do you feel, sweetie?" said the woman with a gruff voice.

Ian, now Jane, looked at the woman with a blank stare. She replied, "What do I feel about what?"

The older blonde woman stood up came over and smoothed out the hem on the Jane's dress. She replied, "About getting wed today. Are you nervous about your wedding day, dear?"

Jane's entire life started to flood back into her consciousness. She remembered that she grew up in a wealthy San Francisco family. Her family's lineage went back to seventeenth-century England. They made their wealth from the 1849 gold rush. They owned San Francisco commercial real estate and had majority ownership in financial investment companies.

She remembered that she attended an eastern boarding school for girls and attained her college degree in international finance from Wellesley College in Massachusetts.

She met her fiancé while she interned at a Boston investment company partially owned by her family. The woman in the room with her was her mother, and today was her wedding day.

"Sweetie, you seem distant. What's the matter?" asked her mother.

Jane looked down at her mother from the pedestal. She replied, "Mother, I just had the most intense feeling that I had lived another life. That I had lived the life of a young man named Ian."

Jane's mother looked at her for a long time with a concerned look. She replied, "Dear, I think you are just having wedding day jitters."

Jane replied, "Maybe so, mother, but it seemed so real."

The seamstress walked into the room and started to work on Jane's wedding dress for last minute touches to make it perfect.

Jane began to think about what had transpired over the past twelve months. She recalled how her fiancé, Patrick, and she fell in love in Boston. How he popped the question at the annual investors' ball given by her family.

How free she felt with Patrick in Boston. So far away from the drama of her family in San Francisco. She thought how first her parents were skeptical about her engagement because Patrick was a self-made man.

He didn't have the pedigree her parents longed for her. His family was of lower caste, not snobbish and emotionally inbred like her family. She felt that he was her soul mate. It had been a whirlwind romance with parties and friends all happy for her new love.

"You know, mother, I love Patrick with all my heart?" announced Jane.

Jane's mother looked at her with a big fake smile. She replied, "Yes, dear, I know. We all love him now, even though he is part of that dreadful Irish Boston family with political connections that go everywhere in Massachusetts."

Jane looked at her mother with a scornful frown. She replied, "I don't know why you continue to admonish Patrick's family. They are hardworking and his father is a state senator."

Jane's mother shrugged her shoulder. She replied, "You know, dear, that I have your best interest at heart. Those kinds of people are just not our kind, and you will better understand this as you get a little older and a little bit wiser."

Jane's mother tightened her lip as the Hispanic seamstress entered the room again with the final fittings. She motioned to Jane that they would continue the discussion later.

Jane's cell phone started to ring. She picked up the skirt of her dress and stepped down to pick up the phone when her mother said, "Stay there, dear, I'll get your phone."

Jane's mother handed her the phone and Jane had a brief conversation with the person on the other end.

Jane put down the phone and said, "Mother, everyone is moving over to the church. I think it is time we wrap this up."

Jane's mother called into the other room, "Alejandra, could you please call Randal and tell him to bring the limousine around?"

Jane stared out the window of the limousine during the drive up California Avenue to the church. She couldn't shake the feeling that this wedding and her love for Patrick was all some test.

She questioned why her parents decided not to fight her marrying Patrick. She started to wonder if the whole arrangement was set up by her family. She instantly shook off the feeling as being fearful. She could not shake the feeling that this moment in her life was a test of some sort. She could not shake a sense that she lived another life, as someone named Ian.

Jane looked over at her mother and said, "Mother, why did you and daddy finally give in to my engagement?"

Jane's mom was fussing with something in her purse while she replied, "I don't know, dear. I guess we just saw that Patrick made you happy. Your father sat down with Patrick and mapped out a path for both of you."

Jane's back tightened as she asked, "Daddy did what?"

Jane's mother stopped fussing with her purse and looked over with another fake smile. She replied, "If Patrick marries you, dear, he is not going to stay at the same little terrible firm in Boston.

"It is all set, he is going to take over as an associate partner of Del Rey Investments and will, in time, make full partner. Don't worry, dear, he doesn't have to come up with any money to buy into the partnership. Your father and I took care of everything. You and Patrick will live near to us. We already put a down payment on the house across the street. Sorry, dear, your father and I were going to tell you the good news when you both returned from your honeymoon."

An annoyed look came over Jane's face. She asked, "Does Patrick know about all of this?"

Jane's mother looked at the window and replied, "Yes, of course, dear. He already put his little condo on the market in Boston."

Jane looked at her mother with a curious eye. She said, "Mother, I wanted to live in Boston with Patrick, and continue working at the same firm."

Jane's mother looked over at Jane and replied, "Oh, no, dear. Now that you are married, you need to think about Patrick's career. We are excited about grandchildren. A career for you was fine while you were single. Now that you are married, you need to think about other more grown-up considerations."

Jane looked at her mother with amazement. In an instant, her life changed from a new beginning in Boston with the man she loved, to a more controlled life in San Francisco with the man she thought she knew.

Jane looked over at her mother with a fake smile. She asked, "Mother, did you and daddy know Patrick before I met him?"

Jane's mom kept looking out the window and consider her answer for a long time. She replied, "I believe your father met him a few times during his business dealings. I can't remember if I met him or not, dear."

The mistrust that was in the back of Jane's mind started to grow. She began to go over the last twelve months with a different perspective.

She and Patrick were introduced by a family friend. A family friend that worked closely with her father and owed her dad his career.

Patrick was a climber. His father's connections got him into Harvard. He received his MBA from Harvard's business school.

Jane started to think that their romance was a whirlwind of fun and excitement. She only knew Patrick for a couple of months before he proposed.

Jane considered that maybe she didn't know Patrick at all. Everything was moving so fast. She hasn't had a chance to breathe much less know Patrick.

A shiver ran down Jane's spine. Then she sat up straight and tried to shake off the feeling of suspicion that now permeated her being.

Jane's mother asked, "What is wrong, dear? We are almost at the church."

Jane looked at her mother, feeling that her mother was not honest with her. She gave her mother a big fake smile. She replied, "Nothing, mother, I just have pre-wedding jitters. I could not be happier."

Jane's mother smiled a fake smile. She replied, "Good, dear, your father and I are so happy for you."

The limousine pulled up to the curb at the church. An older man walked up to the car with two other people, all dressed in tuxedos.

Jane knew the older man as her father, but something struck her with force. The older man looked like Ian's dad in her dream. She shook the thought out of her mind. She told herself that Ian's life was just a dream.

Randall, the limousine driver, jumped out of the car and ran around to open the doors. Jane's father held out his hand. He said, "It's time, dear."

For a long time Jane didn't want to move. She just sat in the car in her wedding dress. Her mother and father and the others looked at each other, wondering what to say.

Her father leaned in and said, "Dear, if you don't get out of the car, you cannot get married. Are you nervous, my love?"

Jane took her father's hand and slowly moved out onto the sidewalk in front of the church. A cold sweat started to show on her face. She began to consider that maybe Patrick was different than she thought.

He was so charming. But underneath she always felt that there was a harder controlling person. He did show his true self a couple of times. There was that time when she didn't want to entertain his friends, and he lashed out, but only for a second.

He knew about her parents' plan for them to live in San Francisco and work at the firm. She wondered why he never told her about his intentions with her parents.

Another shiver ran down her spine. Then she started to try to shake off the feeling of distrust, but she could not stop feeling that her parents and Patrick conspired. If she married Patrick, she would be a prisoner of her situation.

Jane's sister Beth followed everything their parents dictated. She is hopelessly lost in San Francisco society. Everyone knows that Bill is cheating on her, but she's stuck with no career and three young children.

An overwhelming feeling of dread came over Jane. She started to feel like she could not breathe. That she was not moving towards a life with the man she loved, but moving towards a life sentence of misery and dishonesty.

The two men with her father, who she knew to be her brother and Patrick's best friend Eric, walked up the stairs and opened the two big wooden church doors. She looked at both men, and they looked back with fake smiles.

"Good luck, sis," said Jane's brother as she moved over the entrance into the church. She felt as if she was walking into a vampire's realm. She wanted to turn around and run, run for her life.

Jane could see the church was full of her friends, family, and future family. Everyone in the church rose as she entered. Jane could see all the faces looking back at her. They were all smiling the same fake smile she grew up with. The one she knew so well. The one she hated with all her heart.

She started to consider that she made a mistake. It all happened too fast. She began to understand that she didn't know Patrick at all and that she didn't want to give up her life.

The cold sweat she felt earlier was getting worse. Underneath her wedding dress, her garments were soaking wet with sweat.

Her parents looked over at each other as Jane's father escorted her to the pulpit. They both had worried looks on their faces. Jane's father whispered to her, "What's wrong, dear?"

Jane didn't trust her parents anymore. She replied, "Nothing, just a little nervous."

In front of Jane stood the wedding party. Wedding music played on the organ, and everyone in the hall was standing. She slowly made her way to the pulpit.

The wedding party consisted of her best friends, her sister, Patrick's friends, and her brother. Jane grew up going to this church. She knew the pastor since she was a little girl. She thought that he was a good man. He would not deceive her. Maybe he was not aware of what is going on. She thought perhaps she didn't know what was going on.

The pastor motioned Jane to move up to the pulpit. Jane was so nervous that she could not hear anything. Her father leaned over and whispered, "I love you, sweetie, good luck."

Jane stood in front of Patrick with everyone in the church looking at her. She wondered if she could get out of this. Jane just wanted to breathe. She wanted to scream, stop; stop everything. She needed to think, but the pastor's mouth just kept moving.

Then she heard the pastor ask Patrick if he would take this woman for his wife. Jane couldn't make out what Patrick said, but she surmised he said, yes.

Then everything became quiet. The pastor turned to Jane and asked, "Jane, do you take this man for your husband, to love and protect him in sickness and health as long as you shall live?"

Jane looked at Patrick and knew that her demise would be to move forward and say yes. Suddenly Patrick seemed like a total stranger. She looked around the church hall and looked at everyone. Everyone looked like strangers.

Jane stood, not saying a word. The pastor leaned over and whispered, "Jane, you need to answer the question. Do you take Patrick as your husband?"

The church became quiet as everyone looked at Jane with concern. Then small murmurs started to rise in the church. People were wondering what was going on with Jane.

Jane's father moved up to the pulpit and whispered in Jane's ear, "Dear, you are embarrassing your mother and me. Please answer the question."

Jane looked around at everyone in the room. She took in a big breath of air and said, "No, I don't."

She turned around and started to walk out of the church with her wedding dress, dragging on the ground. The moment she opened the two large wooden doors, a bright light flooded into the church, and she was gone. ❦

CƷ

Chapter Forty-Three
Ponzi Scheme

Ian found himself standing back in the middle of the chamber of light. However, this time he had a much different perspective on the nature of the chamber. He looked at the orb and saw that two steady streams of light, one red and one orange, moved from the key to points on the chamber wall. The wall was a brilliant orange with a tinge of red that he could see in the background.

Ian could still feel the intense feminine energy from the life he just lived. It was disconcerting to Ian to feel like a woman because he was now a man in physical form. The feminine energy soon balanced with his masculine energy.

He could see experiences move across the wall like a movie screen. He could see the past, present, and future realities. As if his time and experiences in the different realities were all happening at once.

He realized that the chamber and he were one. The orb was not creating the light. It was drawing the light that existed in him. That the secret of the sphere was that he was a spiritual being, an entity of light.

The chamber reflected the energy created by the being. That's why each person who ventures to the City of Light has a different path.

The journey to the City of Light challenges each's person's perceptions of themselves. Ian started to laugh out loud. The energy processing through his being created a giddiness.

Ian remembered Pecky telling him that the world outside of himself was only a reflection of how he perceived himself. He didn't understand what Pecky was telling him until this moment. Ian felt that Pecky didn't really understand the concept, he said it for Ian's benefit.

It occurred to Ian that he had been in the chamber for either a second or many days. He was not hungry, thirsty, or needed a bathroom break. Since there was no apparent door, this realization gave Ian comfort.

Ian considered he was ready for the next challenge. He knew that his memory of who he was must change for the test. If he were aware that it was a test, then it would not be a challenge.

He did remember who he was longer in the second challenge than he did in the first. He could hear his inner voice with ease in the second task.

Ian contemplated what the tests represent. The most important factor he discerned was that the trial challenge his ability to hear his inner voice over the world. He wondered if the chamber creates real or manufactured realities.

He slowly turned the orb again so that a steady yellow stream of light met with a yellow point on the wall of light. As before, he vanished.

• • •

"Rob, are you in or are you out?" said a young man sitting in an office chair snapping his fingers in Ian's face. Ian looked around the room quickly. He had an absolute recollection of who he was as Ian, but soon the illusion started to overcome him. He tried hard to remember that he was Ian, but all memory of his life before began to slip away.

"Rob, buddy, I'm talking to you, are you there?" said the young twenty-something hipster in an expensive suit.

The life of Robert Evens started to flood Ian's consciousness. He looked around the room and began to recognize his office in Miami, Florida. He remembered that he was an investment broker at a boutique firm, married with one small daughter, and he was twenty-nine years old.

The frustrated man in his office was an associate partner and his roommate at college. He looked at the man for a long time and then remembered his name, "Steve Johnson."

The man looked back at Ian and replied, "Yes, buddy, that is my name. Where are you, Rob?"

Ian, now Rob, sat back his chair and said, "I had the strangest flash move across my mind. I was living another life as a kid named Ian. I had traveled to someplace in Africa. Anyway, the memory is starting to fade."

Steve looked at Rob with irritation. He replied, "You asshole, you mean all the time I was talking you were somewhere else?"

Rob's face tightened with stress as he replied, "No, I was listening. The memory was only a flash."

"Then, are you in, or are you out?" replied Steve with an authoritative tone.

Rob folded his hands on his desk and looked out the window for a long time. He replied, "Look, this is a lot to take in. I need time to think."

Steve stood up and said, "No problem, you have until the end of business. I don't need to remind you that this is between you and me. No one in the office or outside the office can know. This warning includes your wife. Remember, you signed a confidentiality agreement. Are we clear?"

Rob replied, "We're clear."

Steve left the office with an air of irritability. He did not want to leave without an answer.

Rob slumped back in his chair and looked out the window. The conversation he had with Steve flooded back into his mind.

Steve offered him an associate partnership in the firm. But with one big catch. Steve disclosed that the business was a front for an elaborate Ponzi scheme.

Steve's father, a well-respected investment banker, started the investment fraud ten years ago, because of an unexpected downturn in the market.

William Johnson, Steve's father, got the idea for the investment scheme from the subprime mortgage market that was booming at the time. Investment bankers were bundling a thousand home mortgages together and selling them as one investment.

Mortgage investments were popular because of the eight percent return. The market soon went from prime mortgage holders to subprime and then sub, subprime, mortgage holders.

Selling mortgages to people who had no possibility of paying them back. The investors didn't know they were buying high-risk investments. They kept gobbling them up like candy.

William thought that he could sell the same kind of subprime investments for cars. The investment was legitimate at first, and it worked flawlessly. He would buy a thousand car loans from somewhat shady used car dealers and wholesalers. The return on investment wasn't eight percent. It was twenty-nine percent.

Bill knew it was predatory investing. He didn't care. He felt if someone was stupid or poor enough to buy a car at twenty-nine percent interest, he deserved to get taken. When he offered the investment to his clients, they lined up to feed at the trough.

Bill was offered a steady twenty percent on the dollar to his customers with a lucrative fee and commission for his firm. For a couple of years, he had more money than he had ever imagined. Even when his firm was a legit investment firm.

The shit hit the fan in the third year. Bill considered that there were going to be dead beats that would not pay the loan, but he estimated the percent wrong.

By the third year, more than two-thirds of the car loans started to go into default. He couldn't repossess the cars because there were too many. He never got all the paperwork needed to do repos.

Investors kept wanting to buy-in even though the investments were falling apart. He took the money. He convinced himself that it was only for a short time. He would pay back everyone. He needed time to make it right, to get legitimate again. He had his family to consider.

A crucial decision faced Rob. He came aboard the firm four years earlier after an internship with a large Wall Street firm. He had a stellar opportunity, but his buddy from college convinced him that he would move up faster with his father's firm.

It was only six months ago that he started to sell the car loan investments. Up until then, he worked on the arbitrage desk.

"Rob, is everything okay?" said a blonde woman in her forties standing in the doorway of Rob's office.

Rob looked up and smiled with a stressed grin. He replied, "Everything is great, Martha."

Martha walked in and closed the door. She sat down in the chair once occupied by Steve. She disclosed, "I know all about the firm."

A terrified look came over Rob's face as he replied, "You know what, about the firm?"

Martha leaned forward and, in a whisper, said, "The company is perpetuating a Ponzi scheme."

Martha had been Rob's executive assistant for two years. She had been with the company from the beginning twenty-three years ago.

Rob looked at Martha for a long time. He asked, "How do you know that I know?"

Martha sat back in the chair. She replied, "Steve told others, and they always looks the same afterward."

Rob folded his hands on his desk as he often does when nervous. A friend once told him that folding his hands was his tell in poker.

Rob said, "I don't know what to say to you, Martha. I just found out, and I am a little stunned."

Martha nodded her head and replied, "I was, too, when I found out."

"Did Steve tell you?" said Rob with a concerned look.

Martha leaned forward again and whispered, "No, he doesn't know. I found out about a year ago. Mr. Johnson left a financial paper in his wastebasket. I wasn't snooping. I just went to his office to drop off the monthly progress reports. I noticed that the document in his wastepaper basket had his handwriting in red ink. I could read 'Keep the lie going.'

"The report was from someone Mr. Johnson paid to fake financial documents. I often thought that maybe he left it in his wastebasket instead of shredding it so that someone would see it and blow the whistle."

Rob crossed his hands. He asked, "Why did you stay? You know that this whole thing will blow up sooner or later?"

Martha bit her lip and replied, "I thought about leaving right away, but the economy is in the toilet. The job market is tight. When everything went south a few years ago, I thought I would lose my job. Mr. Johnson did not fire anyone. I always wondered how he kept the business going when other firms were downsizing or going out of business.

"All I knew was that I was still getting a check. I have one child in college, and the other is about to start college. I have a mortgage, and my husband has been out of work since the downturn.

"After I found out, I decided just to wait long enough to get another job. But as you know, time goes by fast, and sometimes it is just easier to go along with the flow. Do you know what you're going to do?"

Rob put his hands behind his neck and swiveled his chair to look out the window. He replied, "I don't know what I'm going to do. Steve has given me to the end of the business to decide.

"If I leave, I might not be able to get another job right away. When the shit hits the fan, I might be implicated in the fraud. If I become a whistleblower, I will become a leper in the financial community. I wouldn't be able to get a teller job at a bank."

Martha started to wring her hands. She said, "Rob, if you come out with the lie, you're going to take us all down. I don't think your wife would like to move back to Minnesota and live with the folks."

Rob laughed out loud. He replied, "No, I don't think my wife would like leaving her mini-mansion or all her social clubs. You know I wouldn't like it either. I have gotten quite fond of the country club life.

"I had this intense feeling earlier that I lived another life. That this life, this moment is only a test. I can't quite shake the feeling that today is a trial of something bigger than my life in Miami."

Martha looked at Rob with a confused look, "I'm sorry, Rob, what are you saying?"

Rob replied, "I don't' know. Maybe I'm supposed to do the right thing."

Martha replied, "What's the right thing?"

Rob sat back and took a long breath through his nose. He replied, "I don't think the right decision is to be a whistleblower. I think the only decision I can make is for myself. If that decision causes me problems down the road, then I will have to deal with the consequences."

Martha interjected, "Rob, I don't think it would be the worst thing to bring the lie to light. What I would ask of you is, please wait to give me some time to find another job. I'm tired of waiting for the other shoe to drop. I just want to be free of this place. I don't have what it takes to stop the deception."

Rob patted Martha's hand and replied, "Martha, I promise I won't screw you over. I have a friend who is a criminal lawyer. I'll give him a call."

Martha stood up and slowly opened the door and walked out, saying for all to hear, "I'll get the report to you by first thing Monday morning."

Rob nodded his head and closed the door behind her. Rob needed to talk with his wife, Patricia. He walked over to the phone and pushed the automatic dial for home and put the phone on speaker.

The phone rang for a moment, and a child's voice answered. "Hello."

Rob sat back in his chair and replied, "Hi, sweetie, this is daddy. How is your day?"

"Fine, mommy and I are going out to buy a new dress. I want a blue one because that is my favorite color. Also, because Katy got one for her birthday," replied the little girl.

"That's great sweetie. Is mommy there?" replied Rob.

"Here's mommy," replied the little girl.

"Hey stranger, you never call in the middle of the day. What's up?" interjected Rob's wife, Patricia.

"A tear ran down Rob's face as he replied, "I don't know, just a rough day. I needed to hear your voice."

A long pause on the phone and then, "Are you okay? Is there something you want to talk about?"

"No, I just needed to hear your voice," replied Rob wiping the tear from his face.

Patricia interjected, "We have roast beef for dinner. We got a good size portion from the country butcher. It was a little pricey, but hey, you're going to be made partner soon, right?"

Rob paused for a moment creating an awkward moment in the conversation, "Right, give Izzy a big hug and kiss for me. I will be home early for dinner."

"Is everything okay?" asked Patricia.

"Everything is great; I'll see you both soon." Rob then hung up the phone and sat on the window seat overlooking the Miami financial district.

Rob looked out into the office and noticed that Martha was intently looking at him. She lowered her eyes when he looked at her. He could feel the tension building. He knew what he needed to do, but wasn't sure he had the balls to pull it off. He has gotten too comfortable with his life.

Rob thought to himself that maybe it wasn't as big a thing as he is making it out to be. Maybe Bill will pull the company out of the hole and find a way to become legitimate again.

Rob knew that his work in statistical data and arbitrage was upfront and honest. The fraud was with the car loan security division. He wondered how many other firms were fraudulent in their dealings with clients.

Rob thought about his family and his life in Miami. Rob couldn't pay his house payment with a job at Starbucks. He knew what the right thing to do was, he just needed more time.

Rob grabbed his coat and slowly moved towards the main entrance of the office and said, "If Steve asks for me, tell him I am out getting coffee."

Martha looked up with a fake smile and replied, "Will do, chief."

Rob sat in Starbucks coffee, thinking about his future, his past, and of course, his present dilemma. He was angry. He didn't need this shit. He didn't sign up for this. He should have just stayed at the Wall Street firm.

Rob might not be making the same money, but he would have at least been making honest money. Then consider that maybe if he stayed at the larger firm, he might be facing the same dilemma. Perhaps he would be confronting the same dilemma no matter where he worked in high finance.

His father, who was a flat rate mechanic for fifty years, warned him what chasing gold could make of a man. He, of course, thought his father was an ignorant fool. He felt his father didn't understand the modern world, because he was from another time and place.

Rob saw Steve come in the front entrance of the coffee shop. Steve was erratically turning his head around, looking for him. Once he saw Rob in the back corner, he walked over with a stern look on his face. Steve's father also walked in with the same stern look.

"Hey, buddy, hiding in the corner?" Steve said with a lyrical tone.

Steve and his father sat down. They both looked at Rob intently, wondering what was going on in his head.

William placed his hand on Rob's wrist and said, "You got to understand I never wanted this situation to get to this point. I have been working hard to steer the ship in another direction. You must realize that I had no other choice."

Steve looked around the coffee shop, making sure no one could hear their conversation. He asked, "What are you thinking, buddy?"

Rob looked at them with disconcertment in his eyes and replied, "I'm weighing my options."

Steve replied, "What options? Do you think we are doing anything different than the other financial firms? Everyone is screwing everyone else to make a buck.

"What about your family, what about that big house. What about the stiffs at the country club? Do you think they will understand? All those assholes are stepping on the corpses of others to get ahead. All those years at Harvard, what was it all for if you walk?"

"We're just doing what is necessary," exclaimed William.

A cold sweat started to form on Rob's face. He grabbed a paper napkin, pulled out his expensive pen from his vest pocket wrote, "I resign as of today," signed Robert Herbert Evens. He got up and opened the door and walked out. The outside flashed a brilliant light into the coffee shop. ✄

CB

Chapter Forty-Four
Of the Heart

Ian was back in the chamber of light. Something different occurred this time. He stayed connected to Rob Evan's life. The flash of Rob Evan's life moved over Ian's consciousness. Ian lived Rob's entire life in a second. He knew that Rob lost his house and went into a three-year dark night of the soul. His relationship with his wife suffered.

Their marriage was strained, but they stayed together. Rob's wife had a greater depth to her than he knew. Rob found out a lot about himself.

Rob moved from job to job until he moved back to Minnesota and took over his father's auto mechanic business. He never reaped the gold that he once worked so hard for. His life took on a depth that he didn't know existed.

Ian realized that the realities he had lived in the chamber of light were always part of him. The chamber didn't fabricate the realities. He realized that his decisions did have lifelong ramifications. He grasped that he had made the wrong decision many times in different realities he lived.

Ian remembered what Kasunga had told him about being lost in the chamber and reliving the same life over a thousand times. He knew now that if he made the wrong decision, he would have been lost in Rob's life. He would not come back to the chamber of light until after physical death and the long journey to the Congo.

If he made the wrong decision and stayed with the firm, he might be in prison for taking part in a fraud. He knew that making the right choice took him in one direction. The wrong decision took him in a countless number of directions—some more horrible then he would want even to imagine.

The chamber wall now radiated with yellow light. Behind the light, Ian could see orange and red images move across the wall. Each image that flashed across the chamber represented an infinite array of realities Ian had lived.

Ian comprehended why he was challenged during his journey towards the

Congo and the chamber of light. Each test he had to overcome prepared him for what he needed to understand in the chamber, and when he reached the City of Light.

Kasunga had told Ian that the first three tests are of the world and Legorian. The fourth would be the start of his transition back to a spiritual being. The fourth test is forgiveness and compassion. It is a primary portal to the last three tests and to entering the City of Light.

A single emerald green light moved out of the orb. Ian moved the green light to a single green dot on the wall of light. The other streams of light stayed fixed on their positions, once Ian aligned the flow of light with the green dot. He did not vanish as before but slowly faded away.

* * *

"Aiden, I laid your best suit on the bed," said a woman with a strong accent. Ian looked around the room as he had done during the first three tests, but this time he had a much firmer grip on what was happening.

"Aidan, are you listening? We have two hours until the visiting time is up at the hospital," said the woman moving frantically around the room.

Ian tried to remind himself that this time his forgiveness and compassion would be tested. His life slowly faded away, and Aidan davies's life started to flood his consciousness.

"Aidan darling, are you going to get ready?" asked the woman, now irritated.

Ian, now Aidan, looked over at the woman who he knew was his wife and replied, "Fiona, stop pressuring me. You know I don't want to go to this thing."

Fiona stopped what she was doing and looked over at Aidan. She replied, "For Christ's sake, Aidan, it is your ma's death bed."

Flashes of Aidan's life started to move across Ian's mind. Aidan felt sorry for himself because his childhood was tragic. His mother abandoned him during the great depression when he was twelve.

He could remember coming home from school, and his mother and father were arguing. She had her bags packed and was in her finest dress. The moment he walked in, they stopped arguing. She picked up her suitcase, came over, and kissed him on the forehead and said, "I love you."

Aidan's mother then walked out the door and never came back. She left him and his two younger sisters with their abusive alcoholic father.

Aiden's father would never talk about his mother. His father was a Welsh citizen who immigrated to the United States through Ellis Island, New York, in 1906. He worked in the coal mines in Wales from fourteen until he was in his early twenties. He was looking for a better life in America but found the same poverty that he left Wales for in the Lower East Side of Manhattan.

A few years later, Aiden's father made his way to Pittsburg, California. Aidan's dad scraped together a life in Pittsburg but never quite fit in. He still mainly spoke the Welsh language. For the first few years, he could only get low paying construction or fishing jobs. As time went by, he secured himself better positions with the city working on municipal projects.

When Aidan's father was thirty-six, he finally made a somewhat stable life in California. He decided to marry and knew of a young sixteen-year-old distant cousin in Wales. The family in Wales had many children and was more than happy to see one leave for a better life in America. The family was poor and thought it lucky to have one less mouth to feed.

By the time Aiden's mother, Dona, was twenty-one, she had three small children and an abusive older husband. Dona fell in love with a musician and decided to leave her husband. Aiden's father, Byrne, would only let her go if she left the children and never came back. It was one of the most painful decisions she ever had to make.

Aiden did not know about the decision until he was in his forties when united with his sister at a family reunion. His sister, who, when she was eighteen, decided to leave her father and live with her mother. Aiden did not see his sister until a family reunion twenty years later.

At the family reunion, Aiden was told about how cruel his father was to his mother. How Aiden's mother had to make a hard decision about staying in a miserable situation or leaving. Aiden's mom was so unhappy with the marriage to his father she contemplated suicide but decided to go once she fell in love with another man.

When Aiden heard this story at the family reunion, his heart was still hardened. He always felt a great pain about her abandonment. Even though he now knew that she had to leave and never come back. He still felt angry at his mother.

His mother was not at the family reunion because she had been battling cancer and was in a brief remission. Aiden considered she was not at the gathering because she would have a hard time facing him.

Five years after the reunion, Aiden received word that his mother's cancer had returned, and she is going to die. One of her last wishes is that Aiden visits her in the hospital.

At first, Aiden rejected the notion of seeing his mother on her death bed. Something deep down in his soul kept nagging him to go. He needed to forgive her and have compassion. Aiden knew that this might be his last opportunity to heal the pain.

The drive to the hospital was only two hours, but the anxiety that Aiden felt seemed to make the trip go on forever. Aiden was fifty-three, but he appeared to be much older, and on the way to the hospital he seemed much older still.

His wife kept looking over at Aiden. Aiden and Fiona got married in 1947 after he left the Navy. Aiden served in the South Pacific aboard a minesweeper. Fiona was from an Irish family that lived in his neighborhood.

Aiden often thought about his mother when he was on his tour of duty in the South Pacific. He especially thought of her before the invasion of Iwo Jima.

When he was away in the Navy, he often hoped for a chance to see his mother again, and maybe heal some of his wounds.

When he returned to the states after the war, he was a different person. He was harder and cynical about the world. Fiona softened his heart a little bit, but after a few years of struggling to grow a family of five, he emotionally shut down to the need to reconcile with his mother.

Aiden considered visiting her but always thought that there would be plenty of time. Aiden was not a coward, but to face his mother was a terrifying thought because it would mean facing the pain in his heart.

What made the pain harder was that Aiden's mother lived two hours away in Northern California. He always felt that she was in reach but not in reach at the same time.

Aiden had built his mother into a monster. He could not remember if she was kind or loving to him. Aidan pushed down any pleasant memory of her.

Aiden claimed he didn't think about his mother. Actually, he thought about her every day. He wondered what she might be doing or if she ever thought of him.

A stoplight ahead jolted Aiden out of his stupor. Soon the city, then the hospital, then the parking garage all came into sight. Aiden had not seen his mother in forty one years, but now standing in front of the hospital, it seemed like it was only a moment ago that she walked out the door.

Every step towards his mother's hospital room seemed like a dream. The nagging pain that Aiden had tried so hard to push down started to radiate with renewed strength. The voice in his heart told him to forgive his mother. The sound became louder and louder; the closer he came to her room.

"I can't do it. I can't face my ma." Exclaimed Aiden has he stopped in his tracks.

Fiona put her arm around Aiden and said, "Aiden, this is your last chance to see your ma and make things right. If you don't walk through that door, you will regret it for the rest of your life.

"I know that you have struggled. You can tell everyone that it doesn't cause you pain. I know you better than anyone, and I know the truth."

Fiona opened the door to the hospital room and gently pushed Aiden through. She closed the door behind Aiden and walked down to the cafeteria. She knew that this was Aiden's journey, and she needed to let him travel it by himself.

The moment Aiden walked through the door of the hospital room, he felt like he was twelve years old again. He felt that all the years it took to get to this moment just faded away.

Aiden looked over at the bed and saw a frail old woman. Both his sisters were sitting down in chairs next to the bed. They looked over at Aiden, and everyone started to cry, including Aiden.

"Come sit down, Aiden, and say hello to your ma." Said Aiden's youngest sister Anna.

Aiden's older sister Ellen, the family member who left when she turned eighteen, said nothing. She just looked at Aiden with a warm smile.

Aiden approached his mother's death bed and looked upon the face of the women he longed to know. He looked down and saw the face of an angel. His mother's face radiated with a light that was soft, kind, and loving.

Aiden was surprised that his mother was not a monster. All the anger started to fade away. The woman before him had kind and loving eyes. She was just human, nothing more, nothing less.

Aiden and his mother looked at each other for a long time without saying a word. Then Aiden's mom gently put her hand on his and slowly squeezed his hand. "Son, please forgive me," asked his mother.

Aiden sat up in the chair and looked over at a mirror on the wall. It startled him because he could see the twelve-year-old boy shining through. He realized that he never moved on emotionally from that point in time. That no matter how old he got physically, he had been lost in that moment for all his life.

Aiden looked down at his mother and asked, "Ma, why did you leave me, and why didn't you come back?"

Aiden's mother sat up in bed and replied, "At first I couldn't come back, your father wouldn't let me. Then as the years went by, I felt so much shame that I could face you."

Aiden thought of this moment for so many years that he almost couldn't believe that it was happening.

It was not like he thought it might be when he finally faced his mother. He thought he would be angry and defiant towards the monster he created in his mind. He didn't feel mad anymore or defiant, he just felt sad that he wasted so many years.

"Did you get my letters and the money I sent you, son?" Dona asked.

A surprised look came over Aiden's face as he replied, "What letters and money?"

Dona took a heavy breath and replied, "After I left, I worked as a maid in a large hotel in town and started to write to you and your sisters every month. I would put in as much money as I could spare. I hoped that you would get the letters and money. I considered that your father might not let you have them."

Aiden sat back in his chair and thought for a moment. In Wales, a boy is considered a man when he was fourteen, and it was no different in Aiden's home. When Aiden reached fourteen, he was required to take care of himself financially.

He worked odd jobs around Pittsburg, California, but because it was the middle of the great depression, he had little money for school and other essentials. His father fed him and put a roof over his head, that was it.

Aiden remembered the weekend before he was supposed to go to high school. He had no shoes, and his clothes were old and worn.

He thought that he might have to go to work instead of attending high school when a miracle happened. Misses Ellis from next door asked him to work on her car, and she would pay him $5.00. This kindness was enough for him to buy new shoes, a pair of jeans, and a shirt to attend high school. Back then, $5.00 was a lot of money, more money than what it should have cost to fix the car. Aiden considered that Misses Ellis was helping him out.

"Ma, did you tell Misses Ellis to give me the $5.00?" asked Aiden.

Aiden's mother smiled and replied, "Yes, I asked Veronica if she would make sure that you get the money for high school. She asked you to fix her car so that your father wouldn't know it was from me and take it away."

Aiden looked at his mother for a long time and said, "Ma, I'm sorry, please forgive me."

Dona sat up in bed and hugged Aiden and replied, "Forgive you for what?"

"For wasting time on nothing. I could have been in your life. I was holding onto anger. The anger became part of my life. I couldn't let it go. Now that I am standing in front of you, the anger is gone. My heart is full of love for you, just like that twelve-year-old boy, so long ago.

"I now remember all the fun we had. I remember your kindness and the sound of your laughter. The memories are all coming back." Replied Aiden.

A tear started to move down Dona's face as she replied, "Aiden, you have made me the happiest I have been all my life. You have given me a great gift."

Aiden started to realize that true forgiveness knows that there is nothing to forgive. That time does not heal all wounds, a connection does.

For a long time, he looked down on his mother's face. A feeling of great love started to feel his heart. He leaned over and kissed his mother on her forehead. A burst of bright warm light moved through the windows into the hospital room. ❧

CB

Chapter Forty-Five
Truth to Power

The lack of sound was deafening. Ian was back in the chamber of light, but now the cell had transformed into something much different. The chamber of light was now a perfectly round orb of light with layers of red, orange, yellow, and green.

There was a stillness in the cell that was peaceful. At the same time, Ian could hear everything. The sound of the chamber took on a form and weight that Ian had never experienced before.

Ian could see that the Congo, Africa, and the Earth had all faded away. He could see in all directions that there were other orbs. Spheres of light floating in a cosmic ocean that expanded in every direction.

Ian realized that the other orbs were the physical manifestation of consciousness. Each of the spheres represented other beings and their realities.

Pecky once told Ian, people's perceptions separate them from each other. The world outside reflects how we perceive ourselves in the reality that we have created. Ian finally understood the concept that we are all only separated by our perceptions.

The dark space that held all the spheres in place seemed to have a form that he could not see. A field of energy that moved through all things and bound the universe together.

When Ian watched Star Wars, he wondered what the force might look like—now he knew.

Ian could see the different realities that he lived move across the green field of light that encircled the inner chamber of light. He was aware that he lived a complete life as Aidan. He understood that anger and hate are a prison that we create for ourselves, and that forgiveness and compassion are the keys.

The orb in the center of the cell lost its physical form. It was a single ball of brilliant bright light not unlike the sun. Ian could look directly into the orb without averting his eyes. He could physically touch the sphere and feel a weight.

Ian noticed that his physical being took on a translucent form. He was floating in the center of the chamber. Ian's physical form was not supported by anything seen. He considered that the same energy field that supported the sphere held up his being.

The orb was still directing single beams of red, orange, yellow, and green light to the field of energy surrounding the inner chamber. Ian could not tell if the chamber of light was expanding or he was decreasing in size. The orb seemed to be part of him but not part of him at the same time.

The peace in the orb was without time or form. All the worries that Ian once held onto so tightly were fading away. He felt perfectly at peace, and at the same time, a feeling of purpose still held his existence together.

Ian held the orb of pure light in his hands and turned it so that a single blue beam of light moved to a position on the wall of light. The blue stream of light hit a blue point and then displaced in all directions covering the inner wall of the chamber, and then Ian's physical form faded away.

• • •

The brutal cold hit Ian with force. He stopped walking and looked around. He was standing on a street in a city that he did not recognize. Everyone around him, including himself, was bundled up in large coats and fur hats.

He could hear people talking, but he could not make out what they were saying or even what language they were speaking.

He remembered the chamber of light and knew that soon his life as Ian would fade away. He was aware that his connection to the Source would continue as a faint voice in his heart. He started to understand that the orb was his connection to the infinite.

A man passing by Ian came to close, and their arms clashed, turning Ian and the man around facing each other. The man looked at Ian and said, "I'm sorry. I didn't see you standing there."

This jolt from the stranger snapped Ian away from his connections to the chamber of light, and instantly his life as Pavel Semenov entered his consciousness. He could understand the language spoken was Russian. He looked at the man for a long time and replied in perfect Russian, "No problem."

The man looked at Ian for a moment with a blank stare on his face and then kept walking down the street.

Ian stood on a corner of the city for a long time, wondering where he was going in such a rush and what city surrounded him. Slowly his memory of Pavel's life started to create a clear picture in his mind.

Ian remembered that the city he was walking in was Veliky Novgorod. Ian, now Pavel, knew the city was in the northwestern part of Russian between Moscow and St. Petersburg along the Volkhov River.

Pavel's life in Veliky began to come back. Pavel remembered that he was a chemical engineer for the last fifteen years at the Acron Group, one of the largest chemical companies in the world. The company primarily manufactured fertilizer. Pavel started to remember that recently he found out it made something else, something more nefarious.

He had moved to Veliky with his wife and three kids a year ago. He took over as the chief research engineer at the main office in Veliky. Before he arrived, he worked at the company's fertilizer factor as a research engineer for eleven years in Shandong Province, China.

He was thrilled to receive his new post back in Mother Russia, but after a few months, his research started to unravel. He did not understand why they choose him but soon realized that he had no political connections to anyone in Russia. What they wanted him to do was not mainstream. He had worked on experimental fertilizers in China.

Pavel remembered that he was on his way to meet a western newspaper reporter who had contacted him a month earlier about his assignment. They were to meet at a secluded hotel room in an industrial part of the city.

Eight months ago, the chief executive officer and vice president at the company disclosed to Pavel what they wanted his team to do. They wanted a chemical fertilizer that would temporarily sterilize soil for ten years.

They told Pavel that the Russian government wanted an option to starve an enemy in case of war. They didn't wish to permanently sterilize farmland.

Pavel, at first, had apprehensions but convinced himself that war would be the only use of the chemical. When he was in China, they worked on a compound with the Chinese to temporarily kill invasive bacteria in the soil. The soil would be unusable for ten years but then would have a higher percentage of nitrogen and good bacteria for faster and more efficient plant growth.

The Chinese considered that it was better to remove the soil of toxins than continue to battle invasive pathogens. The Chinese were starting to rotate crops, and this seemed to be the right solution for their modern monoculture farming techniques they learned from the United States.

The reporter who contacted Pavel worked for the London Times Newspaper. Pavel first rejected the notion of any meeting with a journalist. The reporter told Pavel that he would be sending a gift to his daughter.

The reporter put a chemical in a popular girl's doll with a note detailing the chemical breakdown hidden in one of the legs. Pavel had the compound tested in his lab and found it to be the same toxin his team was studying.

Pavel could not understand how the chemical got into the hands of the journalist. It crossed his mind that either the government or the executives at his company were testing his loyalty. Pavel thought that maybe the reporter worked for the company and was a trap.

Pavel felt between a rock and a hard place. He could go to his superiors and disclose what happened, or he could meet the journalist and put his curiously to rest.

He kept telling himself that this whole thing was probably nothing. Pavel grew up in a privileged family in Moscow and went to the top research engineering school. He was not political at all. He did everything he could not to make waves or get in the crosshairs of anyone powerful. Pavel loved his calm routine.

The one time he rebelled against his family was when he married his wife, Sasha. She was a Ukrainian national that he met at the university. She was in her second year of college studying to be a chemist. They fell in love, and she dropped out of college to support Pavel. She got pregnant with their first child.

Their life in China was privileged. Pavel's father was an influential businessman in Moscow and made sure that his family had the best of everything.

Pavel thought as he walked briskly to the hotel that his father would not be happy with him going behind his superiors to meet with a Western journalist. Knowing that his father would be unhappy made Pavel feel a little bit exhilarated.

Rebelling against his superiors also made Pavel a little bit paranoid. The closer he came to the hotel, the more he looked around for anyone that seemed suspicious. He was mindful that most everyone he socialized with would never venture into this part of the city. The area was made up of the lower working class.

Pavel stood in front of the hotel for a long time. He considered that maybe he should just walk away. Something deep down in his heart kept telling him to move forward. He had to know how this reporter got ahold of the chemical.

Once he was aware of how the compound got out in the world, he would go to his superiors and disclose his findings. He thought for a moment that maybe they would make him a full director. He felt that his father would be proud that he stopped something lethal from being used by an enemy of the state.

Pavel walked into the hotel and went over to the phone booth near the registration table. A single young man sat behind the registration booth, reading a magazine. The hotel was a rundown hovel that housed old military pensioners.

Pavel looked in the cafeteria and noticed a few old men sitting around a television watching some western movie.

Pavel thought that he was lucky that he would never have to live in such a terrible place. He thought about joining the military after college, but the company gave him such an excellent package. He had a family to consider.

It didn't seem right to fight a war in Ukraine when his wife's family still lived there. He and his wife never brought up what was happening in Ukraine. It only led to arguments. What the Russian government was doing had nothing to do with him or his family.

Pavel called the room number left on the note hidden in the doll. A man answered and said, "Come to room 235. Everything is ready."

Pavel hung up the phone and climbed to the second floor of the hotel. The elevator had a broken sign attached to the outer door. The bright red and orange carpet was filthy. Pavel kept his coat and gloves on, careful not to touch anything in the soiled hallway. Pavel stood before room 235 and thought that this might be a trap. A voice in his heart told him that it was not. He did consider for the last time to turn around and walk away. The voice in his heart kept moving him forward.

Pavel knocked on the door, and a man in his late thirties instantly opened the door and said, "Come in." The man closed the door behind Pavel and took two pillows from the bed and placed them over the crack at the bottom of the door. He turned to Pavel and said, "Can't be too cautious. Pavel, please take off your coat and hold up your hands over your head."

Pavel stiffened with this request and asked, "Why?"

The man just repeated what he said, "Take off your coat and hold up your hands so that I can check for bugging devices."

Pavel acquiesced to the man's request and took off his coat, gloves, and hat. He then put up his hands over his head.

The man looked through all his clothes and patted down Pavel's body. The man even moved his hand over Pavel's hair and ears and between his legs.

The man sat down on the bed and said, "Good, you're clean."

Pavel, now with an irritated look on his face, replied, "Yes, I'm clean, but what about you? Who are you and who do you work for?"

Pavel was proud that he took an aggressive attitude towards the stranger. He wasn't going to be pushed around by anyone.

The stranger handed Pavel a London Times Newspaper and said, "If you look on page three, you will see a picture of me and my name."

Pavel opened the paper and looked. On page three, there was a picture of Roger Townsend, an investigative reporter for the Times.

Pavel looked at Roger and said, "This doesn't prove anything. This newspaper could be fake."

Roger laughed and replied, "True, but it isn't. I know who you are. I know what you have been researching. I am going to tell you a story, and you are going to believe it, or you are not. It makes no difference to me, because either way, the story is going to come out. The choice you need to make is if you are going to support the story or you are going to deny it."

Pavel noticed that Roger had a strong English accent even though he seemed to speak Russian with perfect diction. Pavel asked, "How did you learn Russian?"

Roger replied, "My father worked for MI6. He was stationed in Russia for many years. My connections to MI6 was how I found out about your research, and what is taking place in Ukraine."

Pavel sat on a chair near Roger making sure he didn't touch anything and said, "So, let's get to it. What story do you want me to hear?"

Roger handed Pavel maps and papers with diagrams on them and said, "These are documents that outline the use of your sterilization fertilizer on farmland in Ukraine. The chemical is being used on remote farms. The records show that the Russian government and your superiors at Acron Group are planning the temporary sterilization Ukrainian farmland.

"Your president is friends with the chairman of your company. They came up with this solution to the rebels in Ukraine three years ago. Your president had hard sanctions brought against Russia by the western powers, because of his policies against Ukraine. He wants this little plan to be secret because he doesn't want any more western meddling."

Pavel stood up and walked towards the door and replied, "This is bullshit. I don't believe it."

Roger walked over to the door and put his hands against the door keeping Pavel from leaving and replied, "Believe it or not, Pavel, it is happening. It will happen to even more farms maybe in Chechnya, Crimea, who knows where else.

"Your government can't kill every Chechnyan and Ukrainian, but they can starve them to death, or make them reliant on Mother Russia. That includes your wife's family farm in Ukraine. Your president doesn't want to destroy the farmland, just decrease the population enough to gain total power. People have a hard time fighting when their bellies are empty."

Pavel moved back into the room. He asked, "So, what do you want from me?"

Rodger replied, "The story is coming out in Monday's Times. What I need from you is support of the article. We have time to get you and your family out of Russia into a safe house in Britain. I need to know what you are going to do."

Pavel asked, "What if I do nothing?"

Rodger replied, "You are implemented in the article as one of the designers of the plot. I believe your government and superiors at the company will hang you out to dry. Why do you think they put you in charge? You have no political pull other than your father, and he is in the shit house with your president."

Pavel asked, "What do you know about my father?"

Rodger sat back on the bed. He replied, "You think your dad is an influential businessman. What you don't know is that your father was a mid-manager at the KGB. He worked over your president for many years during the Soviet days. He just recently tried a power grab and got caught with his hands in the cookie jar.

"He was more than happy to give you up over being sent to the Black Dolphin prison in Siberian. He never did like the idea of his oldest marrying a Ukrainian national."

Pavel sat down in the chair. His face became pale. He sat looking out the window for a long time and then replied, "All I wanted was to have a simple life. I'm an engineer, not a politician."

Rodger replied, "At one point in everybody's life, we become political."

Pavel looked at Rodger with a defeated look on his face. He asked, "What are my options?"

Rodger replied, "You and your family come with me. We will get your family to a safe place. Your wife's family will be taken to the U.S. After the story hits the newsstands on Monday, you will need to work with us.

"Your life will be in jeopardy. Most likely, your government will get to you. Before they do, we need to get the truth out, or many millions of people will die."

Pavel sat back in the chair and started to think about his life in the most honest way he had ever done. He knew from an early age that his father was an evil man. He realized his whole life was a lie. His job was handed to him. He never intended to join the military. He knew that he wouldn't last two days in the army.

He made excuses his whole life for his apathy and indifference. He did everything he could to not bring truth to power, especially against his father. He thought that maybe this was his chance to change his life. To finally stand up to his father. Speak the truth for once in his pathetic existence.

In his heart, he knew that he had but one path. He was aware that his life was always leading up to this point. He could not escape what he needed to do next.

Rodger asked, "Pavel, I have to leave. I have been in this place too long, and too many people have seen me. What are you going to do?"

Pavel stood up, brushed his pants off, and replied, "I'm ready to change my life." Pavel, Rodger, and the hotel all faded away into a point of pure blue light. ☙

CR

Chapter Forty-Six
Dark Night of the Soul

A single point of brilliant light radiated from the center of the chamber where the golden orb once emitted streams of light. Ian could not tell if the single point of light was three feet across or three miles across. The point of clear light seemed to have no form other than to be perfectly round.

Ian could see the layers of different colored lights that surrounded the center point of the chamber. Where before, Ian saw different spheres lined in every direction outside his chamber, there was now only one center of bright clear light.

Ian didn't feel connected to the physical world anymore. He felt as if he was floating in the center of the chamber and observing the world. He felt more connected to the bright light than he did to his body.

The images moved past the different layers of colored light. The inner chamber wall radiated blue light. Ian could still see and physically feel the other colors shined around the center of the cell.

A profound awareness crossed his consciousness. He realized that the reflections that were moving across the cell were not only his perceptions but all perceptions. Where he once felt connected to the Source with his heart, he now also felt connected through his perceptions.

A feeling of peace flowed over Ian's heart. He still had a strong connection to the world through purpose, but this time he felt he had a singular divine purpose.

Something expanded Ian's consciousness and held him tethered to the world. A single purple stream of light sprang from the light at center of the chamber. The purple stream of light moved to the outer walls of the cell and then spread in all directions.

Ian didn't vanish as before. The white light that defined the center of the chamber expanded and filled the cell with bright light. A feeling of warmth washed over Ian's consciousness. He felt both awake and asleep at the same time.

. . .

"Bill, can I call you Bill?" Asked a middle-aged man in a dark suit, gray curly hair, and close-cropped beard.

Ian looked around the room and at the man sitting at a table. Near a window with bars on the outside. The life of Bill Collins began to wash over Ian's consciousness. He recalled why he was in the room and who the man was sitting at the table.

Bill Collin's life flooded Ian's soul, as each reality did before, but something different happened this time. Ian remembered both Bill's life, and he remembered Ian's life and the chamber of light.

Bill Collin's life did not wash away all memory of Ian's life. He found it interesting that he could know the details of both simultaneously.

Ian looked at the man for a long time. He replied, "Yes, you can call me Bill."

The man crossed his legs, pulled out a file from his briefcase. He asked, "So, you were admitted into Ward G three days ago?

"It says here that you took an overdose of sleeping pills. You then called an ambulance, which took you to the hospital. You were administered ipecac to induce vomiting, and then they let you rest for one day before admitting you here."

Ian replied, "Yes, that is what happened."

The man crossed his legs and leaned forward. He asked, "Do you want to talk about your intentions to commit suicide?"

Ian looked at the man with a comical look. He replied, "My story is a long one and will be more bizarre than you might suspect."

A confident look came over the man's face as he said, "Try me, you have my undivided attention for the next two hours."

Ian connected with the transitions that took place in Bill Collins's life over the last three years. He thought about the wisdom of disclosing all that had happened to the doctor sitting in front of him.

Ian realized that he was being examined by a psychiatrist in Ward G of a mental hospital. Three days earlier, Bill had taken an overdose of sleeping pills to end his life. A transformation of souls took place. Ian took on the dominant role of living Bill's life, after Bill made a commitment to end his life.

Ian called an ambulance, which took him to the hospital. A psychologist met Ian at the hospital. The moment wasn't right to disclose all that had transpired. After the hospital, they transferred Ian to Ward G. The orderlies took all his clothing and gave him pajamas, a robe, and slippers to wear.

Ian was confused about why he was living Bill's life. His heart kept telling him that there was a reason, and it would become apparent. Ian now trusted his heart without any trepidation.

The doctor's name was Samuel Bostwick. He was a clinical psychiatrist attached to the St. Helena Hospital in Lincoln, Nebraska. He has been an attending doctor for twenty-three years and feels that he has heard everything.

"Bill, you can trust me," interjected Dr. Bostwick.

Ian knew that he could not trust Dr. Bostwick to have an open mind. He understood this because he could see into the minds of those around him. Ian realized that he's connected to each person's perceptions. He could see into the life of Dr. Bostwick. He could understand his most intimate feelings.

Dr. Bostwick started his career with an open mind. But like many who walk such a path, he had become cynical about spirituality or miracles. The hospital politics and realization that little could be done to heal the mentally ill pounded down his passion year after year.

A strong feeling came over Ian's mind. He felt that this was both an opportunity for him to transition to the next level towards the City of Light, and maybe to give Dr. Bostwick back his passion. He considered that perhaps the last test before he entered the City of Light had nothing to do with him. Perhaps it had to do with helping others at the cost of his own existence.

Ian took a sip of the tea an orderly brought him earlier. He replied, "I will trust you, Dr. Bostwick. Can I call you, Sam?"

Dr. Bostwick replied, "Yes, you can call me Sam. If it makes you more comfortable."

Ian took another sip of his tea. He continued, "What I am about to tell you might support your perception that I am mentally ill. I realize that deep in my heart, there is a purpose to this process."

"I'm glad you feel that way, Bill, please continue," interjected Dr. Bostwick.

Ian sat back and relaxed his chair. He continued, "My story started three years ago. I drowned in Lake McConaughey during summer vacation with my family."

"You mean you almost drowned, don't you?" asked Dr. Bostwick.

Ian continued, "No, I drowned. I was swimming in a small lagoon. I hit a log with my head that was just beneath the surface. It knocked me out cold. I started to sink to the bottom of the lagoon.

"Even though I had passed out, I knew I was drowning. I began to convulse in the water and grasp for the surface. After what seemed like a short period, I gave up and just sat on the bottom of the lagoon.

"As my lifeless body sat on the bottom, I felt scared and sad that I would not see my family again. My life didn't pass before my eyes, but what passed through my heart was a feeling of loss, loss of the people that I loved the most.

"In an instant, a warm, loving light descended on me. A shade of yellow light that was so pure that I felt comforted by its presence. I started to rise towards the light, and then a voice spoke to me. With perfect clarity, I heard a voice tell me, 'Bill, everything is going to be fine. Nothing matters anymore.' At that moment I knew absolutely that nothing mattered.

"The problems and worries of the world had faded. I felt at peace. Peace so pure that I felt one with everything, and with my soul.

"I felt a vibration in the light that communicated with me on an infinite level. The communication was beyond words but with absolute being.

"My spirit rose above the surface of the lake. I looked back on the world and saw a thin veil of black and white. The world wasn't a multi-colored place anymore, but an illusion. I saw the world as an experience in an infinite moment that never happened.

"I looked down on the lake that I had drowned in and saw people running towards where I had been. I couldn't make out specific people, but I understood that my drowning was causing the motion.

"The next thing that I remember was looking up as people were looking down at me. At this moment, I knew that I was back in the world.

"My wife had waded out in the lagoon. She miraculously pulled me ashore. As my wife held me in her arms and tried to comfort me, I felt darkness come over me. This brief experience would drive the last three years of my life."

Dr. Bostwick looked at Ian with an uncomfortable look. He explained, "Bill, it has been proven by scientists that these out-of-body experiences are the brain assimilating the lack of oxygen."

Ian looked at Dr. Bostwick and smiled. Ian could see Dr. Bostwick's past, where he did believe in such things. His colleagues told him that he was crazy. He shut off the part of him connected to the Source.

Ian continued, "Something happened during the process of my drowning. I felt another soul enter my body. I felt that someone named Ian stepped into my consciousness when I was open to the universe.

"From that time at the lake until I arrived here, I descended into a dark night of the soul.

"Before that day at the lagoon, I loved my life. I had bad moments as everyone has during their life, but overall, I had a good life. I owned a local bicycle shop. I had a beautiful wife and three lovely kids. I had lifelong friends and the respect of my community. I owned a small house in the hills near Lincoln. But nothing seemed to matter anymore. I have felt pain in my life — nothing like the emptiness that filled my heart after drowning.

"When I first felt the emptiness, I tried to fight it with alcohol. Not a good idea. I didn't want to get on any meds. I lived in a small community and didn't want anyone to know I was going insane.

"I started to retreat from my family. After a while, I didn't even go into my business. I just didn't see the point. Soon my wife and I started to sleep in different rooms. My child didn't want to spend time with me. I would lash out at my family with fits of anger.

"My wife pleaded with me to get help. All I wanted to do was die. I couldn't find any joy in living anymore. I would just sleep and get drunk every day.

"Two years ago, the bicycle shop failed, and I had to declare bankruptcy. Luckily my wife had a good job. My family didn't descend into poverty. My wife was a senior nurse at a local hospital. She did take a risk and bring home Prozac for me. The medication didn't' help. I was worried that she would lose her job and told her to stop giving me meds.

"A year later, my wife gave me an ultimatum. She told me to get help, or she would leave me and take the kids. I remember the day she told me.

"It was like I was in a dream and merely observing the experience. My disconnection infuriated my wife. A week later, she had a moving truck come and remove all our furniture.

"She is living in a rental house near where she works. Her parents, who used to love me, take care of our kids when she is at work. That was a year ago, and I have not seen my children or my wife since."

"Do you miss your family?" asked Dr. Bostwick.

Ian sat back and took another sip of tea. He replied, "No, they seem to be total strangers to me. Since the lake, I have had no feelings about my family. Slowly a sense of another being has entered my consciousness. Over the last three years, I felt more like Ian than Bill."

"Would you like me to call you Ian?" Asked Dr. Bostwick.

Ian replied, "Yes, I think that would be appropriate."

"Ian, what happened after your wife left?" asked Dr. Bostwick.

Ian continued, "At first nothing. I slowly went through my savings. The bank finally foreclosed on the house. I found myself living in a tent under the freeway.

"The funny thing is that I would walk to the soup kitchen and pass people I used to know. They would not look me in the eye. Good friends would just pass by me in the streets. I entered a dark world that I never knew existed.

"A few months ago, I started to sense that there were spirits around me all the time. I have had ghosts show up at 3:30 in the morning looking for answers. I didn't know what these spirits wanted. I realized that they did not understand that they were dead, or at least their physical form was dead.

"They held onto their perceptions so much that they still believed they're alive. The spirits stay in their homes for hundreds of years, holding onto their belief in this world."

A fearful look came over Dr. Bostwick's face as he asked, "How do you know all this is true?"

Ian looked straight into Dr. Bostwick's eyes and replied, "I know it is true because Ian knows that it is true. When I look into your eyes, I see that you have a real question for me. A spirit has been haunting you for some time now."

Dr. Bostwick sat straight up. His face became pale as he replied, "First, I don't believe in ghosts. Yes, something has been creating problems in my home."

Ian replied, "Your ghost is the former homeowner. An elderly woman who died in the house a few years before you bought it. She has been quiet for many years, but becuase you're renovating her kitchen it has upset her."

Dr. Bostwick asked, "How do you know that she died in my house before we bought it?"

"Because she is standing right next to you," replied Ian.

Dr. Bostwick looked down for a moment and then replied, "Let's say just for a moment that all that you are telling me is right. What purpose would you have to say to me that the world is an illusion if you consider yourself sane? If you know me, then you might find that I would keep you in this mental institution."

Ian continued, "As I was saying before, the emptiness was overwhelming. I felt more pain than I have ever felt in my life. Then something happened. After I took the overdose of pills, I felt a light enter my heart.

"What reached out of the darkness and touched my soul was not of this earth. I started to totally understand that the world outside is an illusion. I realized I was going through a severe shift in perception. We are spiritual beings having a physical experience.

"During our journey through this reality, we hold onto our perceptions. Some hold onto their perceptions so much that they are unwilling to change. I started to understand that there is no death, just a transition of energy."

A warm smile came over Ian's face. He continued, "It is because I know absolutely that this world is an illusion, I can tell you everything.

"I'm not even here. I realize I am in the chamber of light observing this world. The cell is testing my intuitive abilities. If I hesitate in any way, it means that I do not trust my connection to the Source.

"I do not believe or have faith that what I am telling you is the truth. I know that it is the truth. The truth does not rely on you believing it is the truth.

"Yes, I know that you could keep me in this mental institution for the rest of my life. I know who I am and what test I need to overcome to enter the City of Light. I need to know the truth no matter what happens to my physical form, even at the threat of pain, misery, and the perception of death."

Ian's focus on the truth caused the world in the room to change. Ian looked over at Dr. Bostwick and now saw a perfect reflection of his physical form. Ian was aware that he was talking to himself.

In that critical moment of realization, the world around Ian flattened into a black and white mirage and then expanded in all directions with such force that Ian felt his consciousness become infinite. ☙

CR

Chapter Forty-Seven
A City of Light

"You made it. You are the first true heart in a thousand years to get this far," said a disembodied being of light hovering in front of Ian. Ian looked around and saw that he was standing at an apex of bright energy, moving in all directions. Ian laughed because the effect appeared reminiscent of the ending to the movie "2001: A Space Odyssey."

Ian observed that he was not a body. His consciousness, memories, and intelligence were still part of him, but his physical form was not visible. He could see just a slight outline of his shape floating. Ian looked at the being of light in front of him and asked, "Where am I?"

"You already know the answer. You have made it to a City of Light," replied the Entity of light.

Ian asked, "A City of Light, are there other Cities of Light?"

The Entity of light replied, "There are infinite numbers of Cities of Light in the multi-universe of separation."

Ian asked, "I am still in the world of separation. I imagined that when I reached the City of Light, I would be one with the infinite being."

The Entity of light replied, "No, you have reached a higher level of spirituality in the reality of separation. You will be one with the Source once you obtain the highest level of spirituality in the multi-universe. To achieve this will take many lifetimes, reaching a City of Light at a higher and higher level."

Ian interjected, "Who are you?"

"You know who I am. I am you, or the purest spiritual form of you. I am your conduit between the multi-universe and the infinite reality." Replied the Entity of light.

The Entity of light materialized into a three-dimensional physical form and took on a pure reflection of Ian's self-image. It was like looking into a mirror. Ian looked down at his figure and saw his hands and his body appear.

"I thought a physical form would be easier for you to comprehend. It always takes a true heart time to adjust to this level of creation," said Ian's reflection.

"How is it that I can hear you and understand what you are saying as if my ears worked in this place?" asked Ian.

Ian's reflection replied, "You are not hearing me through any physical form you may interpret. You understand me through a profound spiritual connection we have with each other. During your journey through the physical world, you have heard me as a whisper deep in your heart. There are no barriers. The level of communication in this spiritual reality is absolute.

"All Cities of Light have many advantages over the physical world. This City of Light is the closest to pure physical creation. This City of Light can create any physical reality. We can create a reality that might help you feel a little more comfortable. How about your favorite diner in Vermont?"

A flash of light-filled Ian's mind and a second later, he was sitting in his favorite diner in Vermont. His reflection was seated across from him in physical form. A waiter brought them two coffees, eggs benedict, and hash browns. Others were sitting around them talking. Ian could see that outside the restaurant was the apex of light going in infinite directions.

"A little more comfortable?" asked Ian's reflection.

Ian replied, "Yes, but it is still bizarre talking to myself."

"I will remedy that," replied Ian's reflection. "How about your best friend from high school?" Another light-filled Ian's mind and a moment later, Ian's best friend from high school, Max, was sitting across the table from him.

Ian's reflection, now Max, asked, "Better?"

Ian replied, "Yes, much better, thank you. Being a disembodied spirit must take time to adjust?"

Max replied, "A physical body is harder."

Ian sat back in his chair and sipped his coffee. "This is delicious. It tastes just like my favorite coffee. How is that possible?"

Max replied, "It is possible because we are one being in this multi-universe of separation. Whatever you have experienced, I have also experienced."

Ian took another sip of coffee, sat back, and contemplated his next question. He had no idea how long he had or how many questions he could ask.

Max replied, "As long as it takes and as many questions as you need to prepare you for your divine purpose."

Ian replied, "How do you know what I am thinking?"

"Ian, I am you, and we are communicating on an absolute level," replied Max.

Ian laughed at the reality he now occupied. Ian replied, "I'm sorry. I saw my best friend, Max, sitting across from me and became confused. It will take a moment to wrap my mind around this place. I still have a thousand questions."

Max continued, "Good, because most of the knowledge of the multi-universe you acquired during your journey to the City of Light, was what you logically understood. To help the physical world to evolve to a higher awareness, you will need to know the knowledge in your heart."

"Is the City of Light Heaven?" asked Ian.

"Yes, the City of Light is Heaven. The City of Light is the Garden of Eden, Shangri-La, Moksha, Paradise, and Nirvana, to name only a few. The City of Light is the purest spiritual level of energy in the multi-universe of separation."

Ian asked, "When a physical person dies, do they transcend to a City of Light?"

Max replied, "Yes, and no. All beings that physically die transcend to a level of energy that reflects their connection to the physical world. What you may call a ghost, in the physical world, does not know that their body has perished. They stay in the physical realm, stuck in multi-levels of energy. Only hearts that are good, pure, or true can make it to the higher levels in the spiritual realm.

"Only the infinite being occupies a reality beyond the multi-universe of separation. The Source cannot be communicated in the reality of separation, even by a spiritual being existing in the highest level of energy."

"Why can't you communicate the infinite reality?" Asked Ian.

Max replied, "Even though I am a pure spiritual being, we still are separate from each other by our perceptions. If I were to communicate to you what the infinite reality is, you would base the information on the reality of separation that you know occupy, not the infinite reality."

Ian interjected, "During my journey through the chambers of light, my body transcended. I observed that during the last two challenges, my consciousness was symbolized by a perfect sphere of light. I surmised that the sphere was my true spiritual form in this reality."

Max answered, "Yes, when I talk of the physical reality or what you may say is your body, I am only speaking of perception. The seven colors that make up the outer layer of the orb are our perceptions. The inner bright white center is the infinite being. Each being in the multi-universe is an orb of pure energy with different perceptions, but the center is always the infinite being.

"When you watch a movie, you become emotionally engaged. You might consider the perceptions moving across the outer layer of the sphere to be the same as a film for the infinite being. The only difference is that the Source is watching an infinite variety of movies at the same time. The physical body that you occupy is only a self-generated image created by your perceptions of yourself in the reality of separation."

Ian asked, "Since I am still in the reality of separation, and not one with the Source, how am I to change the consciousness of those beings existing in the physical reality?"

Ian's reflection replied, "Just as I stated, the level of communication in this reality is absolute. The level of knowledge is absolute. What you need to learn to help evolve the consciousness of those in the physical world will be absolute. You will know it at such a deep level, almost no ego distraction in the physical world will deceive you off your divine path."

Ian asked, "An essential question most people ask is, if the Source is a loving deity, then why does the infinite being allow so much despair to take place in the physical world? Why does the Source allow innocent children to suffer in misery and die?"

Max replied, "First, as you have realized, there is no death. All life transcends to different levels of energy. Many true hearts over the many millenia have proved that there is no death, but many physical beings misperceive the simple equation that physical death does not equal an end.

"As far as the Source's understanding of misery in the world, when the infinite being created the multi-universe, it was only an idea. The Source is so powerful that the physical world is an illusion created to support the idea the infinite being had. The Source exists 100% in an infinite reality and 100% in a reality of separation. Since the Source exists 100% in an infinite reality, it does not even know that a world of separation exists. This dual existence is a paradox.

"The infinite being's presence in the multi-universe of separation is experiencing a physical reality through every being—from the highest level of spirituality to the lowest, most ego-driven person. This existence includes children living in dire poverty or abusive realities, and adults battling severe addictions. The Source is experiencing everything a reality of separation creates, such as hate, love, fear, compassion, empathy, apathy, jealousy, indifference, to name only a few of the feelings a sentient being would endure.

"Many in the physical world do not understand that they choose their realities. Many think that they are victims of their lives, but not one child of the Source is a victim. Each path that a being of the multi-universe chooses can bring them closer to the Source or father away—it is up to them."

Ian asked, "How do people choose to either embrace the Source or move away?"

Max answered, "To embrace the Source is simple. All one has to do is listen to their true inner self, live an authentic life, and follow their divine purpose."

Ian asked, "To move away from the Source?"

Max answered, "If someone lies, cheats, or steals, they cut themselves off from the Source because they believe they lack something. Each person has everything they need to fulfill their divine purpose, and the universe is 100% behind them."

Ian askes, "What is love?"

Max answered, "Love is the authentic state of a spiritual being. When a spiritual being is in its natural state, it is as close to the Source as it can get in the multi-universe of separation."

Ian asked, "One of the questions that I have yet to understand is, since the world is an illusion, why do I need to bring heightened awareness to humankind?"

Max replied, "The multi-universe is off balance. Each being has the free will to either build a relationship with their authentic spiritual self or connect with the illusionary world of the ego.

"When someone gives meaning to the illusion, they are following their ego-self, and if they give too much importance to the emptiness, they fall into a state of depression, a dark place without light.

"A true heart is born to the world when the reality of separation is off balance. A true heart is the purest conduit between the physical world and the spiritual reality. A true heart is a reminder of the most important relationship a being can have in the physical world, a relationship with their authentic spiritual selves."

Ian asked, "So, what is my divine purpose?"

"Your divine purpose is to evolve all souls in the multi-universe from a lower level of energy to a higher level. We inhabit one of the highest levels of energy that exist in this multi-universe but are still not free from the reality of separation. All souls have lived thousands of lives in thousands of realities. In the infinite reality, this process took an infinite second. In this world of separation, the process takes on the form of linear time. Linear time dictates each life relative to the multi-universe of separation.

"A true heart is a physical entity connected to this level of spirituality. Many beings who exist at a physical level of consciousness will only hear the faint whisper of their authentic selves. Many will never hear their inner voice.

"In all the multi-universes, there has been a handful of true hearts. And of all the true hearts that have journeyed to a City of Light, you are the purest so far," explained Max.

"So far?" asked Ian.

"Yes, so far. You are a crucial intermediary that will help the world move in the direction of light, but you will not be the last true heart to make it to a City of Light," replied Max.

"If the Source is experiencing the world through each person, then ulti-mately, we are all the infinite being?" asked Ian.

"Yes, we are all the Source, having a collective experience in a reality of separation," replied Max.

"What part does Legorian play in the cosmic drama?" asked Ian.

Max replied, "Good, Ian, you see patterns. Legorian, Satan, devil, and ego, to name only a few, were created by the infinite being when it created the world of separation. Legorian's only job is to convince us that we are separate. That we are not spiritual beings having a physical experience, we are physical beings alone and separate from each other, and cut off from the Source.

"Legorian makes sure that we feel fear, doubt, jealousy, envy, happiness, joy, and outside love. These feelings are products of a world of separation, and we need to feel them to the fullest of our abilities to progress out of this reality and go home.

"Even though you have made it to a City of Light, you will still have to pass the seventh test of the chamber of light. Like every test in the chamber, Legorian plays a significant part.

"When you return to your physical life as Ian, Legorian will try to con-vince you that you are the only Source. He will convince others that you are the Messiah, and you alone hold the key to a higher level of consciousness. Your authentic spiritual perception of yourself is the last test Legorian will try to use against you.

"Your purpose is to reflect the highest state of what a physical beings can become. You are a beacon for those lost in the dark. Your higher purpose is to show that each person in the world holds the key to their hearts—that everyone is one with everything."

"What happens if I fail?" asked Ian.

"The multi-universe will fall into darkness for a thousand years. Another chance to evolve will not happen until another true heart is born to the world," explained Max.

"During my physical journey, many have explained to me much of what you have just shared. I didn't comprehend the concepts until now. What you have told me is deep in my heart. Will I be as sure as I am now when I return to my physical life?" asked Ian.

"When you return to your physical life, you will once again feel fear, guilt, anger, hope, and love. I will be there with you guiding you towards your ultimate divine purpose. My voice will be clear if you do not let Lego-rian deceive you."

Ian asked, "So, the last and seventh test of the chamber of light is to transcend the world into a higher level of consciousness?"

Max answered, "Yes, the world that you occupy is grinding down. It is at a nadir of greed, apathy, indifference, guilt, and fear. Most souls are concerned about love and acceptance outside themselves and have moved away from having a relationship with their authentic spiritual selves.

"You are the light that will shift all souls in a positive direction. Your presence in the world will transcend to all creations in the multi-universe of separation.

"When you return to your world, many thousands of souls will know of your return. They are good and pure hearts without having the connection you now possess. They will look towards you for strength and wisdom. They will travel over the multi-universe spreading light."

"When do I go back?" asked Ian.

"You are already there," replied Max.

A flash of pure light flowed over Ian's consciousness. Ian found himself sitting under the apple tree nestled next to his house in the valley of the two green mountains in Vermont. It was a beautiful spring day.

Ian looked out on his family's farm field and saw many people waiting for his arrival. At the front of the gathering stood Pecky, Bee, and Ogden. Ian rose from the apple tree and stood before the crowd. The group was silent. Ian looked out on the world and saw only a thin veil of pure light. He could feel the hearts of everyone in the multi-universe. Ian once again felt endless love in his heart for all things. ⊗

A New Beginning

A True Heart
Journey to the City of Light

Reference Material

The following reference material helped to create the information provided in this book. All learned information in this novel only slightly reflects the information in the reference material. The information was changed to fit the narrative of this novel.

Pages 119-120: Source, Wikipedia: Law of Conservative Energy
Page 116: Source, Wikipedia: Mount Athos Greek Myth
Page 157: Source, Wikipedia: Bedouin

A True Heart
Journey to the City of Light

Reference Material
Material That Helped Me During My Journey

Siddhartha:	Novel by Hermann Hesse
Divine Comedy:	Poem by Dante Alighieri
Odyssey:	Poem by Homer
Narcissus and Goldmund:	Novel by Hermann Hesse
Zen and the Art of Motorcycle Maintenance:	Book by Robert M. Pirsig
The Hitchhiker's Guide to the Galaxy:	Series by Douglas Adams
Dark Night of the Soul:	Poem by John of the Cross
Dark Night of the Soul:	Book by Thomas Moore
Anatomy of the Spirit:	Book by Caroline Myss
The Bible:	King James Version
Sacred Contracts:	Book by Caroline Myss
Complete Book Series:	Dr. Wayne Dyer
Stand Like Mountain, Flow Like Water:	Book by Brian Luke Seaward
The Power of Now:	Book by Eckhart Tolle
Conversations with God:	Neale Donald Walsch
The Matrix:	Written by Wachowskis
No Such Thing:	Movie written by Hal Hartley
The Four Agreements:	Book by Don Miguel Ruiz
The Alchemist:	Novel by Paulo Coelho
The Secret:	Book by Rhonda Byrne
The seven spiritual laws of success:	Book by Deepak Chopra
The Celestine Prophecy:	Novel by James Redfield
A Course in Miracles:	Book by Helen Schucman
Tao Te Ching:	Religious Text
The Seat of the Soul:	Book by Gary Zukav
The Prophet:	Book by Kahlil Gibran
Illusions:	Novel by Richard Bach
Johnathan Livingston Seagull:	Novel by Richard Bach
The Last Temptation of Christ:	Novel by Nikos Kazantzakis